BANISHED Love

RAMONA FLIGHTNER

Ramona Flightner/Grizzly Damsel Publishing
P.O. Box 187
Boston, MA 02128
www.ramonaflightner.com

Cover design by Derek Murphy

Publisher's Note: This is a work of fiction. Names, characters, places, and incidents
are a product of the author's imagination. Locales and public names are sometimes
used for atmospheric purposes. Any resemblance to actual people, living or dead, or
to businesses, companies, events, institutions, or locales is completely coincidental.

Ordering Information:
Quantity sales. Special discounts are available on quantity purchases by corporations,
associations, and others. For details, contact the "Special Sales Department" at the
address above.

Banished Love/ Ramona Flightner. — 1st ed.
ISBN 978-0-9860502-1-3

RAMONA FLIGHTNER

Dedication

A Jefe,
Your unequaled generosity in time, editing, support, and love fueled my creative spirit.
You taught me "Paciencia y Barajar," a priceless lesson.
Mil Gracias.

CAST OF CHARACTERS

Clarissa Sullivan: teaches school in the West End of Boston, a suffragette, clumsy, lives in the South End,

Colin Sullivan: Clarissa's brother, a blacksmith

Patrick Sullivan: Clarissa's eldest brother

Sean Sullivan: Clarissa's father, a blacksmith, from Ireland

Mrs. Rebecca Sullivan nee Smythe: Clarissa's stepmother, has social aspirations

Agnes Sullivan nee Thompson: Clarissa's mother, deceased

Savannah Russell: Clarissa's cousin and confidante, soon to be married to Jonas Montgomery, lives in the South End near Clarissa

Lucas Russell: Clarissa's cousin, works at his father's linen store, "Russells," is a talented piano player

Martin Russell: father to Lucas and Savannah, uncle to Clarissa, owns and runs the linen store, "Russells," store and home in the South End, near the Sullivan home

Matilda Russell nee Thompson: Savannah's mother and Clarissa's aunt, sister to Agnes and Betsy

Betsy Parker nee Thompson: childless, lives in Quincy, married to a wealthy man, free-thinking, cryptic comments, Matilda and Agnes' sister, Clarissa and Savannah's aunt.

Gabriel McLeod: the eldest McLeod brother, a cabinetmaker, lives in North End, fascinated by Clarissa

Richard McLeod: Gabriel's middle brother, a blacksmith, friend to Colin

Jeremy McLeod: the youngest McLeod brother, in the Army, fighting in the Philippines

Aidan McLeod: uncle to the three McLeod boys

Ian McLeod: father to the three McLeod boys

Geraldine McLeod nee Sanders: wife to Ian and mother to the McLeod boys

Patricia Masterson nee Sanders: sister to Geraldine, aunt to the McLeod boys, helped raise them.

Henry Masterson: cousin to the McLeod boys

Nicholas Masterson: cousin to the McLeod boys

Florence Butler: orphan teacher who works with Clarissa in the West End

Sophronia Chickering: feisty suffragette who befriends Clarissa, lives on Beacon Hill, distantly related by marriage to the piano Chickerings

Jonas Montgomery: wealthy New Yorker, Savannah's fiancée

Cameron Wright: a suitor for Clarissa's hand

Maid Mary: Clarissa's maid who is loyal to her

Maid Bridget: the other maid in the Sullivan household, more loyal to Mrs. Sullivan (Smythe)

Maid Polly: Uncle Martin's maid

CHAPTER 1

MY CLUMSINESS WOULD BE my downfall. So I had been told, and so it seemed when, at twenty-two, I remained single with the possibility of marrying appearing increasingly elusive. Thus, I never suspected my ungainliness would, in the end, be my saving grace. I never imagined that one small stumble, the fall of a ladder and a minor head wound would lead to life-altering events.

It was a typical day in early March at the public school I taught at in Boston's immigrant West End. I had a tiny classroom with a small, drafty window overlooking a metal fire escape, teaching children of a variety of ages and skill levels throughout the day.

After I closed the door to my schoolroom, I entered the next-door room of colleague and friend Florence Butler. I walked past rows of battered children's desks to stand behind Florence's larger one at the front of the room to help her wipe clean the well-used chalkboard. Books in need of a proper bookshelf or cabinet lay piled on the floor.

"Florence, I'm heading home soon," I said.

"Did you bring your umbrella?" she asked as she moved to peer out the miniscule window in her room. "It looks like the sky will open up any minute."

"Of course not. I just hope I'll make it to my uncle's store."

"Enjoy your time with Mr. Russell, away from talk of your cousin Savannah's wedding," Florence said with a small teasing smile. Her black curly hair formed a riotous mess around her oval face as she pushed her glasses more firmly onto the bridge of her nose.

"Oh, it will be wonderful to speak of politics or literature."

"Rather than flowers and linen," Florence said.

I nodded in agreement. "I can't believe the ceremony isn't until June."

"Maybe that fancy aunt of yours can help them with the wedding plans so they will stop pestering you."

"Aunt Betsy is lovely and sure to help. Hopefully Savannah and her mother's stay with Aunt Betsy in Quincy will quell any desire to speak of Savannah's wedding with me. I hope Aunt Betsy will exert a calming influence over her sister, aunt Matilda."

"I doubt that will happen with Savannah marrying such an important man as that New Yorker, Mr. Montgomery. Be careful, my friend, for now your aunt Matilda will begin to find you such a man. Or even worse, she will join forces with your stepmother."

"Please, not even in jest," I said with a small shudder at the thought of my cousin Savannah's fiancé, Jonas Montgomery.

"It will be interesting to see what this wedding brings out in your family," Florence said.

I shrugged, knowing that, if I were completely truthful, I dreaded another wedding after my own disaster two years ago.

"Do you miss your etiquette classes?"

"Teaching me how to behave properly, especially with the upcoming event, has now become Aunt Matilda's main focus. Well, other than preparing Savannah's wedding trousseau," I said with a long sigh. "I wish my mother were alive to advise her sister that I am well schooled in this realm already."

"You do seem to have near weekly mishaps, Clarissa," Florence said, breaking into my thoughts.

"Of course I know that," I said. "Mr. Duncannon is no worse for the wear from my visit."

"His storefront is," Florence said with a lift of one eyebrow. "I should count myself very fortunate he is not demanding you pay for a replacement window. I can see why your aunt is concerned that you will embarrass the family."

"Renewed lessons on proper ways to pour tea and converse about nonsensical topics are not what I need."

"True grace is either inherent or lacking," Florence teased. She glanced again toward the window and the ever-darkening sky. "I fear the rain will start soon. Are you taking a trolley?"

"Yes, although you know how I hate them," I said. "I must go. Don't dally too long!"

I gave her a quick wave before rushing out the door. As Florence had predicted, the ominous gray clouds threatened rain. I turned from the school entrance with a spring in my step and a silent prayer I would beat the rain.

As I rushed toward the streetcar stop, I passed rows of brick tenement houses duller than usual in the dim light. I looked around and stopped short as a man with a narrow back, perfect posture, blond hair curled at the nape and finely cut clothes turned quickly away. Breathless, I stood rooted in place for a moment, panic and excitement warring inside me. I quickly shook my head in disbelief and chastised myself, starting a silent mantra of *It's not Cameron*. Consumed by memories, I stared for a few moments at the spot where the man had stood.

I continued, bending forward against the wind to the trolley stop. Vendors circled the area moving in a synchronized dance, peddling cheap umbrellas, hats and other protective wear. They groaned as the thunder sounded just as the public transport finally approached.

After squeezing onto the crowded streetcar, I jerked forward and back with each stop, barely avoiding treading on others' shoes. I extricated myself at the South End to severely blowing wind that nearly blinded me. My long skirts billowed around my legs, and my hat almost flew off with a strong gust. I realized the storm was about to hit and laughed. I knew I would not make it to my uncle's, but the challenge and adventure would be exhilarating. I began to run as fast as possible, one hand firmly on my hat. The wind whipping my skirts nearly made me fall a few times causing me to laugh again.

Half-running, half-stumbling, I approached the store on Washington Street. I glanced up toward the dark clouds upon hearing another loud clap of thunder. I grimaced as sheets of rain began to pour down, instantly drenching me. I arrived at Russell's, a fine linen store, named after my uncle Martin Russell's father. I barely noted the small handwritten Closed sign propped in the window. I ignored it, knowing I would always be welcome. Besides, I refused to remain soaked and shivering outside.

I thrust open the door with a quick laugh, shaking my head from side to side to rid myself of the raindrops gathered in my hair, only to have the laughter end in a gasp as I tripped over the doorjamb. My misstep caused me to barrel into a ladder, standing akimbo next to the entrance. I nearly fell to the floor but, instead, rammed my right side into the wall. Wincing in pain, I glared around the room to determine why such an obstruction had been positioned here. I panicked as I saw the ladder, now swaying, had a large man near the top holding on with a death grip. I froze and then reacted to his precarious situation by lunging for the ladder.

Instead of stabilizing it, the force of my movement and another small stumble caused the ladder to overbalance. I watched the man's torturously slow fall to the floor, knowing the panic I saw in his eyes was mirrored in my own. He fell backward, landing with a loud thud on the wooden floor. Although his descent seemed slow, it took only a few moments. Unfortunately the ladder skidded to the man's side and its downward momentum pulled me with it as I did not have enough sense to let go. I landed half on, half off, the man, causing him to grunt. His arms reached up around me, holding me protectively.

"Are you hurt, ma'am?" he whispered.

"No," I gasped, shocked to be in such a situation. I stared down at his closed eyes, aghast. The reality of my position, half prone on an unknown man, made me flush. From the amount of heat generated in my face, I knew I must be beet red. I began to wriggle, trying to rise with no success.

"Do you think you could get up then?" he asked, a hint of amusement in his voice.

"I'm trying," I murmured. "My skirts are tangled."

I accidentally kicked him a few times in my attempt to stand as I squirmed around. I eventually scooted to the side to a sitting position where I could work on my skirts in a slightly more dignified manner. I heard a few grunts and muttered words, but thankfully could not make them out. I knew from my brothers that such utterings were best ignored. I finally freed my skirts—with a small ripping sound—and stood. I frowned, trying to determine how badly I had damaged my skirt, but I quickly became focused on the prone man.

"For the love of God, woman, couldn't you read the Closed sign?" asked the stranger. He wrinkled his brow, watching me through barely opened eyes.

The amusement I had detected seemed to have disappeared. I continued to study him, wondering who he was. I knew most people at Uncle's store, but this man was unknown to me.

"Are you always such a menace?" he asked, letting out a long sigh and closing his eyes again.

I took a moment to appraise him. He had a straight patrician nose, and his mouth was full, though turned down in a scowl. Lying prostrate on the ground, he seemed as tall, or taller than, the six-foot ladder. He had broad shoulders; long arms; strong, lean legs; and a narrow waist. It appeared that the ready-made clothes he wore did not quite fit, as his shirtsleeve ended partway up his forearm and his pants showed his boot-covered ankles. I smiled, enjoying my silent perusal of him.

"Do you find me amusing, miss?" he asked.

I realized he had cracked open his eyes and had caught me staring at him.

"Oh! I do beg your pardon," I said, feeling the inadequacy of my words. "I am sorry! I tripped when I came in the store and…" I broke off, making a circular motion with my hands to try to explain what had happened. I bit my lip, trying to hide the fascination and the irritation I felt in equal measure toward him. "The rain, the storm," I continued, allowing my voice to trail away. I finally lowered my hands, feeling like the proverbial village idiot, waving my arms around for no reason.

He merely grunted, watching me through slitted eyes. "Do you think, Miss Calamity, that Closed signs don't pertain to the likes of you?" he asked.

I shrugged my shoulders, having no good response.

Uncle Martin entered the room, an apron covering his fine clothes of black linen pants, white cotton shirt and black waistcoat. His chocolate-colored eyes shone with curiosity as he furrowed his bushy eyebrows. He stood in the doorway, frowning, studying my torn clothes and my disheveled hair. I smiled sheepishly toward him, hoping he would understand and find humor in my latest mishap. I glanced down at my rose print dress, blanching to see the large tear along the left side nearly up to the knee.

Uncle Martin moved toward me, gently stroking my shoulder, looking into my eyes. "Are you harmed, Clarissa?" he asked in a worried tone. He began to relax, with his expression becoming more inquisitive as his gaze moved from me to the ladder and the man lying next to it.

"Clarissa, can you find Polly and send her for the doctor while I help my friend Gabriel McLeod to the parlor?" He reached down to help Mr. McLeod to his feet.

He leaned against my uncle, unable to stand without my uncle's support. I nodded as I noted the blood soaking the back of Mr. McLeod's shirt.

I hurried across the store, through a back door for family or workers, and into the part of the building for family only. I passed Uncle's study and descended the sturdy oak stairs to the kitchens. Polly, one of my uncle's maids, looked up from kneading bread as I clambered down the stairs. She broke into a friendly smile, her dull blond hair pulled into a tight bun. "You're a bit earlier than usual for tea, Miss Sullivan, but I can bring it up to you."

"Polly, I don't need tea. Can you go for the doctor? I…a man has been injured in Mr. Martin's store."

"Of course, Miss Sullivan," Polly said as she wiped her hands clean. She removed her flour-covered apron, revealing a simple cotton shirtwaist in faded navy. "Where should I bring him?"

"The family sitting room." After Polly departed from the basement entrance,

I walked up the stairs continuing to the second floor. The steps from the first floor to the second, covered in plush carpets, dulled my footsteps. I entered the large sitting room at the head of the stairs.

I glanced immediately at the injured Mr. McLeod, expecting to see him in a worsened state, but he appeared to be resting peacefully on a settee. He was lying on his right side, his head wrapped turban-style with a towel covering any blood. His legs dangling off the end of the sofa emphasized his height.

Faint light shone through the north-facing window. The Russell family parlor, though not formal, was rather stuffy. Aunt Matilda preferred fancy, decorative, often impractical furniture. Thus the settee Mr. McLeod laid on was crafted in a very ornate Rococo style with a sleigh back, faded gold fabric, intricately carved wood with a floral motif tracing the top of the sofa and delicate legs. It appeared almost too fragile to hold his weight. There were various mismatched chairs, ottomans, side tables and lamps scattered throughout the room, all to create conversation areas. The faded pink silk wallpaper was haphazardly covered with paintings of scenes from Boston and New England. The small piano sat in a far corner—to my knowledge seldom used, with my cousin Lucas being the only accomplished player. I shivered appreciatively at the warmth of the room and moved toward a heating vent, standing directly over it to warm myself.

After a few minutes of silence Polly bustled in with the doctor. For a small man, Dr. Mitchelson commanded immediate respect. He spoke in a calm, confident manner that assured all present that he could resolve whatever calamity had occurred. His eyes shone with the intelligence and weariness of years of medical practice. As the doctor began to speak with Mr. McLeod, Polly left to find towels and bowls of water. Thankfully, when Polly returned, she acted as the doctor's assistant, and I was able to remain an interested observer.

"Well, young man, you seem to have trouble with ladders," Dr. Mitchelson said as he began to examine Mr. McLeod. He moved a chair to seat himself next to the patient to study him more closely. Gently he began to unwrap the towel around his head.

"No, sir, I don't have trouble with ladders. Just with people who can't follow instructions or read signs," muttered Mr. McLeod, wincing with the removal of the towel. I remembered Uncle Martin calling him Gabriel, and I began to call him Gabriel in my mind. I stiffened defensively, knowing he had referred to me. I glanced at Uncle Martin, smiling with chagrin.

"Let's take a look at you," murmured Dr. Mitchelson.

He looked at Gabriel's eyes, the back of his head, and closely watched Gabriel's reactions and responses. It appeared at one point that Gabriel nearly fainted, and I found myself holding my breath to hear what Dr. Mitchelson had discerned.

"Tell me what happened," Dr. Mitchelson encouraged.

"I was working at the top of the ladder…" Gabriel began in a low, melodious baritone.

I listened, with my cheeks reddening.

"It was jostled. I fell off it and hurt my head."

I let out a sigh of relief that he did not share the details of my entrance. I met Polly's amused light blue eyes and blushed even more.

"The pain in my head…" Gabriel continued. "It hurts worse than it's ever hurt. I couldn't open my eyes 'cause of it." He softly hissed as the head wound was cleansed with alcohol.

I focused on Gabriel to find his piercing blue eyes watching me. I felt pinned by his gaze, unable to break the connection.

Uncle Martin, standing at the foot of the settee, attempted to control his amusement. Gabriel looked away from me and glanced in Martin's direction, glaring at him. Uncle Martin was of medium height but had an impressive build with broad, muscular shoulders; thick arms; and strong hands. He was capable of lifting tremendously heavy objects and parcels. Although not a particularly handsome man—with a receding hairline, a slightly crooked nose and a gap between his front teeth—his thoughtfulness and compassion had led to tight bonds between our branches of the family.

"Oh, I wish I could have seen this one!" chortled Uncle Martin. "Dear Clarissa is famous for her mishaps, and I think this is the worst one yet."

I frowned in consternation to see him laughing while the doctor attended to Gabriel's wounds.

"I am just sorry it was at your expense, Gabriel," he said with a final chuckle, taking a deep breath in an attempt to calm his mirth. "I should have realized instantly that she would hurt *you*, not the other way around."

Gabriel glanced at him with slightly closed eyes, brows furrowed, as though trying to figure out a puzzle, but then Dr. Mitchelson began to sew up the head wound, and Gabriel jerked in pain, quickly closing his eyes on a groan. With his eyelids shut, I was able to study him again.

"I saw her torn skirt, her hair falling out of its pins, and for an instant thought that someone had again harmed my favorite niece," Uncle Martin said. "Then I saw you on the floor and realized my initial reaction was wrong."

My eyes widened at his comments, unable to comprehend why Uncle Martin spoke so frankly about me in front of Dr. Mitchelson and this near stranger,

Gabriel McLeod. I wanted to slink quietly out of the room but remained rooted to the spot. Had he forgotten I was present? Why would he refer to Cameron in this oblique way? No one ever referred to Cameron. He was a taboo topic.

A sudden pounding on the storefront door jerked me from my silent reverie, nearly causing me to fall over. Uncle Martin turned to leave, as Polly continued to help Dr. Mitchelson.

"Uncle, I'll answer the door," I said a bit too eagerly.

"No, Clarissa, you stay here. I'll answer it," he commanded. He strode purposefully from the room.

I remained to one side, watching Dr. Mitchelson and Polly finish their work. Polly began to remove the soiled towels and dirty water. Dr. Mitchelson excused himself to wash up before leaving. I remained, feeling awkward, unsure what to do.

"Still there, miss?" Gabriel asked in a low, weak voice with closed eyes.

"Yes," I replied, moving toward him. I sat in the chair vacated by Dr. Mitchelson, taking in Gabriel's pained expression. "I wonder if there is anything the doctor can give you for your headache," I murmured, worried about his well-being.

"I certainly hope so," Gabriel whispered.

"I am terribly sorry."

"Yes, so you've said, miss," he said, opening his eyes to meet mine. "Do you always wreak such havoc?" he asked. "Or am I just extremely unlucky?"

"You are unfortunate," I replied. "Most of my mishaps involve no one else, so you have the honor of being my first, ah…casualty. For lack of a better word," I whispered ruefully, flushing softly.

"Hmm, I *feel* like a casualty," he said, the hint of a smile playing around his lips.

"Do you have anyone to care for you?" I asked. "I fear you won't be able to tend yourself for a few days."

"I have family, miss," he said, a flash of amusement shining momentarily in his eyes. "I thank you for your concern."

"It's the least I can do."

"That's true," he replied. There was another moment of silence. "Oh, talk to me about something interesting," he said, closing his eyes again in pain.

"Something interesting," I said, faltering. "I read in the paper that President McKinley has authorized the first withdrawal of troops from the Philippines."

"Did you?" he asked, opening his eyes and meeting mine with a sharp glance. I nodded, attempting to think of other interesting news. Gabriel's eyes fluttered and closed as though too heavy for him to keep them open, and asked, "Did he say when all the troops would come home?"

"No, I didn't read that," I said. "Yet I believe it is progress if some of our troops return."

He grunted. "Is your uncle always overprotective of you?" He cracked open one eye, watching me.

I tried to calm my blush and shifted uncomfortably in my chair. "Yes, he's been protective of me for quite some time. More so the past few years," I admitted in a near whisper.

Gabriel continued to study me intently through eyes barely open, as though trying to understand what I did not say. He appeared on the verge of saying something else when footsteps sounded in the hallway. I jumped at Patrick's booming voice and noticed Gabriel's grimace, as my eldest brother strolled into the parlor, with Uncle Martin following him.

"What have you done this time, Rissa?" he asked with a short laugh. He raked a hand through his windblown chestnut-brown hair peppered with gray, further disheveling it.

I stood hastily, battling a furious blush. "Patrick, this is Mr. McLeod." I waved toward Gabriel lying on the couch. "He's the one I hurt in the fall in the storefront. Thankfully the doctor has patched him up, and all is well." I heard a snort of disbelief from Gabriel and wished he would remain silent.

Uncle Martin began to regale Patrick with "poor Gabriel's" fall from grace and the subsequent visit from the doctor. I flinched as they shared a hearty laugh at my expense. Anger kindled inside me, because no one had bothered to ask me what had happened, nor worried about how I felt.

I observed Gabriel studying Patrick and Uncle Martin. I flinched again as they continued to enjoy my inherent clumsiness. However, I noted that Gabriel did not join in their joviality but observed them in apparent fascination. Once again he appeared to be attempting to solve a riddle. I continued to watch him through partially lowered eyes. Our eyes met briefly, and I felt a moment of kinship, his eyes showing compassion and concern. I glanced away quickly.

"What did the doctor recommend for Mr. McLeod?" I asked.

"The doctor, yes," Uncle Martin said. He looked chagrined as he glanced at me. "I should find a way to get you home, Gabriel," he said, looking at Gabriel with concern.

Gabriel nodded, then grimaced. "If you could send word to my brother, he would come to help me," he murmured.

"Of course," Uncle Martin replied. "Patrick, I am sure you and Clarissa need to return home. I will see you out as I send a message to Gabriel's brother." He stood, motioning for us to leave the parlor. Uncle Martin led Patrick out of the room, and I turned to follow them.

"Won't you say good-bye to me, miss?" Gabriel called out as I had almost left the room. I turned, startled to hear the deep baritone again. I met his eyes, mesmerizing blue eyes, staring intently into mine. I knew I openly stared, but his eyes were beautiful. Hypnotizing.

"Oh, yes. Good-bye, sir," I stated quickly, breaking eye contact. I smiled vaguely at a point over his shoulder before turning to leave. However, before I exited the door, I looked back to find him still staring after me through a haze of pain. "I wish you a quick recovery, sir," I whispered. I turned and hurriedly followed my brother and Uncle Martin.

CHAPTER 2

"COME ALONG, CLARISSA," Patrick urged as I trudged beside him on the short walk home. "Mrs. Smythe is upset enough without your tardy arrival." After a short pause, he said with a mischievous chuckle, "I can only imagine what she will say when she hears about your latest misadventure."

Rather than worry about the teasing I would receive from Patrick and my other brother, Colin, when I arrived home, I tried to focus on the beautiful evening after the deluge. I inhaled the fresh after-rain scent of the air, the storm having washed away the worst of the city smells.

"I love our street," I said to Patrick as we turned onto the serenity of Union Square. The bow-fronted row houses lined a centralized oval park. The park, surrounded by black wrought-iron fencing, had a fountain at either end, and rose bushes bloomed there during the summer. It lay dormant now, waiting for spring to officially come and then burst forth.

Upon our arrival home, Patrick patted my arm and said, "Good luck with her." He acted as though I had to tame a dragon. I watched with envy as he slipped into the house unnoticed. Mrs. Smythe had married our father a few months ago, and we three siblings knew we should address her as Mrs. Sullivan or Stepmama. Our continued usage of her first married name was our subtle way of expressing our discontent with her addition to our family.

As I entered the warm front hall and began to thaw out, I glanced around appreciatively, having always considered it a welcoming space. I stood on the slightly worn red carpets, admiring the narrow mahogany table which had been one of my mama's favorite pieces. I glared at the new gold-tinted card receiver resting on it—a horn of cornucopia turned on its head, with a flat area on top overly embellished by an abundance of flowers. A small dog sat in one corner at the ready, as though to guard the calling cards.

I held my stomach to try to quell its rumbling at the delicious smells wafting from the nearby dining room. Roasting meats, rosemary and thyme, and the hint of fresh bread scented the air. After Mama's death and our cook's unfortunate defection to the house of Mrs. Parker, Mrs. Smythe had aided in training our new cook. She had appeared eager to help a grieving friend's family by sharing her extensive cooking knowledge, although Colin and I soon realized her true objective was our *da*. I never would have thought she had neither the patience nor the perseverance to wait seven years for a marriage proposal from Da, yet she had.

"Where could that girl be? I have tried and tried with her to no avail," I heard Mrs. Smythe wail, the rapid click of her heels on the dining room floor showing her agitation.

I cringed, knowing she referred to me. I decided to slip up the stairs to my bedroom on the third floor. Unfortunately she sailed into the front hall, her skirts billowing behind her, wheat-blond hair perfectly done, looking like a life-sized doll. Her eyes flashed with anger, and she studied me as though I were an insect. I glanced down at my ripped dress, soaked clothes, disheveled hair and grimaced. I attempted to pat down my skirts to improve my appearance but quickly realized the futility of my actions.

"Good Lord, dear, what happened to you?" exclaimed Mrs. Smythe, concern flashing momentarily in her eyes as she took in my appearance. I glanced toward the mirror in the hallway, blanching at my reflection. I raised my eyebrows and shrugged my shoulder in resignation to the damage already done. She rushed toward me, patting my blouse with a gentle hand, and then glared at me in distaste as her hand became dampened.

"I hope you weren't seen by many people on the street looking like that, or you will be the brunt of much talk, dear. *Much* talk. You *know* how people *love* to talk," she continued in her singsong voice. "How many times have I told you to take care, be cautious, prudent, yet you never seem to listen. Why won't you listen to me, Clarissa? All I want is your well-being." She paused, gasping for air. She ushered me farther into the front hall, refraining from touching me, continuing to stare at me with distaste and a look that bordered on disappointment.

"Why can't you listen to my advice, Clarissa? All I have longed for was for you to heed me on my extensive knowledge. I could aid you with your clothes and manners, if you weren't so intent on spending your days teaching those immigrant children," she said with deep derision in her voice. "I should think that one such as you, Clarissa, would begin to look toward your own future. Or you might not have one."

I sighed as she continued to prattle. I knew by now that trying to speak was a pointless endeavor.

"Really, Clarissa, you should take more care to prevent becoming wet. I can't understand why you haven't retired to your room to change. You'll catch a cold if you aren't careful," she admonished. "Have I not told you, over and over again, to stay dry? We can't have you catching cold now, of all times," she wailed, unceremoniously pushing me toward the stairs.

Mrs. Smythe followed on my heels up the stairs to Da's study, calling out for him, I was convinced, to report on my unladylike behavior.

As I hastily changed clothes with the aid of my maid, Mary, I heard the guffaws coming from the dining room, and I realized that Patrick had begun regaling the family with today's tale. I quickly descended the stairs and entered the dining room, as Patrick, Colin, and Da were known to eat my share of supper as well as their own when I arrived late to the meal.

I glanced around the room as I settled into my chair. Da sat relaxed at the head of the table, light brown eyes lit with pleasure at the storytelling. His broad shoulders and muscled arms were the only indication of his profession as a blacksmith.

Colin, the middle sibling at age twenty-five, sitting next to me on my right, was as tall as Da, at least six feet, though not quite as stocky. Instead of brown, his hair was a thick, wavy auburn. His light blue eyes were generally filled with merriment, and he was the least serious of us all, loving a good joke and story. He worked with Da as a blacksmith.

I glanced toward my eldest brother, seated across from me, as he continued to expound on a particular detail from today. At twenty-eight, Patrick had just finished apprenticing to be an architect, and we were all extraordinarily proud of him. He worked hard, and his chestnut-brown hair already showed a little gray. His rather plain "muddy brown" eyes—as he liked to call them—hid his inquisitive nature. He rarely found himself home at night due to the long hours at his new job.

My eyes rested on the final person at the supper table, Mrs. Smythe, seated at the other end of the table and thus some distance from the rest of us. I watched her through lowered eyes, noting that her posture, hair and clothes all seemed perfect. She was slightly shorter than me, about five foot four. Her golden brown eyes appeared dull unless you looked closely and caught the cunning glimmer hidden within. Her petite frame, expertly draped in an immaculate, crisp white shirtwaist with a burgundy red skirt, highlighted her tightly corseted figure. Her long, thin face portrayed flashes of displeasure, although she tried to quell any outward reaction.

Tonight we ate in the dining room, one of my favorite rooms. We had shared many wonderful family meals here when my mama lived. The dining room table was long and made of sturdy maple with eight matching chairs around it. Along the wall toward the butler's pantry sat a simple maple sideboard with drawers to hold linens. A small oak table separated the twin windows in the room, with a small overflowing potted fern. Plush red drapes covered the windows, an addition from Mrs. Smythe. The pale slate-blue wallpaper, slightly faded, had been chosen when my mama had first decorated the room.

"Hey, human catapult!" Colin said with a wink. I blushed, realizing Patrick had already told the worst of the tale. I wondered what they would think had I been the one telling it. That thought made my cheeks redden further, as all I seemed able to recall were Gabriel's eyes and his intense, inquisitive stares.

"As long as the man wasn't hurt badly," Da said with a note of resignation, the pleasure dimming from his eyes at the realization I had hurt someone this time. He focused his light brown eyes on me. "I thought your aunt was giving you lessons?"

"Yes, in manners."

"Though clearly not in comportment," Mrs. Smythe said with a disdainful sniff. "You should never have been out in such weather. And then to stumble into a store?" she asked with a hand to her breast. "One must always exude calm and a sense of grace."

Colin snickered. "I doubt Clarissa is on very good terms with grace, Mrs. Sm…Sullivan. She probably has trouble spelling it." I poked him in the side, but he just winked at me.

"And to think they let her teach impressionable children," Mrs. Smythe said.

"Yes, Rebecca," Da said. "You know Clarissa has my approval until her wedding."

"Whenever that may be," Mrs. Smythe muttered.

"She has the right to work, like any man," Da insisted.

I smiled at him as he sat at the head of the table, thankful some of my suffragist lessons had been effective.

"What would her mother think?"

"Mama would…" I began but was interrupted by Da.

"She's not as fortunate as poor Agnes. You know that, Rebecca," Da said. "Clarissa doesn't have a generous dowry like her mother."

"Well, walking about the streets without the sense to use an umbrella does not improve…"

"Enough," Da said in a firm voice. He rubbed a hand through his thick brown hair in agitation. "Be thankful we have the smithy."

"And Colin to work in it with you," I said.

"Of course," Da said. "I inherited it from my da. We moved here from the old country when I was a young lad. My da, a poor farmer, God rest him, learned all he could when he arrived. He was fortunate enough to work as an apprentice for such a man as Mr. Wayland. An unbiased man, willing to teach my da all there was to know. And now, I have a good trade, one I can teach my own son. One day Colin will inherit it from me."

Colin turned toward me and rolled his eyes. He leaned back in his chair stretching out his long legs. "Da, you stole Patrick's job. He generally makes every conversation as boring as the ash pile with talk of his architect work." He flashed Patrick a quick smile.

"Ah, 'tis grand to see us so well settled," Da said with a fond glance toward Mrs. Smythe. She sat with impeccable stillness, her back poker straight.

"Yes it is, Sean," Mrs. Smythe said. "I am very relieved we have finally returned to the dining room from the wretched eating area in the kitchen. I can't imagine what you were thinking, eating in there when you have a perfectly functional dining room."

I glanced toward Colin and he rolled his eyes again at me.

She asked, waving in the direction of the sideboard, "Do you like the new vase that was delivered today?"

We all glanced toward the large, ornate oriental vase with a blue-and-red scene glazed on the front. It was the exact antithesis of my mama's style, clashing with the room's other simple furnishings. "It's, ah…exotic," Da said after a long pause. He continued to frown at the vase as he studied it.

"Of course it is!" she responded with enthusiasm. "I am greatly looking forward to bringing the home and the furnishings up to modern standards. It is 1900 after all. The turn of a new century."

"I always loved how well Mama decorated the house. She had an unparalleled ability for both thrift and beauty," I said.

"Pshaw…who need concern themselves with the budget? The smithy is successful, and I couldn't possibly entertain in such shabby rooms. You wouldn't want to humiliate me in such a manner, would you, Sean?" she asked, her brown eyes full of tears.

"Now, Rebecca, don't fret so," he said. He glanced around as though trying to discover a new topic.

"Not wanting to sound too much like Patrick, but I believe there is something serious that needs to be discussed," Colin said, watching me with grave blue eyes.

My fork clattered out of my fingers, my hearty appetite fleeing after only finishing half my supper. I watched Colin with dread. Colin was rarely serious.

"I have heard, though it's not confirmed, that Cameron is back," Colin said, watching me intently.

I paled and began to feel light-headed. I wished I could let out my corset and take a deep breath.

"Rissa, if you see him, you need to tell us," Colin admonished. "You shouldn't have to speak with him, not after what he did."

Da grunted in agreement.

"Is that wise, dear?" Mrs. Smythe asked, looking me up and down.

I frowned defensively, not imagining she could take offense with my current attire, a satin lilac evening dress.

"If a man is interested in you, I'd hate to think you would turn him away due to a minor lapse of judgment."

I gritted my teeth at an angry retort, breathing heavily. "I believe my brothers, Da and I know best when it comes to Cameron," I replied, nearly choking on his name.

"Aye, you do, Clarissa," Da replied. "You remember now, any trouble from him, you send word to us. We'll be there in no time."

I nodded my agreement.

"May I be excused, Da?" I asked. I had no desire to listen further to Mrs. Smythe nor had any appetite for the remainder of my supper.

***

I ENTERED MY ROOM, closing the door to the sounds of Da and Colin settling in for their cribbage match in the second-floor family parlor. I leaned against the door for a moment, allowing the calm colors of my bedroom to soothe me. The walls were decorated in blue-and-white wallpaper with a flowing bird-and-flower motif. I pushed away from the door, moving toward my four-poster bed, reaching for the pile of pillows to rearrange them. I fluffed one before moving on to the chaise positioned in front of the windows, to the right of the bed. I sat for a moment, looking out into the darkened back garden and skeletonlike tree limbs.

A quick knock heralded my maid's expected arrival, and I moved behind the privacy screen, to the right of the door. After freeing myself from layers of petticoats, corsets and my chemise, I slipped into a comfortable nightgown and wrap. I emerged from the privacy screen as Mary left my bedroom. I wandered along the opposite side of my room to the tall maple dresser to stare at one of the few pictures I had of Mama. A piece of lace covered the top of the dresser, one of my mama's school projects. I fingered a few of the seashells I had collected with Mama the last time we had gone to the beach together. "Oh, Mama," I whispered, trying not to cry. "I wish you were here."

I scrubbed away the tears as I faced the dark mahogany vanity, which had also been my mama's. I collapsed onto the stool, pulling out compartments on either side of the mirror to place within my earrings, bracelets and hairpins. Every time I stared into the long mirror, I imagined my mama looking into the mirror and felt closer to her.

I sat on the stool in front of the vanity, staring at my reflection in the mirror. My long chestnut-brown hair, freed from its pins, cascaded down my back in waves. I had an oval, almost round face, with high cheekbones and lips that appeared turned up at the corners as though always on the verge of smiling. My almond-shaped light blue eyes reflected my inner turmoil.

I remembered the first time I had met Cameron at one of Aunt Betsy's functions in Quincy. I had decided to visit her to raise my spirits after my mama had died. While there, Aunt Betsy had held a party in my honor. She and Uncle Tobias were of the highest social class. One of their friends' sons, Cameron Wright, had been coerced into attending the soiree. He had stood aloof to one side of the room, dispassionately studying those present while appearing formal and stiff-necked. Even so, I had felt an instant interest in him.

That night, for one of the first times since the death of my mama, I felt my spirit lighten. I gaily joined in conversations with a large group of fascinating guests. After a few lengthy, lively discussions, Cameron strolled toward my group and joined in. I cannot remember what was said, yet I remember feeling a thrill of energy race through my body to be near him. I sighed, staring into the mirror into my devastated eyes, wondering if I would ever feel such a thrill again.

CHAPTER 3

AS I WALKED DOWN MY STREET, I noted once again that our home was one of the last on the block occupied as a single-family home. Most were filled with working men with rooms to let and no board provided. Mrs. Smythe often simpered in disdain as the neighborhood became increasingly working class. All of the houses were built in a style similar to mine: simple four-story bow-fronted brick row homes with a basement. Each had steep staircases leading to the front door with intricately carved metal railings. A set of stairs in front of the house led down to the kitchen area, and I often used this door as a means of escape. With that thought, I attempted to banish Mrs. Smythe from my thoughts and to enjoy the day.

I sighed in contentment to be outside, turning my head up to the blue sky, imagining the street in full bloom with the warmth and rebirth of spring. I envisioned the budding trees, the branches forming a green canopy overhead from which hidden birds trilled. I suddenly tripped on an uneven brick and reentered the present moment again with the last of winter and its barren trees.

I continued my walk down Union Street before turning right onto the busy storefront-lined Washington Street. Horses pulled carts as their drivers ably avoided streetcars rumbling by on tracks in the middle of the road while numerous carriages lined each side. I glanced down the street at the steel monstrosity being created to elevate the streetcar. It had not yet reached Russell's, although it would by the end of the year. The huge metal beams glistened in the sun, although the farther it encroached, the darker the street below became.

I walked along the sidewalk, looking at the windows under large storefront awnings. I passed many familiar businesses: a Chinese laundry, a hat cleaning shop, a coffeehouse. Mr. Jeffries, the tailor, seemed particularly busy this morning, and I nodded to him as I continued toward my uncle's store.

I had always loved the store. As a child, I thought it a magical space with all the linen, ribbon and interesting people visiting throughout the day. Although a small shop, Uncle Martin managed to obtain and sell some of the most sought-after linens in Boston. He rejected the idea of ready-made clothes, believing there still existed a market for people to make their own clothes or visit a tailor.

After entering, I glanced around, absently noting the unfinished display Gabriel had been working on. There were stacks of fine linens along three walls; in front of each was a low glass case. Inside these were ribbons, patterns and the most expensive linens. Lucas, Uncle Martin or Aunt Matilda took turns standing behind the glass cases, waiting on the customers. During busier times, both Uncle Martin and Lucas worked out front together.

Lucas bounded into the storefront from upstairs, full of energy. "All ready, Rissa?" he asked, his amber eyes filled with good-natured mischief. Lucas wore a well-tailored suit with white shirt, black pants, waistcoat and jacket. He reached for a hat, covering his light brown hair. He and Uncle Martin always wore well-tailored clothes, believing themselves to be walking advertisements for the linens they sold.

"Let's go," I agreed. I linked my arm with his, exiting Russell's and strolling toward the trolley stop. "Lucas, have you heard that Cameron might be back?" I asked.

Lucas stopped walking abruptly, staring at me in concern. We were jostled as other pedestrians had to scramble around us. He nodded his apologies to them and then focused his attention on me, studying me with squinted eyes, surprise and concern in his expression.

"How do you feel about that, Rissa?"

"I honestly don't know," I said. "Shocked. Saddened. Disappointed."

"Why disappointed?"

"I want to forget about him, and I thought that at last I was succeeding. I feel that now, two years later, I have the chance to forge a new life and new dreams. I don't understand why he would reappear again," I said, my voice laced with bitterness.

Lucas nodded. "I'm sure we'll know in time."

***

"CALM DOWN, RISSA," Lucas murmured as he sat next to me as I fidgeted on the streetcar. "You will see that he is fine and then you can forget meeting him."

I nodded, expelling a pent-up breath at his words. "I wish I had sent a note," I said.

"It's a little late now," Lucas said as he rose to get off the streetcar at our stop. He held on to my elbow so I would not fall. "And Father would be very upset if we didn't visit."

Lucas led me into an immigrant part of town mainly composed of Italians. Da used to say that the Irish were here in years past but had the good sense to leave. The North End was a virtual rabbit warren of narrow streets, with few traversing the entire neighborhood. The buildings ranged from three to four stories high, many with a storefront on the first floor and living quarters in the upper stories. Small alleys led off the main streets to homes that were so close together it appeared they rarely saw sunlight.

All thought of the upcoming visit fled as we turned the corner onto Salem Street, and I suddenly found myself in the middle of a street market. I inhaled, closing my eyes, smelling the new, unfamiliar scents wafting from a nearby bakery. It smelled like licorice. People pushed impatiently past us to reach their favorite vendor, muttering in Italian at our slow progress.

The fresh fruit stalls had their selections perfectly positioned so that I did not dare touch an orange for fear of causing an avalanche to cascade onto the street. We passed by buckets of salted fish, with women haggling in Italian over the price. I watched, fascinated to see how expressive the women were, using their hands and arms to show their displeasure, their voices raised as they argued over a price. I shared a smile with Lucas, enjoying this view into an unknown area of Boston. I nearly tripped a few times on the uneven cobblestones, but the street was so packed I merely stumbled ungracefully into someone else, preventing a fall.

"It's fantastic, isn't it?" Lucas said. "I don't have cause to come here much with deliveries, but I always enjoy my trips to the North End."

We emerged from Salem Street onto a quieter street that almost seemed like an alley. I breathed deeply. Lucas nodded in passing toward a group of men lounging at the mouth of the walkway, taking my arm.

"How do you know where we're going?" I asked, breathless from the crowd.

"I have been to the area before, Rissa," he said.

We turned onto a small opening between buildings, walking nearly half a block and entered a tiny courtyard. Another row of houses stood behind those that fronted the main street, faint sunlight permeating the courtyard. Lucas glanced at the number of one of the homes in this hidden row of residences and said, "Ah, here we are," before gently letting go of my arm and reaching out to knock on the door.

Suddenly all the pleasure I had felt at the impromptu street market fled, and I felt like I wanted to be ill. Nervous energy raced through me at the thought of seeing Gabriel again. *Mr. McLeod*, I resolutely told myself. I clasped my hands together, standing poker straight with my shoulders back. I wanted to appear strong and capable, even if I was quaking inside.

I heard a loud thud and muffled voices from inside the house. Finally heavy footsteps approached. The door slowly cracked open to reveal a tall youngish man with icy-blue eyes, black hair and a fierce frown. I took a small step backward at such a welcome. I couldn't remember if this was the Mr. McLeod I had injured or not.

"Please pardon the interruption," Lucas said in a cold, formal voice, squaring his shoulders and lifting his chin. "But we were hoping to inquire after the health of a Mr. McLeod. He was injured at my father's store, Russell's, a few days ago. We wanted to ensure his return to health."

The young man's frown eased with Lucas's words, and he became curious, glancing from Lucas to me, tilting his head to the side as he looked at me, before smiling. The smile transformed his face from forbidding to very handsome and welcoming. His eyes lit with humor.

"Aye, Gabe's had a few rough days, though he's on the mend now. Please come in."

He stepped aside, fully opening the door, and waved us through. He did not offer to take coats or hats but simply waited for us to enter, secured the front door, then led us through a dark, dreary hallway.

"Richard, who was it? Not Aunt Masterson again?" a deep, melodious baritone called out as we approached the back room. I paused, closing my eyes for a moment in recognition of this voice. A chill raced down my spine in anticipation.

I opened my eyes to exchange a furtive glance with Lucas, who gave me a quick, encouraging smile as we entered the room. I scanned it, looking for Gabriel, and saw him sitting at a table. As we entered, his eyes focused first on Lucas, and he stared at him with frank curiosity. Then he turned his dulled azure-blue eyes to me, and ruefully shook his head and continued to watch me in apparent fascination. At that, Lucas stepped in front of me, attempting to block me from view. Annoyance swept through me, and I quietly sidestepped Lucas, allowing myself to see the room and Gabriel.

Gabriel sat in a sturdy chair in a clean but threadbare gray shirt and black pants. His thick ebony hair was disheveled, and his cheeks and chin were darkened with day-old stubble. The man who had led us here walked to the rear wall.

They both remained silent.

I continued to stare about the large multipurpose room, curious, and attempted to dispel my nervousness. Along the far wall, there was a tiny clean window, overlooking what appeared to be a rear garden. Near this window there was a kitchen area with a small stove and open shelves over the sink to hold plates and bowls. Along the left side of the room was a fireplace, with a small perfunctory fire smoldering in the grate. It did not give off much heat, as the room maintained a damp coldness.

Along the right wall were bookshelves, filled to bursting with tomes that appeared to be well tended with little or no dust visible. In the center of the room I saw a finely wrought square wooden table with three chairs, big enough for tall men to sit comfortably, with Gabriel occupying one of them. Finally along the fourth wall was a small settee covered with blankets. That wall also contained the door through which we had just entered. A tattered rug lay in front of the settee. A black-and-white cat curled up on one of its many blankets, blinking open its eyes to study the new arrivals.

"So, you finally decided to come and see if I survived?" Gabriel asked, a trace of amused bitterness in his voice after watching my silent perusal of his home.

I was startled at his words, not knowing what to say. He didn't look ill, sitting in his chair. I returned his gaze, mesmerized, searching for the proper response. Lucas forestalled anything I might have said.

"I am Lucas Russell, and I'm here on behalf of my father to inquire after your health." Lucas spoke in his most proper voice and accent. I glanced at him worriedly, softly biting my lower lip, as he rarely spoke in such an unfriendly tone.

Gabriel watched him with squinted eyes, taking in his well-tailored fine linen clothes and highly polished shoes. Gabriel nodded once, as though in understanding.

"Begging your pardon, miss and sir, for not getting up," Gabriel replied, in an equally formal tone, all trace of amusement gone. "I continue with a headache, and I still can't see straight when I'm standing." A wisp of a smile crossed his features as he waved toward me. "Thanks to the disaster known as a person standing beside you currently, sir."

I flushed.

I gripped Lucas's arm, silently indicating I wanted to speak. I nodded toward Gabriel, attempting to disarm him and charm him. I noted again another small smile lurking around his mouth as he studied me. I moved toward the table and

Gabriel, needing to ascertain for myself how much he continued to suffer from his injury.

"You must allow me to apologize for the harm and pain I have caused you, sir—" I stopped short in front of him, examining him with worried eyes. "I have never before hurt anyone in one of my, ah…" My voice trailed off.

Gabriel had watched my approach warily, leaning away as I neared. "Again, begging your pardon, miss, I do not want to be in too close proximity to you. Especially while you are in motion."

I heard a snigger from the man who had let us in and sent a frown in his direction.

I gritted my teeth in frustration and moved toward the back window, glancing outside. Sunlight streamed into this room. The two buildings that should have abutted the rear of this one were missing. The empty space in the back, which I had originally thought consisted of a garden, was two empty weed-filled lots.

I stared at the scene outside, surprised to see washing hanging out to dry. I marveled at his neighbors' apparent lack of inhibition in displaying their clothes, including their most intimate apparel, for all to see. A small smile tugged at my mouth to see a tiny multicolored, though worn, pair of baby's booties hanging out to dry. It seemed whimsical to me, the incongruity of them hanging next to a large pair of men's faded gray working pants.

"You find my neighbors' wash entertaining, miss?" Gabriel asked in a flat voice.

I turned toward him with a frown. Uncertainty spread through me, self-doubt quickly replacing the pleasure I had felt upon admiring the innocent domestic scene moments before. I looked away and shook my head in denial. "No," I contradicted him. "Not amusement. Pleasure."

I turned back to face him in time to see shock flit through his eyes before he masked his expression. I admired his ability to hide his feelings.

"So, you're the infamous sister," called out the other man, the one who had answered the door.

He stood, leaning against the back wall, avidly watching our interaction. He pushed away to move toward me. I looked up and up as he towered over me. He appeared not to want or need to hide his expression, and watched me with open fascination. "You don't look like a walking disaster," he said in an amicable tone. "Though Gabe suffered enough on your account."

"I am sorry to hear that you know of my, ah…"

"Your lack of grace?" the man asked with a friendly smile. "You are quite famous at my smithy, thanks to Colin's frequent visits. His tales of your latest misadventures are some of our favorites. I just never imagined you'd end up harming Gabe."

I blushed at Colin's lack of discretion.

The man reached out his hand to shake mine, saying, "My name is Richard, and I am the middle McLeod brother."

I detected a note of pride in his voice at the name *McLeod*. He and Gabriel shared the same height, blue eyes and black hair; though if I were honest, I would say that Richard was the more handsome of the two.

I nodded an acknowledgment, belatedly taking his hand. I waited for Lucas to provide the formal introductions for me, as was proper. Lucas, however, remained stubbornly mute, engaging in a silent staring match with the elder brother. After a few moments of uncomfortable silence, I spoke up.

"My name is Clarissa Sullivan," I said to the two McLeod brothers, "of the unfortunate mishaps." The last was said with a small, regretful smile. I brushed at a wisp of hair that had come loose and tucked it behind my ear. I continued to glance around the room, looking at everything but Gabriel McLeod or his brother.

"Nice to meet you," Richard responded, smiling, flashing a dimple in his left cheek, seemingly entertained by our visit. "I know your brother well," he said. He continued to smile, watching me with a similarly intense gaze as his brother.

I studied him. Tattered suspenders held up a pair of faded black trousers, the worn dark blue shirt's sleeves rolled up to his elbows. No amount of polishing would make his shoes black. He wore no tie, vest or collar, and his shirt was slightly open at the neckline, revealing a small tuft of black hair. He appeared more casually dressed than any man I had ever seen. I tried not to stare at him, but his beauty and evident charm intrigued me.

"Nice to *formally* meet you," Gabriel said, interrupting my perusal of his brother. At that, I glanced over and met Gabriel's eyes again. There remained a trace of humor in them, but, more than anything, I saw pain. He appeared to be doing his best to conceal the discomfort, but it was evident.

I gentled my voice and addressed him. "Is there anything I can do to help?"

He closed his eyes, preventing me from being further entranced by his piercing blue eyes.

Richard spoke up for his brother. "He hates to admit it, Miss Sullivan, but he is in considerable discomfort." Worry furrowed his brow. "I had thought he would be recovered by now, but he can still barely stand up without help, and he has terrible dizzy spells."

Gabriel spoke, interrupting Richard in a gruff voice. "Don't exaggerate so, Rich. I'm fine. Just a little ache. Nothing time won't heal. I'll be back to work soon."

I looked from one to the other, unsure who to believe. I turned toward Lucas, but he remained determinedly silent. "Let me look at your head," I entreated, then moved toward him, but he scooted his chair away.

"Again begging your pardon, miss, I would rather you didn't," he said, eyeing me warily. I noted sweat on his brow, the clenching of his jaw. I reached out as though to feel his brow for fever but stopped myself in time, realizing it would not be proper. I stood stooped over him, studying him.

"You are truly unwell," I whispered. "Lucas, we must find a doctor," I commanded, turning to look at Lucas, who rolled his eyes at me in apparent exasperation.

"Oh, that won't be necessary," Richard blurted out, flushing.

"I thank you for your concern, miss," Gabriel gasped out, his gaze momentarily unfocused. "You have done your duty by ensuring I survived my…misadventure with you. I am sure you have much more important matters to fill your time."

I frowned at him, uncertain why he would refuse a doctor's help.

"Mr. McLeod," I entreated once more, reaching out and gripping his hand. "I really believe you need to see the doctor." I saw shock flit through his eyes as I took his hand. "Please let me call for one for you?"

"No, miss, I'm sure I'll be just fine," he replied. "You've done your duty here. You can forget this last accident ever occurred."

"But, if you are in pain…" I continued, noting the exchange of uncomfortable looks between Richard and Gabriel.

"I don't want your charity, miss," Gabriel muttered.

I jerked, taken aback. I watched Richard kick Gabriel in the leg, and heard Gabriel grunt softly. I stood, moving toward Lucas. He glanced at me sharply and leaned over, hissing in my ear, "Doctors cost money, Rissa. And I doubt they could afford one."

"Well, then we should pay, as it was my fault," I whispered back, glaring at Lucas and his blatant snobbery, wishing I could kick him in the shin as Richard had just kicked Gabriel.

After a long pause and a deep breath, Lucas spoke up and said, "Yes, Rissa, let's fetch the doctor and send him on his way here. When you are feeling better, Mr. McLeod, I hope you will return to the store to visit with my father." At this, he nodded, nearly imperceptibly, first to Gabriel, then to Richard. He gripped my elbow, turning me in the direction of the door. I resisted for a moment, wanting to say a farewell to Gabriel.

"I do hope you will recover soon, Mr. McLeod," I stated, noting the inadequacy of my words as I allowed Lucas to usher me out of the room.

"Miss Sullivan?" Gabriel's baritone voice gently called out as I turned to leave. I glanced back at him to see his pensive, troubled eyes. "I thank you for your concern."

I nodded, unable to think of anything adequate to say. Richard led us down the hallway, thanking me for the visit while subtly ignoring Lucas.

As we walked along the small alleyway, I gripped Lucas's arm painfully. "Why were you such a boor?" I demanded.

"Rissa," he said, exasperation tingeing his tone. "Are you seriously concerned about me offending two poor laborers who live *here*?" He stared at me incredulously as he waved around the poorly lit area, stopping to stare at me. "You can't actually tell me you care one whit about them?"

"They're Colin's friends," I insisted.

"Yes, and Colin has some regrettable associations," Lucas said. "Clarissa, are you so naive?" He gripped my arms lightly, as though he wanted to shake sense into me. "The elder brother looked at you with such…" Lucas broke off, muttering under his breath.

"With such what, Lucas?" I demanded.

"Insolence," he nearly roared. "How dare he look at you like that?"

"Like what? Like he found me attractive?" I said, louder than I had meant and heard a faint catcall in response. I noted we had a small audience, and, though I wasn't sure they could understand all we were saying, I felt uncomfortable. "Lucas, we shouldn't be arguing in the street." I gripped his arm, trying to propel him into motion.

"So now you worry about propriety?" Lucas ground out, remaining stock-still. "Rissa, what's come over you?" he asked, finally allowing me to drag him toward the main street and home.

"I don't like it when you sound like Jonas Montgomery, that insufferable fiancé of Savannah's, all pompous and stuffy, as though you are better than other people," I said. "I don't like it when you stand sullenly by, glaring at an injured man, then insult him in his own home by pointing out his poverty!" I hissed. "Don't you think he knows he is poor?"

"As long as you understand it, Clarissa," Lucas whispered. "Don't get any ideas about the McLeods. They're not good enough for you."

I shook my head futilely. "Lucas, you misunderstand. I have no ideas, romantic or otherwise, about the McLeods," I said. "I just want to see him well, to move on with my life."

"Rissa…" He let out a long sigh. "I'm sorry if I acted improperly, in your opinion. I didn't like either of them. One too friendly and sure of himself, the other too…" Again he wouldn't finish his sentence. "Rissa, just don't plan to be around them much. It's not a good idea."

"I doubt either would want to see me," I muttered as a wave of self-pitying thoughts washed over me.

CHAPTER 4

"UNCLE," I CALLED OUT as I entered the store, only to find myself nearly deafened by a high-pitched squeal. I almost toppled over as Savannah threw herself into my arms.

"Where have you been? I've been here for ages, and I even had to wait on a few customers," she said, widening her sky-blue eyes in mock horror. Her wispy strawberry-blond hair was fashioned in a loose chignon with tendrils framing her heart-shaped face. "Come, tell me of the past few weeks!" Savannah said, grabbing my hand and pulling me up the stairs.

We passed through the darkened hallway, careening into a side table. A vase of flowers almost tipped over, but Savannah reached out to right it before it toppled to the floor. We continued through the hallway to the stairs, passing hung scenes of New England and small cross-stitched pieces that Aunt Matilda and Savannah had created. Bright sunlight streamed in through the windows as we entered the Russell family sitting room, where tea had been prepared for us.

"Does Aunt Matilda ever see you like this?" I asked on a laugh as I sank onto an overstuffed, uncomfortable settee.

"Rarely. She would frown and remind me of the need for propriety at all times," she said as she mimicked her mother before she burst out laughing.

"Then why am I to model my behavior on yours?" I asked.

"Because I can act the part. I know their rules are ridiculous, and so do you. But you have to play along if you want to join their group," she said, resting against the cushions.

"So you say," I said thinking of Jonas Montgomery, her fiancé.

"Don't you want to marry, have children? That was always our favorite topic as children." We shared a long look as we both reminisced. "We'd have little girls, months apart, and they'd grow up close, like sisters."

"Like us," I said.

"Yes, like us," she said with a wistful sigh.

"I may have a sister in a few months' time," I murmured.

"You mean she's…expecting?" Savannah sputtered, then bent forward to pour us some tea.

"Yes, a 'blessed event.' That's what Mrs. Smythe calls it." I shook my head as I imagined having another sibling.

"What bothers you, Rissa?"

"The idea that I may be looked upon to care for the child if I am still at home."

"Yes, the spinsterly older sister," Savannah said with a theatrical sigh.

I glared at her, fighting resentment at the reference to spinsterhood.

"I imagine your stepmother would consider it your duty."

"I'm not that old. And, yes, she most assuredly would."

"Old enough. And if we are to have daughters who are more or less the same age, you need to find an acceptable man."

"Well, seeing as I haven't met an eligible man in years, that may prove a challenge," I said with a frown.

"Mr. Montgomery and I might need to move to New York City after the wedding," Savannah said, some of her vivaciousness dimming as she spoke of her fiancé.

"What? You are to stay here. Or is this part of the bargain for him to marry—"

"There is no bargain," Savannah snapped. "You know I want to marry him, and he wants to marry me. I want to be a part of his important world. I'm simply fortunate the family approves."

I stared at her, for once at a loss for words as I thought about Jonas, who exuded power and self-confidence. Whereas he thought he appeared upper class and debonair, I found him stuffy and pompous. Colin would argue that those words were synonymous for the truly rich. In any case, I believed Jonas's personal convictions were dangerous misconceptions to have about oneself and feared for Savannah's future happiness.

Jonas stood at about my height with brown hair and topaz eyes that appeared deceptively dull. However, they hid a rapier sharp mind, waiting to detect the smallest weakness in an opponent to expose him or her to public ridicule. I sensed that his greatest joy came in detecting when someone was not thoroughly engaged in a debate, or did not know all of their facts, and having them look a fool in front of a crowd. He lived to debate and prove his prowess with the spoken word, preening as he showed his superior verbal skills. He believed it showed a nobility of mind to expose the weaknesses of others. I disagreed. I believed it showed a poverty of spirit to relish the humiliation of others only for personal pleasure.

"I think you will find that Jonas is very caring when you know him better," Savannah said as she broke into my thoughts.

"Does he know of our interest in the suffragettes?" I asked.

Savannah choked on her sip of tea before gasping out a response. "Never mention any interest that I might have had. I am recovered from such foolish notions."

"Such as wanting to have the same rights as men or to be able to vote? To have some say on our own lives when we marry?"

"Hush, Rissa, you speak nonsense. Women can and should want for no more than what we already have. Men have been good to us."

"What has happened to you?" I asked, truly alarmed.

"I know what I need to do to marry. You should learn the same," she said with a pointed glance. After an awkward moment she said, "Do you want to hear Aunt Betsy's ideas for the wedding?"

I picked up my teacup, staring into it instead of answering.

"Hmm…" she said at my long pause. "I can see my time away did not make you any more eager to hear about my plans." She tucked her feet up under her burgundy satin skirt, sitting comfortably, with her hands folded in front of her.

"I'd rather tell you about my adventures of the past few days."

"Adventures? Plural? Oh, Rissa, after all Mother has done to help." Savannah watched me with fond despair.

I shrugged as there was nothing to say. "I stumbled into the store a few days ago and knocked a man off his ladder. He crashed to the floor, hurting his head. I couldn't believe a head wound would bleed so much, Savannah. How could I have been so clumsy again?" I sighed as I remembered that day. "We had the doctor here, and the injured man was sent home to recover. I visited him today with Lucas because Uncle Martin told me that he wasn't improving. I thought it better to visit rather than send a note." The tension that had bloomed between us with the mention of Jonas slowly dissipated.

"What was his home like?"

"Well, he lives in the North End…" At Savannah's knowing nod I realized I did not need to explain further. "He has a shelf full of books."

"Are you saying all you noticed was his books?"

"No, of course not. Mr. McLeod—"

"Are you telling me that your adventure was with Mr. McLeod? The tall, black-haired, broad-shouldered carpenter?"

"Yes, of the brooding stares."

"Oh, my. I've seen him," Savannah said with feigned breathlessness, grinning and unable to hide her delight. "I can't say I've met him, but I've definitely seen him." She sighed melodramatically, causing me to laugh again.

I sighed too, thinking about his blue eyes. "He is somewhat handsome, isn't he?"

"Somewhat? Somewhat? Do you need to have Dr. Mitchelson examine your eyes?" Savannah asked.

"If you can believe it, the brother's even more attractive," I said, leaning in as though imparting a great secret. Savannah's eyes widened in glee, and she smiled broadly.

"Oh, this is delicious. A fun story when I've just arrived home. You know how I love Aunt Betsy, but it can be so tiring being with her. It's as though there're always hidden meanings in everything she says. I don't have your wit or patience to puzzle them all out." Savannah pouted, closing her eyes briefly before opening them to meet mine. "So, tell me more about today's visit."

"Oh, Sav, that too was a disaster! I think Mr. McLeod, the injured one, thought I was there just for charitable works, a sense of duty." At this Savannah cocked her head toward me with eyebrows raised. I huffed slightly. "All right, he was right. I admit, I *was* there out of a sense of duty, yet I truly wanted to know how he was. Though on reflection I think a card might have sufficed." I pinched the bridge of my nose, feeling a headache coming on.

"Rissa, you must know I am teasing you. I am sorry you are so upset," Savannah said. "Tell me all of it, all that happened."

"When we arrived, his brother let us in. We moved to the back room, a surprisingly sunny room in the midst of a dark alley. Gabriel—Mr. McLeod—seemed upset I was there, didn't want me near him. I think he was afraid I would cause him harm again. I fear he thought me a snob." I grimaced as I thought through my visit to Gabriel's. "Lucas was obnoxious and stuffy, acting all superior, and I felt like a mute who could barely speak coherently. Then, when I realized Mr. McLeod should see a doctor, Lucas pointed out they were too poor to afford one. I was mortified to have money brought up, and then disgusted with Lucas for being so rude and pompous. Thankfully Lucas finally agreed to pay for one."

"Rissa, you *know* how Lucas can be." Savannah looked at me knowingly and rolled her eyes. "You have just always chosen to see the better parts of him and ignore his worst aspects. He can be *awful* to others, especially if he feels uncomfortable. And he would feel uncomfortable around two tall, gorgeous McLeod brothers."

I blushed and looked away, finally betraying my personal reaction to Savannah.

Savannah squealed with laughter. "Oh, I knew there was more to this story! Which one did you like? Was it the injured Gabriel? Or the friendly, more handsome brother?"

She sat up excitedly, and I almost expected her to begin to bounce up and down on the settee with her enthusiasm.

"Sav, calm down!" I glanced worriedly toward the door, but Savannah waved her hand at the door in dismissal.

"Don't worry so much, Rissa," Savannah admonished. "Mama is too tired from our time at Aunt Betsy's to hover outside listening to our jabbering, and the shop's too busy today for Father or Lucas to join us. We have our privacy." She squeezed my hand in encouragement. "So, which one is it?" When I remained silent, she said, "My guess is on Gabriel. You had an open and friendly man last time, and what did it get you? I bet you go for brooding and temperamental this time."

I looked away for a moment, before meeting her gaze with entreating eyes, silently asking her to be kind. "I don't know what it is, Sav," I whispered, pausing, trying to find the words to describe my feelings. "I felt alive again, like I had before, yet also nervous. And I couldn't understand why he kept staring at me. It made me very uncomfortable. Gentlemen don't stare."

"Oh, this is promising!" Savannah said with a look of triumph. "And when have you ever cared about proper manners? You know we have despaired that you would ever fully master the rules of society." Savannah looked at me knowingly. "We must find a way for you to see him again. Do you think you could manage another visit? Hmm…no, of course you couldn't. That would make people talk. You being *you* makes people talk enough," she said, stopping to think, biting her lip, deep in thought.

"Well, there are potential problems. First off, he's the carpenter you injured. He might not want much more to do with you and your clumsiness. Also I imagine there will be opposition from the family, as he isn't of the same class if he's too poor to send for a doctor for himself. He must not be a master carpenter yet? Hmm… Plus you may not find him interesting as he might not be educated enough to even hold a decent conversation. Well, what you consider decent, not the rest of us. However, if you don't care that he is a carpenter, and he *is* interesting, why should anyone else?" she concluded, smiling broadly.

"Sav," I responded in a serious tone, as a ball of anxiety settled at the pit of my stomach. "You are getting ahead of yourself. I have just met him twice. There is nothing going on between us. I doubt I will see him again."

Savannah made a circular motion in the air with her hand that looked elegant rather than vapid, continuing the vein of conversation that most interested her. "That's exactly my point, Rissa. We must find a way for you to see him again. We'll have to contrive something!" She leaned back, laughing and clapping her hands together in her excitement.

At that moment, the parlor door creaked open, and I said a small prayer of thanks for the momentary warning.

"Savannah, dear," interrupted a cold, nasally voice. "I do hope you are not planning any more mischief with Clarissa. I doubt she needs your help in that regard."

The cultured voice made me shudder. I glanced up to see Jonas leaning against the door, one foot crossed against the other, sneering at me. He was impeccably dressed, his thin frame clothed in fabrics of the highest quality. His sandy-blond hair coiffed with pomade, not a hair out of place. I smiled tightly in his direction in an attempt to feign pleasure at seeing him. He did not move to enter the room but stood there, surveying the two of us.

"Hello, Jonas," Savannah demurely called out, extending her hand to him in invitation to join us.

He entered the room, walking with military precision toward a formal wing-back chair. I watched Savannah subtly change: she sat straighter, talked in hushed tones, and became less vivid and vivacious. He sat stiffly in the chair, taking Savannah's hand, and stared at me thoughtfully.

"Have you extricated yourself from this latest mess yet, Clarissa? I would hate for you to have to continue to associate with such people for long."

"I can understand your concern, Jonas, but really you must quit being such a snob," Savannah chided. "Clarissa will do what she must, and we will all be happy for her."

Jonas studied Savannah intently, attempting to decipher the full meaning of her statement, then shook his head ruefully and half smiled at Savannah. "You are the only person I know who can continuously speak in riddles." A trace of warmth had finally entered his voice as he addressed Savannah. He again glanced at me with icicle-cold eyes, speaking with his customary chill. "I hate to interrupt your reunion, but Savannah and I must attend a previously agreed upon engagement. Savannah, we must leave soon, and you need to tidy your appearance." He pointedly glanced at her hair, which had come loose from its pins. Savannah agreed, blushing to have been seen thus, and turned to me.

"Rissa, it has been so good to see you again. Will you be at home for supper tonight? I thought I would come by to visit everyone, and to congratulate your father and Mrs. Smy…er, Mrs. Sullivan. Let's continue our conversation then," she concluded with a wink and a grin. I leaned over to give her a half hug, after which she rose and quietly left the room.

Jonas remained sitting in the parlor, relaxing in the high-backed chair with his legs crossed, watching me intently. I quietly met his gaze, refusing to break the silence. Finally he spoke. "I have tried to determine for quite some time now why you and Savannah are so close, and it remains a mystery to me. Do you have any insight into your relationship, Cousin Clarissa?"

I took a deep breath to calm myself at being called his cousin and said, "I believe it is because we are the same age and are more like sisters than cousins. I am as close to her as to my own brothers."

He continued to watch me and nodded his head as though in agreement. "That may be the reason why your relationship started, Clarissa, but you have shown me no *insight* into why it continues to be such a strong one. You seem as different to me as two women can be. One full of decorum and good manners, the other lacking all common sense and gentility while only causing havoc wherever she goes. I can't imagine why she continues to associate with you." With that, he flicked a piece of imaginary lint off his trousers, uncrossed his legs, arose and left the room. A few moments later, I heard Savannah and Jonas call out their good-byes.

As I continued to sit in the parlor, thinking over the last exchange with Jonas, Uncle Martin entered. Concern flashed in his brown eyes, and he rubbed the ridge of his slightly crooked nose.

"Ah, they've left then," he said. "Let's have a cup of tea, and then why don't you stay for dinner, and you can tell me all about the visit to see Mr. McLeod."

I was slow to respond, envisioning a conflict-free meal with Uncle Martin, Aunt Matilda and Lucas. I shook my head regretfully. "I wish I could stay, Uncle, but I know I should return home soon. Mrs. Smythe expected me to return home after today's visit. She'll be angry enough I came here for a visit." I was unable to hide the remorse from my voice.

He nodded, appearing to understand. "Before you depart, tell me. How did the afternoon go?" he asked with thinly veiled curiosity.

I settled into my seat as I described the afternoon. "We went to the North End and Mr. McLeod's home, Uncle Martin. His brother answered, and I soon realized that Mr. McLeod is still quite ill. He continues with terrible pain in his head from the fall."

"I would have thought he'd be improved by now."

"I was very upset, Uncle, and insisted on a doctor. At first they declined one, but when I insisted that we would pay the doctor's bill, they accepted."

"It's the least we can do," he said. His chocolate-brown eyes darkened slightly with puzzlement. "I am surprised Lucas did not think of that first."

"There was quite a bit of tension in the air, Uncle," I said, waving my hands about, trying to explain the mood of the room.

"Was there?" inquired Uncle Martin. "I wonder why? I shall discuss this with Lucas." We stood and walked down the stairs together toward the store. He seemed to place the injured Mr. McLeod out of his mind as we entered the storefront. The store had closed for the day, and I knew Aunt Matilda would wait supper for him.

"Clarissa, I need your help with a project for Savannah," he said as he helped me into my coat, handing me my hat. "Can you come by the store in two days, prepared for a bit of an adventure?"

"An adventure?" I asked. "Haven't I already had enough of one?"

"One not caused by you," he stated, watching me with amused, patient eyes.

"As long as you promise it will not wreak havoc on my life."

"I promise," Uncle Martin replied with a laugh, ushering me out the door toward home.

CHAPTER 5

I HURRIED TO UNCLE'S STORE after work. The air felt heavy and humid, as though it wanted to rain, and the wind on my cheeks felt like shards of ice. Any hint of spring from the previous week had disappeared. March always seemed interminable in Boston, and it was one of my least favorite months. The only consolation was that the air held a briny smell, as though I were walking next to the ocean, and I inhaled the scent appreciatively.

As I entered the store, I smiled at Lucas and Uncle Martin working behind the linen counter. Lucas turned to attend a customer who entered after me, and I moved toward Uncle Martin.

He winked at me and mouthed *shh*. After he retrieved his overcoat from his office, he shrugged it on and held out his elbow for me. "Ready, Clarissa?"

I smiled in agreement.

"Where are you going?" Lucas asked in a hushed tone as his customer debated between three fabrics.

"I wanted to spend a little time with Clarissa, and she came by this afternoon so we could go for a stroll. If you need extra help manning the front, call your mother." Uncle Martin smiled toward Lucas and the waiting customer, donning his hat as he opened the door and ushered me outside.

We walked the short distance to the trolley stop and boarded one headed toward the North End. There were plenty of seats available, and Uncle and I sat on the hard wooden benches, slipping forward and back with the lurching movement of the trolley. "What sort of adventure are we having, Uncle Martin?"

"All in good time, Clarissa. All in good time." We disembarked at the Haymarket Square stop, and I stood paralyzed with fright at the thought of crossing the street. The trolley stop was in the middle of the bustling square where numerous roads met. Horses, carts and other trolleys passed in a constant flow of traffic.

"Uncle, how will we ever traverse here?" I gripped his arm as he began to walk.

"We will be fine. Just keep moving. And whatever you do, don't fall!"

I clasped his arm tighter with both hands and followed him into the traffic. In a matter of moments, he had circumvented a team of draft horses and a fine private carriage, and we stepped onto the sidewalk moments before another trolley passed.

I heaved a sigh of relief to be on the sidewalk. Uncle Martin patted my hand and began to walk more quickly. I did too to keep up and soon found myself short of breath.

We headed up Canal Street, a side street packed with commercial buildings. A few fine carriages made their way down the street, but the main traffic consisted of delivery carts pulled by mules or draft horses. Wagons and carts lined the sides of the road, with men busily loading and unloading the carts with boxes or sturdy flax bags. It seemed as though everyone had a job to do.

I skirted around a boy with a small pushcart selling pickles out of large barrels. He strained against the heavy weight of the cart but still managed to smile as we walked hurriedly by. An emaciated woman hustled down the boardwalk, trying to hawk sandwiches from her basket. A number of the men paused to speak with her and buy some.

I turned my thoughts away from the street scene toward Uncle Martin. "I haven't spoken with Savannah or Aunt Matilda about Aunt Betsy," I said. "How is she faring?"

"Her rheumatism is acting up and may prevent her from attending the wedding," Uncle Martin said with regret. "Savannah and your Aunt Matilda are busy trying to find a solution for her to come see the 'blessed event' in person."

"She can't miss the wedding! It wouldn't be a family event without her." I remained lost in thought for a few moments. "Quincy isn't that far away, Uncle."

"I know, Clarissa, but she is having more trouble managing stairs, and train travel is becoming difficult."

I continued to think about Aunt Betsy, the middle sister between my mama and Aunt Matilda. As a young woman, she had made a brilliant match and married a very wealthy man handpicked for her by her father. However, her one dream had been to have children and a family of her own, a dream that remained unfulfilled. Instead, she had showered her love on her nieces and nephews. I still saw sadness and a sense of wistfulness in her eyes at times, especially when she watched us interact. Uncle Tobias was a kind man, although he appeared somewhat distant, emotionally and physically. I rarely saw them together, and I never saw them hold hands or embrace in any way.

"Ah, here we are then," Uncle Martin said. I glanced at the gray stone building, a four-story warehouse with glass windows fronting the street. A closed outer doorway was at the left of the building. "Let's hope the front door is open." He pushed open the outer door, motioning for me to enter.

I stood uncertainly inside the dark, dreary hallway, unsure where to go.

"Up the stairs, Rissa," Uncle Martin encouraged. I stumbled over the first step but righted myself quickly and rapidly ascended to the second floor. I noted another set of stairs leading to a third floor and glanced at Uncle Martin. "Just one more set of stairs!" Uncle Martin called out.

I sighed, turning toward the stairs, clomping up them gracelessly. I was breathless as I arrived at the top. The miniscule landing had one closed doorway and a tiny window. I wandered to it, looking out at the view. "I wish we could see the harbor," I murmured, but realized Uncle Martin was not paying attention to me. I looked down to watch the people on the street below.

Uncle Martin knocked on the door, and someone opened it. I stiffened when I heard a familiar baritone answer. I whirled around. "Mr. McLeod!" I gasped, eyes opened wide, mouth slightly agape. I quickly closed my mouth but continued to hold Gabriel's gaze.

"Miss," he said toward me, eyes twinkling with humor. "I had not thought to see you, ah, so soon," he said. "Mr. Russell, always a pleasure." He turned toward my uncle, shaking his hand. "Please come into my workshop." He stepped back, inviting us in.

Uncle Martin turned to Gabriel. "You remember my niece, Miss Sullivan, Gabriel?"

He smiled, murmuring, "How could I forget?" He gently massaged the back of his head. I blushed, though in truth felt relief as he appeared much better today than two days ago.

"Are you improved, sir?" I asked.

"Yes, miss. I am much improved," he said. He continued to watch me intensely, finally seeming to remember Uncle Martin and glanced at him to include him in the conversation.

"It is a pleasure to see you, sir, though I had not thought to see you at my workshop again so soon," Gabriel admitted. "I assure you I will return to your store to finish the display tomorrow." He appeared nervous, rubbing the sides of his faded black pants with his hands.

"Never fear, Gabriel," Uncle Martin replied, waving his hat to show he was unconcerned. "I know you will finish that display case. It's that I have another, a secret project, in mind and wanted to discuss it with you privately."

Gabriel appeared puzzled, pointedly looking toward me.

"Ah, yes, and I shall need the assistance of my niece."

As I listened to their conversation, my glance took in various saws, a saw-horse and numerous wooden contraptions. A variety of tools hung along one wall within easy reach of what appeared to be a workbench. I slowly meandered toward it, wondering at the numerous holes along the front. The table was tall, hitting Gabriel at midarm and looked to be over six feet long. The left front had drawers at the top with cabinets beneath. The right-hand side was open with a few planks of wood stored below.

"What is it that is such a secret, sir?" Gabriel asked, leaning against another high table, arms crossed, curiosity lighting his expression.

"I need a handsomely made, finely carved piece for my daughter for her wedding," Uncle Martin said. "When I saw your display, I thought to myself you were the man for the job." He raised his eyebrows as though expecting Gabriel to disagree. When Gabriel merely continued to watch him, Uncle Martin resumed. "I am thinking a sideboard, in mahogany with rosewood inlay. Something simple, yet spectacular."

"Simple, yet spectacular," Gabriel mused, looking toward me. I met his gaze and then turned away. He shook his head quickly. "Do you have any other ideas about the piece? Do you know the size of the room it will be in?"

Gabriel strode over to a dust-covered draft table, picking up books and odd pieces of wood until he found a blank sheet of paper. He blew on it to remove the dust, found a pencil and turned toward my uncle.

"If you would come over here, sir," Gabriel said, hastily clearing off a pile of wood, pulling out a ruler to begin a rough drawing.

I inched closer, fascinated to see him at work. He deftly sketched a rectangular sideboard with three long drawers at the bottom. At the top of the base piece, there were three small drawers in a row.

"I imagine the long drawers on bottom are good for linens 'n' things," he said. "And the smaller drawers for silver and other dining room necessities. I should think you'd want them lined with felt."

"You disagree, miss?" Gabriel asked. He looked at the beginnings of the rough sketch with a critical eye.

"No, not at all," I replied. "I think it is a good design."

"Yes, good, but not spectacular," he mused, continuing to sketch. "I envision a back panel with small shelves on either side leading up to a large shelf along the top. This is where you could display family heirlooms or important china." He continued to sketch, bringing his words to life. "If you want it simple, I would not carve much into it but allow the rich mahogany to be the main decoration. I would use a minimal amount of molding." He finished the picture with a small flourish.

I studied the drawing, envisioning the furniture in my dining room—my imagined dining room—and felt pleasure at the thought of having such a grand piece. I tilted my head to one side, trying to find a way to improve upon the design. "I don't know what I would add," I admitted.

"It seems lovely to me," Uncle Martin said.

Gabriel nodded, pleased with the design. "Well, it should be a pretty piece," he agreed. "When do you need it?"

"Mid-June," Uncle replied. "It's a gift to my daughter and her new husband. I want it to be a secret," he said. He turned to me, impressing upon me his last words.

I nodded my agreement.

"I should have just enough time to finish it, sir," Gabriel said. "I thank you for your patronage," he added. They shook hands, sealing the deal.

I wandered away again as they began to discuss the particulars of payment and cost. I looked at the workbench more closely, wondering how each tool was used. I picked up a few small pieces that appeared to be different types of chisels and imagined seeing Gabriel at work.

"I will not be able to continue to leave the store to come and see to the progress, Gabriel," Uncle Martin said.

I turned to watch him study the basic drawing.

"However, it is very important that I am informed of the progress you are making and of any difficulties." At this, he raised his head and shared a long glance with Gabriel.

Gabriel shook his head in disagreement. "I'm not sure how I will make a sideboard if I can't speak with you, sir," Gabriel said, sounding disgruntled. "I need to be able to discuss my progress with you."

"Hmm…yes," Uncle Martin agreed, appearing deep in thought. "Would you object with speaking with my niece, Miss Sullivan? She knows what Miss Russell and Mr. Montgomery like, and I have complete faith in her judgment. If possible, I would like you to meet with her once weekly to discuss your progress. Is that acceptable to you?"

"Well, Mr. Russell, I do not know realistically how it would work. I would not want to damage a young lady's reputation by meeting with her regularly. Would it not be better that I meet with your son, the young Mr. Russell?" Gabriel nodded in my direction as he spoke.

I choked on a laugh, trying to imagine him working with Lucas.

Gabriel watched me with amused eyes, seeming to understand my unspoken sentiment.

"I have thought about this long and hard. Lucas will not do. I heard he was not as cordial as he should have been on Saturday," Uncle Martin admitted, a grim line about his mouth. Gabriel's eyebrows rose in surprise at Uncle Martin's words, again looking toward me.

I met his inquisitive gaze with a noncommittal shrug.

"Therefore, I have thought of a solution. Clarissa had mentioned to me that she needs bookshelves for her schoolroom. I imagine something like that is very simple for a man of your talents. Wouldn't you agree, Mr. McLeod?"

Gabriel nodded with lips quirked and humor lighting his rich blue eyes.

I felt I could drown in those eyes, and hastily looked away.

"Therefore, it will be necessary for you to visit with her at her school, at my request, to create the bookshelves that she needs, and then you can give any updates needed. Is that satisfactory to you, Mr. McLeod?"

Gabriel again nodded but, after glancing at my glazed expression, replied, "I am fine with the arrangement as it means more work for me. However, I still do not believe it is proper for a workingman to visit her at her school. I would not want to risk her reputation as a teacher. Miss Sullivan, what do you think?" he asked me.

I straightened my shoulders, attempting to breathe through my tight corset. "I, ah, there would need to be at least one other person present when he visited," I said. "Or there could be talk, Uncle. I can't give the school board reason to suspect my character." I looked toward my uncle.

"Yes, of course, Clarissa. I would wish no more scandal for you. I know the school board has stringent rules regarding the moral fiber of its teachers." He paused for a moment clearing his throat, squinting while he thought. "That teacher friend of yours could act as a chaperone, don't you think?"

"Yes, I suppose," I said.

"Good. I will also speak with your principal, explain my plans for the new bookshelves, and that Mr. McLeod will be visiting your rooms for the sake of the project. If problems arise, we will meet them as they come," Uncle Martin said.

I furrowed my brow, uncertain how well the plan would work, but nodded my agreement. I turned toward Gabriel, who again appeared to study me. He watched the emotions flitting across my face in apparent fascination, causing me to wish I had the ability to mask what I felt. "Mr. McLeod, when would you like to visit the school?" I asked.

"Is tomorrow too soon?"

"Oh." My mind seemed to go blank. I needed to speak with Florence. "Why not the day after? When the children have left for home. That should be fine."

He nodded his assent, turning his attention toward Uncle Martin.

"Well, then, we are agreed that you will make the sideboard and the bookshelves for the school. Can you assure me that you will have it ready in time?" Uncle Martin said, leveling a stern glance at Gabriel.

"The sideboard will be ready by your daughter's wedding day. The bookshelves might not be finished until the start of next school year. I will want to put most of my energies into the creation of the sideboard."

"Excellent. Clarissa will let you know where her school is," Uncle Martin said.

When I remained silent for a few moments, Gabriel cleared his throat. "Ahem, miss, could you tell me where your school is?" Gabriel inquired gently.

"Oh, of course. It's the Wells School on Blossom Street."

"But that's a school in the West End," Gabriel said, sounding confused.

"Yes, it is," I replied.

He simply smiled, seemingly pleased, and nodded in agreement. "Well then, it will be my pleasure to visit you there. It's been some time since I've been to the West End."

CHAPTER 6

THE BRIGHT SUN SHONE through the schoolroom window as I tidied the room, erasing some of the day's lessons from the chalkboard. I turned expectantly when I heard steps at the door, my heart racing at the thought of seeing Gabriel again.

I exhaled loudly. "Florence! So good of you to come help me." I smiled warmly, feeling foolish at the disappointment it was not Gabriel.

"Oh, yes. I wouldn't want to miss this," she said with a quick grin. She looked around the room, searching. "It is an exciting day when one of us has need for a chaperone." Her voice was tinted with wistfulness before it turned serious. "You must be careful, Clarissa. You know Mr. Carney would like nothing better than to find fault with another one of us. I still can't believe how they shamed Ursula."

I grimaced at the thought of the principal, Mr. Carney, reporting our former colleague to the school board. "She told me that she never thought the school committee would fire her."

"For immoral behavior," Florence said with a shake of her head. "And all for being seen walking with a man not of her family. In the middle of the afternoon. Can you imagine? Now she is without work because she was deemed 'of loose moral fiber.'"

"Even though my uncle spoke with Mr. Carney, I want to ensure they have no reason to reproach me. It's why I wanted you here, Flo. I have no desire to be seen in the same way." Florence and I shared a knowing nod of agreement.

"Let's tidy your room for tomorrow as we wait," Florence said as she moved toward the chalkboard. "I just finished mine. The girls were quite rambunctious today. Only wanting to be outside. I had half a mind to just let them go but knew there'd be *repercussions*." She wiggled her eyebrows at me with her final word, causing me to laugh. She pushed a strand of black curly hair behind her ear that had escaped her tight bun.

"Do you remember what happened to Miss Lewis? I'd hate for us to suffer her punishment." She shuddered at the thought.

I shook my head, thinking of poor Miss Lewis and her garnished wages for a few hours of freedom for the students.

"Oh, but we did have a fun time of it today," Florence continued as she cleaned the chalkboard. "We painted and sewed and a few are learning to knit."

I grimaced at the thought of attempting so many of the domestic arts in one day.

"Of course there are always accidents," she said, wiping a hand down her skirts.

I looked toward her skirt and gasped, noting the dark green paint marring the pretty pink linen. Thankfully, there were no stains on her cream-colored shirt. "Florence! How will you get the paint out?"

"Oh, a little of this 'n' that. And I'm sure someone at the Chinese laundry will have an idea," she said, wiping at her skirt again. "I shouldn't like my clothes so much. But I do. If only I could entice you to window-shop with me."

"Oh, Florence, you are good medicine," I said with a laugh.

"When is this man going to show up, so I can finally enjoy some of the sunshine myself?"

"Ahem," a low voice said.

Florence and I twirled around toward the door, nearly tripping on our long skirts. I caught myself on one of the children's desks, flushing with embarrassment to be seen in such an unladylike way again.

"Mr. McLeod!" I called out, straightening, though feeling short of breath. "Thank you for coming by." I walked toward him extending my hand in greeting. He watched me intently, taking my hand in a firm yet gentle grip.

"Miss," he replied. He looked pointedly over toward Florence, watching her with apparent fascination, before guarding his expression. Florence seemed rooted to the spot, watching him as though in a daze.

"Richard," Florence whispered.

Gabriel's eyes flashed before he hid his emotion. "No, ma'am," he replied. "I'm *Gabriel* McLeod." His voice sounded cold, clipped.

Florence nodded, then collapsed into a chair, looking as though she had seen a ghost. Her ashen color made me worry she would soon faint. Finally she looked up toward Gabriel and in a small voice said, "I'm Florence Butler."

Gabriel nodded curtly, hiding any further recognition he may have had. "Nice to, ah…meet you, Miss Butler." He glanced quickly around the room, hiding his features from us.

I had a few moments to study him. His strong hands gripped his hat as though in anger. His broad shoulders tensed under his dull off-white shirt and gray jacket, and he kicked at the foot of a student's desk with a rough brown boot before turning to face me again.

I glanced toward Florence, but she still seemed overcome with shock. I itched to hear her story. Wiping my hands on a rag, I tried to clean them and prevent dirtying my crisp white blouse. After a few moments, I set down the rag and crossed my hands on my waist, covering a simple silver belt, and hoped no chalk would mar my pretty rose-colored skirt. I smiled nervously, welcoming Gabriel.

"I'm here about the sideboard and bookshelves, if you recall." There was silent mirth in his eyes as he focused on me.

I nodded my assent. "I have thought about bookshelves for a long time. Ideally I would like to have glass-fronted ones to help keep out the dust, but those are too dear and impractical with children." I paused, lost in imagining the ideal shelves in my mind. "Therefore I would like them to go from the floor to at least shoulder height. There are a lot of books here," I said, pointing to a pile stacked against a far wall.

He nodded, taking in the space and dimensions at a glance. "I will need exact measurements. Have you given any thought to how you would like the bookshelves made?"

I had thought he would make all the shelves at a standard spacing and had not imagined he would customize the project for me. Gabriel took my silence to mean I did not understand his question.

"I can make them any height you would like, miss. For example, if you have tall books, I can make some higher for those, shorter for smaller books. I'd need you to tell me the proper dimensions and number of different types of shelves." He was studying me again.

I felt like a simpleton, unable to form any coherent words when looking into his eyes. I nodded, glancing away, clearing my throat. "Oh, of course," I replied, a small smile escaping. "How wonderful to be able to create whatever you want with your hands and knowledge!"

"Not everything, miss," he replied. "Just what I can build out of wood. Richard's the real magician in the family, conjuring what he likes out of bits of iron."

I noted he watched Florence when he had said Richard's name. However, Florence remained in a state of shock, sitting on a child's chair, staring dully ahead. I had never seen my vivacious spinster friend act in such a way.

"I would recommend that they not be flush on the floor. Sometimes there is moisture there, and this could lead to wood and book rot. Therefore, I suggest the shelves start a few inches off the floor. Would that meet your expectations?"

"Yes, that sounds very good. Do you have any drawings of the bookshelves to show me?"

"Not yet, but I will soon. However, about the sideboard," Gabriel said, pulling out a few pieces of paper, which were vastly improved sketches of the secret project. "This is an expansion of the drawing from the other day," he said.

He had added detail to the front and sides, and I had a better perception of depth. "Oh, that is lovely." I sighed. "Savannah will love it."

"May I see it?" Florence called out as she rose from the child's desk.

"Of course, Florence," I answered, holding my arm out to draw her into our discussion. "This is the sideboard Mr. McLeod will make for my cousin Savannah."

Florence silently studied the drawing, nodding a few times. "She is very fortunate, *very* fortunate, it seems," Florence said in a small voice.

I detected a trace of bitterness in her tone.

Gabriel had watched Florence the entire time she examined the sketch, confusion and animosity playing across his features. "Well, Miss Butler," he said, "it appears her family thinks she deserves it." He turned away, dislike emanating off him.

Florence blanched, moving toward the chair behind my desk, collapsing into it.

"If it is all right with you, miss," he said in a slightly warmer voice, "I'd like to take a few measurements."

"Of course," I replied, watching him and Florence in confusion.

Florence continued to look ashen and despondent. "Florence," I whispered. "Are you all right?"

"Fine," she replied in a flat monotone. "Just fine." She looked toward me with a lost look in her eyes.

I recognized this look. I had seen it enough times in the mirror the months after Cameron had disappeared. I moved toward her, gripping her hands.

"How much longer will you need to be here today, Mr. McLeod?" I asked, concern for Florence invading my sense of contentment at the time spent with him.

"If I could have a few minutes more to measure, miss, that would be helpful."

"Of course," I replied, turning toward Florence. Her color had returned, and she met my eyes with patent embarrassment. "Just a little longer, Florence, then we'll be out in the sun!" I said. I looked around the room, trying to find something to keep us busy until Gabriel had finished, but we had already tidied the room.

Florence watched me as though understanding what I was looking for. "Why don't you read to us, Clarissa, to pass the time?" she asked. "You have the loveliest reading voice."

"Yes, I just went to the public library and was able to borrow *The Red Badge of Courage*. Would you like to hear it read?" It didn't seem the type of book to raise one's spirits, but the only other books I had were school primers.

"Yes. Why don't you read out loud and entertain us all?" Florence said with a weak smile. She had settled in my comfortable chair behind my desk, and I didn't have the heart to ask her to move.

I went over to my bag and retrieved the book. My brothers had loved it, but I had not yet read it. I wasn't sure I would enjoy reading a war story but thought I should try. I had nowhere to sit now, except for a student's seat, so I reluctantly sat in one of those, with my knees next to my chin, feeling rather silly. However, as soon as I started reading, I lost all sense of self, as though becoming part of the story.

I read for the next half hour, slowly relaxing, enjoying the quiet, peaceful room and the sounds of Gabriel walking around my area, working as I read. After a while I realized that the sounds of working had abated and that I was reading to a rapt audience. I looked up to find Florence curled up in the chair, with her eyes closed, appearing contented. I glanced over to Gabriel to find him studying me unabashedly. I blushed but met his gaze, holding it for a long moment.

Finally Florence stirred, asking, "So, is that all for today then, Clarissa?" She sat up primly, watching Gabriel warily. She stood and righted her appearance, not looking at either of us.

As I realized the time and that I needed to return home, I closed the book reluctantly. "I'm sorry, but I need to go. I won't be able to read anymore today. I, ah…" I was at a loss for words, unsure if he wanted me to read more to him.

He smiled fully for the first time, and I was startled anew by his handsomeness. "I greatly enjoyed your reading, miss. Maybe you could save that book for me, and we could keep reading it together?" His eyes twinkled a little.

"Of course, Mr. McLeod. If you like, the next time you come to the schoolhouse, I can read to you then. However, I can only keep the book out for er… fourteen days, so we will have to continue to make progress."

He watched me intently. "I will come visit your school soon, miss." His voice was a gentle, rich baritone, and it felt like a caress. I flushed, looking away, nodding my agreement. He bid Florence and then me a good day, and left quietly.

"Well, Clarissa," Florence stated. "I am glad you found a competent carpenter." A bitter grimace turned down her mouth. "Now I must return home."

I gripped her hand as she moved past me, stopping her. "Florence! What is there between you and Mr. McLeod?"

Florence closed her eyes wearily. "Nothing but a terrible past, Clarissa." She opened her eyes, pleadingly. "Not today, Clarissa," she entreated. "Not today."

I let her hand go. "Florence, I hate to see you so sad," I whispered.

Florence stood only a few feet from me, but she held herself as though she were miles away.

I felt an impenetrable wall between us and longed to be able to help my friend.

"You would never understand, Clarissa," she whispered. "You, who have always had your family around you. You have no idea what it is to be truly alone," she said wearily, clamping her mouth shut.

I looked into her devastated eyes, reaching out to comfort her, but she shook her head, fighting tears, and fled from the room.

CHAPTER 7

I SAT RELAXING in the Russell family parlor with Savannah. Lucas had gone out with friends, and Aunt Matilda and Uncle Martin were working in the store office, organizing and pricing a new batch of cloth that had just been delivered.

"I envy Uncle and Aunt," I mused aloud as I sprawled lazily on the faded rose-patterned settee.

"Why is that?" Savannah inquired, almost startled by my statement. She looked up in surprise, interrupting her calm progress on her needlepoint. Her hair was made more strawberry than blond by the glow of the fire.

"Well, they seem so well matched, and she is able to help him with the business. I think it must be a good marriage. They seem very happy," I said. I sat with my needlepoint on my lap, halfheartedly attempting to work at it but knowing that no intelligible design would ever be discerned when I finished.

"I think that a good marriage is a marriage where the wife is not expected to work, except within the home, of course," Savannah replied, raising an eyebrow toward me waiting for my response.

"Sav, it's just you and me here, no Jonas. Is that truly how you feel? Is this all you want to do the rest of your life? Plan dinner parties and work at needlepoint? I think it would be very satisfying to have other things to do with my life."

"Well, I am not so sure Mother would have the same sentiments as you, Rissa. She wasn't raised to work, as you well know. Our grandparents' wealth should have assured her of a life of leisure, not toiling over bolts of cloth. I think our grandparents are shocked at all that she does."

"Uncle Martin is very respectable."

"Yes, in his way," Savannah said. "But he is in trade. You must know how that seems to the grandparents. They are very refined, Clarissa."

She watched me with a raised eyebrow as I frowned at her further mention of our grandparents. I never liked discussing them. Unlike Savannah, the favored grandchild, I had never been close to them. Their wealth seemed to grow on a daily basis, yet they were remarkably stingy with what seemed truly important to me: their love and acceptance.

I exhaled a long, weary sigh. "I guess the only one of the sisters to make an acceptable marriage in their eyes was Aunt Betsy. For I know that, in their opinion, my mama's marriage to my da was a mistake." I glanced at her, daring her to defend them.

"Rissa, you have to look at it from their point of view," Savannah entreated. "They are genteel, upper-class people. They've only become wealthier, more socially important, as the years have continued. They have never understood why our mothers married men beneath them socially and economically. It's nothing personal."

"Nothing personal when they tell Da at my mama's funeral that she would have been alive, if not for him? Nothing personal when they tell my brothers and me that we aren't what they desired when they thought of grandchildren? Nothing personal when they say that, in their minds, it would have been better had I not been born than to live through the scandal of two years ago?" I rasped out, my voice growing louder with each question. I felt the old bitterness, resentments and anger rising in me. I shared a long look with Savannah, daring her to contradict me, but she remained resolutely silent while I took a calming breath.

"Oh, Rissa, I know it hurts, but you must not think too much about what they have said in the past. Deep down I know that they are good people at heart," she insisted.

"Good people, Sav?" I asked. "Good people don't treat servants that way, never mind their own families. And why shouldn't I think about what they have said?" I leaned forward, a red flush on my cheeks, emphasizing my anger. "These are the people I have been instructed my entire life to emulate. And yet I have never felt one moment's worth of warmth or love from them. Why should I want to be like them? Why wouldn't they worry about *me*?" I asked, feeling tears prick the back of my eyes.

"I will not try to defend them to you, Clarissa," Savannah said as she collapsed against the back of the settee. "I believe that life is easier if you don't go through it trying to always cause problems or change things. Sometimes it's best to just accept it the way it is."

"That's not living, Sav. You're already dead if you do that," I snapped. I moved to rise, ready to go home.

"Rissa, don't go yet. There are other more pleasant things for us to discuss." Savannah looked at me with pleading eyes, setting aside her needlepoint, fully focusing on me.

I sat back against the settee, still feeling very tense. I closed my eyes and pushed away the unsettling emotions I felt about my grandparents. Discussing them never failed to upset me, and I silently berated myself for thinking about them.

"Let's talk about your handsome Mr. McLeod. When are you going to see him again?" Savannah said brightly.

"I saw him today, Sav." I smiled, unable to hide my joy.

Savannah sat upright, in shock. "Are you telling me that you saw him hours ago, and you've sat here for tea and supper, yet this is the first you are telling me of it?"

"We weren't alone before," I demurred, grinning. Savannah hated my ability to keep a secret.

"You are impossible!" she cried. "Tell me all! What happened? Did you run into him on the street? I bet he wanted to see you, so he sought you out."

I laughed again, at last feeling joy at his visit rather than misgivings due to Florence's reaction. "Uncle Martin has contracted him to make bookshelves for my schoolroom," I said, unable to hide the excitement from my eyes.

"Oh, really?" Savannah said. "I didn't think my father was capable of being so forward thinking."

I stared at her in confusion for a moment and then gaped at her. "Sav, he's not matchmaking!" I blushed at the thought. "He merely wants me to have my much-needed bookshelves and give a young carpenter work."

"Think that if you will, Rissa," Savannah replied with an indulgent smile, "but I know my father, and this is something more than ensuring you receive your bookshelves." Her grin remained for a few moments before she became worried. "You weren't alone with him, were you?"

"No. My friend Florence was there."

"Good choice, Rissa. It's always best to choose someone less attractive as the chaperone. That way he'll always notice you."

I looked up, startled. "You are horrible!" I protested. "Florence is…" My voice trailed off as I pictured Florence. Her impossible-to-control curly black hair, myopic eyes, thin mouth, round face. "Fine, I agree, she may not be a beauty. But she is a special person, always in a good mood, trying to make the best of all situations."

"Why?" asked Savannah. "She's like a thousand other poor spinster women living in this city. I see nothing special about her."

"Well, she's my friend, and I like her," I replied. "Not that it, in and of itself, makes her special." I blew out a breath. "Each one of us is special in our own way, Sav. You just may need a person like Florence someday to help you."

Savannah scoffed. "I doubt that. Once I marry Jonas, I will have no need for the likes of her."

I watched Savannah sadly. "Careful you don't turn into an insufferable snob, Sav. I'd hate to lose you."

Her light blue eyes grew round, then she turned the conversation back to Gabriel. "So, tell me more. What was he like? Was he still fascinated by you?"

I giggled, sighing in contentment when thinking about Gabriel. "There's so much I don't know about him. But what I do know, I like."

"When are you seeing him again?" Savannah asked.

"I'm not sure. I think he will come by the school in about a week."

"I can tell you don't want to wait that long to see him," Savannah said as we shared a rueful smile. "I have an idea! Why don't we find out where his warehouse is—or shop or whatever it is called—and go visit? We can think up some excuse and call around. What do you think, Rissa?" She watched me intently, nearly vibrating with excitement.

"I think that would be the height of impropriety, as you and Aunt Matilda would like to say," I replied as a nervous tremor thrummed through me. "I'm sure it would be inappropriate for us to look for a carpenter's warehouse, Sav, and then show up unannounced."

"I thought you *wanted* to see him again," Savannah replied, picking up her needlepoint once more, although I could tell she was upset because she nearly spiked her own finger rather than the cloth with the needle.

"Sav—"

"Rissa, at some point you are going to have to decide that you really do want to have a life of your own and go for it. Are you interested in this man or not? If not, just say so, and that's the end of it. If you are, I am willing to help. It's really as simple as that." She speared me with a ferocious glance, determination in every line of her face. "Yes, I am sure we would be going against what is deemed proper by society, but I've never known you to care. And we would be together, so neither of us would be unchaperoned. You helped me with Jonas. I want to help ensure that you are happy. Just tell me what *you* want, and we'll do it." Savannah leaned over and gently grasped my hand, giving it a gentle squeeze.

I gripped her hand but looked away, fearful that I would cry. "I want to see him again, Savannah, but I am so afraid. What if it is like my last…? I don't think

I could live through that again. It hurt too much," I whispered, taking a deep breath, trying to steady my thoughts and my racing heart.

"Rissa, I have no idea what you truly felt, but I can imagine after witnessing how you suffered. I never knew what heartbreak meant until I saw you live through it. However, you have to have hope that this time will be better. Can you?"

"I just don't know, Sav," I murmured. "I like to think of myself as strong and capable, but I feel so weak sometimes."

"Well, then, let's be daring and visit Mr. McLeod," Savannah said sitting up straight and giving me a wink. "At the bare minimum, we will have another adventure to add to our stories to tell our children when they grow up."

"When should we go, Sav?" I tried to hide the eagerness from my voice, but, at Savannah's amused glance, I could tell I had failed.

"Why not the day after tomorrow? I will spend some time in Father's office. Maybe there is a receipt in there for the display. If not, then we will find another way to find his workspace."

"I'll ask around as well. Between the two of us, we should be successful," I said, not wanting to let on that I already knew where his workshop was. I felt my spirits lift and smiled at Savannah, the anticipation of seeing Gabriel again rushing through me.

CHAPTER 8

TWO DAYS LATER, Savannah met me at my West End school, and we walked toward the nearby Haymarket Square area where Gabriel had his business. As we walked, we passed rows of somber, dull redbrick tenement homes. The good weather enticed everyone to be outside; although, with few parks in the area, the options for the children were limited. They played in the streets and on the sidewalks, their mothers on the stoops half watching and enjoying a chance to chat with their neighbors. Most of the women held babies, or little ones clung to their skirts, afraid to join the antics of the older children. I smiled toward them as we passed, knowing I taught some of their daughters.

I gripped Savannah's arm in nervous apprehension, and she grinned conspiratorially toward me.

"Rissa, you need to calm down, or you will have another mishap," Savannah warned me.

"Don't say that, or you will cause me to have one merely by thinking about it!" I pleaded.

We walked down the street, arm in arm, at a sedate pace. Not wanting to garner any undue attention, we had donned our most dreary outer coats and dullest hats, and were trying to be as demure as possible.

"What a lovely spring day," I said, tipping up my face to the sky for a moment. The late afternoon sun penetrated the narrow, windy streets we traversed, further elevating my mood. I ignored the rancid smells of rotting food and horse dung.

"I doubt it is the sun that has put that bloom in your cheeks, Rissa," Savannah teased as we emerged onto a larger street bustling with working men and carts pulled by large work horses. We shared a smile as I tried to quell my nervousness at seeing Gabriel again. I had worried about spoiling Uncle Martin's surprise and, to that end, had sent Gabriel a note warning him of a potential visit.

After entering his building and climbing the flights of stairs, we found the door to his workshop ajar. I could hear low whistling coming from inside. I turned to Savannah. "Maybe I should go in first, as I am the one doing business with him." Savannah rolled her eyes, although I knew she would be right behind me.

"Excuse me, Mr. McLeod?" I called out in a carrying voice. "I came by—along with my cousin, Miss Savannah Russell—to discuss the bookshelves with you." I had entered into the workshop a few steps but stopped suddenly.

Gabriel had not heard me. He was busy flattening one side of a piece of wood. He used an object that seemed to whittle it away, little by little. His mouth was drawn up into a frown of concentration, as though he could not afford to have it broken. His arms were extended along a long piece of wood as he slowly evened one side, and I could see rippling muscles beneath the thin linen of his shirt. He stepped back from the wood to peruse his work. He tilted his head to one side, shaking his head as though disappointed in what he saw.

I cleared my throat again. "Ahem."

He jumped, startled and surprised not to be alone. For an instant I thought I saw alarm in his eyes, but then I saw only pleasure in them as he focused on me. Light streamed in the workshop windows, illuminating the quantity of boards and wood piled to the far side of the room. A fine dust covered everything and seemed to dance in the air when the light hit it. Above his workbench, I saw sketches similar to what he had shown me for the bookcases. Nothing but the large piece of wood he had been working with lay on the workbench.

"Miss, good to see you again. I had thought I wouldn't see you until next week when I visited the schoolhouse." He moved toward the door to greet us, smearing wood dust on his brown trousers as he attempted to wipe his hands clean.

"Please pardon the intrusion, Mr. McLeod. I am here with my cousin, Miss Russell, whom I am sure you remember." I waved vaguely in Savannah's direction. Sav nodded her head once, attempting to look regal, as she tried not to smile.

"It is no intrusion. Please come in. I will put the kettle on for tea."

He motioned us to enter the room fully and led us to a table covered in wood dust, tools and drawings. There were a few finished chairs at the table, and he invited us to sit down. He moved drawings away from the chairs and quickly tried to clean off some of the dust there with his hand.

"Please pardon the state of things. I wasn't expecting company," he said, although I thought he nearly winked at me as he cleared the table.

"Mr. McLeod," I asked. "What were you doing just now?" I had a newfound curiosity in carpentry.

"I was planing a board, making it even," he said, sending a small smile my way.

Savannah moved toward a chair apart from the table and began to sit down. "Oh, no, don't sit at that one!" He grabbed Savannah's arm, hauling her to a standing position. "I am still working on it. The leg is loose, and I'm afraid you'd end up on the floor." He smiled, chagrined, and let go of Savannah's arm.

He motioned to other chairs around the table. "Please, be seated in one of these. I have just finished them and would like your opinion. Do you find them comfortable?" he inquired as he turned toward the small stove to place the kettle on for tea.

On a shelf over the area, I noted a few chipped earthenware mugs and a peeling teapot. I knew it was too much to hope for milk and sugar.

He turned toward us smiling apologetically as he set the mugs out onto the table. "I am afraid all I have is sugar, no milk. That's how I always take my tea. The milk goes bad too quickly here." He seemed to choose his words carefully and spoke quietly.

"Any tea will be lovely, thank you, sir," replied Savannah, looking around the warehouse. "Is all of this your work?" she asked after her quiet perusal.

"Most of it, though some of it came from the man I used to work with."

I waited for him to speak more on that subject, but he remained silent and turned to steep the tea. I enjoyed watching the fluidity of his movements. However, more than anything, I wanted to learn more about him.

"Did you have a particular reason for visiting today, miss?" he asked over his shoulder, amusement lighting his eyes.

I quickly looked around the workshop. I realized that until the sideboard was being pieced together, it would be hard to determine what was being created here. I smiled at Gabriel, hoping to express my thanks in maintaining the secrecy over uncle Martin's wedding gift.

"Miss?" he asked again after the long pause.

"Oh, yes. Well, we came today because I forgot to speak with you about which type of wood you would use in the bookcases."

He watched me, as though seeing through my ruse. "As to the type of wood, miss, I was going to discuss that with your uncle when I finish the project at his store. Now that I have the measurements, the type of wood will affect the price," he said.

I looked away, uncomfortable to discuss money matters with him.

"Do you have a particular preference?"

"I hadn't realized the price would change depending on the wood. How interesting carpentry must be! And how complicated." I found myself rambling, running the risk of babbling, and I looked to Sav to save me. However, she would not look up even though she must have felt the weight of my stare.

"Yes, miss, all in all, it is a fascinating profession," he said.

I was unable to tell if he mocked me or genuinely agreed.

"Though I'm a cabinetmaker, not a carpenter."

I squinted at him, unsure of the difference.

"What do you think of the chairs you are sitting on? I have altered a traditional design, and I am not sure if they will be comfortable to all. I may like them simply because I made them," he admitted.

"I find them comfortable, though they seem a little tall."

"Tall? In what sense?"

I blushed. "My feet barely touch the floor."

He looked and noted for the first time that my toes were touching, but the rest of my foot dangled in midair. "Hmm…I can see that would be a problem." He seemed to become lost in thought and then addressed Savannah.

"And for you, Miss Russell, what do you think?"

"I agree with Clarissa. I'd like a chair where my feet touch the ground. However, I am sure Lucas, Patrick or Colin would love these chairs," she replied.

He looked from her to me, apparently thinking over those names, although I thought they should all be familiar to him.

"Lucas is my cousin, Lucas Russell. If you remember, you met him a few days ago," I said.

A grim expression flitted across his face then vanished.

"Patrick and Colin are my brothers," I explained. "They are very tall, though not quite as tall as you." At that last remark, I looked away.

Savannah nearly choked into her tea and had the presence of mind to act like she was coughing.

Gabriel merely smiled and nodded. "Yes, well, that makes sense now. I should have them out to the workshop to see what they think. I believe Colin and Richard are good friends," he said. He smiled and sipped his sweetened tea.

I nodded my agreement.

"If you don't mind me asking, miss, if your main concern was the type of wood I would be using, maybe as we finish our tea you could read more from your book?" he asked with a hint of longing in his voice.

"Oh, I would have liked that, but I didn't think to bring it with me," I apologized. Savannah shook her head at me and rolled her eyes in exasperation, as though I were a complete idiot. After a few more moments, Savannah and I stood to take our leave.

"I thank you for your visit here today, Miss Russell," Gabriel said with a slight nod in Sav's direction. "Miss," he murmured in a husky voice, nodding more fully at me with warm eyes. "I will see you again at the schoolhouse."

I said something that hopefully sounded like an agreement and then turned to leave. Thankfully Savannah gripped my arm, or I would have spun myself to a sitting position on the floor.

Savannah propelled me into motion, tugging me down the stairs. We clattered our way down the increasingly dark hallway until we reached the ground floor and the street. We stepped onto the sidewalk, dodging the bustling peddlers. I tripped on the uneven stones, smiling my thanks as a fish peddler prevented me from falling. Turning toward Savannah, I gripped her arm once more, and we began to stroll away from the workshop. We looked at each other with wide eyes.

"Wow, that's Mr. Carpenter up close," Savannah breathed. She acted as if she were fanning herself, then looked around the street, remembering we were in public. "No scenes, Rissa. Let's walk and talk quietly." She gripped my arm and again propelled me faster into motion. It never ceased to surprise me how such a small woman could be so strong.

"Yes," I agreed, "that's him. What do you think?"

"I think he is the handsomest man I have ever seen. *Virile* is the word that comes to mind." She sighed, giving me a teasing smile. "Just be thankful I've already agreed to marry Jonas, or I might try to entice him away from you."

"Sav, he's not interested in me," I protested.

"Hmm…if you say so. Now I understand why Lucas disliked him so much," Savannah said.

I watched with confusion, waiting for her to say more.

"Not only is he handsome, but he looks at you…" She paused, in a similar fashion as Lucas had, but, rather than displeased, she seemed pleased.

"Looks at me how?" I demanded.

Savannah studied me for a moment, surprise evident in her expression. "Are you telling me that you don't see it? The way he studies you?" Savannah demanded, speaking to me as if she thought I were a simpleton.

I shrugged my shoulders, unsure.

"Well, start paying attention, Rissa," Savannah encouraged with a broad smile. "This could be a grand adventure."

CHAPTER 9

I SAT VISITING WITH FLORENCE after school in her room. It was a cold, blustery day, and I did not relish going outside. Florence had the gaslights on due to the weak light coming in from the window. The chalkboard had been erased, prepared for another day of teaching, and Florence sat behind her desk with a stack of papers in front of her. I sat in the only other adult-sized chair in the room, an uncomfortable straight-backed chair that I had moved toward Florence's desk.

"Florence," I asked, "what happened to your family?"

"They all died when I was young," she replied.

I watched her, sympathy and concern flooding me.

As I remained silent, she continued to speak, "Baby Sam got sick first and then it spread to everyone else. We didn't have money for a doctor, and there we were, all crammed into our one-room tenement, in pools of…" She broke off, embarrassed, not finishing the sentence. "Mama 'n' Papa never thought about taking us to the relief station. Maybe by the time they did, we were too sick," she whispered.

I gripped her hand, unsure of any other way to show my sadness at her story.

"They all died, left me alone," she whispered. "Left me all alone."

"What did you do?" I asked.

"When the neighbors finally came in, they found only me. They took me to the relief station, got me well," she said, wiping away a tear. "Then I went to an orphanage." She stopped, shaking her head, as though she couldn't say any more.

"Oh, Florence. I am sorry." I grimaced, feeling the inadequacy of my words.

"There are hundreds just like me, Clarissa. Except I made something of myself, got a good job," she said with pride.

"Why did you never marry?" I asked, curious about her relationship with the McLeod brothers.

She watched me warily before asking, "Why didn't you?"

I looked at her in confusion, then in dawning understanding. I nodded with a rueful smile. "Come, let's go home. Why don't you join us for tea?"

Her eyes flared in concern, looking at her stained dress. "Oh, thank you, Clarissa, but not today. Maybe some other time. I wouldn't want to shock that stepmother of yours too much."

I stood to gather my things. "I understand. But we will go for tea one of these days," I said as I donned my jacket and hat.

***

I RETURNED HOME after an uneventful walk to find Colin pacing our family parlor. He skirted the ottomans, chairs and settees, making an agitated pattern across the floor. The rose-colored wallpaper appeared darker than usual on this dreary day with little sunlight streaming in the large front windows. A small fire crackled in the marble-topped fireplace to the left of the door.

"Why are you here, Colin?" I asked rushing toward him. "You are never home midday. Is it Da? The smithy?" Colin studied me for a moment as my anxiety mounted.

I looked entreatingly at Colin, and he met my gaze with mournful eyes. "Rissa, sit."

I dutifully sat on the pale gold settee.

He took a deep breath and seemed to brace himself as he met my eyes again. "Rissa, Cameron is back."

I frowned at him, unsure why he acted like this was news. "You warned me that you thought he was back a few weeks ago. But he wouldn't come back," I scoffed. "And if he has, it has nothing to do with me."

"He's back. I saw him. He was asking about you today at the smithy."

"Why would he come back? Why would he be interested in me?" I sat dazed, unsure where to look. My mind couldn't make sense of it. I had known, deep inside, when I had seen a glimmer of his profile a few weeks ago, that he had returned. Yet, I didn't want to believe it possible.

"Rissa, don't be childish. He's clearly still interested in you," Colin chided. "There will be a lot of talk."

"When have you ever cared about what people said, Colin? And when was the last time you were left at the altar? Don't you *dare* tell me you know what that feels like, because you have no idea," I snapped at him, hastily wiping away a tear, hoping that I could keep the rest of them locked inside.

"I care what people say, Rissa, when they are maligning my baby sister. I care when the ba…man who hurt her comes back into town, as though he's done nothing wrong," Colin nearly shouted, seething with anger.

Colin took a moment to collect himself. "There's every chance you'll meet him on the street, Rissa. We can't protect you completely from him. He's proven he's no gentleman, and I am sure he'll not wait for you to acknowledge him before speaking with you. None of us can be away from work as much as would be needed to always escort you."

"I don't want to always have an escort," I cried. "I want my freedom."

"Rissa, be realistic," Colin said. "You must know that's not possible now."

I sat, mutely staring at him, a kaleidoscope of memories rushing through me. Once again I found myself waiting, waiting on Cameron, while trying not to think too much about the past. I silently squeezed Colin's hand, unable to speak, overcome by emotions.

"I sent for Aunt Matilda and Savannah. I thought you might want their support."

I blinked a dazed agreement.

Colin nodded and gently patted me on my shoulder. Soon he left to return to the smithy.

There was a commotion at the front hall door as Aunt Matilda and Savannah arrived. Aunt Matilda demanded tea and cakes be delivered immediately to the parlor. Savannah exuded calm although she was unable to hide the concern in her light blue eyes. She sat next to me on the settee, with Aunt Matilda across from us in a comfortable lady's chair. I felt cocooned by their love and support.

I leaned into Savannah and finally began to cry. I hadn't cried in my bedroom waiting in vain for him to show or in the days after the wedding, while waiting for a reason for his disappearance. I hadn't cried through all of the pitying looks and the snide, not-so-subtle write-up in the newspaper or my grandparents' scorn. I realized now how much I had held in and how much I needed to let it go. I sobbed quietly into Savannah's shoulder, and she simply held me, saying nothing.

I finally stopped weeping and let go of Savannah. She smoothed away the hair from my forehead with a gentle touch. "All better, Rissa?"

I gave a start of laughter, as I knew I was far from "all better." I looked at her, mumbling, "I think crying should be recommended. I feel much better now."

"Well, maybe in the privacies of our own homes, but we wouldn't want men to see us this way, would we? Not at all becoming," she said with a small smile.

Aunt Matilda began to fix cups of tea. "Have some tea, Clarissa. It will calm you." She overlooked my red puffy eyes and pink nose. "Tomorrow will be a trying day, dear, as you will be worrying about seeing him, though I doubt he will seek you out so quickly. He seems more subtle and cunning than that," Aunt Matilda mused.

"I wouldn't call going to the smithy cunning nor subtle, Mother," Savannah retorted.

"True, but now that he has us all up in arms, he can see how we react and then decide what to do. I think the best thing for you, Clarissa, with Cameron roaming the streets again, would be to have no set schedule, so he would not know where to find you at any given time."

I looked at her blankly. "Are you saying…?"

"Yes, for now, give up the teaching. It's almost end of term anyway," Aunt Matilda said.

"Aunt, I can't stop teaching now. It's the most important time for many of the students!" I looked toward Savannah but realized I would get no support from her. My heart raced as one thought was paramount in my mind. *If I am not at school, I won't see Gabriel.*

"Clarissa, the family has indulged this whim of yours to teach for long enough. You have no need to teach. You should be spending your time at home, refining your knowledge on how to run a proper house." Aunt Matilda spoke with a note of chastisement in her voice, as though the decision had already been made.

"Aunt Matilda, I want to teach. I like teaching. I like being outside of the house," I protested.

"Clarissa, you do not realize how badly it reflects on the family, you leaving the house each day for employment. It makes people wonder if it is a necessity. I shouldn't wonder that your father's customers worry that he is in financial hardship, with his daughter *working.*" She emphasized *working* as though it were a bad word.

"You work with Uncle Martin," I replied.

"Only out of necessity," she retorted, her eyes flashing at me as though in anger at the reminder. She lifted up her teacup to forestall any more conversation. I noted Savannah watching the conversation avidly.

"Aunt…"

"Clarissa, we yielded to your desire to teach as it appeared the only way to have you emerge from the sadness after dear Agnes's death. It should have ended two years ago. However, you have been pampered long enough. Think of the effect it may be having on Savannah and Mr. Montgomery. The last thing we would want would be for Mr. Montgomery to lose esteem for the family."

I spoke in a determined, confident voice. "Aunt Matilda, I am truly sorry if my teaching reflects poorly on the family. However, I am sure there are many other things that I have done that have tarnished the reputation of the family much worse than my helping to improve the lives of young children."

"Clarissa, I will be discussing this with your father. I believe I have the agreement of Mrs. Sullivan?" Aunt Matilda inquired, raising her eyebrows, looking toward the door, where Mrs. Smythe now hovered.

"Of course, dear Mrs. Russell," Mrs. Smythe simpered. "You have my full support. I have despaired for a long time over Clarissa's lack of social graces."

I watched as Mrs. Smythe looked ready to start on her favorite topic and knew I needed to escape.

"I am sorry. It has been a trying afternoon," I said. "I have a headache. If you will all excuse me?" I rose and left the room, heading upstairs to the relative tranquility of my bedroom.

CHAPTER 10

FOR DAYS I WAITED anxiously for Cameron to approach me. Da had continued to support my teaching, and there had been very little discussion about me leaving before term ended. I was able to continue with my daily routine, and I enjoyed the sense of normalcy. One day nearly two weeks later, I heard heavy footsteps approaching my school door. My stomach tightened.

At the gentle knock, I turned to see Gabriel at the doorway. "Hello, Mr. McLeod," I said, unable to hide the flash of joy in my eyes at seeing him. I bit my lip, worried for an instant that I was alone with him, unchaperoned in my schoolroom, but soon focused on Gabriel and his visit rather than propriety.

"Miss Sullivan," he said in a formal tone. "I am sorry for the delay in coming by the school." He looked down, running the edge of his hat through his fingers as though nervous. "I…" He broke off, looking up to meet my eyes.

I met his gaze, my interest heightened by his hesitation. I raised my eyebrows in encouragement, signaling him to continue.

"I don't have much news about the bookcase. Or the sideboard," he said. "But I wanted you to know I'm still working on them."

"Excellent," I said with a small smile, feeling comforted by his presence.

"If it would not be improper, miss," he said, meeting my gaze, "do you think you could return to my workshop some day?"

I inhaled shortly, taken by surprise.

"It's just that I have a few ideas but wanted, needed to discuss them there."

I continued to watch him silently. He ran his hand through his hair. "I would like your opinion on a few design ideas and wood choices, Miss Sullivan."

I remained silent as though incapable of speaking.

"The wood's too bulky to cart around the streets."

I blushed, glancing down. "Of course, the sideboard. I'll come by tomorrow."

He nodded once, smiling, "That would be fine, miss." He paused, studying me. "How is the school year progressing, miss?"

I nodded at him. "Well enough. Though the students are becoming anxious to be out of school. As am I," I murmured, flushing softly at my escaped comment.

His lips quirked a quick smile, and I saw a small dimple in his right cheek. "At least you're an honest teacher," he said. He perused the room, taking in the chalkboard and the maps on the wall. "Do you teach geography, miss?"

"I teach a little of everything. Well, except homemaking arts. That would be a true disaster," I admitted.

He wandered toward the map of the United States pinned on the wall. "Do you ever dream of traveling?" he asked in a wistful voice. At my quick shake of my head in denial, he said, "I do. I dream of California. Seeing the San Francisco Bay. I think it must truly be a land of opportunity there." He continued to study the map. "Or anywhere out West. It seems a magical, wild place. Full of possibilities."

"I should think you have plenty of opportunity here, in Boston," I replied. "With family and friends nearby."

"Why should you be content in the place you were born? Shouldn't you want to see more of the world than that?" he asked.

"You sound like Colin," I said. "He's always talking of adventure, doing something new and different. I should be happy to stay here forever."

"You say that now, but you never know what could induce you to travel, miss."

"It's hard to imagine what that would be, sir," I replied, anxiety filling me at the thought of any leave taking.

He nodded again, seeming to sense my anxiety. "Well, then, Miss Sullivan, I will bid you good day. I will see you tomorrow. Good afternoon," he said, smiling and nodding toward me. He turned and left, leaving my thoughts and emotions in disarray.

***

THE FOLLOWING DAY, after school, I set out for the workshop after trying unsuccessfully to convince Florence to accompany me. Although I knew I took a risk visiting his shop alone, I owed it to Uncle Martin not to ruin his wedding gift surprise for Savannah. And, if I were truthful, I wanted to have a few moments alone with him.

I enjoyed the now familiar walk to the workshop, cataloging spring's arrival. The trees were finally in bud, and a few hardy birds braved the city environs. I smiled at the faint birdsong I could hear over the *clip-clop* of hooves on the cobblestones and the rattle of streetcars as they roared by. I turned my face toward the sun, thankful I did not have to ride a streetcar today but could walk.

I approached the workshop, enjoying watching the busy activity of the street, noting today's fruit du jour in the pushcart was oranges. After a slow climb to the third floor, I saw that the workshop door was once again ajar, and I poked my head in to see if I could catch a glimpse of Gabriel working. Instead, I saw Gabriel and an older woman glaring at each other in a tense silence. I remained mesmerized in a shadow near the doorway, silently watching the exchange. They were leaning toward each other with fists clenched, as though they were merely pausing in the middle of a heated argument. Both breathed heavily, and they seemed to be conducting a battle of wits, daring the other to look away first.

I must have leaned against the door or stepped on a squeaky floorboard, because a loud creaking noise rent the air. I flinched guiltily at being caught witnessing such a scene.

The short, rail-thin woman whirled to look at me. Her fashionable clothes were hanging off her like a scarecrow, and she had piercing, almost turquoise-blue, eyes, with her dull, limp brown hair pulled back severely in a bun and a slightly hooked nose. Her eyes lit on me.

"And who do we have here, Gabriel? She seems a little fancy for you," she taunted, her thin lips pulled back into a sneer. "Or maybe you think you've moved up in the world?" she jeered as she looked again toward Gabriel. "Don't be thinking you're better than you are. You'll always be gutter scum."

Then she addressed me in a sinister, low voice, "You'd better find out exactly what you're getting into with this one, young lady. He's a good-for-nothing, just like his father. He'll bring you nothing but pain, disgrace and an early death."

"Get out!" Gabriel roared, marching to the door and pointing at the stairway. "I have heard enough about my family from you. If I never heard another word, it would be too soon. Leave." He hissed out a long breath, waiting for her to depart. They shared a long glaring look, icy-blue eyes clashing.

Finally the older woman left, looking over her shoulder toward me, but addressing Gabriel. She spoke with a slight smirk on her lips, stating, "Nothing good will come of your association with the Russells. I'll see to that." She then walked past me, slipped out the door, and I could hear the clatter of her heels down the stairs.

"Argh!" groaned Gabriel, walking toward his workbench where he picked up a piece of wood and threw it across the room where it splintered into fragments against the brick wall.

I stood still, transfixed, as I had never seen such displays of anger before. It was as though I were frozen in place, unsure if to run or to stay. Gabriel continued to breathe forcefully but finally began to calm after a few moments. He leaned heavily on the workbench, bent over at the waist, gripping the edge of the table so hard I thought it would break in his strong hands.

After a few moments he looked up at me, with his piercing blue eyes starker today than I had ever seen them, and said, "I'd ask you to forget these past few minutes, but that won't be possible, will it?" He now appeared weary, as though the emotional exertions of a few moments ago had drained him.

I stared at him dumbfounded. "How could I forget what I have just seen? Who was that woman? Why is there such animosity between the two of you?"

"Ah, Miss Sullivan, you of the thousand questions." His deep baritone had dropped to a gentle tone and was laced with wry humor. He shook his head ruefully and said, "I won't be getting much more work done today. Will you walk with me, and I'll tell you a story?"

I noted that he did not meet my eyes, one of the first times that had happened in our acquaintance.

I agreed and, as I had yet to take off my coat, was ready to leave. Gabriel carefully extinguished the gaslights and locked the door. We descended the stairs quietly, and then turned down Canal Street toward Causeway Street. He appeared to be gathering his thoughts.

Finally after a few blocks of silently walking side by side, I asked, "Penny for your thoughts?"

He said with a dry laugh, "Ah, Miss Sullivan, I thought they'd be worth more than that to you. However, you are right. I have a long story to tell you. I just hope you don't tire of the telling."

"I don't wish to intrude," I whispered.

"I want you to know who I am," Gabriel said, determination lacing his voice. "And after witnessing that scene, you can only have doubts."

I nodded in silent agreement, thinking of Florence.

We walked to an overlook of the harbor where we could see ships coming and going. The bustling port was filled with ships, many now with steam engines, although there were still quite a few sailboats traversing the harbor. Across the waterway in East Boston, large passenger ships were docked, recently arrived from Europe. Small ferries skirted the larger ships, bringing passengers to and from the different areas surrounding the harbor. Bunker Hill Monument gleamed in the late afternoon sunlight. This overlook was a beautiful place for we could see the harbor, watch men unloading ships and still have a sense of privacy while remaining in public.

"I had a good childhood," Gabriel began in a low tone, carefully choosing his words. "My parents were strict, yet there was no doubt that we were all cherished. We didn't have much money, but I think we were too young to notice. Or else my mum did a wonderful job of hiding our poverty from us. Either way, Jeremy, my youngest brother, Richard and I grew up creating harmless mischief and learning from our mistakes. My da believed in schooling, since he hadn't had much himself and was barely able to write his own name. My mum was very educated, a well-read woman. She read to us every night and taught us our letters at an early age.

"It was expected of us to go to school, to learn and to make something of ourselves when we grew up. I wanted to be a lawyer, learn fancy words and be paid to argue. That was one of my favorite things to do when I was young—try to outargue my da. I never won, but I enjoyed the challenge. Richard wanted to be a doctor. Jeremy didn't know what he wanted to do, but he figured he had time to decide, being the youngest. We lived in a protected cocoon, in our tenement in the West End, with sporadic visits from my da's traveling brother, Uncle Aidan."

He paused, sighing, and seemed to brace himself, not looking at me, but out to sea. As he continued, his voice hardened. "One night—a cold early fall night in November when the chill had just hit—I heard screaming and woke up. I was twelve and knew waking up and smelling smoke meant something was wrong. I shook Richard and Jeremy, grabbed them, somehow moved us in the right direction, and we escaped the house. We stood huddled together, in front of the house, waiting for Da and Mum to come out. I remember calling out, over and over again until I was hoarse, for my mum and da. But they never came."

"What had happened?" I whispered.

"A neighbor's lantern had tipped over, and the fire had spread to the back of the house first, killing my folks, but giving us time to escape." His bleak eyes reflected the torment of reliving that long-ago night and the loss of his parents. He shook his head, as though trying to shake free of the memories.

"We just continued to stand huddled together in the street, not knowing what to do. We didn't understand death, the finality of it. This was our home. We had nowhere else to go. Thankfully a neighbor across the way took us in for the rest of the night, rocked Jeremy to sleep and consoled us as best she could. But she had five little ones herself, and she couldn't take us on. I remember watching the door all that first night, waiting for Mum or Da to come in to tell us everything would be fine, it had been a mistake, but they never did." He paused, staring out at the harbor as though lost in thought. He shook his head, continuing to speak in a low, flat, emotionless voice.

"Finally the next afternoon, Aunt Masterson, my mum's sister, came around looking much imposed upon that she had to see to her sister's children, horrified she had to set foot in the West End. However, her idea of appearances and social standing had to be kept up, and she didn't want the apparent social disgrace of forcing her parentless nephews into an orphanage. So she took us.

"Am I boring you?" he turned to me, addressing me for the first time during the retelling of his childhood nightmare. Torment lit his eyes. "I can stop at any moment."

"No! No, I'd wish to hear more, if you'd like to speak of it," I replied, reaching out to touch his arm, unable to hide the eagerness in my voice.

He smiled wistfully and looked out to sea again. A slight breeze blew, ruffling his black hair.

"We rode to the Mastersons' home in a carriage—the first time I had ever been in one—and were introduced to cousins we had never met. Nicholas and Henry." His voice was laced with disgust as he said their names. "They disliked us immediately. They were dandies. All dressed up in proper clothes, though a bit too fine, if you know what I mean? And using proper words and no rough accents. They looked at us like we were beggars, come to live in their home, and they treated us as such. We learned quickly that there was no love to be spared on us—no hug when we scraped our knees, no extra help with our studies."

He closed his eyes for a few moments.

"I dreamt of escape from that house, almost from the moment I entered it, and Old Mr. Smithers helped provide that escape. He had no sons and was looking for an apprentice. He had caught me a few times in his shop, skulking around, hiding from Aunt Masterson. We struck a bargain. He'd teach me his craft, and I'd behave for my aunt and uncle. In the beginning, I often wondered who got the better part of the bargain." With that, he let out a long sigh and turned to me. "Well, that's enough of the past for one day. I'll walk you home."

I frowned, startled at the abrupt ending of the story. There was so much more I wanted to know, especially why the woman I had met, who I assumed to be his aunt Masterson, disliked him so greatly. However, as I glanced toward the harbor and East Boston, I noted that night was quickly falling. I knew I needed to hurry home to forestall any unwanted questions from my family.

"I would not want to put you to the trouble of walking me home, Mr. McLeod. I am used to making my own way, and I can ride a streetcar."

"No, I'll see you home. It's best not to wander these areas at this time of day alone, miss." He smiled at me, almost shyly, and offered me his arm as we walked toward the streetcar stop.

I was pensive, thinking through what he had told me, and what had not been relayed. I hoped he would tell me more as we walked, but, instead, we fell into a quiet camaraderie. We arrived at the streetcar kiosk after a short, brisk walk.

"Richard worries about you, you know," Gabriel said, breaking the silence between us.

"Richard?" I asked perplexed. I couldn't imagine Richard, who had only met me once, worrying about me. "Why?"

"He heard a rumor at the smithy that an old friend is looking you up," he said, watching me intently.

I felt my eyes go round, surprise flitting through me. "And they say women are the worst gossips," I muttered.

Gabriel laughed. "Men say that of course. Though we're just as curious as the next about the latest news." He continued to watch me. "You still haven't answered my question."

"I hadn't realized you'd asked one," I said primly.

"Who's the man, and what does he want from you?" Gabriel asked, leaning down to fully meet my eyes, daring me to prevaricate.

"A ghost from the past."

"A welcome one?" he inquired, studying me.

"Unexpected."

Gabriel leaned away, sighing. "I apologize, miss. It's not my place," he said with a hint of regret.

I nodded, feeling sadness course through me. "We all have pasts that haunt us, Mr. McLeod," I whispered before clearing my throat. I worried I had revealed too much with that simple comment. "Thank you for sharing part of yours with me. I'd like…" I closed my eyes, breaking off any further comments, feeling foolish.

"You'd like what, miss?" Gabriel asked, intensity in his voice again.

I met his eyes. "I'd like you to know that I enjoy the time I spend with you."

His eyes flashed momentarily, as though in triumph, then focused on the approaching streetcar. "I should let you arrive home without me in tow," he stated. "I bid you a good evening, Miss Clarissa."

I looked up at him sharply, at his use of my first name, pleasure flooding me. I could not hide a smile and nodded a few times before hastily boarding the streetcar.

"Come see me again, so we can discuss the project," he called into the open streetcar door, just as it began to move. I watched him shove his hands into his pockets, happiness filling me as he continued to watch me until the car disappeared around a bend.

CHAPTER 11

I ASCENDED THE STEPS, finding the workshop door closed, although I thought I could detect a hint of light below the door. I knocked on the door, hoping for a response. Unable to find an acceptable chaperone, I visited alone. The compulsion to see him again outweighed any concern I had at being seen by a member of the school committee.

After a few moments, the door creaked opened to a frowning Gabriel. He looked at me, shrugged his shoulders as though to ease tension and let me pass into the room. He firmly shut the door, and I realized why as soon as I entered: the warmth of the room enveloped me after the cool dampness of the walk. The pile of wood in the corner appeared smaller and more drawings were tacked up behind his workbench. The small stove set on bricks on the far side of the room was the source of the heat.

"Hello, Mr. McLeod. I've come by to help with the project," I said. Gabriel raked a hand through his short ebony hair, his dark blue eyes shuttered of any emotion. I glanced around the workroom, but I could make neither heads nor tails of any of the pieces of wood on the workbench, uncertain if they even pertained to the sideboard.

"So, you finally decided to come back. It's been a week. Your absence has delayed my work," he grumbled. He moved toward the workbench, not watching me, emanating frustration.

"This is the earliest I could return, sir."

He nodded, studying something on the workbench. "Of course." He turned toward me with a smile that didn't reach his eyes, nodding repeatedly as though trying to talk himself into something.

"I need your opinion on the sideboard, Miss Sullivan," he said. He turned again toward the workbench, and I construed that as an invitation to approach him. I nodded, nearing the workbench, waiting for him to continue. "Which do you like better?" he said, pointing to two small pieces of wood. "That carving or this one?" he asked.

I studied both pieces. One an ornate curved molding with flowers along the edge, whereas the other was simpler with fine lines and a geometric pattern.

"I know what *I* like," I replied. "I'm trying to determine what Miss Russell would like."

"Which one do you like?"

"I like the simple one," I replied. "I like the clean lines and the graceful beauty of it."

"Then that's the one I'll use," he said.

"But the piece isn't for me," I protested, turning my head to look at him with alarm.

He shook his head, a smile twisting the corner of his lips. "No," he said, "it's not for you. Thankfully."

I felt breathless and confused, and turned away from the workbench. "If that is all, Mr. McLeod," I stammered out, "I should head home."

"Would you like a cup of tea on this cold day?" he asked, moving toward the small stove. I noted the pot of water already warming on the grate. He reached for the teapot, watching me expectantly.

Even in the warm room, I still felt chilled after the damp walk. I had just begun to feel my toes again and did not relish the thought of returning to the cold so soon. I nodded my agreement, happy for a reason to linger. "I brought a new book," I called out, as I turned away to further study his workshop.

"Did you, now?" he asked, a smile evident in his voice. "Which one?"

"It's by Mark Twain. *A Connecticut Yankee in King Arthur's Court*," I replied, reaching for my bag. "The librarian told me it was entertaining, and I think Colin liked it when he read it."

"Hmm…Twain's always a good read," Gabriel said.

"If you've already read it…" I began.

"I'd love to hear you read it, miss," he said, forestalling any further protestations. I watched as he continued to prepare the tea, enjoying the domestic scene. I sighed with contentment, relishing the thought of a quiet cup of tea with no formalities.

Gabriel moved toward the table, brushing off dust and random pieces of paper to make room for the mugs and teapot. "Sugar, miss?" he asked, holding up the cracked sugar bowl. I shook my head, wishing for milk. He scooped out two heaping mounds of sugar, dumping them in his mug before adding the scalding tea first to my mug and then his. I eagerly reached for my mug, warming my hands. I sighed again in contentment.

"You might find this chair more to your liking, Miss Clarissa," he said, appearing embarrassed. I turned in the too-tall chair, noticing a small new delicate-looking rocking chair off to one side. I hopped down from the tall chair, thankful I refrained from spilling my tea, and moved toward the rocking chair. I sat, concerned it would give way as I did. I leaned into the chair, relaxing as the back of the chair seemed to have been made for someone of my proportions.

"Do you like it?"

I smiled as I relaxed in absolute comfort into the chair, gripping the arm of the chair with one hand. "It's very comfortable for someone my size."

"Exactly," he murmured, turning away.

I watched as he picked up his mug, moving toward the workbench. He began to work in silence, and I wondered if he liked to talk while he worked. I rocked gently, lulled into a sense of well-being. After a few minutes of silence, I set my mug on the floor and reached for my purse, pulling out the book.

I cleared my throat and began to read, quickly becoming lost in the new story. I had to check myself a few times from laughing too loudly. I found myself enjoying the book and the travails of the main character as he awoke to find himself in a new time period. After losing myself in the story for nearly an hour, I realized the time. I needed to leave.

Gabriel glanced toward me as I rose, placing the book aside. I set my mug on the table, unsure if I should offer to help wash up.

"You've a very pleasant reading voice, miss," he said.

"My family thinks so," I agreed. "I remember you said your mother read to you."

"My mum would read to us every night," Gabriel said, a distant look in his eye as he gazed toward me.

"What were your parents like?" I asked.

He considered his answer, appearing to weigh his response. "Truthfully?" he asked with quirked eyebrow.

I nodded, waiting.

"My da was a poor laborer, uneducated, worked to bring up his younger brother, Aidan. They were orphans, too, you see?" he said. "Uncle Aidan remained in school, though only for the requisite time period, until age fourteen. He learned his letters well, though. Loved to talk over books with Mum. Uncle Aidan always said there were plenty of hours to fill while out to sea.

"Da worked hard, working on the project to fill in the Back Bay," he said.

"Where your cousin will live." He nodded toward me, as though I were unsure where the Back Bay was. "He took tremendous pride in his work. Believed that no matter what a man did, he should do it well. Work hard. Earn his wage."

"And your mother?" I asked.

"My mum, she was from another world. She came from a middle-class family, a learned woman. She was a free spirit. Believed each person makes their own way. Loved transcendental poetry and their beliefs," he recalled, the distant expression overcoming him again. He glanced toward me wistfully, shaking his head as though to clear the memories.

"How did they meet?" I asked.

"I'm not sure," he admitted regretfully. "I never thought to ask while they lived. Now it's too late."

"No one ever told you?" I asked.

"Aunt Masterson loathed my da. Never wanted to speak of him. Thought he and his offspring were beneath her. Beneath notice," he said, anger lacing his voice. He had picked up a piece of wood and a chisel but refrained from working.

He watched me, as I thought about what he had related. "Have I answered all your questions, miss?"

I nodded. "I must go, or they will worry." I donned my jacket and hat, girding myself for the blast of cold air when I left the workshop.

"I'll be by the school in a week or so to tell you of my progress."

"That seems a long time," I replied attempting not to appear too eager to see him again.

He smiled. "Yes, well, anything sooner might seem…" He shrugged his shoulders, still watching me. "I'll see what I can do, miss."

I felt breathless, watching him as he studied me. From the added heat to my face, I knew I blushed a darker shade of red, nearly tripping over a low bench as I turned to leave.

"It will be lovely to see you again," I whispered, and turned to leave.

CHAPTER 12

DURING AN EVENING when Mrs. Smythe and Da had a dinner engagement, leaving Lucas, Colin and me the parlor to ourselves, I decided to read one of my suffrage newspapers in the parlor, rather than sequestered away in my bedroom. The *Woman's Journal* never failed to inspire me. My eyes lit up as I read that a meeting would take place in a few days in the Back Bay in the late afternoon. I focused on the article, feeling nervous, purposeful energy roll through me. I closed my eyes, exhaled slowly and determined that this would be a gathering I would attend.

After I made my decision, my attention returned to the room. Lucas sat at the piano, playing lyrical, hypnotizing music. I remembered hearing occasional strains of it whistled by workers as I walked down the street but had never heard the complete song played before on the piano. I rose, quietly walking toward him to watch him play. The music was joyous, filling me with happiness and a desire to dance.

Lucas's brow furrowed in concentration. His right hand seemed to flow over the keys, emphasizing sounds and chords in contrast to the rhythmic beats from his left hand.

As the song ended, I began to clap, causing Lucas to look up from the music for the first time. He smiled, playing out the last few notes in a dramatic fashion. I laughed with delight, twirling around, nearly falling over as my skirts became entangled with my enthusiasm.

"Lucas! That was fantastic! What was it?" I asked.

"It's called 'Maple Leaf Rag,' Rissa," Lucas said, wiping his brow. "And it sure is hard to play." He touched the piano keys fondly a few times, striking a few chords here and there from the song.

"I've never seen you practice before, and Savannah never speaks of you playing the piano at home. Where did you learn to play it, Lucas?" I asked, curious.

Lucas smiled widely. "From friends of mine." His cryptic remark only fueled my curiosity.

Before I could question him any further, Mrs. Smythe barreled into the room. "What on earth was that horrid music?" she demanded, hands across her chest, gasping for breath after her hasty entrance.

"It's called ragtime, Mrs. Sullivan," Lucas replied, smiling sweetly at her. "I can play it again if you feel deprived of hearing it."

"Why, of course not, Lucas," she snapped. "I should think you would have better taste than to bring *that sort* of music into this house."

"Well, I'm afraid that sort of music is going to be the music of the future, ma'am. This will be the song of the year, so you'd better become accustomed to hearing it." He winked in my direction, showing no contrition. Then we both stood and walked to our seats, him settling in the chair next to mine.

"Colin, anything in that paper interesting enough to share? You read it like you are hoping to find some long-lost treasure," Lucas cajoled.

"Hmm…no, nothing uplifting like that song. Just more tales of death and woe around the world. The Boxers are getting more powerful and dangerous." Colin sighed, setting aside the *Boston Evening Transcript*.

"And why should we care about a bunch of pugilists?" Mrs. Smythe demanded, her thin face even longer with her disapproval.

I giggled; Lucas snorted before acting as though he were sneezing to hide his amusement, but Colin stared at Mrs. Smythe with frank fascination.

"Do you read the papers, Mrs. Sm…Sullivan? Talk with your friends?" At her cold stare, he continued. "The Boxers are discontented Chinese on the verge of rebellion who are indiscriminately killing Christians in China. Including American Christians," Colin said helpfully. "I thought it was the topic of conversation these days." He glanced toward Lucas and me, and we both nodded our agreement.

"A genteel woman," Mrs. Smythe began, with a sniff in my direction to indicate I must be lacking in that regard, "would not know of such vulgar goings-on halfway around the world with a bunch of savages, my dear Colin. I do read the papers but only the parts that pertain to my world and me. The parts about running a good home, a good kitchen. About decoration." With this, she waved her hand around the room to indicate its frightful state. "Decorum." Yet another censorious glare was sent in my direction. "These are the important matters of *my* life," she stated with one more sniff, showing her displeasure at the topic.

I gaped at her, unable to imagine finding happiness with such a restricted life. Lucas, in the meantime, had reached over and grabbed my paper. I tried to snatch it back but did not want to make a scene in front of Mrs. Smythe. He tucked it under his arm, as though it had been his all along.

"And I do not see why I should be made to suffer listening to music such as yours, Lucas," she snapped. "I am sure your mother would be most displeased."

Lucas smiled. "I'm sure she would, except she hasn't heard me play recently."

"I expect to hear calming, soothing music in my parlor in the evening, not a riotous mixed-up jangle of melodies. I am sure a simpleton with no musical abilities wrote that piece and duped you into thinking it had merit."

"Well, ma'am, I never like to contradict a lady, but I think you'll find you are wrong. I did just learn a much more basic song, with quite simple words. Would you like to hear it?" His feigned innocence, so like how Colin acted at times, put me on edge.

"Of course, Lucas, as long as it is more appropriate for the parlor," Mrs. Smythe simpered, settling back into her chair with a sigh.

Lucas rose, walking back toward the piano bench.

I followed at his heels, unable to do anything more than hiss, "Careful, Lucas!"

His angelic smile did little to calm me.

Lucas sat at the piano bench, placing my paper away from me, stretching his fingers in a theatrical manner. Colin had moved over toward the piano, to distance himself from Mrs. Smythe and to better hear the performance. Lucas began to play a ponderous, plodding gospel hymn that I vaguely recalled from my sparse church attendance. I looked toward Colin, and he whispered the title, "'Hold the Fort.'"

I nodded. Of course. A gospel hymn from the Civil War would be exceedingly acceptable to Mrs. Smythe. I looked toward her to find her humming along contentedly, swaying side to side with her eyes closed.

Lucas looked up at me, winked, and then began to sing.

Hark the sound of myriad voices
Rising in their might
'Tis the daughters of Columbia
Pleading for the right.
Raise the flag and plant the standard,
Wave the signal still;
Brothers, we must share your freedom,
Help us, and we will.

At this, point, I peered around Colin to look at Mrs. Smythe to find her watching Lucas with a horrified expression. I knew she had not meant a suffrage song, adapted to an acceptable gospel hymn, was to be sung in her parlor.

Think it not an idle murmur,
You who hear the cry;
'Tis a plea for human freedom
Hallowed liberty.

"Lucas!" Mrs. Smythe screeched, storming toward the piano. Lucas barely had time to snatch his fingers away before she slammed down the piano key cover. "How dare you sing such a song in my house? You know that such a song will never be acceptable," she hissed. She glowered at the three of us, considering all of us as part of a conspiracy against her. "I know Clarissa has backward ideas, but they will never be acceptable, do you hear me?" she shrieked.

I grimaced from the high pitch of her voice, and Colin actually touched his ear as though in pain. Lucas smiled, seeming pleased that he had riled her so much.

"Mrs. Sullivan, I believe my musical talents are wasted on your discerning ear," he said without a trace of mocking in his voice. "It is time I headed for home." He rose, slipping my paper under his arm again. "Rissa, will you see me out?"

I walked by his side from the room, gripping his arm firmly as though expressing my displeasure with his outrageous actions.

"Lucas, how could you?" I whispered in the front hall as he donned a light jacket.

"The question, Rissa, is how could I not? She was begging for something like that. It was almost too easy," he said with an impish grin.

I stifled a giggle as I thought back to her antics.

"Though I fear I might have lost the ability to hear a few octaves, sitting next to her as she shrieked," Lucas said with a rueful shake of his head. He handed me my newspaper, winking at me again. "Careful with that one," he said, nodding toward the parlor. "She won't be kind if she finds this kind of paper in your room." He gave me a quick hug and left.

I stood in the hallway a moment, battling my anxiety at what she would do if she were to find out about my planned attendance at the suffragette meeting.

CHAPTER 13

"FLORENCE," I SAID two days later, twitching nervously, delaying my departure from school for a few moments, "won't you come with me this afternoon?"

Florence glanced up from correcting ledgers, her black curly hair falling out of its pins, her dress sleeves pushed up around her elbows, her hands chalk and ink stained from a strenuous day of teaching, to study me curiously.

"Clarissa, I've told you I won't go to hear those suffragettes belabor their lack of freedom as they sit in their expensive parlors, drinking tea, with servants waiting on them." She eyed me severely, over her horn-rimmed glasses, daring me to contradict her.

"It's a good cause, Flo," I argued.

"So is correcting these ledgers so I can walk home in the daylight," she countered with a hint of a smile.

I nodded, feeling somewhat dejected, yet mainly nervous. I had no idea what my reception would be at today's meeting. "Well, in that case, good luck with the ledgers and I'll give you a full report tomorrow."

Florence nodded absently, already absorbed in her work.

I gathered my purse, gloves and shawl. As I pinned on my hat, I was thankful I had taken a few moments this morning to consider my appearance. My mint-green long-sleeved poplin dress and matching jacket with lace at the collar and wrists had been too fancy for school. However, I had known I would not be able to return home to change before the meeting, as Mrs. Smythe would have prevented me from leaving again.

I walked outside, attempting to breathe the fresh scents of spring. I focused on the positive to calm my nerves. I turned left from the school, down Blossom Street, right on Cambridge Street, and then onto Charles Street, which would allow me to circumvent Beacon Hill.

As I walked toward the Back Bay, I thought about the recent expansion of Boston. It had been a very small city before its leaders had decided to fill in the Back Bay. The bay had been a festering tidal flat until about fifty years ago when it was gradually drained for the filling project. Though controversial at the time, the filling project had been enormously successful, and the Back Bay was now the most desirable place to live in Boston with all the many modern amenities such as central heating, electric lighting, telephones, modern plumbing and a sewage system.

I continued to walk along Charles Street passing numerous stores including rope builders, carpenters, tailors, coffee shops and grocers. I crossed Beacon Street into the Public Gardens through wrought-iron gates and breathed in the fresh air, enjoying the momentary peace and the sensation of being in an oasis in the midst of the city. The trees were in full bloom, the tulips striking in their beds, all of one color. I paused on the bridge over the pond to bask in spring's sunshine and to calm my nerves. Reluctantly I began walking again, exiting onto Commonwealth Avenue, slowly approaching my destination.

I crossed over from the central tree-lined, shaded mall in the middle of Commonwealth Avenue to stand across the street from an imposing redbrick mansion with its slate roof and a garden at the front of the house. Many of the bow-fronted windows had lighter brick inlay, outlining and highlighting their shape. The large, highly polished oak door with brass knocker gleamed in the sunlight. I tried to work up my courage to cross the street, ascend the steps and knock on the door.

I remained rooted to the spot, watching elegantly dressed women and a few men enter the house. I fretted that I didn't have an invitation. I dithered a few more moments, attempting to gather my courage. As I exhaled loudly, a refined voice at my elbow interrupted my thoughts.

"It's a bit overdone, wouldn't you agree?" a scratchy, nearly hoarse female voice said.

I turned toward the voice, noting a stout middle-aged woman in an eggplant-colored dress in bombazine fabric with pearls sewn into the front. She wore a matching hat covering gray hair with ivory gloves reaching to midforearm. Her piercing aquamarine eyes assessed me as quickly as I had her. I must not have been found wanting as she looped her right arm through my left arm and started across the street, dragging me along with the force of her momentum.

I found myself ushered into the enormous, opulent front hall. Floor to ceiling was paneled in gleaming dark mahogany. A large mirror sat over an onyx fireplace with two chairs on either side of it. I had never seen a hall so large as to merit a fireplace. The marble-topped entryway table held an enormous bouquet of flowers including daffodils and tulips. Dark blue plush carpets covered hardwood floors.

"Mrs. Chickering," a high-pitched voice squealed, causing the hair on the back of my nape to rise. "How wonderful you could make today's soiree."

I could not tell if the speaker was sincere, but the grand dame next to me smiled with apparent delight.

"Ah, Bertha, always a delight to see you and to partake of one of your events. And of your fabulous teas," Mrs. Chickering replied with a smile, patting Bertha's hand with her free one but keeping her right arm looped through mine.

Bertha smiled, tilting her head toward me. Her thin lips, now turned down in disapproval, did nothing to improve her emaciated appearance.

"Bertha, I don't know as you've met my dear friend?" Mrs. Chickering asked, pointing at me, then raising an eyebrow toward Bertha as though daring her to turn me away.

"Oh, no. It's an honor, I assure you, to meet a…a dear friend of *yours*," Bertha stammered out, her voice more whining and high-pitched than when she had first approached us, causing me to attempt not to grimace at the sound.

I wondered why she, the mistress of such a grand home, would be solicitous of Mrs. Chickering. "Clarissa Sullivan, ma'am," I murmured, nodding demurely.

"Of course," Bertha effused, her thin lips turned up in a slightly feral smile. "You always were a forward thinker, Sophronia. Just like you to invite the *immigrant* masses to our gatherings."

I squinted at her emphasis on *immigrant* but knew now was not the time for clarification.

Bertha eyed my dress critically, raised an eyebrow and sniffed as though to imply my presence was tolerated solely due to my association with Mrs. Chickering. "Please, make yourselves welcome," she called out in her grating voice.

Mrs. Chickering and I moved on; she cut a wide swath through the room with me following in her wake. Either the other guests did not like her, or they were in awe of her, and attempted to appear busy with their own conversations. I imagined it was a mixture of the two. We arrived at a black walnut settee covered in mauve-colored satin with an ornately carved back panel of a hunting scene.

"Harrumph," Mrs. Chickering muttered. I glanced curiously toward her, wondering what had upset her. Mrs. Chickering murmured, "I've always hated this settee, never understood why a suffragette would own the piece. And I've told Bertha. Now for some perverse reason, I find this is always the settee open to me."

I unsuccessfully attempted to glance at the carving to determine why it was offensive, craning my neck to decipher the scene.

"You'll pull a neck muscle, and you look like a simpleton, turned around like that," Mrs. Chickering barked. I hastily faced forward, flushing fiercely. I began to doubt that meeting her had been providential.

"It's a scene of Apollo hunting Daphne and her running away," Mrs. Chickering hissed. "I *know* it's from mythology. I *know* we must respect the past and ancestors. But don't you think a good suffragette would turn and fight? Not run away and want her father to turn her into a tree, but to give her quivers and arrows and *shoot him?*" she demanded with righteous indignation. I laughed, caught completely off guard by her outrageous comment.

She turned toward me, her aquamarine eyes bright as though fire-lit. I sensed she, too, was trying not to laugh. I finally said, "It would be a nice twist to the story and a wonderful conversation piece." My eyes danced with mischief and merriment. I began to relax in her presence.

"Exactly, my girl," she said. "Unfortunately, Bertha, not the smartest woman of her day, married an even simpler man, a *banker,*"—this word said with absolute derision—"and he wants everything as basic as possible. Lest he become confused." She grunted as though she couldn't imagine such people. "Though of course the Searles are exceedingly wealthy and the 'right' sort of people," Mrs. Chickering said with a quirk of her eyebrow.

Mrs. Chickering attempted to settle back against the uncomfortable carving of the settee, grimacing in disgust.

I too wished for a cushion to protect my back. I lowered my voice, afraid of being overheard by too many attendants. "What exactly happens at one of these events?"

"Depends on the day and the mood of those here," she murmured. "Some days I just partake of delicious teas and cakes and give my cook the afternoon off." She raised her eyebrows again, and I found myself enjoying her irreverence. "Other days someone or other has a fire in their belly, and there are good discussions on our cause. Not that we've made much progress lately."

"Surely keeping the public aware of the need to vote is essential," I argued, feeling my excitement and passion for the cause rising.

She waved her right hand in a somewhat dismissive manner. "Of course it is and always will be. But the public has been aware of our wishes for decades now and has had no desire to treat women as anything other than a herd of sheep who follow the will of their men." She looked at me, arching her eyebrows again, daring me to argue.

"Not all men expect women to be that way," I countered, thinking of Gabriel, silently hoping he was different.

"If you are fortunate, my girl, if you are fortunate," she murmured, nodding a few times, a wistful expression in her eyes.

I smiled, thankful she had agreed.

"No, back in the day, we were filled with fire," she said, raising her fisted hand slightly at the word *fire*. "We had finally emerged from that dreadful conflict,"—at which she nearly crossed herself—"and we women had hopes of being treated as equals. It turns out that white men weren't serious on that front, no matter what the amendments say," she whispered, looking at me.

I merely nodded.

"Back then we thought it would be a short fight. That we'd have the vote by now. Some—" and she nodded vaguely toward the room so I didn't know whom she truly meant "—thought we'd be included in the scope of the Fifteenth Amendment." A long sigh followed. "But here we are, more than thirty years after the war, still toiling."

"It's worth it, surely," I said.

"Of course it's worth it, my girl. Just like it's worth my believing that someday I'll meet my maker in heaven. Though I believe He'll be too busy for more than a quick salute." She eyed me closely, and I again felt the full effect of those aquamarine eyes.

I chuckled, imperceptibly saluting her. I hid my actions to anyone watching our conversation by acting like I was checking my coiffure. Mrs. Chickering guffawed, seeming to enjoy me as much as I was now delighting in her.

"Why are we alone to one side?" I asked in a low voice, glancing around the room, watching all the well-dressed, demurely attired men and women surreptitiously watch us in return.

"I am a bit outspoken for their tastes," Mrs. Chickering proclaimed. "Many of them prefer the insipid commentaries of Bertha to anything of true substance. They live in fear that one of my statements will be quoted in the newspaper. Harold Zimmerman, one of our few male members,"—she nodded toward a balding man with a large paunch—"endeavors to ensure that nothing that has not been approved by him appears in any printed press." She sniffed her disapproval, glaring in his direction. He sensed her attention, glancing toward her. He blanched at noticing the full effect of her displeasure and quickly looked away.

She moved restlessly on the settee, I imagined in an attempt to find a comfortable position.

I had given up, accepting that, from my backside down, I would be numb for the foreseeable future.

"Now, tell me about you, Clarissa Sullivan, the so-called immigrant upstart." She pinned me with an intense stare, making my heart race at having her full attention.

"I live in the South End with my da, stepmother and brothers. My mama died eight years ago from a wasting disease. My da runs a successful blacksmith shop and my brother, Colin, works for him. As I am not yet married, I wanted to have a profession." After a short pause, I murmured, "Needed one, really. I work as a teacher at the Wells School in the West End."

"You mean to tell me, my girl, that you teach, and teach a mass of poor children in that wretched West End?" Again the near crossing of herself. "Though you don't need to?"

I looked at her, trying to determine her real question. Finally, I answered, "I need to. For me. For my sense of purpose."

A full smile bloomed on her face, and she sighed with contentment. "You've been a suffragette for a while, my girl, and not known it." She patted my hand affectionately, and then seemed to lose all interest in our conversation as tea was brought out on large trays.

Most men and women slowly rose from their seats to wander toward the teapots and trays of food. However, Mrs. Chickering and I had an overflowing plate of sandwiches, cakes and cookies delivered to us along with perfectly prepared cups of tea by a gracious maid. I smiled my thanks to her, unsure why we had been granted the courtesy.

"It's done for all of the older generation," Mrs. Chickering said, nodding toward a few of the other women, "and anyone who is sitting with us. It shows their respect. In the beginning I railed against it and marched up there to pour my own tea. Now I simply enjoy not having to balance a cup of tea with my cakes as I walk. I enjoy their solicitude, makes me feel welcome here, even if some of them wished I lived in Wyoming. Though at least I'd have the vote there."

I choked on my tea, unable to imagine living so far from Boston.

"Eat up, my girl, Clarissa. Bertha's cook makes some of the finest pastries you'll ever eat."

We ate slowly, drank cups of tea and watched the room. A handful of women wandered over to speak a few words with Mrs. Chickering, although none remained in her company long. I enjoyed watching the room and seeing everyone interact, yet began to feel purposefully ignored. I stiffened my spine, intent on maintaining a placid expression. Finally, after everyone had settled again, it seemed as though the meeting would start.

At first, I sat enraptured, listening to the speakers, both women and men, discuss current concerns and strategies.

Then a young plump woman, with a face appearing to be in a perpetual state of frowning, stood to speak in an upper-crust Bostonian accent that grated on my nerves and reminded me of my grandparents. "I am sure we are all in agreement that the current course, the present argument, is the correct one," she said in a husky voice, expecting approval from those gathered.

I heard an overwhelming murmur of agreement from most of the attendants, though I heard Mrs. Chickering snort in disapproval. I felt like a fish out of water, as if I had entered a room in the middle of the conversation and had missed the crux of the argument. The severe-looking woman, attired in a dull gray dress, continued speaking. "The argument against the immigrant vote and for educated white women's vote is quite sound," she said.

I gasped, then tried to cover up my alarm with a few coughs. Mrs. Chickering harrumphed again, as though echoing my sentiments. The disapproving plump woman looked severely toward Mrs. Chickering. "You disagree, Sophronia?"

"As well you know, Gertrude," Mrs. Chickering ground out. "Why the lot of you could ever put your pea-brained heads together and create an argument denying anyone the vote and then think this helps the women's cause is beyond me." She exhaled loudly, staring fiercely around the room, daring anyone to countermand her previous statement. "Shouldn't we work toward the rights of all people? Isn't that what the movement is for?"

Another woman—with lips that seemed to be perpetually turned up, mockingly at the corners—spoke softly. "Your generation had your chance to do it your way and failed. Now it is our turn." She tilted her head toward Mrs. Chickering in a challenging way.

"You think, Mrs. Cushing, that disenfranchising some will lead to the enfranchisement of others?" Mrs. Chickering shook her head, seeming at a loss for words.

Mrs. Cushing spoke up in a soft, gently derisive voice. "I am sure you can find guidance in your *Woman's Bible*."

Mrs. Chickering glowered at the young woman as a few of the attendants snickered. My eyes grew round at the reference to the controversial rewriting of the Bible by one of the earliest founders of the suffragist movement, Elizabeth Cady Stanton.

Mrs. Chickering tilted up her chin, meeting Mrs. Cushing's gaze. "Yes, I might just learn more about my own sense of self and worth outside the control of the preacher man. Thank you for your kind suggestion," she replied.

Mrs. Cushing flushed red, losing any semblance of a smile.

"Now," Mrs. Chickering spoke up in a loud, authoritative voice, "I know our leaders have not spoken openly against these ideas. However, no one in the suffrage movement would truly wish for one to gain the vote at the expense of another. Even if they are currently poor and immigrant." She paused to pass a severe look around the room. "Many of you seem to have forgotten that your forebears were all immigrants at some point. Though, unfortunately, many of you were never poor."

"Mrs. Chickering," Gertrude interrupted, "how dare you compare us to these immigrants? They are uneducated. They don't speak English. Or if they do, it's an accent you cannot understand. And they are not good Protestants," she finished with a fervor, so upset she nearly stammered.

"As our esteemed leader, Susan B. Anthony, said, 'There is no true freedom for women without possession of all her rights.' I like to think that is true for all people. Immigrant or well established. Woman or man. Educated or undereducated." Sophronia sat tall, appearing at peace.

I glanced at the others in the room, and they seemed deflated, as though their argument had lost steam. I feared it had merely stalled for the day and that it would resurface again soon.

After a few tense moments, another woman spoke up. "I believe it is time to discuss the celebratory preparations for Mrs. Ward-Howe." At this, a boisterous discussion began, with petty arguments over the cake and music. "It is in less than two months' time, and all are expected to come. There is still much planning to be done."

Excitement coursed through me at the thought of seeing, maybe actually meeting, Mrs. Ward-Howe, a legend in the suffragist movement. After a few more moments, Mrs. Chickering turned to me during a particularly long-winded talk by a Mrs. Audley, pinning me with an intense stare. "You will be there, my girl," she intoned.

"I will do my best," I murmured.

"*Humph…*" she said, pursing her lips in displeasure. "Do your best to come to tea at my house in a few days," she whispered in a carrying voice. She handed me a calling card with her address on it. I nodded a few times, uncertainty filling me at how I would manage tea at her house.

The discussion about the ceremony for Mrs. Ward-Howe ended, signaling the completion of the meeting. I quickly stood, knowing I had tarried too long. "I must hurry home," I whispered to Sophronia. "I will call in a few days." I clasped her hand, then slipped out of the ornate room and house.

CHAPTER 14

THE SCHOOL YEAR CONTINUED, although my students became increasingly restless. I found my mood mirrored theirs perfectly, although my restlessness derived from inner doubts and turmoil rather than a desire to be outside. I had enjoyed the suffragist meeting and encountering Mrs. Chickering, but the gathering had stirred up my deeply suppressed longings for more from life.

One afternoon after a meeting with the principal, Mr. Carney, I returned to my schoolroom to find Gabriel there. It had been a particularly harrowing day with my students Susie and Debra nearly coming to blows over a piece of ribbon. I began to enter my classroom, only to stop short upon the realization Gabriel was not alone. I remained in the hallway, skulking outside the door, listening to the discussion, fascinated by the play of emotions across Gabriel's face.

Gabriel stood amid the pupils' desks, his tall frame rigid with anger. The day's lesson about comportment remained on the chalkboard behind him. He turned to watch Florence as she moved around the room, farther away from him. I saw Florence's ashen face for a brief moment, and I realized that, by luck or misfortune, Florence had decided to visit me at the same time and was now confronted with an irate Gabriel.

"How is my cousin Henry, Miss Butler?" Gabriel asked.

Florence gave a start, as though she had been struck. "I do not know what you mean," she protested.

In a low voice, Gabriel said, "Oh, I think you do."

She glared at Gabriel, standing up straight, bringing her shoulders back. She stood as tall as her five-foot-six-inch frame allowed. "Who are you to speak to me in such a manner?" she asked. "You, who would sacrifice your own brother's happiness out of pride."

"Is that what I did?" he demanded, fire filling his eyes.

"You tell me, Gabriel," Florence demanded. "One minute, Richard and I were to marry, the next, he won't even acknowledge he knows me. Scorning me," she nearly sobbed out.

"And why should he acknowledge the likes of you?" Gabriel asked.

"How dare you!" Florence cried out, looking as though she were about to hit him. "How dare you treat me in such a manner?" Tears began to pour down her cheeks. "Was it because I'm poor? Unattractive? Forward thinking for a woman?" she demanded.

Gabriel watched her without emotion. "You know damn well that's got nothing to do with it, Florence," he bit out.

"Then what, Gabriel? I've waited four years to know why. Why?"

"You're a liar. How could we ever trust the likes of you?"

"What?" Florence gasped, confusion evident in her expression.

"You heard me," Gabriel stated, taking a deep calming breath. "After I found out about your true past—and about you and Cousin Henry and Aunt Masterson—no way in hell was someone with ties to them marrying my brother," Gabriel hissed. Florence watched him with dazed eyes, the fight and bluster slowly seeping out of her. She collapsed onto a chair, staring vacantly into space, as though remembering long-ago scenes.

"How could you get it so wrong?" Florence asked. She looked at him with devastated eyes. "Be thankful you have no idea what it is to be truly alone, to be so unloved, Gabriel," she whispered in a tortured voice, the words sounding more like a curse than a benediction.

Gabriel straightened. He tightened his jaw and stiffened his shoulders. "Stay away from my brother," Gabriel ground out. "He's doing just fine without you." He turned to leave, stopping short when he saw me witnessing the scene from the doorway. He flushed and brushed past me, leaving the schoolroom abruptly.

I moved toward Florence, unsure how to approach her. She seemed as fragile as one of my beloved seashells, and I did not wish to cause her further pain.

"Florence," I whispered, kneeling by her side, grasping one of her hands gently in mine. "How can I help you?" I asked.

She shook her head futilely, tears seeping out of her eyes. "You can't, Clarissa. I made this mess, and I have to find a way to make it better." She began to sob, and I enfolded her in my arms, comforting her as best I could.

CHAPTER 15

"SO YOU MEAN TO TELL ME that he yelled at poor Florence?" Savannah asked over tea the following day. We sat in the Russell family parlor, the door closed for privacy. I glanced around, noting the subtle changes to the artwork. Aunt Matilda had replaced a few of the scenes of New England with European ones. I sat on the ugly lime-green settee, choosing comfort over beauty.

"Yes, Sav," I replied, absently biting into a piece of sweet bread. "I think there is an awful history between them. I just don't know what it is." I sighed, hating being ignorant of the full story.

"Rissa, maybe this is a sign you should forget about him. I'd hate to think of you with someone with an evil temper," Savannah said with a shudder. She daintily took a sip of tea, abstaining from eating during teatime. Her strawberry-blond hair was perfectly pulled back in a relaxed bun with no hair out of place. She wore a fine navy-and-white striped silk day dress with a navy belt highlighting her petite figure.

I shook my head in disagreement. I continued to chew on the sweet bread, marveling at Savannah's ability to abstain from eating any of the delicious foods on the tea tray.

Savannah rolled her eyes, in frustration. "Rissa, I know he's handsome. And he's clearly fascinated with you. But I think we should try to find you someone reasonable," she urged. "Someone more from our class. I've come to realize he is completely inappropriate for you."

"Why are you allowing Jonas to change you so much?" I whispered.

"Rissa, if, *when* you marry, you will realize you must believe, act, feel exactly as your husband," she replied. "It is as it should be."

"How can you believe that, Sav?" I asked, deciding to ignore the sting her words wrought about me possibly not marrying. "Shouldn't you want to be with someone who wants you to be your own person?"

"Rissa, quit reading those suffragists' publications and enter the real world," Savannah demanded. "No man wants a free-spirited, forward-thinking wife. He wants a compliant woman to create a soothing home environment in which to raise children."

"Can't you think your own thoughts while creating that environment and raising those children?" I asked.

"I know it's the turn of the century, but you really must not be too modern," Savannah warned.

"I don't agree with you, Sav," I replied. "I never will. I...my mama wasn't like that."

"Promise me that you will start to consider acceptable men. Though, of course, I would never mean Cameron."

"I have come to believe he will never surface," I said, a tinge of exasperation in my voice. "I think there must have been some mistake."

"Do you think he would have come to find you so quickly?"

Though she had asked her question in a gentle tone, I sensed a criticism. "Yes, I would have thought he'd speak with me by now. I thought I had meant more to him…"

"Rissa, you meant something to him, that much is obvious. Just not enough." Savannah looked at me knowingly, not attempting to soften her words in any way.

"Enough talk about me! Any news on wedding plans?"

***

AFTER THE SHORT WALK HOME, I entered the front hall dreading another lecture from Mrs. Smythe. I turned toward the coat rack to hang my hat and jacket. As I headed toward the stairs, I noticed a small envelope on the front hall table. I glanced at it with no real interest, certain it did not pertain to me. However, in bold male handwriting, I saw my name scribbled on the front. My heart leapt at the unfamiliar handwriting. I grabbed the letter, stuffing it into my purse to keep its presence a secret.

"Is that you, dear?" called out Mrs. Smythe from the formal parlor. She sailed into the front hall, hair perfectly coiffed, impeccably dressed, her posture so straight I thought she would topple backward.

She realized I stood in the front hall lost in thought, with no purpose, and sighed with exasperation. "Oh, it's you, Clarissa. What are you doing, just standing in the hallway?" She tugged my arm, pulling me into the parlor.

I tripped on the edge of the rug, nearly causing the two of us to tumble to the floor. Mrs. Smythe let go of my arm, righting herself by grabbing a nearby chair. I banged into a wall, smashing my shoulder.

"Really, Clarissa!" she hissed. "You could do with learning a little grace!"

I meekly nodded in agreement as I rubbed my shoulder. I entered the parlor, noting a new plush rug, wondering idly if it were oriental. "Nice rug," I said unable to feign enthusiasm.

"Is that all you can say, dear?" Mrs. Smythe chided. "No other words of encouragement as I take on the monumental task of refurbishing this albatross of a house?"

I watched her closely, noting she considered this a house, not a home. I wondered if she only viewed it as a project to show off to the neighbors. I glanced around the room, liking what I saw, memories of happy times flooding me, each piece provoking a sense of nostalgia. I saw no need for redecoration. I tried to see it through her eyes but failed. She wanted everything to change, be modern and new. I wanted everything to be as it had once been and realized neither of us would be completely satisfied.

"I'm sure you will have…" I began.

"It's not as though I receive any support from you or your brothers," she wailed. "And Sean only wants me doing minor alterations. *Minor* alterations. As though this home is acceptable with so few changes," she sniffed, looking affronted.

"Mrs. Smythe." I attempted to speak gently, feeling a terrible headache coming on at the thought of having to attempt to reason with her. "The house is well furbished."

"Well furbished!" she scoffed. "If you call fading wall hangings, threadbare carpets and out-of-date furniture with dreadful covers *well furbished*." She glared at me. "I thought I would find a little support in you, Clarissa."

I shook my head, unsure why she would look to me as an ally.

"I thought, surely, as the only other female in the house, you would understand my plight."

We sat in awkward silence a few moments with me unwilling to engage in this discussion. Finally I excused myself, escaping to my bedroom to read my letter. I walked up the stairs at a sedate pace, not wishing to cause any suspicion in Mrs. Smythe. I opened my door, latching it shut behind me, as I pulled the letter out of my purse.

I sat on my bed and held the correspondence, noting the unfamiliar red wax seal with the indent of a chisel. I smiled, gently caressing the seal before breaking it open. I unfolded the paper, careful not to rip it, and scanned to the bottom for the signature, *Gabriel*. I sighed in pleasure, my eyes moving to read the letter from the beginning.

April 18, 1900

My Dear Miss Sullivan,

Please excuse my presumption in writing to you. I want to apologize for the scene you witnessed. I would never wish to cause you any distress, though I fear I have done so by the expression in your eyes. I never meant to cause you pain.

There is a long, difficult history between me, Richard and Florence Butler. But I don't feel I'm at liberty to speak with you about it. At least not yet. Just know I have acted to protect my brother. As I would act to protect anyone I care for.

I feel most regretful at not speaking with you. May I come to the school again to see you?

Yours sincerely,
Gabriel McLeod

I stared at the letter, frustration roiling through me. Why couldn't he have written more? I reread it, hoping to find a hidden message, yet there wasn't much more to read into those simple words. I sighed in exasperation, already composing a return letter in my head. I moved to the desk, pulling out a piece of paper, and began to write.

April 19, 1900

Dear Mr. McLeod,

I thank you for writing me your short missive. I must admit to a sense of shock at the scene I witnessed between you and my dear friend Miss Butler. Since your first visit to the school, I have wondered at the history between you and realize it must be extensive for you to react so strongly to her. I am conflicted as to how to correctly answer your request but do enjoy your company and know you will explain your family's history with my friend when you feel it to be appropriate. I, too, wish we had been able to speak. Perhaps it would be less awkward if I were to visit the workshop.

Sincerely,
Miss Sullivan

I examined my reply, not completely satisfied. I had never corresponded with a gentleman before and was not certain what was proper.

I addressed the letter, sealed it and placed it in my purse, keeping it from inquisitive eyes, to post tomorrow. I carefully hid Gabriel's letter, as I knew Mrs. Smythe enjoyed snooping around my room when I was out.

CHAPTER 16

SOPHRONIA LIVED IN A CHARMING bow-fronted brick town house on Beacon Street across from the Common with green shutters on each side of all the windows. I walked across Beacon Street and knocked on her door. A formally attired butler answered, requesting my card. I stood in the front hall, a mauve-colored room with a large black walnut hallstand and mirror with chairs on either side. When the butler returned, I followed him up thickly carpeted stairs, moving soundlessly. The mahogany banister gleamed as though recently polished. The upstairs sitting room with white wainscoting and soothing yellow wallpaper over-looked the street and the Common.

"Mrs. Chickering," I asked after I had settled, "why does there exist such animosity between you and the younger suffragettes?"

Sophronia leaned back in her lady's chair, perfectly at ease. "Ah, my girl, as you age, you will realize that the younger generation lives to find fault with their elders, and they relish the belief that all of their current miseries are due to our failures. In their minds we failed to get them the vote here in Massachusetts in '95. And now there is a faction of women, mainly upper-class wealthy women who have never thought for themselves a day in their lives, who are calling them-selves the Massachusetts Association Opposed to Suffrage for Women."

I set my teacup down carefully, wanting to pay full attention and to prevent any possibility of an accident. "Are you saying there are women who are actively working against us getting the vote?"

"A frightful herd of sheep," Sophronia spat out. "They spout all sorts of useless facts and proclamations, believing that if one such as Queen Victoria is against suffrage for women, then all women should be opposed." Sophie *har-rumphed* her disgust. "I can't imagine anything worse than not wanting better for your daughter or niece."

I sat in silence, thinking about what I knew of these women. "Maybe they think the life they have is the best life for their daughters. Change can be very frightening."

"You have a kind heart, my girl," she said in a gentle voice, "but these women don't deserve your compassion." Her voice had turned to steel. "Would you have them deny your schoolgirls a brighter future merely so those women could hold onto their sense of superiority, their sense of place in the world?" she asked, raising her eyebrows in challenge.

I frowned, furrowing my brow. "Of course not. And I wouldn't have them deny *my* rights, either." I paused for a moment, unsure how to ask what had really been bothering me. "Mrs. Chickering, why are the young women anti-immigrant?"

"You are recent immigrant stock, aren't you, girl? And call me Sophie, all my friends do," she said.

I nodded once in agreement to both her question and her dictate.

She settled into her chair, thinking through her response. "These young women have not lived through the ups and downs of life like some of us have. They see all of this change—the large number of immigrants, the modernization of the world, the new inventions, the social upheaval, the strikes—all of it with distrust. And they see, in a simple way, the perceived injustice of uneducated immigrant men, some who can barely speak English, being granted the right to vote. They are reacting against it."

"What do they have against the immigrant?" I asked, feeling naive.

"It is as Gertrude said last week. They are uneducated. They don't speak English. They do not necessarily follow traditional customs. Many drink more than we are accustomed to and go against the temperance movement. And most are not Protestant." She paused before sharing a rueful glance with me. "And you must never forget the suffrage movement is all about getting the vote. But to get the vote, someone must vote for us. Therefore, it is a very political beast. Currently it is fashionable to be anti-immigrant."

"But they are hard workers," I argued.

"That is immaterial to most."

"Don't they deserve a chance at the life we have?"

"Many would say no. The greedy ones. Or the scared ones. The rich ones like the immigrant because they work cheaply and rarely complain."

"Shouldn't the immigrant have a right to vote, a voice, just as much as women, to help improve their lives?" I argued.

"One should think so, Clarissa, but there are many who would disagree."

I settled back in my chair, lost in thought for a few moments, before deciding to change the topic. "What is your background, Sophie?"

"I married well, married young. To a handsome young doctor from a very wealthy family. He was distantly related to the Chickerings who make pianos, though the only contact I have ever had with that branch of the family was to be gifted a glorious instrument on my wedding day. We married, quickly had three children and then war broke out." She glanced away for a moment, gathering her thoughts. "He wanted to help the wounded. Insisted on traveling with the Union Army."

"I remained here, in Boston, caring for our children," she whispered. "Letters couldn't come soon enough to suit me. Then one came that I wish had never arrived. He caught a severe case of dysentery in '63 and died. My loving Eustace. Gone from this world forever."

"Oh, Sophie. I am so sorry."

"Not nearly as sorry as I am, my girl," she said with bright eyes. "I finally recovered from his loss, emerging from my grief at the time when increased suffrage activity occurred in Boston, and I wanted to be a part of it. I had done a small amount of antislavery work before the war and had a sense of what activism was like.

"Now," she said, "tell me about your immigrant roots. I am most curious about them."

"I am only half immigrant," I said, "though I do not identify well with the nonimmigrant half. My father emigrated from Ireland when he was a child with his family. He is a blacksmith, owns his own blacksmithing shop that he inherited from his father." I was unable to hide the pride in my voice. "My mama's family, the Thompsons, are from an old New England family and have been here for generations. They live here on the Hill, in Louisburg Square."

Sophie gave a bark of laughter. "So you're the disappointing granddaughter?"

I gasped, unaware I had such a reputation.

"Your grandmother and I pay a social call on each other once or twice a year. We stave off having to see each other any more frequently by sending our cards around and having them do the visiting for us." She smiled at that. "But, on the few times we do meet, she speaks of how worried she is about her jilted blacksmithing granddaughter."

"I am not a blacksmith," I protested.

"Of course not, but you are descended from one, and, to her, there isn't much worse. Except maybe a chimney sweep. Such dirty professions."

"And honorable. My father provides very well for our family, and he loved my mama. He is a good da, as she would know if she had ever bothered to spend time with us," I snapped out, then blushed beet red at my outburst.

"Though you were jilted?" Sophronia inquired, raising her eyebrows again and giving me the full effect of her aquamarine eyes.

"A few years ago. Nothing exciting," I murmured.

"Hmm…well, a story for another day then," Sophie said, taking a sip of tea. "It seems to me that one such as you is wasted on the narrow-minded likes of your grandmother." Sophronia patted my hand. "I wouldn't mourn the loss of her in your life. You could spend years trying to please her, and she would never cease finding fault."

I beamed at Sophronia, realizing she truly understood them and their type of people. Then Sophie clapped her hands together with malicious glee and said, "Oh, I hope I am there when she hears you have joined the suffragist movement! I can't wait to see her face become ruddy and see her at a loss for words!"

My smile dimmed as I fervently hoped I was not present when my grandmother heard the news.

CHAPTER 17

"EXCUSE ME, MUM," BRIDGET SAID. "Ye've a caller for tea." She bobbed a quick curtsy, handing the silver salver containing the crisp calling card to Mrs. Smythe.

I had been lounging in my favorite chair, imagining the letter I wanted to receive from Gabriel as Mrs. Smythe prattled on about new carpets, drapes and furniture coverings. Thankfully this interruption had forestalled any further discussion about her grand plans for the redesign of the room, yet it now meant I would need to sit through a formal tea with a friend of hers. I bit back a groan, forced myself to sit upright and pasted a pleasant smile on my face.

Mrs. Smythe reached for the card, raising one eyebrow in surprise at the fancy paper. She frowned as she read the card. "I am not acquainted with a Mrs. Chickering," she said quietly before pinning an intent gaze on me. "Clarissa?"

My eyes grew round before I could hide my reaction.

"You do know her," Mrs. Smythe hissed accusingly. "Now is not the time for me to discover illicit associations with inappropriate persons of questionable backgrounds, Clarissa." She fingered the expensive card as though determining her actions. She turned toward Bridget, replying in a cool voice, eloquently expressing her dislike at the task at hand. "Please invite her in. Prepare another pot of tea and fresh sandwiches."

"Yes, mum," Bridget said, bobbing another quick curtsy before making a hasty retreat.

A moment later, Sophie sailed into the room in a burgundy taffeta dress with decorative gold buttons down the front, head held high, as if her inclusion in our afternoon tea had never been doubted.

"Clarissa, my girl," she called out in her scratchy voice, her aquamarine eyes sparkling with delight. "Wonderful to see you again." She leaned toward me to grip my hands. I smiled fully, delight filling me and momentarily banishing the anxiety of having her meet Mrs. Smythe.

"Sophie, it is wonderful to see you. Please, make yourself comfortable." I gestured toward a settee, though worried it would be as uncomfortable as the Searles'. "Please, sit here. This has always been my favorite chair." I stood and ushered her into my seat, farther away from Mrs. Smythe.

She settled herself, holding herself regally, back straight, feet curled under the chair, surveying the room. Her gaze met Mrs. Smythe's frown, and they sat studying each other for a few moments.

I eyed them warily, uncertain of the outcome of this impromptu meeting. Bridget entered carrying a tea tray that she placed on a small table. She was dismissed with an absentminded flick of the wrist from Mrs. Smythe. I began to prepare cups of tea, thankful for the activity as I watched them silently assess each other.

"Mrs. Chickering," Mrs. Smythe simpered, primly folding her hands on her lap. "We are honored you desired to have tea with us this afternoon. I was unaware that you had any association with a member of my household."

Sophronia leveled her piercing blue eyes on Mrs. Smythe, causing Mrs. Smythe's cheeks to flush. "I called to ascertain how my favorite protégé progresses. I worried because I have not seen her at our recent meetings." Her authoritative tone brooked no argument.

"Your protégé, you say?"

"Hmm… The most promising new suffragette I've met in a while."

I choked on my bite of shortbread, causing paroxysms of coughing, although neither woman paid me any attention.

Mrs. Smythe glared at Mrs. Chickering, avoiding looking in my direction, raising her eyebrows inquiringly. "Suffragette?"

Mrs. Chickering met Mrs. Smythe's glare with a look verging on a smirk, nodding a few times.

I briefly closed my eyes.

Mrs. Smythe paled for a moment before her cheeks became even rosier, belying her anger. "Well, I never! The insolence." At this, she sent a fierce glare in my direction. "And when I think of all I have done to try to give her proper guidance. Instill a sense of propriety. And she does this? Decides to associate with a group of extremists who terrify men? How will she ever marry now? Who would *want* her?" she wailed.

I watched her, beginning to feel amusement and a kernel of pity for her as I realized I was overturning her perception of the world. I had finally calmed my coughing fit by this point, although my voice emerged as a weak gasp.

"You've known my beliefs for some time," I croaked out.

"A schoolgirl's idealism," she snapped. "Nothing to be acted on."

Mrs. Chickering cleared her throat, as though to remind Mrs. Smythe she remained present. "I think it takes a tremendous strength of character to have beliefs and then actually act on them," she said with her own fervor. "I would hate for women to lock away their desires for a better world once they leave school or marry. They, as women, have lives, have hopes and dreams for the future, independent of what a man might want."

"How dare you come into my house and tell me that what I have is not sufficient?" Mrs. Smythe gasped.

"I am saying no such thing, Mrs. Sullivan," Mrs. Chickering replied. "I believe you need to understand that your stepdaughter has beliefs and aspirations that are different from yours."

"Aspirations that include the vote?" Mrs. Smythe scoffed. "Men have voted in the past, they will continue to vote, and I have no desire of it. I feel as my husband does on all things to do with politics, so it would only be giving the same politician two votes rather than one. There's no purpose to women having the vote." Her eyes flashed, true enmity in their depths as she glared at Mrs. Chickering. "And didn't we women of Massachusetts show you suffragettes we didn't want the vote in'95? No one voted for women to become enfranchised then, and they won't now." She sighed loudly, as though trying to calm herself.

"An aspiration for independence?" Mrs. Smythe continued, unable to stop speaking. "Are you telling me that someday it should be lauded, hoped for, that young women become independent and have no need for marriage? No need for children? How could that ever be a hoped-for future? You and your group want too much for women. Women should focus on their home, on creating a moral, upstanding environment in which to raise children. She will want for nothing if she has such a home," Mrs. Smythe argued.

"So I suppose women should remain tied to the kitchen stove with children at their ankles, and a husband who might, or might not, come home with a paycheck as their only recourse?" Mrs. Chickering countered. "Relying on the benevolence of men to write laws and enforce them without women having any involvement in the legislative process? Sitting at home knitting, hoping that men will ensure that our rights are protected? That is all you envision for women? Nothing more?"

"It has been enough for generations. I do not know why it should need to change now," Mrs. Smythe snapped, banging down her teacup with such force I thought she might crack it.

"Was that enough for you in your first marriage, Mrs. Sullivan?" Mrs. Chickering asked, pinning her with an intense gaze.

Mrs. Smythe flushed all the way down her neck to her dress, and her mouth turned down mutinously, but she refused to respond.

"I heard you never knew if your first husband would come home with a paycheck. That he, more often than not, drank away every cent of his pay each Saturday night after payday. And was none too pleasant when he came home from the saloon. That you lived on credit to survive, and you barely eked out a survival with that."

"How dare you?" Mrs. Smythe whispered, tears threatening, though they appeared to be tears of rage.

"I dare because I envision a better future for your stepdaughter than you do," Mrs. Chickering argued. "I dare because only through obtaining the vote for ourselves will we begin to be independent women who do not have to depend on drunken, at times brutish, men for survival. We will have more than the hopes of a good marriage. We will have educations. We will have vocations. We will be at liberty to choose the futures *we* want." Her voice rang out with the sincerity of her beliefs.

"You simply fill her mind with empty promises, and, in the end, she will only be disappointed in life," Mrs. Smythe countered. "When you learn not to expect too much, it is harder to be disappointed." She pursed her lips after that whispered statement as though she had admitted too much.

I sat in rapt attention, fascinated by their exchange.

"I had hoped to invite you also to Mrs. Ward-Howe's birthday celebration in a few weeks, but I think that might be more than your constitution could handle," Sophie said. "I sincerely hope Miss Sullivan will be allowed to attend." Another long clashing stare was exchanged between the two women.

Mrs. Smythe took a deep breath as though considering her answer. "I shall have to discuss this with her father."

Sophie nodded a few times as though realizing she could hope for no more. "Then I will take my leave. I thank you for this delicious tea, and I hope to have Miss Sullivan's company at the celebration." She nodded toward Mrs. Smythe before smiling in my direction.

I returned to the chair recently vacated by Sophie. Mrs. Smythe settled into her chair, tapping its wooden arm in a nervous tattoo. Outside a mockingbird sang, its repetitive calls jarring rather than soothing today. I glanced around the room, noting small changes. The faded table coverings had been replaced with new purple satin cloths, and many of the small items I remembered from my mama's time had been replaced with impersonal ready-made effects purchased during one of Mrs. Smythe's recent shopping excursions. Discolored areas appeared on the rose-colored wallpaper, the paintings either rearranged or replaced. I studied a scene of a wave crashing onto the seashore, one of the few remaining paintings from my mama's time.

"Clarissa," Mrs. Smythe said, distracting me from the ocean scene. She leveled me with her most severe glare. "How dare you associate with the likes of her? Have you not better sense, girl, than to mingle with extremist women?"

"I believe in our cause. I believe in what she says. I have the hope of a more independent future and that I do not have to depend solely on a man." As I spoke, a true passion rose in me.

She waved her hand as though my last comments were of no consequence. "And how are you to survive in this independent women's utopia?" she snapped. "Do you honestly believe you earn enough money, on your own, to live comfortably as a teacher?"

"There is no reason I can't believe in suffragism and have a full life. Many of the suffragettes are married. Look at Elizabeth Cady Stanton. There are men who admire independent women," I argued, silently hoping it was true.

"Is that what you talk about at your meetings? This mythical man who would want any of you Amazonian women who think and act independently? It's about time you learned something about life, young lady. I would have thought you would have learned it by now after your earlier disappointment. Men don't want women who act and think like you, Clarissa," she said. "They want women who agree with them, who do not challenge them. Who believe in the traditional running of the world and aren't trying to turn everything upside down. Women like your cousin."

"Yes, of course. Savannah." I looked away for a moment. "If you will excuse me?" I asked as I rose and left the room without gaining her permission.

I trudged up the stairs, snippets of conversation flickering in and out of my thoughts. I needed to discuss what had just transpired with someone, yet knew no one in my family would understand. Upon entering my bedroom, I collapsed into the chair in front of my desk, fidgeting and trying to tidy the desk, although Mary kept my room spotless. I reached into a desk drawer and extracted writing paper, pen and ink. As I tapped the pen a few times, uncertainty and desperation warred inside me.

I decided to write to Gabriel.

May 3, 1900

Dear Mr. McLeod,

Please forgive me for writing today. I feel so alone with my thoughts roiling around me, and I desperately need a friend. I hope I do not offend.

I just finished a very trying tea with my father's new wife, Mrs. Smythe. One of my new friends called, and Mrs. Smythe took an immediate disliking to her. I now must admit to you that I have attended a suffragist meeting without my family's knowledge and that this new friend of mine is a fellow suffragette. She is very loyal, smart, forward thinking and committed to the cause. She also enjoys rousing the ire of those who are not as convinced of the rights of women to vote and particularly enjoys riling unsupportive women as, in the end, it will benefit all women.

Of course, Mrs. Smythe was horrid to her, doubting our cause, doubting my ability to find any happiness with my beliefs. But, I ask, why should independence in a woman scare a man so that he wouldn't want to marry her? Shouldn't he want a woman who can think and be concerned about topics outside of the home sphere?

As I reread this letter, I realize I should not send it to you, but it has brought me comfort to write it. I miss you, Mr. McLeod. I miss our discussions. I hope you are well.

Yours sincerely,
Miss Clarissa Sullivan

After I finished writing the letter, I quickly folded it in half, crammed it in an envelope, and scrawled Gabriel's name and address on the outside before freezing in place. I closed my eyes in resignation. Sighing, I sat back in my chair and took solace in the fact that the mere act of writing him had relaxed me. I collapsed onto my bed in exhaustion, falling into a fitful sleep. I slept soundly, awakening a few hours later. When I awoke, I knew someone had come into my room while I slept because I now had a throw blanket over me, and my letter was gone.

CHAPTER 18

I ROSE, PANICKED. I searched unsuccessfully behind my desk with the unrealistic hope that my letter had fallen behind it. I looked at myself in the mirror to see my ashen reflection and panicked light blue eyes. After leaving my room, I slipped down the back stairs, hoping to meet Mary.

I arrived in the kitchen to find her and Bridget busily helping to prepare supper. The basement room was cooled in part by the slate floor, although it was still quite warm. A small window was propped open and a faint waft of fresh air entered. A pot bubbled on the stove, drops flying out and making singeing noises every few moments. The air was redolent with the smell of freshly baked bread, and I saw the loaves cooling on the table. I glanced guiltily toward the clock, not realizing I had slept so long. After a few moments, Bridget rushed upstairs with a tray, while Cook stepped into the nearby larder, and I was alone with Mary.

"Mary," I whispered, "did you enter my room this afternoon?"

"Yes, miss," she said smiling. "The missus sen' me to fetch ye, but ye were sleepin' so peaceful, I couldn' wake ye." She continued to slice vegetables and prepare the meal. I stood in the kitchen, feeling useless. Being a horrid cook, I knew the worst thing I could do was to offer to help.

I glanced toward the stairway, listening for Bridget. I began to fidget, wringing my hands a little. "Did you happen to see a letter? On my desk?" I tried to hide any anxiety or urgency from my voice, although I knew I failed when Mary watched me curiously.

"Aye, miss, I saw the letter on yer desk. The mailman was on 'is rounds. I posted it for ye," she said, smiling.

"Ah, you posted it. Right." I felt like fainting, and gripped onto the back of a nearby chair.

"Ye did want it posted, miss?"

"No harm done," I said, flushing at the thought of Gabriel reading my letter. "I should go up." I smiled wanly to Mary before ascending the stairs to the parlor.

***

FOUR DAYS AFTER Sophronia's visit, I received a letter from Gabriel.

May 6, 1900

>*My Dear Miss Sullivan,*
>
>*I opened your letter, delighted to hear from you again. I had not hoped to read such a letter from you. Your honesty and passion for life jumped off the page, making me feel as though you were here with me. I could easily envision your afternoon tea and the two elderly dragon ladies fighting over you. I can see why both sides would battle so fiercely for you. They are attempting to propose their vision of the world as the vision to be emulated and desired.*
>
>*Take care, Miss Clarissa. As you watch these two duel, and as you spend time with each woman separately, continue to determine what it is you envision for yourself, not what anyone else wants. It may be an amalgam of the two.*
>
>*Not all men are frightened so easily by independent, free-thinking women. Some actually like a woman with spirit.*
>
>*I, too, miss you, Miss Clarissa. I hope you are well.*
>
>*Gabriel.*
>
>*P.S. Please come by the workshop with your cousin. I am sure we can find more to talk about than the sideboard.*

The following day, after an interminable wedding gown fitting with Savannah, I cajoled her into accompanying me to the workshop. In reality, I had bartered my time watching her preen in a mirror for her time in a dusty workroom. Savannah was convinced she had received the poorer part of the bargain, but, after three mind-numbing hours of watching a dress be pinned at varying lengths, I no longer felt any sympathy for her.

The balmy spring weather from earlier in the week had disappeared, replaced by a cold, blustery wind with a heavy fog but no rain. I liked the moodiness of the day, although Savannah believed it to be a bad omen. She attempted to convince me to postpone the visit to Gabriel's, but I would not be forestalled. We rode the trolley to Haymarket then walked the short distance to his workshop.

As we reached the top of the stairs, I shushed Sav, who was gasping in an unladylike manner after the climb, because I heard voices arguing. Two deep male voices were in blatant disagreement. I inched toward the door, fully intending to announce our arrival, but stopped short when I heard my name spoken. My eyes grew large, and I grabbed Savannah's arm to keep her in place, out of sight. We both leaned in, listening avidly to the discussion.

"Gabe, I know you're fascinated by this Clarissa, but you must see it can't go anywhere," the unknown voice stated. He blew out a breath, and I imagined I heard pacing. "Granted, she is beautiful, smart and appears kind. But can you really see her interested in one of us?"

"Listen, I enjoy her. That's all there is to it. There is nothing going on that is indiscreet or scandalous," Gabriel's indignant voice replied, with the sound of him sanding wood filling the air.

"Gabe, don't be such an *eejit*, as Da would say. I've seen your elation at the arrival of her letters. You can't fool me that there is nothing growing between the two of you," the voice argued.

I felt Savannah poke me in the side at the mention of letters but ignored her.

"You know society's rules. You had them drummed into your head, just like I did," the unknown voice continued. I heard a long sigh followed by pacing. "Listen, Gabe, I've heard rumors on the street and at the pub. And if I am hearing them, they will quickly spread. You know that she has brothers who would love to hurt you if they found out. For God's sake, I *know* her brothers. I *like* her brothers. And they'd still hurt you." A quiet thump followed; a sound like something thrown against a wall. "What is your goal here?"

I peered into the room, desperate to see more. The unknown voice belonged to Richard. I watched him pace like a caged animal, his arms moving back and forth as though he couldn't keep them still.

Gabriel watched him with a cautious, guarded expression. "Don't bring Mum and Da into this. You should have learned from them that societal rules, all that garbage taught to us by Aunt Masterson, are only important up to a point. Other aspects of life are more important. Or maybe you just don't remember well enough," Gabriel retorted, now glowering at Richard.

Richard turned to glare furiously at Gabriel

Gabriel raised his eyebrows in mock challenge before turning back to his work, appearing to work calmly, tracing pieces of wood with a pencil.

"Gabe, are you listening to anything that I am saying?" demanded Richard.

"What do you want me to say, Richard? I have finally found a bit of happiness, and I am going to see where it leads. I shouldn't think it would worry you."

"For God's sake, Gabe, people are talking. This can't go anywhere. It will only lead to pain. For pity's sake, she's just a woman. Find another one, more suitable, more of our class."

At that, Gabriel threw down the pencil he had been using and gripped the edge of the table, fully looking at Richard for the first time, glaring at him. "It's not like I can just choose a new shirt. Maybe someday you'll realize that there is a woman in the world worth taking a chance on."

"Why shouldn't you, Gabe?" Richard asked in a low, menacing voice. "You expected the same of me."

I watched as they glowered at each other before Richard turned to leave. He began to look for his hat, and I realized Savannah and I had moments to spare if we were to look as though we were just arriving.

I grabbed Savannah's arm and dragged her down a few stairs. I clambered up the top stairs, making plenty of noise, acting as though we had just arrived. As we came up to the door, I knocked on it, calling out "Mr. McLeod?" in a breathless manner.

I watched Richard appear, startled by his near growl of greeting as he stormed past us and down the stairs. I turned to look for Gabriel. His movements were restless, and he emitted a new energy today. I was unable to tell if it was anger, frustration, embarrassment or a mixture of all three.

"I'm sorry, Miss Clarissa, er, Miss Sullivan, Miss Russell. The tea is not quite ready to be steeped," he said.

"Would you rather we came back another day?" I asked.

"Truthfully I am not having a good day, and, after the recent visit from Richard, I am not much use for a social visit. You two should leave and save yourselves a miserable afternoon here. I am sure there are numerous other things you could do to entertain yourselves." He looked very alone.

I looked to Savannah for guidance, and she pointedly nodded to the door. I shook my head in disagreement, moving farther into the room.

"It is a rather cold day out. If we could warm up with a cup of tea first, then depart, would that be acceptable?" I asked. I sat down in the rocking chair, noting Savannah's assessing look at the perfectly dimensioned chair built for me. I began to rock gently, calming my racing heart.

"Yes, of course." Gabriel turned toward the kettle and gathered the necessary mugs.

"If you don't mind me saying so, Mr. McLeod, you seem quite domesticated," Savannah said in a haughty tone.

Gabriel laughed. "Like a favorite pet, Miss Russell?" He glanced toward her with humor. "I always think domestication ruins the better part of the beast."

"But you wouldn't want a wild dog in your house," Savannah protested. "And horses must be tamed."

Gabriel nodded. "I would hate to think you compared me to a horse or a dog, miss. I hope I have better manners than that?" he asked, raising his eyebrows mockingly toward Savannah. "Though, I agree, horses are most useful for our purpose when tamed, but I wonder if they truly enjoy working for us?" He looked toward me, although he did not push me into the conversation.

He let out a long theatrical sigh. "Domesticated cats, dogs. Domesticated women. Wonderful creatures. Wouldn't you agree, Miss Sullivan?" He looked toward me wickedly. I had bolted so hard in the rocker at his words I had nearly flown onto the floor. I watched him with wide eyes, wondering why he pushed Savannah so.

Savannah replied, "Now you are offensive, sir." She vibrated with anger.

"Isn't that what all young women long to be?" Gabriel asked Savannah, setting down the filled mugs with a clunk. "Domesticated. Demure. Tamed to the needs and ways of their husbands?"

"You know perfectly well you are describing the ideal wife," Savannah spat out.

"Am I?" he asked, sounding unconvinced. "What do you think, Miss Sullivan?" he turned to me. "Is that what you long to be, a domesticated woman?"

"No!" I blurted out before I could stop myself.

"Rissa!" Savannah scolded me, eyes flashing. She had begun to breathe heavily, and I feared she would faint with her tightly laced corset.

I blushed but met Gabriel's eyes. "No," I said. "I have no desire to match that description. Slightly less clumsy, perhaps," I muttered.

"Yes, I agree," Gabriel said, causing me to worry he agreed with my assessment about my clumsiness. "Domestication is akin to docility which is an unattractive trait in a woman." He smiled knowingly at me, and I felt a flash of pleasure.

"Do you speak in earnestness, sir, or are you in jest?" Savannah demanded. When Gabriel merely turned to look at her, she continued. "Men want docile, demure women," she expounded, as though teaching a rudimentary fact to Gabriel.

"Well, pardon me, ma'am, for not learning my lessons well," he replied, nodding his head deferentially.

I watched Savannah's face become flushed red with anger and was worried she would erupt. She generally kept her temper under control, but, when it blew, it was a frightening thing to behold.

"I'd actually like to meet a young woman who can think for herself and doesn't want only what her father or husband wants." His quiet statement made my pulse quicken.

Savannah scoffed, "That path leads only to misery."

"Or tremendous contentment," Gabriel countered.

Savannah stood, knocking into the table with such force she caused tea to spill out of the mugs. "I will not sit here any longer and listen to your insolent beliefs," she declared. "Rissa?" She turned toward me expectantly, then headed toward the door.

I looked at Gabriel with remorse, wanting to have spent longer time in his company. "I enjoyed our conversation. Maybe we could continue it one day at the school?" I watched him, hopeful he would agree.

He smiled, releasing a sigh of relief. "I would enjoy that very much, Miss Clarissa."

I had forgotten how his voice could feel like a caress. I closed my eyes for a moment, having missed hearing his gentle baritone. No matter how much I had enjoyed his letters, I had missed him. I gathered my purse.

I raced after Savannah, understanding that she must be well and truly angry because she had already clambered down the stairs and was marching up the street toward Haymarket. I skirted a pushcart seller peddling flowers, avoided a nip from a cantankerous horse and rushed after her.

"Savannah, slow down!" I called out. I walked as quickly as I could, then began to start a slow run. I placed one hand on my hat after it nearly blew off with a strong gust of wind and was soon gasping for breath from my ungraceful gallop down the boardwalk, feeling as though I would faint. "Sav!" I called again, gasping out her name with what little air I could spare.

She turned around, appearing to have been possessed by demons. I had a sudden thought of the *Strange Case of Dr. Jekyll and Mr. Hyde* I had read once, as Savannah's generally placid facade had been transformed into that of a maddened woman. Her flushed face, hair blowing in the wind and rigid stance all expressed her extreme anger. I nearly burst out laughing at Savannah's uncharacteristic, unladylike appearance but caught myself in time.

"Don't you dare try to act as though you could *possibly* be interested in *that man*," Savannah hissed, closing her eyes, taking a deep breath in an attempt to calm herself. I looked around, seeing that we were earning a few interested stares. I smiled, nodding, acting as though a rabid-looking woman was a normal, everyday occurrence.

I hooked my arm through hers and began to tow her down the street. "Sav, you must admit he's interesting," I replied, attempting to soothe her wounded pride.

"He was criticizing all women, Clarissa," she chided. "Not just me and what I want to do. But all women."

"I think you misunderstood."

"And I think you only hear and see what you want to!"

"Savannah, why have you changed so much?" I whispered.

"If I have, I've only changed for the better."

"How is it better to look down at everyone?" I asked, truly confused. "How is it better to believe yourself so superior?" I felt adrift, lost without the Savannah I knew, her support and love.

"Clarissa, you are such an innocent. Someday you'll realize that there are people who are inherently better than others."

"Do you really believe that? Or do you think if you say it enough times you will convince yourself it's true?"

"Don't be insulting. Of course I believe it."

I continued to walk beside her, occasionally gripping my hat against a burst of wind, mainly lost in thought. "So, those people who you believe to be naturally superior," I began, "you actually believe they'll accept you just because you agree with their beliefs?"

"Don't be so insulting, Clarissa," Savannah snapped. "Of course they will accept me. Not because I believe them to be superior, but because I will be one of them once I marry Jonas," she said with an upward tilt of her chin.

"Will that really make you happy?" I asked as tears threatened.

"Of course it will. It's what everyone should want."

CHAPTER 19

I SAT WATCHING LUCAS play the piano in his family parlor, marveling at his tremendous talent. The Sullivans had been invited for dinner with the Russells, one of the last dinners we would all have together before Savannah's wedding.

I tried to sit properly in my lady's chair but found that difficult after eating too much of the delicious meal. I glanced around the room to see if others were as pleased with Lucas's playing. Aunt Matilda and Uncle Martin appeared determined to ignore his music. Mrs. Smythe seemed disgruntled. Da, deep in conversation with Uncle Martin, tapped his fingers and toes in time with the music. Colin listened to the music intently, his eyes closed and a small smile on his face.

I turned toward Savannah. "I really had no idea Lucas had such talent," I whispered in awe.

Sav sniffed. "It really isn't something we like to discuss or promote, Rissa. He prefers such *common* music. If he played more acceptable music, like Beethoven or Mozart, that would be agreeable."

"But, Sav, you know he can play that type of music. He just doesn't want to. This is what intrigues him," I replied.

"Well, it is entirely inappropriate," she hissed.

I opened my mouth, hoping an articulate argument would emerge, when Mrs. Smythe spoke up.

"Do you know, not only does he play this type of music written by, well, those I would rather not discuss, but that he also sings suffragist songs?" she said to the group.

"Yes, I know it is all quite shocking," Mrs. Smythe said after Aunt Matilda gasped. "Imagine my surprise when a new friend of Clarissa's called for tea not long after he sang such an outrageous song in the peaceful haven of my own parlor."

Lucas, who had ceased playing his new favorite ragtime piece, began to play a lyrical, haunting piece by Beethoven as though he were taunting Savannah. I could tell by his tilted head that he listened avidly to the conversation across the room.

"Imagine my surprise to discover that not only was this woman a suffragette but that Clarissa had met her at a suffragists' meeting," Mrs. Smythe wailed.

Aunt Matilda gasped again, clutching her breast. Savannah sat next to me in shocked silence. Da turned toward me, looking at me as though he had never really seen me before. Colin started to laugh, as though it were all quite entertaining.

"Did you have a good time?" Colin asked, an irreverent grin playing around his mouth.

I smiled toward Colin, thankful for his presence. "I did. They are a fascinating group, and their cause, or I should say, our cause, is so vital. I have had an interest in becoming active in the movement for a long time," I said with a touch of defiance. "It shouldn't come as a shock to anyone."

"In the quiet of your own home, you might have an interest. In the doubting of your own spirit, have interest," Aunt Matilda snapped. "You don't go off, on your own, to meet with a group of radical, firebrand women, with no regard for propriety or common sense." Her eyes flashed as she watched me. "What would your mama have said?"

"Really, Clarissa," Savannah said, "what could you possibly have been thinking? Have you no sense? Have you not been listening to all I have said these past months about the ideal women for men? You really should learn to pay attention and emulate. Otherwise you are truly bound to be alone."

"Is that all you are worried about? That no man will want to marry me?" I asked, staring at the mutinous, angry faces of the women of my family. A sharp pain pierced my chest at the mention of my mama, and I glared at Aunt Matilda at her uncalled-for attack. I knew, deep inside, that Mama would have supported me. Da sat silently beside Uncle Martin with an unreadable expression.

"All? All?" Aunt Matilda and Mrs. Smythe yelped at the same time as though twinned in their beliefs.

"Why shouldn't I live a full life? Be able to truly express what I feel, rather than be a parrot to my husband?" This comment provoked further outraged gasps from the three women present, and snickers from Colin and Lucas. Uncle Martin continued to study me curiously and Da appeared extremely uncomfortable. Before anyone could interrupt me, I continued. "Why shouldn't both the husband *and* the wife be allowed to have their own opinions, opinions that don't always agree? Why shouldn't I have interests outside of the home? Why shouldn't

I want more for myself and for women?"

Da shifted uncomfortably as I saw him pinned under a fierce glare from Mrs. Smythe. Finally he spoke. "Clarissa, darlin', you must understand you are asking for quite a lot of changes." As I began to sputter, he watched me with an intense gaze, quieting me. "I don't say I don't agree with you."

Mrs. Smythe gasped, clutched her breast and fell back against the back of her lady's chair as though she would faint.

"I think you just need to be a bit more understanding of those who aren't as progressive minded as you are," he said, with a small smile.

I shared a long glance with Da, a wellspring of happiness bursting forth inside me because he understood.

"Now," Da stated, "as for having these women as friends, I'd like to meet them. Sound interesting. And you should continue to attend your meetings."

"Thank you, Da," I whispered, grateful for his support and for not having to hide my involvement with them. I looked at Mrs. Smythe, her rosy cheeks and shiny eyes eloquently expressing her displeasure with Da.

Aunt Matilda sat rigidly, nearly vibrating in her fury. "Really, Sean, what can you be thinking?" she hissed. "To encourage your daughter, who is already headstrong to a fault, to attend these meetings with women who do not know the limits of propriety? She will only bring pain, disgrace, ruination on the family if you allow her to continue her untoward ways."

Uncle Martin reached over, patting her on her hand as though to calm her, but she slapped away his hand.

"I'm thinking that I know me daughter better than ye, Matilda. She may be yer niece, but she's my daughter. She may be headstrong, and I'm thankful for it," he snapped, his anger betrayed by the thickening of his accent. "She's needed spirit to continue on through all that's happened, an' she's done better than any could have hoped."

"You seem to be confusing her ability to persevere with a willingness to act with propriety and abide by the mores of society," Mrs. Smythe retorted.

"Give me one example when my Clarissa acted out of bounds. When I would have reason to chastise her," Da demanded, breathing harshly, his cheeks ruddy with anger.

I blushed.

"Sean, simply because I do not have a litany of offenses to lay at that girl's feet does not mean she knows the bounds of propriety. Young women do not go off to meetings without their family's permission. It is not done," Mrs. Smythe said, holding a wadded up handkerchief in her hand.

"I will hear no more on it. Rissa's a good girl. She knows what is right 'n' wrong. She has my permission, whether she needs it or not, to continue with the suffragettes," Da said, his tone brooking no argument. I beamed at him, thinking of the upcoming party for Mrs. Ward-Howe and my longing to attend.

Then, as the conversation moved on, I heaved a sigh of relief, leaning against my chair, hopeful Da never discovered my unchaperoned meetings with Gabriel.

CHAPTER 20

THE AFTERNOON WAS DELIGHTFUL as I started my walk home from school. I paused to bask in the bright afternoon rays and tilted my face to the sun, closing my eyes, happy to finally feel completely warm all the way to my toes. At that moment, I heard the nasally light-toned voice from my memories.

"You look well, my dear. But you should be careful with the sun. I would hate for you to lose any of your looks." His voice sounded full of good cheer and joy, but my insides turned to ice. I lowered my head, turning to meet Cameron's smiling face. My gaze scanned him quickly, cataloging any changes. Slightly thinner hair, droopier eyes, more wrinkles at the corners of his mouth. I did not speak, but stood still, thunderstruck.

"What, dear Clarissa, you will not speak to me? What will people say when they see us on the street, and you ignoring your old beau?"

My eyes flashed with anger, thankful for the ire to help hide the anguish washing over me as I continued to study his once-cherished face. I made myself stand even taller, watching him. "My name is Miss Sullivan, sir." I began to cultivate the chilly facade of a society woman as a barrier between us.

"Oh, so we are to play that game, then, *Miss Sullivan*. I have had to be patient to find an opportunity to speak with you." He continued to watch me, with slightly hostile honey-brown eyes. He seemed content to study me, taking in my appearance, as though drinking in the sight of me after a long drought.

"Sir, I am sure I am unaware of any reason you would have to speak with me," I replied in my coldest tones, thankful for once I could mimic Jonas.

"What has happened to my Clarissa? Where is the vivacious, warm-blooded woman I knew? Who is this woman of ice?"

I continued to stare at him with scorn. "As I am sure you are well aware, I am not your anything. You ensured that a few years ago. I wish you a good day."

Hundreds of questions roiled through my bewildered mind, yet I clamped my lips together, forestalling any further inquiries. Cameron leaned toward me, gripped my arms, and continued to stare at me as though trying to determine how I had changed so greatly.

"Why are you acting this way with me? What is this about?" Cameron pleaded.

"Again, sir, I am no longer your concern. Please let go of my arm, and let me *pass*." I was becoming angry as my icy veneer began to crack. "There is no other way I should act with you."

I wrenched my arm free and stepped away from him. "Please desist in attempting to speak with me." I turned and began to walk down the street, noting the curious stares of the women sitting on their front steps minding their children playing on the sidewalk.

When I reached the busy intersection of Blossom and Cambridge Streets, I glanced behind me, but he was gone. I sighed, my shoulders stooping for a moment before smiling at Richard McLeod. He walked with a purposeful stride down Blossom Street, away from the school.

"Hello, Miss Sullivan, good day to you," Richard said. "I was hoping to find you at your school, only to arrive after you had left. May I walk a ways with you?" He proffered his elbow, and we began a slow stroll down Cambridge Street.

After a few blocks, at a snail's pace, Richard leaned toward me and whispered with a rueful smile, "I am sorry to interrupt your reverie, Miss Sullivan, but I don't know where we're going."

"I live on Union Square, in the South End."

"Of course. Why don't we take a streetcar?" At the quick shake of my head in denial, he said, "Let's take the more scenic route then. I hear the Public Gardens are particularly lovely this time of year."

"Sir, if I might ask, why did you come by the school today?"

"Well, Gabriel's been in a right foul mood, and I worried part of it had to do with me." He smiled. "Most of the time when Gabe gets fed up, it has to do with me. Though this time I realized it really had to do with *you*."

I shook my head in confusion, certain Gabriel had no reason to feel upset with me. "You talk nonsense," I whispered.

"Do I?" he asked. "I am at the workshop, carrying on like I do on my free afternoons, and you stop by with a rather handsome if snobby-looking woman, and now you won't speak with Gabe," Richard said. "Makes me wonder."

"He's the one who won't visit me," I protested, and then realized I had admitted too much.

"Well, isn't that curious?" Richard mused with a quirk of his eyebrows. "I know for a fact he's come by the school twice this week and hasn't seen you. I thought for sure you weren't the type to frighten off too easily after your visits to his workshop. But then you disappeared."

"As you can see, I have clearly not disappeared," I said, unable to hide my smile. My spirit lightened at this silly conversation after seeing Cameron again. It lifted further at the thought Gabriel had come by to see me and wanted to see me still. "I've had to leave school early for teas with my stepmother."

"Well, I'll let Gabe figure that out for himself. I shouldn't be running interference anyway."

After a moment's pause, Richard looked down at me. I could see his eyes gleamed with curiosity. He had a similar way of studying me as his brother, although he was less intense.

"Who was the man you were talking with before I approached?"

"Someone who wanted to reacquaint himself with me. Although I have no matching desire."

"Hmm…" Richard said. "He's the one who's been making inquiries at the smithies about you, isn't he?"

"Why would he ask at other smithies about me?" I gasped. I hated the thought of being the object of gossip. Again.

"Seems no one will talk at your father's place. Your father and Colin are rather fierce, and I don't reckon many would want to get in a tussle with them." Richard chuckled. "And this man wanted more information about you. Were you married? What you've been doing these past years? Innocent questions but not so innocent if you really listened to the man," he said, with a slight frown. "Not that many would know such things. Only friends of Colin would know, and I wouldn't talk with him." He glowered at the thought.

"That was very kind of you, Mr. McLeod."

"No, no kindness, when I was a boor the last time you saw me." Regret shone in his eyes. Then Richard laughed, looking at me, assessing. "Don't fret, Miss Sullivan. You handled yourself well without help from anyone. He seemed a bit too informal, if you ask me. No wonder you don't mind Gabe," he said with a quick smile.

"How is Mr. McLeod?" I asked, trying not to sound eager to hear news about him.

"Well, like I said, he's moodier 'n usual for him. But, he'll get over it. I almost suggested he write you another letter. Though he's not much of a writer, more of a reader, you know? But, hopefully he won't have to."

"Can you ask him to come by tomorrow to see me?" I entreated.

"I sure could, Miss Sullivan, but I'm sure he'd rather hear it from you. Maybe you would like to write him a letter. I could deliver it myself." Richard glanced at me with a slight twinkle in his eye. "That way he'd get it in time for tomorrow."

"Oh, that would be lovely."

We walked through the Public Gardens, though I paid little attention to the scenery. I considered Richard's news, silently composing a letter in my mind to Gabriel.

A short time later, we arrived at the house. "Here we are," I informed Richard. "Why don't you come in for a cup of tea?"

"I thank you, Miss Sullivan, but I have been away from work too long already. However, if I may, I will stop by this evening to inquire after your health?"

"Yes, please do." I smiled a good-bye, watching him walk down my street.

Taking a deep breath, I turned for the house and the conversation to come with Mrs. Smythe. Upon entering the parlor, I was shocked to see it set for another tea. I knew this must be important company, because the best china and the silver tea set were to be used.

"Mrs. Smythe?" I called out. "Who are we having for tea?" I was exhausted and could not imagine maintaining the charade of polite, meaningless conversation over a cup of tea.

"Oh, just an old friend of mine, dear. I am sure you will like her. She is the loveliest woman. Helped me through the rough times after my husband died. So refined, so genteel, a true lady." She sighed in contentment, happily looking at the fancy china teacups and silver tea set laid out for her guest. "She will be here any moment. Will you ensure that the tea set has been polished, no unbecoming fingerprints on the silver?"

I sighed inwardly, swallowing back my retort that the silver tea set was only used on special occasions, never for mundane afternoon teas. It had not been used since my engagement two years ago, sparking a further reminder of Cameron today. I wondered who could be so important as to warrant the use of the slightly tarnished set. I scrubbed part of the blackened silver, turning the most tarnished side away from Mrs. Smythe's seat in hopes she would not notice. I sat sullenly in an armless, low lady's chair, trying to appear comfortable, glancing at the food, hopeful this guest liked to eat.

I heard a gentle knock at the front door while Mrs. Smythe and I sat demurely in the parlor, waiting to greet her guest. Though I remained in the warmth of the parlor, I longed to be outside, upstairs, anywhere but here.

I could hear the sounds of a strong voice admonishing Mary to be careful with her cloak. Once the woman entered the parlor, Mrs. Smythe rose eagerly to greet her, and they began chattering away, tittering with laughter, and my hopes that the societal norm of a short visit for tea were dashed. This was an old friend and confidante, and she would be here for a few hours. I glanced up to greet the newcomer, blanching white with shock.

"Miss Clarissa Sullivan, I would like you to meet my good friend, Mrs. Masterson." Mrs. Smythe beamed at her friend.

"H-h-h-how do you do?" I stammered out. My mind reeled back to that day in Gabriel's workshop.

"How lovely that you are able to come to the Sullivans for tea, Mrs. Masterson," simpered Mrs. Smythe. "I am not sure you have heard of my news, but I am soon to experience a blessed event. In about six months." She nearly preened as she spoke, patting her lap primly. She motioned for Mrs. Masterson to be seated and then sat. After pouring tea into cups already laced with sugar, she added a drop of milk to each before passing a cup to Mrs. Masterson, one to me and then settled back with her own cup.

"I had heard. Congratulations, dear Mrs. Sullivan. I had begun to worry that it would never happen. I know how you longed for a child in your first marriage but were not so blessed. How exciting, first the wedding a few months ago, now this! That took some time, didn't it? It took quite some time, indeed, for him to finally stop mourning that dead wife of his, hmm?"

They giggled together over their tea cups while I gaped at them in shock, my cup arrested halfway to my mouth, unable to comprehend that they would speak like that with me present. I was thankful I had not taken a sip or I would have choked on it.

"I had always been taught that patience is a virtue," Mrs. Smythe said.

"Yes, well patience is all well and good when you are young and attractive. At your age, you must expect a quicker response from the gentleman. Though of course, he's not exactly a *gentleman*, is he?" Mrs. Masterson said. She reached out and picked up a small sandwich, daintily biting into a corner of it. She frowned as though finding it lacking.

I opened my mouth, feeling the need to defend both of my parents but was cut off by Mrs. Smythe.

"You are correct. He is not a gentleman in the purest sense of the word. His manners and way of speaking are a bit rough," Mrs. Smythe simpered in her candy-cane-sweet voice. "But what can I expect from a man not born in this country? His children will never be *truly* genteel, as I fear they lacked the true sense of guidance and knowledge from birth about society that only one such as I could have given them. However, one must make do, don't you agree?" Mrs. Smythe replied with a note of resignation in her tone.

Mrs. Masterson looked around the parlor, shuddering at the sight. "Well, dear, the first thing you must do is refurbish the house. It needs proper draperies, furnishings, wallpaper, everything. Now that you are mistress here, you will be able to make all of the necessary alterations. Do not allow that new husband of yours to deny you your proper furnishings. Men like to claim they do not have funds for the household, but they always do," she intoned. "Most importantly, do not allow sentiment and misplaced nostalgia for the past and the artifacts once owned by the now deceased to prevent you from making the changes you feel are necessary." Mrs. Masterson sniffed again as she looked around the room, her gaze finally alighting on me.

"Ah, Miss Sullivan, I had forgotten about you. Do I know you? You seem quite familiar to me." She studied me for a few moments but never seemed able to determine where she had seen me before.

"No, Mrs. Masterson, I believe we have never been introduced before today," I replied with an outward calm, although inside I seethed. How dare Mrs. Smythe want to replace all of Mama's beautiful furnishings? How dare Mrs. Smythe think she could have raised us better?

"I am sure you are delighted to have a new stepmama," Mrs. Masterson said, arching one eyebrow, watching me intently.

"Mrs. Smythe is a welcome addition to our family, I'm sure," I replied.

"Mrs. Smythe? Mrs. *Smythe*? She is Mrs. *Sullivan* now, dear." She glanced around the room as though looking for support. "Well, I never! You really need to learn how to address your elders. She is your stepmama and should be addressed as such," she scolded me. "I am surprised your father hasn't addressed your blatant disrespectfulness toward his wife." She exchanged a long look with Mrs. Smythe.

Mrs. Smythe brought a handkerchief to her eyes, as though blotting a tear. "It has pained me that my stepchildren don't think of me as their mama." She let out a shaky sigh.

I stared at her. The only interest she had in me was to mold me into her idea of a vapid society woman. I squinted my eyes, unsure as to the objective of this tea.

"Well, *Mrs. Sullivan*, I suggest you have a long talk with your husband about the disrespect and insolence of his children," Mrs. Masterson instructed.

I intended to wish them each a lovely day as I breezed out of the room. However, I quickly leaned back in my chair with fascination, expelling my pent-up breath as they continued to talk.

"Any news about your infuriating nephew?" Mrs. Smythe asked.

"Which one? They are all such horrid people. I will never understand why my sister married that awful McLeod and then had to die and leave them to *me* to raise," she stated.

She picked up a dainty cookie, tapping it absently on the side of her plate to remove any crumbs, only succeeding in causing a cascade of crumbs to fall from the fragile sugar cookie. She picked up a napkin in distaste, wiping her hands.

"The only positive aspect I can see is that one of them is away in the army, thus I do not see *him* regularly."

She took a long sip of tea, sighing again. "Richard, the middle one, had an incident with my dear son, Henry, nearly causing me the expense of having to call for a doctor. Could I get Richard to apologize? Impossible. He is such an ungrateful, overbearing oaf, working at a smithy of all places.

"Gabriel is no better," she continued, "insisting that he would rather continue to work as a carpenter rather than train with my husband. You know what an asset he would be to the company. Can you imagine, wanting to work in manual labor rather than work in an office? However, I have never been able to reach them, not once. Never since their parents died."

She and Mrs. Smythe soon turned the conversation toward people I did not know, and I excused myself from the room. I retreated to my bedroom.

I sat on the edge of my bed, puzzling out the afternoon tea conversation.

After a few minutes, I reminded myself that I needed to write a letter. I closed my eyes and took a few deep breaths to calm myself.

May 17, 1900

Dear Mr. McLeod,

Richard visited me today at the school, a most welcome visit as he took my mind off of a surprise visit from my ghost. I had lingered at the schoolhouse today in hopes of seeing you, to no avail. I found my ghost to be unwelcome and would like for him to depart as mysteriously as he returned. However, I know life rarely proceeds as I desire.

Richard escorted me home, during which time he informed me of your recent visits to the school. I am sorry I have been absent. My father's new wife has deemed it necessary for me to attend her afternoon teas. Please know I would rather have spent my time with you.

Sincerely,

Miss Clarissa Sullivan.

***

THAT EVENING, DURING SUPPER, I sat silently, listening to Colin recount a tale about a brawl at another smithy where a dandy had left worse for wear. I attempted to feign interest but found my mind wandering.

Partway through dinner, a faint knock sounded at the front door. I heard Mary answer, who then discreetly interrupted Da, quietly speaking with him about the visitor. Da nodded his assent for the visitor's inclusion into the dining room. Colin paused in his storytelling, glancing toward the door and giving a hearty yell of welcome. He bounded out of his chair, clapping the newcomer on the back.

"Richard! Great to see you. Come in." He spread his arms open, motioning him to enter the room. Richard stood tall, in dulled black pants almost turned gray from numerous washings, off-white shirt and faded black jacket. His icy-blue eyes scanned the room as he remained in the doorway waiting for an invitation to enter from Da, tapping his fingers on his right leg.

Da looked toward Richard questioningly, unsure why Richard would call. He then looked at me inquiringly, noticing for the first time how little I had eaten and my distracted air. "Richard," he intoned, "what brings you by?" He waved to an empty chair at the table, inviting Richard to join us.

Richard sat gracefully, nodding to Da and extending his hand to Patrick. "How do you do? I am Richard McLeod."

Mrs. Smythe jolted as though a pincushion had stuck her. I watched her intently, wondering what she was thinking.

Colin spoke up, clearing his throat. "That's my older brother Patrick. This is my baby sister, Clarissa. And this is my *step*mama, ah, er, Mrs. Sullivan. Would you like something to eat, Richard?" He leaned over to the small sideboard, pulling out another dish and silverware. "Though of course, you've met Clarissa, right?" Colin continued.

Richard looked embarrassed. "I don't want to impose."

"It's no imposition, tuck in." He piled food onto Richard's plate, handing it to him and forestalling any further protestations. I smiled at Colin's thoughtfulness, as I doubted that Richard had yet had dinner.

"Richard, what brings you by?" Patrick spoke up, raising intense brown eyes to Richard.

Richard threw a questioning glance at me, and I demurely shook my head. He put down his silverware and cleared his throat. "Ah, well, I happened to be walking by the area where Miss Sullivan teaches today. She seemed to be having a bit of, er, a discussion, shall we say, with a gentleman. And she seemed none too pleased about it."

"Rissa!" Patrick exclaimed. "Why didn't you tell us immediately?" His face had turned an ugly red, the way it always did when he was excited or angry.

"Please, I am fine. It was Cameron. I just spoke with him for a moment, asking him to leave me be," I said. I gripped my hands together, hidden under the table.

"Clarissa," Da said in a stern tone, "you will tell us this instant what was stated."

At this, I blew out the breath I had been holding and tried to gather my thoughts. "He greeted me, commenting on the nice day, and called me 'dear Clarissa.' I instructed him that I was Miss Sullivan to him and that we had nothing further to discuss. We parted, and when I looked behind me to ensure he was not following me, I saw Mr. McLeod, whom I recognized from the visit to see after his brother's welfare. He graciously escorted me home."

Colin watched me with a shrewd intensity. "I know Cameron, and I know there was more to it than that, Rissa."

I raised my chin and met his eyes. "There's nothing more to tell."

Richard joined the conversation, interjecting, "I came by this evening to check on Miss Sullivan's health, Mr. Sullivan."

I smiled briefly at Richard, as I had the impression he was trying to diffuse the tension in the room.

"Clarissa Sullivan, how could you not have told me about your encounter with Cameron this afternoon? As for dissuading him from speaking with you, I would think you would encourage such attention from an upstanding, wealthy young man who exhibits an interest in you," Mrs. Smythe said. "It is the type of good news I would have enjoyed sharing with my dear friend."

I stared at her confused as to why she would want me to see Cameron. "I did not wish to interrupt your tea with such news, Mrs., err, *Sullivan*."

"Sean, this is what I am talking about! Your children do not care for me! They do not share things with me as they should as I am their stepmother. I spoke of it at length this afternoon with my dear friend, Mrs. Patricia Masterson. She understands my pain," she nearly wailed, bringing a handkerchief up to her eyes.

At the name *Masterson*, I saw Richard jolt. He stopped eating, bent over his plate, fork partway to his mouth, staring with wide eyes first at Mrs. Smythe, then at me. I shrugged my shoulders and shook my head slightly. I glanced toward Mrs. Smythe and saw her watching Richard's reaction to his aunt's name.

Da looked at Mrs. Smythe. "Not now, dear."

I hoped that I heard a touch of exasperation in his tone.

"I thank you, Mr. McLeod, for ensuring my daughter arrived home safely," Da said gruffly.

I heaved a small sigh, hopeful that the worst was past.

Richard finished his meal and stood, taking his leave. "I thank you for a delicious meal and your generous hospitality." He nodded to the table in general, and Colin escorted him to the door. I bit my lip, hoping my Mary had been successful in giving Richard my letter.

As Colin returned from the front hall, I was excusing myself from the dining room table. Colin's furious voice prevented my departure. "Not so fast, Rissa. We know there's more to that story than you're telling us."

"Colin," I entreated, "there really isn't any more to tell." I felt about ninety years old as I collapsed into my chair. I had forgotten this feeling of exhaustion, although I remembered it well, having felt this way frequently after Cameron's disappearance. I massaged my temples, determined to overcome the overwhelming sense of sadness that gripped me.

I closed my eyes, trying to gather my spinning thoughts. "I left school a little later than usual today. I had work that needed to be completed. As I left, pausing to enjoy the sunshine, Cameron spoke with me. He called me Rissa. He said he had been biding his time waiting to find a time to speak with me. When I asked him to leave me alone, he gripped my arm, demanding to know why I had changed so much. Why I was no longer vivacious."

"You know he speaks lies, Rissa?" Colin asked. He waited until I nodded. "What does he *want?*" Colin fairly shouted. His eyes were lit with anger, and I could see how much control he exerted to hide the true extent of his ire.

"I don't know, Colin. I really don't. But I think he may want me back, as farfetched as that seemed to me a few weeks ago," I replied with a touch of bitterness in my voice.

"He treats you abominably and now thinks he can waltz back in as though everything is fine!" he nearly roared. "He has no idea what you lived through the past few years. You've finally begun to act like yourself again. He stole your spirit and your vivaciousness," he hissed, breathing heavily.

I watched him, mouth agape, surprised and grateful at the depth of his feelings.

"I can't stand the thought he might hurt you again. I just can't." With that he stormed out of the room.

I rose to follow Colin, but when I reached the front hall, the front door vibrated from the force of Colin slamming it shut. I turned toward the stairs, pausing to study myself in the mirror. A subtle radiance emanated from my topaz-blue eyes, a joy from within that would not be contained. I studied my reflection, having expected to see despair, due to Cameron's presence in my life again. At that moment, I understood the truth behind Colin's words and knew I had no desire to see devastation looking back at me ever again from a mirror.

CHAPTER 21

THE NEXT MORNING, Colin escorted me to school. I had not slept well, my mind filled with fanciful thoughts and wayward dreams. I had even dreamed about being married to Cameron and the life we shared. In the dream, I lived in a small house, surrounded by fine objects, with maids and all of the material items I could want. No matter how many objects I had in the dream, I was always alone. The entire dream I searched for Cameron and something I had lost, something incredibly dear to me.

"Colin," I asked as we trundled along on a trolley toward my school, "how well do you know Richard McLeod?"

"I've known him a few years," Colin replied. "He works with Old Man Harris, and he is a quick learner. I think Da would still be tempted to hire him but wouldn't want to offend Mr. Harris. Besides, Da's not hiring right now.

"Richard was raised by his older brother, Gabriel. They have a younger brother, but I've never met him. Gabe's the one you injured, right? He seems nice enough, though not as cheerful as Rich. More quiet.

"Richard only has good things to say about his older brother. Rich mentioned once he would have been lost had it not been for Gabe." At this he carelessly shrugged his shoulder. "Richard was the smithy fighting the dandy, that story I was telling you about last night." Colin smiled at me, winking. "Here you are, sis. Have a good day. Wait for Lucas, you hear? He'll come to escort you home."

I nodded my agreement, feeling foolish to need an escort. However, I had agreed to my family's demands if it meant I could continue to teach.

I wearily taught the lessons of the day, finding it difficult to focus on the reading, writing and arithmetic I needed to teach. The reading lesson of the day had been a poem by Longfellow about a smithy in *McGuffey's Fifth Eclectic Reader.*

Thankfully, due to Da and Colin and my knowledge of blacksmiths, I did not have to focus on the lesson and could allow my mind to wander.

I continued to speculate about Cameron's reasons for returning. I could not fathom why Cameron would pursue me now. My mind was in turmoil, and my students could sense it. I longed to grant them an early release, but I struggled valiantly to finish the day.

I waited for Lucas in the schoolroom, patiently tidying. However, no one arrived, and I suspected that Lucas had forgotten or had become busy at the store. After waiting nearly an hour, I decided to go home. I gathered my belongings, squared my shoulders and emerged out onto the street. I surreptitiously glanced around, looking for Cameron, but did not see him. After a few steps I sensed someone following, and I spun to face whoever was behind me.

Gabriel took a quick step back, startled at my expression.

"I'm glad I didn't arrive too late, Miss Clarissa," Gabriel murmured, studying me with intense blue eyes, brows slightly wrinkled, black hair blowing in the soft breeze. "I thought I might escort you home." He offered me his elbow and a soft smile.

My spirits rose as I smiled. "Yes, Mr. McLeod, that would be much appreciated. You received my letter?"

"Yes, I thank you," he replied. "I must say I am more intrigued than satisfied after reading it. I had to badger most of the information out of Richard."

"I was concerned that, if for some reason it didn't reach you, others might read it," I attempted to explain.

"It's of no consequence now. We're here together. Walking down the street on a pretty, sunny day." He glanced at me with a small smile. "Would you care to enlighten me at all as to the story behind the ghost?"

I blew out a long breath, looking away from Gabriel. "We were to be married two years ago." I glanced at him, and noted his intense gaze on my face. I hastily looked away again. "On our wedding day, he failed to show. I remember waiting in vain, in all of my finery, for him to arrive, and he never did. He never sent a letter or a reason why he did not come." I lowered my head, feeling ashamed.

"What a fool," Gabriel murmured, sounding almost lighthearted.

"Don't you dare laugh at me," I demanded in a cold voice, feeling my pleasure at our walk dissipate.

"Oh, now, I am sorry. *You* aren't the fool. *He* is. I can't imagine not showing up to a wedding day with…" Then his voice trailed off. He sounded almost wistful. He shook his head ruefully.

"With?" I asked.

"Let's just say, a man knows when to run and when to stay. And he's a fool, for not knowing the difference," Gabriel said.

It was my turn to stare at him, trying to puzzle out his remark. As his eyes met mine, I saw longing and tenderness. I blushed, looking away. "Well, he's back, and I don't know what he wants." My hand gripped his arm more tightly as panic set in.

"He wants you, of course. Men are rather simple, Miss Clarissa." He smiled at me, flashing his dimple in his right cheek. "What does your family think?"

"They want me to stay as far away from him as possible. Which is fine, as I don't relish being made to look a fool again."

"Is it that you just don't want to look a fool? Or is it that you no longer care for him?" he asked, studying me.

I did not answer him for a few moments. "I am tired of providing constant amusement for my family."

"You still haven't answered my original question. But I wouldn't let a little teasing by your family prevent you from living your life," Gabriel murmured.

As we continued our walk, I stumbled once on the trolley tracks. Gabriel gripped my arm to prevent me from falling.

"Miss," Gabriel said, "you know it would be much safer for you if you didn't walk everywhere."

I recognized a rhetorical question, deciding not to answer it.

"You should consider taking streetcars whenever possible."

"I like to walk," I replied, as I jumped out of the way of a horse and buggy. Gabriel simply watched me, making me believe he did not agree with me, but that he would not argue.

We arrived at my home, and I could think of no way to prolong my time with him.

"We seem to have arrived, miss. I believe you have some thinking to do. I wish you a good day."

"Wait, do you think you could walk me to my uncle's? It's only a little bit farther."

"Of course, Miss Clarissa." We turned from my house and headed toward Uncle Martin's store.

"Mr. McLeod, I can't remember if I have told you, but my father just re-married." At this I had to clear my throat before continuing. "I call her by her first married name, Mrs. Smythe, though I have been told to call her Mrs. Sullivan. Anyway, she had tea at our house yesterday, with someone I believe you know well. A Mrs. Masterson?" I felt his body jerk, and he stopped short to stare at me.

"You had tea yesterday with Aunt Masterson?" Gabriel asked.

"Yes, and it was very unpleasant."

"Well, most things to do with her are." He continued to look at me as though trying to figure out a puzzle. Finally, he gave a small nod and turned to continue walking toward Russell's. "Did she have anything of interest to say?"

"She had nothing complimentary to say about anyone except her own family," I replied.

"Did she mention me or my brothers?"

"Yes, she did."

"And?"

"It appears that you were always a trial to her, and she can't imagine why you would want to be a carpenter rather than work in an office with her husband. She didn't appear to like either of your brothers."

"No, she can't imagine I would want to be my own boss rather than work for her miserly husband. Working for a pittance." He took a deep breath, then smiled at me. "I am sorry you had to have tea with her."

"So am I. She managed to insult everyone in my family. The only person she seems to like is Mrs. Smythe, who she also insulted." I waved away my thoughts on Mrs. Smythe. "However, I am curious about one thing. What argument did Richard and her son have? Colin also alluded to it last night before Richard joined us and again this morning while escorting me to school."

At this, Gabriel laughed. "Oh, that's a good tale. But one that should be told by Richard. He's the storyteller of the family. Ask him next time you see him." Gabriel continued to smile.

We arrived at Russell's, and I turned to Gabriel to take my leave.

He looked at me intently, finally murmuring, "Don't take too much time deciding what you want." He then took my gloved hand, kissing my knuckles. "I bid you a good day, Miss Clarissa," he whispered with a warm smile before turning and walking away.

CHAPTER 22

IT WAS A CRISP SATURDAY EVENING in late May, and earlier in April I had accepted an invitation from the Dickersons for a dinner party with Jonas and Savannah, which I now felt obligated to attend. The Dickersons were important members of Boston society and Jonas' good friends. I was tempted to beg a headache, but, once an invitation had been accepted, only death was an acceptable excuse, or so Jonas said with a fiercely disapproving frown.

I entered the Dickersons' house, trying not to feel overly awed by the elegant furnishings. The house was far grander than the simpler homes I was accustomed to, and I had to force myself not to gape in awe. It seemed as though I had entered a miniature palace.

The front hall was at least three times as large as our entryway, with a towering black walnut staircase at one end, each spindle elaborately carved. The rail formed an animal like paw as it met large newel posts at the landing in the front hall. An ornate lamp exuding a gentle light was mounted on top of the newel post in the hallway. Upon glancing up the stairs toward the landing, I saw a beautiful stained-glass window featuring a Romanesque woman sitting in her bowery. I wished I could see the stained glass lit from behind on a sunny day, its kaleidoscope of colors cascading down onto the surroundings. The hardwood floors, polished to a high gleam where visible, were covered in plush green-and-black oriental rugs. The elaborate mahogany hall stand had enough coat pegs for at least ten coats, although we gave our wraps to a waiting maid.

"Miss Russell," the hostess, Mrs. Dickerson, greeted us, delicately taking Savannah's hand. "What a pleasure to see you again. I do hope you enjoy yourself tonight." She turned toward me, an assessing glance taking in my appearance. I glanced down, thinking that my ice-blue satin evening dress, white gloves and matching shoes were quite stylish. I had even worn an extra petticoat and silk stockings.

"Mrs. Dickenson," replied Savannah, with a small nod, "thank you for the invitation. I would like to introduce you to my cousin, Miss Clarissa Sullivan." Mrs. Dickenson nodded her dismissal and departed to greet arriving guests.

Savannah hooked her arm through Jonas's elbow, entering the formal parlor. I followed behind into the sumptuously large room, continuing to marvel at the molding, the gold-colored silk wallpaper, the thick cranberry-colored damask draperies, the grand piano in the corner. All flat surfaces were covered with different types of cloths, with red the dominant color. A prominently displayed bust of an imposing-looking man on a pedestal stood to one side, and an étagère of travel knickknacks hung on the wall near the piano. Scattered throughout were potted plants and ferns, lending an exotic feel.

After entering the room, I accepted a glass of wine and headed to a quiet corner. I felt lonely, noting I appeared to be the only unattached guest, so I decided to stand next to the marble bust to give myself the illusion of a companion. My goal for the evening was to be as unobtrusive as possible. Savannah hoped that by watching polite society interact, I would begin to learn how to better compose myself. Listening to the guests' discussions throughout the room, all the mingling voices sounded mildly bored or authoritative; I had no desire to join any of their conversations.

"Enjoying the scene, Rissa?"

I jumped, nearly spilling my wine, hoping I had not actually shrieked. I gave silent thanks I had not knocked over the bust of some long-lost ancestor. I turned toward the invader of my calm musings. "Please leave me alone. Go away. Now." I spoke in a low, nearly hissing, voice. I attempted to paste a peaceful, serene expression on my face.

"No. I finally have you in a place where you can't run away from me, and I am going to speak my piece."

Cameron looked up and smiled at Jonas, who nodded in acknowledgment. Savannah looked over at us with a horrified expression, which she quickly masked. She tried to make her way toward us, but Jonas prevented her from walking toward me by firmly gripping her elbow and steering her in the opposite direction.

"You know Jonas?" I asked, eyes narrowing as I contemplated that bit of information.

"Of course. We go back a ways. Families and all that. We know each other best from law school. He owed me a favor, and this is it," he said with a smug smile.

"If you wanted to see me, you should have called at my door and asked permission to speak with me," I retorted, beginning to lose my calm facade.

"And be humiliated by being refused admittance? No, Rissa. I had to think of another way to see you."

I glared at him at his use of my nickname.

Then with gentle urgency in his voice, he leaned toward me asking, "Who is that big hulking brute who walked you home the other day?"

"Cameron, I am not your concern anymore. Please desist asking such questions."

"Oh, you most definitely are my concern, my Clarissa." He looked at me. "We almost married, Clarissa. Or did you forget that?" At my sharp indrawn hiss of breath, he smiled, though with a touch of malice. "Ah, I see that you remember. We were in love, and I never forgot you. Why do you think I am back?" He looked at me with intense brown eyes.

"We *were* in love. We *almost* married. Neither are the case anymore. Everything changed when you failed to show on our wedding day," I retorted, trying to maintain a calm countenance for the sake of the other guests and for my own pride. I had a sense I failed miserably as my cheeks felt hot, and I was short of breath.

"Rissa, it's been to my everlasting regret that I did not come to our wedding. What can I say? I panicked. I felt like I was being trapped into a world, into a life, that I didn't want. You must admit, marrying you wasn't gaining me any social standing. Unfortunately I realized after I left that I did want that world. I did want you."

"You speak to me like this, after years of absence and abject silence, thinking this is the way to woo me? Court me?" I snapped, though kept my voice low. "Do you really think insulting me and my family are the way to my heart? If you truly wanted me, you could have had me, Cameron. You are about two years too late."

"You can't mean that, Clarissa," Cameron pleaded. "You must give me another chance."

I sighed, the anger leaving as quickly as it had come, desolation at his perfidy nearly overwhelming me. "Cameron, you were the one who spoke so confidently about our future lives together. But I've come to realize it was all just talk with you, wasn't it? You didn't really want *me*, just the talking about it. The danger, the excitement, of going against your exalted family." I heard the bitterness in my voice but couldn't mask it.

I paused to study him for a moment and realized he seemed *less* to me somehow. Less vivacious, less charming, less handsome, less endearing. Nothing at all like the memory I had clung to for the past two years.

"How dare you speak about my family's social standing? We are an upstanding, successful, hardworking family. You should be proud to know us. To marry me," I snapped, turning from him. He gripped my arm, preventing me from walking away.

"I never realized how weak a man you are until now," I said.

At my words, he blanched and finally released my arm. "Rissa…" he pleaded.

"I am Miss Sullivan to you, sir, please don't forget that. You owe me that modicum of respect," I replied.

I turned my back to him and walked toward Savannah, who watched me from across the room with worried eyes. A sense of calm settled over me the more distance I put between Cameron and myself.

The dinner party continued endlessly, with the women content to continue their tittering and gossiping in the parlor, finally sitting in small conversation groups. I smiled, fearing I seemed a vapid simpleton, but could not muster the energy to engage in a conversation. Thankfully Savannah busily entertained the small group with details from her upcoming wedding. Finally after an interminable dinner, Jonas, Savannah and I were able to take our leave.

"What could you have been thinking?" Savannah asked Jonas in the carriage. "You should have separated Cameron and Clarissa immediately."

"I will do what I deem best, Savannah," Jonas said. "No matter what your family decrees."

"He has no right…"

"He has every right to speak with her if he wishes. And that is enough on the topic," Jonas said in an authoritative voice.

I sat next to Savannah, shaking in fury, but unable to form a coherent sentence.

***

AFTER I ENTERED THE FRONT HALL, removed my coat and walked up the stairs, I peeked into da's study. He sat in a dilapidated chair near the fire studying the smoldering flames in the grate. A lamp was lit near the doorway, emitting a weak light. Long shadows highlighted the bookshelves on the far side of the room and his desk piled with mounds of paperwork.

"Da?"

"Ah, Rissa darling, you're home," da said. He motioned for me to enter and I sat next to him on a padded footstool. "How was the party?"

"Cameron was there." I whispered the words, hoping the gentle delivery would temper da's ire.

He reached down, gripping my shoulder. I turned to face him. "Savannah and her Jonas kept you away from him." I closed my eyes at his statement, as for him there was no question that they would prevent me from being in Cameron's presence.

"No, Da. They didn't." He pursed his lips and his grip on my shoulder tightened. "Jonas knows Cameron. Says he owed Cameron a favor and helping Cameron find a way to speak with me was a way to repay the debt."

"And they say that those in society are genteel?" Da hissed. "Do they have no sense, leaving you to listen to the filthy lies of such a man?" He reached down to cup the left side of my face. "Are you all right, my Clarissa?"

"Yes, Da. We were in a roomful of people and although I would prefer not to speak with him again, I am fine."

"When does the school year end?"

"In a few weeks. But please let me finish it, Da. Please. I need to teach. I need that purpose to my life. I can't be confined to the house. Not with…" I grimaced at the thought of being in the house with Mrs. Smythe. Of having no way to see Gabriel.

"Rissa, I know you need to teach, but keeping you safe must be my first priority. I wish your mother were here to give me good, sensible advice."

"She'd want me to be happy, Da."

"She'd want you safe." He said as he tucked a piece of hair behind my ear. "For now, you can continue to teach, but it's open for discussion if you see him again." He raised his eyebrows as he watched me. I nodded. I stood, kissed him on his forehead and left to prepare for bed.

***

SAVANNAH FOUND ME HOME ALONE the following afternoon, sipping a strong cup of tea in the parlor, lost in thought. Mrs. Smythe followed her in but, in an uncommon act of kindness, realized we needed to be left alone.

"Rissa, are you all right?" Savannah asked in a tremulous voice, taking my hand in hers as she sat next to me on the settee. She appeared near tears, gripping my hand almost painfully in her agitation.

I continued to lean back against the settee without the strength or inclination to sit up properly. I had been deep in thought, thinking of the night before and the conversation with Cameron. I continued to turn it over again in my head, unable to stop puzzling it. I turned to face her and silently shook my head, unsure of what to say.

"Rissa, I assure you, I had no idea Jonas was going to arrange a meeting. I did not even know he *knew* Cameron. Should I discuss this with father?"

"No, I spoke with my Da last night. He's quite upset with Jonas."

"Rissa, I didn't know it was going to happen." Savannah blinked rapidly as she fought tears.

"Sav, I saw your face. I know you were as shocked as I was," I admitted, squeezing her hand. "I don't understand why Jonas acted as he did toward me. It seems disrespectful. Ungentlemanly." I looked at a spot on the wall, reenvisioning the scene from last night. I murmured, "I always knew he disliked me. I just hadn't realized how much."

Savannah raised her eyebrows, trying to find words to contradict my last statement, but I forestalled her, saying, "No, Sav, don't disagree. This is proof of his dislike toward me. Everyone is trying to prevent me from speaking to Cameron, yet he arranges it." I sighed, leaning my head fully against the settee.

"Rissa, what can I do to make it up to you?"

"It's not for you to make up to me. You didn't do anything to me," I replied, smiling at her.

"What did he say to you? You seemed upset when he spoke with you." She released my hand, turning toward the tea table to prepare herself a cup of tea. At her grimace upon her first sip, I realized the tea had turned cold and was now too strong for her.

I focused on her question, my thoughts returning to Cameron and last night. "He told me why he didn't show up."

"Really? What was his reason?" Savannah leaned in, holding her breath.

I turned dull, pained eyes toward her. "He told me that he felt trapped into a life he didn't want, and it was the only way he could see out." A tear leaked down my face, and I wiped it away. I felt impatient with myself for crying over him; I had cried enough for Cameron and needed to move on.

"Oh, Clarissa, how wretched!" Savannah covered her mouth with her left hand. "I can't believe he is trying to blame you for his own weakness."

"Yes, that is what he is trying to do. Blame me for his weakness. However, I won't let him. I told him that he should have only felt pride to be marrying me. That I thought he was a weak man." Speaking with Savannah aided in lifting my spirits, eased my insecurities.

Savannah gasped when I mentioned the weak man comment and then grinned. "Oh, that must have hurt his pride. I know I should not take joy in that, Rissa, but he seems like Jonas in many ways, and that type of comment would cause Jonas no end of distress."

We shared twin evil smiles for a moment before I finally broke the silence. "I said that mainly to hurt him. A part of me wanted him to hurt as he had hurt me." I let out a long sigh. "But it didn't make me feel any better, Sav. It just made me feel worse."

Savannah gently tapped my hand and said, "That's because you are a decent, kind person." After a few moments she gently cleared her throat and said, "Clarissa, I know this sounds horrible, but isn't it better to know, before you married him, what type of person he really was? At least you didn't marry him, only to find out what he truly thought of you and your life together. That would have been horrible. *And* you would have been stuck with him."

I nodded my agreement. "Yes, Sav, you are right." I sighed, stretching, sitting up fully. "I am tired of being inside. Let's go for a walk."

"Yes, let's. It's a beautiful day. Let's walk toward the Public Gardens. I imagine the flowers will be in bloom by now."

We gathered light wraps in the front hall, pinning and adjusting our hats in the mirror before descending the front steps. I looped my arm through Savannah's, and we began our walk. The calm oasis of Union Park disappeared as we entered the larger thoroughfares. We skirted trolley tracks, carriages and delivery carts as we continued toward the Back Bay.

We entered the Public Gardens through the Arlington gate and began to stroll around the manicured grounds. The swan boats moved slowly around the pond. The roses were not yet in bloom, although I smiled at the whimsy of flowers with long stems and large mauve-colored orbs at the top. They seemed the type of flower one could pick and then blow on to spread the flower petals, like a dandelion. I finally began to relax, enjoying the fresh air, seeing the gardens in their springtime glory.

Savannah and I continued to walk, although Savannah seemed more pensive than usual. Suddenly she turned to me, and blurted out, "I envy you, you know, Rissa."

"Envy me. Why?"

"You are living your own life. You teach, even though no one is particularly happy with it. You are free to marry who you want."

I looked at her, sensing there was much she wasn't saying. "Savannah, you of all people know that my life isn't that easy." I paused for a moment. "Tell me what you are really trying to say."

"I feel as though I am keeping up expectations. Meeting everyone else's desires for me. Mama's so happy about the wedding, as are the grandparents. I feel..." A long sigh, a quiet shake of her head and a softly rueful laugh followed.

"Sav, are you saying you don't want to marry Jonas?" I asked, trying to dampen my nascent hope.

"Do you know how I met Jonas?" she asked.

"Wasn't it at a party?"

"No, I met him at Grandpapa and Grandmama's house one afternoon when I called for tea. They had transpired for the two of us to come for tea on the same day. This has been their dream. To have one granddaughter marry well."

I stared at Savannah in surprise, shocked by our grandparents' plotting. "Savannah, if you don't want to marry him, then don't. You should be happy, too."

"That's such a simple way of looking at life, Rissa," Savannah chided gently, making me feel about ten years old.

Before I could take any true offense, she met my worried gaze with devastated eyes, and I began to understand her despair.

"I don't know as I believe in love, Rissa. At least, not that grand, all-consuming feeling you described with Cameron at the beginning. I feel great affection for Jonas. I believe that will be enough for me," she finished with a hard, resolute edge to her voice and a quick nod. Her words had become more determined and firm as she spoke. It seemed as though she were trying to convince herself, rather than me, of this truth.

I stopped walking, staring at Savannah with an expression of despair. "For pity's sake, Sav, don't marry him if you don't love him!"

"What did love get you, Rissa?" Savannah asked.

I recoiled as though she had struck me. A lone tear escaped, and I hastily wiped it away. I continued to watch her, attempting to understand why she would strike out at me. "Pain, heartbreak." My voice cracked slightly. "But at least I wasn't afraid to live. Taking risks in life is part of living, Sav." I looked away, taking a steadying breath. "Let's go back. It's grown chilly."

Savannah nodded, and we turned for home. "Rissa, I didn't mean…"

I waited for her to finish, but she said no more. I realized she had no more to say, and I knew, deep inside, she was not truly upset with me. This really was about her. We walked toward home in tense silence, lost in thought.

CHAPTER 23

MY STUDENTS HAD LEFT, but I sensed I was being watched. I glanced up impatiently from correcting ledgers at my desk to see Cameron standing in the doorway. He looked every inch the successful gentleman in a formal black suit and waistcoat with crisp white shirt and dark tie.

"Cameron, what are you doing here?" I demanded. I rose from my seated position at the desk.

"I knew of no other way to speak with you than to be bold, so I decided to come to your schoolhouse. I never realized you wanted to continue to teach, Clarissa." He glanced around the schoolroom, taking it in, smirking at the students' simple drawings. "I would have thought you could have taught at a better school than this." He sniffed.

"Cameron, I teach here because I choose to teach here, because I *want* to teach these children. They have as much right to an education as any other."

"Yes, of course," he murmured. "However, that is not why I am here. There is much still for us to discuss, Clarissa." He turned to me, looking at me with his pale brown eyes lit with a strange light.

"Is there? What would you like to discuss?"

"Rissa, I fear you did not understand me the other evening." He stood with his legs slightly apart, with his hands gently holding his hat, fingers repeatedly tracing the edges. "The pain you felt at the altar surely has faded by now, and we can move on from that, can't we? I realize I do want a life with you. I miss *you*. I miss the fact that you are full of life and vitality and that you show your emotions, even though that is not always proper. I have met other women, and no one compares to you, Rissa. What do you say?" He spoke in a rush, the words pouring out of him as they always had. He finished, smiling, as though I would be pleased to agree with him.

"The hurt has faded by now?" I seethed, as I approached him. "We can move on? As though we disagreed on the color of wallpaper? You failed to show up at our *wedding*. Do you know the kind of ridicule and disgrace I had to endure? I may not be a genteel, upper-class woman, as you pointed out. My family may not be up to your standards, as you so kindly made clear the other evening. However, let me assure you that I felt the full censure of my family, neighbors, friends and society in general. Do you know what that feels like?" I demanded, eyes flashing, breathing heavily.

"Rissa, I'm sorry."

He looked at me with a half smile, the half smile he had always used to excuse any misunderstanding between us. In the past, I had found it endearing; now it simply enraged me.

"Sorry doesn't take away the pain, doesn't begin to ease the heartache. You left me to scorn and pity. You left me alone. How could you?" I stared at him with tears in my eyes, gasping for air, begging him for a valid explanation, and then suddenly realized there would be no valid explanation. None existed.

"Get out, Cameron. I don't want to hear any more excuses. That's all they are, and I want nothing more to do with you." I started to turn away, but he grabbed my arm, spinning me toward him.

"Don't tell me that we are through, Clarissa," he demanded in a low, urgent voice, fire in his eyes. "*Don't.*"

I wrenched my arm but was unable to break free. I tried kicking him in the shin, but it had no effect. "Let me go. Now," I ordered. We continued to stare at each other, both angry, breathing heavily.

"I believe Miss Clarissa asked you to let her go, sir," a deep baritone voice interjected, breaking the tension of the room.

I jerked back, nearly falling, as Cameron suddenly freed my arm. I leaned heavily against my desk with my hand, still facing the room. I glanced at Gabriel standing in the doorway, delight and relief flooding me.

"I would thank you to not interfere in other people's private business," Cameron replied, half turning toward Gabriel, glaring at him.

Gabriel nodded mockingly with lips quirked. "Generally I do not, sir. But I do have business here."

"You can't mean…Rissa!"

"Cameron, leave," I demanded, leaning more heavily against the desk for support.

He continued to stare at me and then glanced at Gabriel. "We aren't finished," Cameron said to me, eyes flashing.

"Cameron, we finished two years ago. Please accept that," I said in a flat voice. I stared at him, attempting to betray no emotion.

Cameron noted my expression, though his appeared more mulish by the minute, until he finally turned and stormed out of the room.

Gabriel continued to study me, noting how I began to lean more and more heavily against the desk. "I'd sit, Miss Clarissa, before falling down," he suggested.

I took his advice, turned toward my chair and collapsed. I had no reserves of strength left, feeling exhausted after the confrontation with Cameron. I glanced toward Gabriel. "Why can't the ghosts of the past stay in the past?" I mused.

Gabriel gave a small smile. "Because then they wouldn't be ghosts, darling." He seemed to blush after using the endearment, but he crouched down in front of me taking my hand. He met my eyes, staring at me. "I should lie to you. Tell you that I didn't hear most of that exchange. But I won't. I couldn't help but listen. A fascinating man, your Cameron." He attempted to tease, but he continued to watch my reaction closely, concern for me evident in his expression.

My face crumbled, and I started to cry. He pulled me gently into his arms, easing me to a standing position, cradling me against his chest. He simply held me, brushing my hair softly with one of his big hands, crooning a song in my ear. I slowly started to calm, hiccupping against his chest.

"If I were a true gentleman," Gabriel stated self mockingly, "I'd have a clean handkerchief to offer you. I don't." He smiled his apology, wiping the remnants of my tears away with his thumbs.

Belatedly I realized I did not want him to see me like this—red-eyed, with a blotchy face and a runny nose. However, he gently held onto me, looking into my eyes, not letting me turn away.

"You'll be fine, Miss Clarissa," he murmured. "You're a strong woman with great spirit." He watched me another moment before letting me go.

I turned away, searched for a handkerchief and dried my face. I turned back to find Gabriel watching me. "Why do you do that?"

"I am trying to discover the hidden aspects of you," he replied, a warmth lighting his eyes.

"Mr. McLeod, I am sure that you will be disappointed. I am really rather simple."

He chuckled. "With that, I must disagree."

"Yes, well, be that as it may, I should return home soon. My family will start to wonder about me." I turned toward my desk to gather my things.

"Of course. Might I escort you?"

"Yes, thank you. Mr. McLeod, why did you originally stop by today?"

"I came by to discuss the sideboard with you. You are no longer visiting the workshop. Therefore, I thought I would visit you. However, I need you to come to the workshop soon to give me your opinion on an idea I had."

"Yes, of course. I could come by tomorrow, if I am not delayed by family members."

He nodded in agreement, then offered his elbow to me as we departed.

I was unsure how to reestablish the relaxed camaraderie we had previously shared. It was a cold, damp afternoon, and I shivered with the chill. We walked slowly toward Cambridge Street, a large bustling venue crammed with carriages, delivery carts and trolleys. Nearby, two men yelled at each other as they attempted to right a cart that had tipped over, spilling sacks of flour. The sidewalks were crowded as people hustled to do their shopping or to hawk their wares. I shook my head "no" at a boy peddling half-ripened bananas.

As we entered Cambridge Street on my usual route home, Gabriel turned toward me, raising one eyebrow. "Trolley?" At my quick shake of denial, he sighed then said, "Home or Russell's?"

"I'd like to go to Russell's today." After a short pause, I said, "I'm sure you are wondering about Cameron." I peered up at him, to try to detect any signs of interest.

He glanced at me, nodding once.

"I met Cameron at one of my Aunt Betsy's soirees in Quincy," I began. "His family is well-to-do. Their wealth is from one of the railroads. And he studied to be a lawyer, though he never really worked. He was filled with light when my world had been in darkness for so long." I whispered the last part, my voice trailing off as I became lost to memory.

"You don't need to explain," Gabriel said. "I have a decent understanding of what transpired."

"Yes, well, then, that's good." I cleared my throat, desperately trying to think of another topic.

"Did you finish the book by Mark Twain, Miss Clarissa?" He gently steered me away from a pushcart, filled to overflowing with horse dung. I held my breath, trying not to inhale the smell. Gabriel watched me with a small grin, noting my reaction.

I let out my pent-up breath with a gasp. "Oh, the book! Yes, I did, and I found it quite enjoyable." I smiled up at him.

"Yes, it is. I enjoy his storytelling. It's interesting at the end, wouldn't you agree?"

"You'd already read it?" I exclaimed.

"Of course. I can never resist a good book." He smiled at me.

"Why did you have me read it to you then?" I demanded, flushing with embarrassment. I looked around Charles Street, noting the other fashionably dressed couples walking by.

"Miss Butler and your family were right. You do have a nice reading voice. It and your face come alive as you read. As though you travel to another place while you are in a story. Have you thought any more on travel, Miss Clarissa?"

"No. Why would I want to leave my family? Leave Boston? I have everything I want here." I felt panic at the thought of another leave taking. I thought of Cameron, his departure from my life. My mama's death. I looked up at Gabriel, meeting his inquisitive blue eyes, focusing on him. "I know you dream of travel."

"Every time I open a book," he agreed. "I promise myself I will travel to the place I read about."

"When in my school room, you seemed fascinated by the western part of the United States. Was it Oregon?" I asked, curious despite myself.

"Yes, the West. But California, not Oregon. It still seems wild to me. Yet a man could build a life there." He sounded wistful.

Our pace slowed, and I looked up to realize we had arrived at Russell's. I had not focused on the walk, but on Gabriel and the conversation, almost completely unaware of the passing scenery.

"Ah, it appears we have reached our destination," Gabriel murmured. He turned toward me, kissed the back of my gloved hand. "Come visit me soon."

I felt shy, watching him leave until he was out of sight.

CHAPTER 24

COLIN ARRIVED AT THE SCHOOLHOUSE a few minutes after the children left and waited patiently as I tidied the room. He had learned, through gossip at the smithy, that I had been visiting Gabriel's warehouse. After a tense conversation—where I explained I had visited to help Uncle Martin with his project for Savannah and where Colin appeared unconvinced there was not more occurring—he agreed to escort me to Gabriel's workshop.

"Clarissa," Florence called out, breezily entering the room. She stopped short when she saw Colin leaning against the far wall, looking out the window. "Oh, I beg your pardon. I didn't mean to interrupt," Florence said, twirling on her heel to scamper away.

"Florence!" I called out as she turned to leave. "Florence, please, I'd like you to meet my brother." I rushed toward her, knowing I would drag her into the room if necessary. She had been very distant of late, and I needed to find a way to bridge the distance. "Colin, this is my friend Miss Butler. Florence, my brother, Colin Sullivan," I said.

"Nice to meet you," Colin said with a small nod.

"And you," Florence said, smiling up at him. "It's nice to meet someone from Clarissa's family."

"Where are you headed, Miss Butler? We could escort you part of the way, if it is in our direction," Colin offered as we left the school.

"I am headed toward home, which isn't far from here. I thank you for your kind offer," she said, nodding to us both, walking in the opposite direction.

"She seems nice enough," he commented. Colin turned us toward Gabriel's warehouse and began walking at a measured pace, allowing me a chance to talk while I walked. We turned onto busy Causeway Street, dodging trolleys as we crossed to the other side. The large arched central entrance to the North Union

Station bustled with passengers rushing toward trains. Carriages clogged the streets with those looking for their recently arrived friends or family.

"She's very nice," I replied. "I have invited her to the house a few times, but she has resisted."

"Hmm…" Colin appeared lost in thought. "I doubt Mrs. Smythe would like her. She seems a little too…*simple*…for her."

I grimaced at his choice of words, feeling that they did Florence a disservice. "She is poor, Colin," I contradicted him. "And yet she is making her own way in this world as a single woman. I have to admire her." I looked at him with a challenging tilt to my chin.

"Don't get all worked up, Rissa. I didn't mean it like that. I just meant, I wouldn't want her to have to suffer Mrs. Smythe's snobbery."

I laughed. "Yes, I can agree with that. Florence is all alone in the world now. No family."

"None?" Colin asked, the sadness lighting his eyes mirroring mine.

"No, none. Although I think Florence knew Richard McLeod, maybe quite well in the past, but I haven't heard the story yet."

"You mean you haven't tricked her into telling you the truth?" Colin teased. "Don't look to me to help you ferret out information, Rissa."

We arrived at the workshop about twenty minutes after leaving the school. The door was slightly ajar, and Colin knocked lightly but stuck his head in before waiting for a response. "Hello there!" Colin called out.

"Hello."

I heard Gabriel's deep voice. Colin pushed open the door, and we entered.

I watched Gabriel approach us, unable to suppress a smile. Colin glanced at me, grinning, sending me a quick wink.

"It's Colin, isn't it?" Gabriel asked. At Colin's jaunty nod, Gabriel said, "Great to see you." He shook Colin's hand then clapped him on the back.

I watched, amazed at men's interactions and greetings. This informality seemed much more welcoming than a bow, a nod or tipping one's hat.

Gabriel turned toward me. "Miss Sullivan. Nice to see you again. I've just brewed a pot of tea." He motioned for us to follow him. We walked over to the dust-covered table where Colin sat comfortably at one of the large chairs. I moved toward the rocking chair. Colin took in all the details, missing nothing, noting my different chair and my familiarity with the room.

I looked around. "Mr. McLeod, you have worked on many new pieces," I said in an attempt to turn Colin's attention from me.

"Yes, miss. I have had plenty of work lately. There has been an increased interest in my work since the display for your uncle."

Colin nodded, smiling. "Uncle has always had good taste. It's one of the reasons he's so successful as a linen merchant."

We sat in a pleasant silence for a few moments before Colin spoke up. "Gabe, has Rich recovered from his fight with your cousin?"

"Richard is fine. I think you have the story backward, Colin. It's Cousin Henry who needed to see the doctor, not Richard," Gabriel said with pride.

Gabriel smiled tenderly at me, and I smiled back. We shared a long glance, interrupted only by Colin's noisy slurp of tea. I jolted as I glanced toward Colin, appalled to have been caught staring at Gabriel.

"I imagine you came about the sideboard," Gabriel said. We rose from our chairs to walk toward his workbench.

"Now, miss, I would like your opinion," Gabriel said. "I have been looking at the sideboard design, and I've constructed the bottom part. It seems rather plain to me. I know your uncle stated that he wanted a simple, clean piece. 'Simple but spectacular' are words I think he used." He paused to study the drawings pegged over his workbench.

I leaned in too, noting the various changes to the sketches that had occurred as he had progressed on the piece.

Gabriel studied me as I examined the drawing. He turned to Colin, including him in the conversation. "But I can't imagine your uncle wanted something this plain."

"What do you suggest, Gabe?" Colin asked. "You could have Richard make you some fancy door pulls, which would spruce it up."

Gabriel nodded, seeming to think over Colin's words. "I think Rich will help me with that." He pointed to his sketch with a sharpened pencil. "In this original drawing, I had a simple shelf over the main serving area. Perfect for displaying knickknacks, china, whatever. But it's not spectacular."

He pulled out a revised sketch. "My new design is to continue with the upper shelf but add more decorative molding to the top." He paused to tap on the area for emphasis. "I think this area would benefit from a mirror, with minimal molding around the edges. It would enhance the beauty of the piece, allowing candlelight's reflection."

I squinted, studying the sideboard's before and after drawings. Then I looked toward the already finished portion. "As long as the simple beauty, the fine lines of the bottom half, are continued along the top, I think a mirror would be a nice addition," I said in agreement.

"This is beautiful." I moved toward it, tracing the wood gently with my fingers leaving tracks in the dust. The sideboard's main shelf tapered out to curved edges. The feet were simply carved, not the ornate lion's feet I was accustomed to in the more decorative sideboards. Around the edge of each drawer was a delicate inlay of lighter colored rosewood. I traced it, asking, "Will you stain the wood?"

"Yes, though I will use a clear stain. More like a sealant. I like the natural color of mahogany." Gabriel also reached out to touch the sideboard. His hands came away covered in fine wood dust before rubbing his hands on his pants.

"Gabe, this is great work," Colin said. "What else are you working on?"

Gabriel turned toward Colin, guiding him through the workshop, with Gabriel showing Colin partially completed pieces.

Colin seemed impressed. "When are you going to take on an apprentice?" Colin inquired.

"I haven't decided yet. The recent upswing is still relatively new for me. I want to wait to see if it lasts. Also, as I am sure you understand, more and more of what I do is now done by machines. I worry that I soon won't be needed in this new economy."

"Gabe, when people see your sideboard at the wedding, you will be in demand," Colin effused. "No machine can create what you can make."

"Hmm…maybe not. But I'm finding many willing to sacrifice quality and craftsmanship for price."

"Yes, I understand," Colin murmured. "Da worries we'll soon be obsolete in this new world of machines." He and Gabriel shared a long knowing look filled with understanding of the other's concerns.

"Well, I must return to work. And Rissa should travel home before anyone misses her. Thanks for the tour, Gabe," Colin said, extending his hand, firmly clasping Gabriel's.

"Good-bye, Colin. Good-bye, miss, ah…Miss Sullivan," Gabriel said with a soft smile and a small nod.

"Good-bye, Mr. McLeod."

We made our way down the stairs, and I stepped onto the sidewalk. A group of men sat outside a warehouse relaxing between jobs, their sweat-stained shirts partially unbuttoned in the heat. I looked down the street to see a cart overturned.

"One man's misfortune…" I said with a smile as I nodded toward the cart blocking the street entrance and the men relaxing.

"I bet they're excited to finally have a short rest," Colin said with a smile. "It's a warm day for such work, although it's only going to become worse with summer approaching."

We continued to walk down Canal Street toward Haymarket Square. "Gabe does great work," Colin said.

"Beautiful work," I agreed, attempting to hide my enthusiasm.

"I imagine a man with his talents will never be out of work," he replied. "I would think he makes a good living."

"I suppose," I said. I smiled toward Colin as though I did not know his game.

"Come on, Rissa," he said, exasperation tingeing his voice. "You know you think he would make someone a good husband."

"I've said no such thing," I replied.

"I'm just saying you should think about it, Rissa," he responded with a smile in his voice. "You could do worse." We maneuvered our way to the trolley kiosk, narrowly avoiding a pair of draft horses and a determined driver. Colin called out his anger to him, raising his fist as I'd seen people do in the North End, and I smiled at his antics. He squeezed my arm, but before he left me for the rest of my trip home, he leaned in, murmuring in my ear, "If you want to see him again, just ask."

I nodded, a smile breaking out, unable to hide my pleasure.

"Tomorrow, then?" he asked with an answering grin.

I nodded with a lightened spirit. He watched me board the trolley, leaving me to the rest of my trip home, as he returned to work with Da.

***

COLIN SAT ON THE FRONT STEPS of the school, twirling his hat in his hands as he waited for me the next day. The sunny day highlighted the red in his auburn hair. He smiled to those who walked past and called out encouragement to a group of young boys playing soccer in the street.

"Ah, I love spring," he said when he saw me, soaking in the rays of late May. He rose, donning his hat, offering me his arm. As we walked toward Gabriel's workshop, Colin turned toward me with a worried expression.

"How long has it been since you've seen Cameron?"

I tripped on one of the cobbled bricks. "Cameron? Not since he came by the school after the soiree."

"I'm pretty sure I saw him walk by the school today. He saw me sitting on the steps and kept on walking. I became distracted when the ball the boys were kicking around in the street nearly hit me, and, when I looked again, he was gone."

"He knows I'm not interested in him, Col. I'm sure I won't see him again."

Colin raised one eyebrow. "Well, if you see him, tell me. I won't talk with Da about this, but I will have to if Cameron tries to speak with you again."

"No, Col. Don't tell Da. Then you'll have to explain to him why you are away so long from the smithy with me. About Gabriel..."

"Let's not worry about it yet. As it happens, I'm afraid I will only be with you a few short minutes today. I'll need to leave you soon after we arrive 'cause I don't want to make Da suspicious. He hasn't heard any of the rumors, and I don't know how he'd react."

Colin and I shared a long look.

Then Colin smiled impishly. "Don't let my early departure shorten your visit."

"Colin!" I gasped. "I thought you were worried about my reputation."

"I am, that's why I am escorting you there," he said.

"And that's why you should also escort me *home*," I said as I tried to hide a smile.

"Oh, well, you know me. I'll never be completely proper," he said with a mischievous grin, wriggling his eyebrows at me.

We arrived at Gabriel's workshop, with sunshine and fresh air streaming in through the large open windows. "Hi, Gabe!" Colin called out.

Gabriel stood at the workbench, bent over, chiseling a piece of wood. He spun around at our arrival, surprise then happiness flitting across his features. "Colin, Miss Sullivan. It's nice to see you again so soon." He wiped his dusty hands on his workpants, though only succeeded in making them dustier. He reached out his hand to shake Colin's and nodded at me. "I'm afraid I wasn't expecting you."

"Don't worry. We thought we would just come by, see if there was any progress," Colin said.

"There won't be much in just one day, Colin," Gabriel said.

"Yes, of course," Colin agreed. "Well, I must leave Clarissa to discuss the bookshelves with you and return to work." He looked at me with amusement in his gaze. "Gabe." He nodded to us, winking at me as he strolled out the door. I listened to the heavy thumps of his steps down the stairs, feeling an awkward silence descend.

I blushed, knowing that Colin had been quite transparent. "Mr. McLeod, please pardon the interruption." I waved toward his workbench, encouraging him to keep working.

He watched me closely before nodding his agreement. "Please make yourself comfortable, Miss Clarissa," he encouraged. I saw the hint of a small smile at the corner of his mouth.

I moved around the room, watching him continue to work. I walked toward the table and the rocking chair. I gingerly sat down and slowly relaxed in the rocking chair Gabriel had made, closing my eyes for a moment, relishing the opportunity to listen to him work. He began to whistle off-key an unknown tune. A whimsical, joyful tune that continued on and on with few repeats of any one part of the song. I heard a whisper of the ragtime song Lucas had played last month, but the piece quickly changed, and I couldn't place it.

"What are you smiling about?" he asked, interrupting my peaceful reverie.

I opened my eyes, a slight grin playing around my mouth, tilting my head toward him to find him studying me with a tender expression. I continued to rest my head against the back of the chair, meeting his gaze. "At the whimsy of your whistling," I admitted. "You whistle with such enthusiasm, though it's all off-key," I teased, making him laugh. "I don't know the song. What's the name of it?"

He studied me, as though weighing his answer. He gently cleared his throat and met my gaze with a chagrined expression. "I only whistle when I am happy," he admitted softly. "And I make up it up as I go along. I tend to combine different songs that I have heard into one long piece."

I smiled again, my heart lifting at his quiet admission. "So it's called 'Gabriel's Happiness'?"

He smiled fully, the smile that always took me by surprise because of its rarity, the dimple flashing in his right cheek. "Yes, I guess that's what it's called," he agreed, holding my gaze. We continued to stare into each other's eyes until there was a loud knocking at the partially open door.

I started, nearly toppling out of the rocking chair. I knew I blushed beet red at the further evidence of my clumsiness and hastily righted myself. Gabriel, upon seeing me nearly land on the floor, rushed to help me up, yet found his help was not necessary. By the time he maneuvered his way around the table, I was sitting crimson faced in the rocking chair. I was reluctant to meet his gaze, not wanting to see what it held.

I finally glanced up to find Gabriel stared at me with tender understanding, a trace of humor lurking in his eyes. When I continued to blush, he smiled fully. I waved toward the door.

"Yes, Miss Clarissa," he murmured, "I will go to the door. But first, are you settled?"

"Yes, perfectly settled," I said. I patted the arms of the rocking chair, trying to indicate it was a sturdy seat but instead felt silly.

He continued to smile as he walked toward the door, his boots sounding on the floor.

"Hello? Can I help you?" Gabriel asked in a jovial voice. I heard quiet murmurings from the doorway and then footsteps retreating down the stairs.

I looked toward Gabriel. "Who was that?" I asked.

"Oh, the mailman," he responded, throwing down a pile of mail on the dusty desk in the corner. "He knows I am looking for a letter from my brother, and I can tell by his face when there isn't one."

I nodded, unsure what to say. "It must be hard to be separated from him," I said, feeling like an idiot the minute the words were out of my mouth.

"Yes, terrible," he admitted. "But he wanted to enter the army, and he got his wish. I am very proud of him." Then he sighed, smiling at me sadly. "Now I just wish he would come home, in one piece."

"Where is he?" I asked.

"The Philippines. I hope that every time they announce a treaty, he will return to us. But, Richard and I've heard nothing," he said.

I half smiled, not knowing anything to say to comfort, but wanting to give encouragement. "I hope he comes home soon to you. Healthy and happy."

"'From your mouth to God's ear' as my da would say, miss," Gabriel said, smiling at me. He turned toward his workbench.

"I must return home," I said. I rose, gathering my purse. I stood fidgeting by the table, fingers nervously tapping the tabletop.

"I hope you are able to return soon, Miss Clarissa," he said, watching me longingly before he began to walk toward me, stopping in front of me.

I held my breath uncertain what he would do, watching him with curious, nervous eyes. He gazed at me intently, slowly leaning toward me. I felt my heart begin to race. My eyes fluttered closed as his lips neared mine, and I subtly leaned in toward him. He gently kissed me, a whisper of a kiss. His lips were soft, softer than I had imagined they would be. He slowly leaned away, and I felt him gently caress the side of my cheek as my eyes slowly fluttered open again. I watched him in wonder, feeling my heart beat an erratic tattoo in my chest.

"Until you return, Miss Clarissa," he said, dropping his hand, backing up a step.

I nodded, unable to say anything. I turned absently, pausing on the landing to gather my thoughts and to calm my racing heartbeat.

I stumbled onto the street, feeling blinded by the bright sunlight. Cameron had kissed me, although all I remembered from his kisses was a hard pressing together of lips. I could not remember ever being affected in such a way.

CHAPTER 25

ON A HOT SUMMER DAY in early June, Colin escorted me to Gabriel's workshop. The sideboard was virtually done, only needing a few coats of varnish. I enjoyed watching the subtle changes, cataloging the alterations Gabriel made on a near daily basis.

Today, after Colin left, Gabriel continued sanding a piece of wood at his workbench. He appeared lost in thought, enjoying his work.

"Do you mind my visit today?" I asked.

"Well, miss, I welcome the company but must keep working." He looked at me as though hoping I would understand.

"Of course," I said. "I'll just sit for a few minutes, if you don't mind."

He smiled, waving me toward what I considered my chair. "Did you bring a book today, Miss Clarissa?"

"No, I haven't been by the library recently."

I slowly began to rock, relaxing with the sound of sanding wood. I waited a few moments to see if he would whistle, but he remained silent. "May I ask you a question, Mr. McLeod?"

"You may. Though I may not answer it," he replied, looking at me over his shoulder with a grin. I enjoyed watching him work, his long arms and strong shoulders fluidly moving together to sand the wood.

"If you had such a hard time with the Mastersons, why didn't you live with other family members?"

"You are very curious, aren't you, Miss Clarissa?" he asked. He sighed, massaging the back of his neck. "Well, I think you've earned the right to your curiosity."

He turned back toward the wood, beginning to carefully sand, although I couldn't tell if he was concentrating on the story or the wood.

"You must understand, I had no other family to live with, or I would never have lived with her. My brothers and I, we always dreamt about escaping the oppressive atmosphere of the Mastersons. But we knew we had nowhere to go. Our only other living relative, our father's brother, Uncle Aidan, had never returned to Boston after the fire. For all we knew, he died at sea during one of his journeys." His gaze appeared distant, as though remembering long-ago scenes. He sanded once more, the sound a soothing balm to his difficult tale.

Then he stopped sanding, turning toward me and met my gaze with a sad smile. "I slowly lost hope that he would ever return and look for us. We were too young to live on our own, and we had heard enough about the hard life of children living on the streets or in orphanages. I didn't relish being sent on one of those orphan trains, being separated from my brothers. Aunt threatened us with it weekly."

He rolled his shoulders, as though dispelling the thought of being separated from his brothers. He turned back to the wood, picking up the sandpaper, although lost in thought, for he didn't begin to sand.

"Even though we were shown no love, no affection, we always had food and shelter and received an education. As the elder brother, I tried to be mother and father to my younger brothers.

"There was very little love in the Masterson household. What there was of it, none was spared to come around to us. Aunt rarely hugged her children. Their only praise came when they did well in school. It seemed she often forgot she had children. She had three maids, and they appeared to do most of the child rearing. Uncle Masterson was never home, always working. I began to suspect that he preferred the office to home. Aunt Masterson did not complain, as his success led to more prestige for her. And more wealth."

I continued to rock, watching anger and sadness flit across his face as he spoke of his past.

"Aunt Masterson believed that if we did something wrong, we needed to be punished. She relished corporal punishment and took great joy in beating us. To prevent punishment, our two cousins often blamed us for their misdeeds. Our punishment was always more harsh than theirs." I saw him flex his fingers while he pondered this. "Aunt Masterson could not believe that her children were capable of wrongdoings when her sister's brats were the true hellions. Because my brothers were younger, I frequently tried to take the blame for them. I wanted them to have a decent childhood. I had known happiness until age twelve. I didn't want them to only think of loneliness, fear and pain.

"For me, Old Mr. Smithers was the man, other than my da, who helped shape me. He let me spend time in this carpentry shop. I enjoyed it here. The workshop was always warm. He had food and a pot of tea. He also listened. Never judging. Only listened," he said with a small smile. "You can't know how much a young boy just needs to talk sometimes. Mr. Smithers had that uncanny ability to listen, say a few words and point me in the right direction."

Gabriel glanced around the workshop, as though envisioning the space with Mr. Smithers.

"He put me to work. Over time, he taught me all he knew about carpentry and cabinetmaking. I eventually left school to apprentice with him full-time, learning the craft, and spent seven years as an apprentice, though I didn't live with him."

"Why not?" I asked.

"I would have found that much more agreeable, but I couldn't leave my brothers alone with Aunt Masterson. When I had learned all I needed to learn to be a master cabinetmaker, I built a sideboard for the guild. They liked it, and I was considered a Master." His voice rang with pride as he remembered that day. "However, I didn't leave Mr. Smithers like so many thought I would. I liked working with him. There was enough work for the two of us, and he was like family to me." He smiled at the memory.

"When did you finally move away from your aunt?" I asked.

"After I became a Master, and after nine years with the Mastersons, we moved out. I had learned enough from Old Mr. Smithers to start selling my own furniture. I knew it would be hard. I couldn't stay there any longer. Richard and Cousin Henry were in near daily fights. I worried that Richard would eventually run away. I wanted my brothers to have a chance to live elsewhere. We rented a cheap tenement room with Mrs. Capuano in the North End and eked out a living. I continued to work with Mr. Smithers in his shop. We survived." He paused, as though finished.

"What happened to Mr. Smithers?"

"He died two years ago. He left me his workshop and his tools. More importantly, he passed on his great knowledge. His customers had met me, known me for years. I thought my business would continue to grow." He sighed, massaging the back of his neck, rolling his shoulders, trying to calm the tension he appeared to be feeling.

"However, Aunt Masterson started to spread rumors about me, insinuating that I had led to Mr. Smithers's death. When I first heard the rumors, I thought it a joke. Why would I have hurt the man I loved like a father? But the murmurings continued. I had been the one to find him dead at the shop. The doctor said his heart gave out. He was over seventy. Smoked like a chimney, though not in the workshop."

Gabriel looked at me. "But the damage was done. My business slowly dwindled. Thankfully, by this time, Richard worked at the smithy, and we could continue to live independently. I am hopeful that your uncle's patronage will restore my reputation as a cabinetmaker."

"Why did Aunt Masterson dislike you so much?" I knew I had already asked him this, but I couldn't imagine one of my aunts treating me in such a manner.

Gabriel sighed, tossing the sandpaper back and forth in his hands before finally tossing it onto the workbench, bitterness lacing his voice. "I am not certain. She did say numerous times that my mum had married a worthless man. In her eyes, my mum's children were worthless due to their father."

I rose, walking toward him. I gripped his arm gently, looking at him beseechingly with large rounded eyes. "You are not worthless," I said.

Gabriel blushed, looking at me abashed. He appeared uncomfortable at all that he had revealed to me.

"I am confused about something," I stated, thinking back to the conversation that his Aunt Masterson had had with Mrs. Smythe at my house over tea. "If she thought you might have killed someone, why would she want you to work with her husband?"

"Oh, she is a sly woman, never underestimate her. She came by one day, as my business was at a standstill. She appeared very worried about the rumors. Very solicitous of my well-being. Ensuring me that she did not believe a word of what she had heard. However, since I was having such a hard time making a living as a cabinetmaker, why not join my uncle's firm?"

"That was her intention, wasn't it?"

"Exactly, ruin me, make me desperate to the point where I would feel my only choice was to work for my uncle. I had no intention of entering her sphere of influence again. She continues to come by the warehouse every few months, to determine if I am still in business. It is her way to taunt me, show me that she can still manipulate my life."

"Ga…Mr. McLeod," I quickly corrected myself, absently reaching out to grip his hand for a moment. "I know how hard it can be to speak of the past and the pain that still seems too fresh though it is from years ago. Thank you for sharing it with me."

Gabriel sighed, gripping my hand, meeting my gaze with deep blue eyes. "I never like talking about what happened. I want you to know about me. I want *you* to know *me*." He gently took my other hand, clasping it lightly, continuing to watch me intently.

"It explains so much," I said. "I wondered, when I saw your display for Uncle, why you were not well-known and why people were not clamoring for your work. Then when you agreed to make bookshelves for a poor schoolroom, I became more curious." I shook my head at the cruel twists of fate.

"Don't be too upset, Miss Clarissa," Gabriel replied. "Else we never would have met."

I nodded my agreement, continuing to smile.

"May I ask you questions, now?" he inquired, tilting his head to one side, watching me with frank interest.

"If you like, though I may not answer them," I replied, repeating his words back to him.

He gave a bark of laughter before asking, "Why did your family scorn you after Cameron left?" He stared with fierce intensity, looking deeply into my eyes.

I broke eye contact, blushing. "My grandparents are society-type people. Well, the ones on my mother's side, anyway. They were mortified that I caused such a 'scandal.' That was the word they used. It was snidely written up in the papers. Tongue in cheek. My grandparents disliked anything unflattering to be reflected toward them, and that reeked of it." I paused, and a few tears escaped. I whispered, "My grandpapa even stated that there must be something inherently wrong with me for a man not to show up on his wedding day. That now no one would ever want to marry me as I had been shown to be so undesirable, so unlovable."

Gabriel pulled me into his arms. "Oh, darling. They call themselves 'genteel'? They may be rich in the amount of money they have in the bank, but they are poor in spirit." He continued to cradle me against his chest, murmuring soothing words into my ear.

"I swear I did nothing wrong! I just stood in my room, waiting and waiting. Cameron never came. I never knew why. I still don't, not really. His pathetic excuses now will never explain his reasons for not coming." I leaned against Gabriel, sighing into his chest, trying to regain a modicum of control.

Gabriel eased me away from him, smiling at me. "Darling, I've told you before, and I'll tell you again. The man's an idiot. No one who has the chance to marry you would fail to show up." He spoke in a fervent yet gentle voice that soothed me.

He cupped my face in his palms, tilting up my face to meet his worried, tender gaze. He softly stroked my cheeks with his thumbs, the light touches a balm. His deep, rich baritone stirred a long-dormant part of me buried inside. A part of me I thought had died after Cameron.

"Why are you so good to me?" I asked with a teary smile.

He studied me for a few moments as though weighing his answer. Finally, he murmured, "Clarissa, I like to think we would be good to each other."

My eyes widened slightly, unsure if this were a declaration. I found my voice, asking, "Would you mind clarifying what you mean?"

"Clarifying?" He smiled with wry humor. "I'm saying I'd like to court you. Have the chance to know you. Properly." He watched me, waiting for my response.

"I'd like that," I said in a strong voice.

"That's good, Clarissa," he murmured, leaning toward me.

I closed my eyes in anticipation of his kiss but felt disappointment pour through me like a bucket of ice water when he merely brushed his lips against my cheek.

"I'd hate it if you thought I took any liberties," he murmured, a teasing note in his voice.

I opened my eyes to meet his amused gaze. After clearing my throat, I said in as firm a voice as possible, "I do not believe you have taken any liberties."

"I may not have taken any yet, Clarissa," he whispered, "but I thought it only fair to warn you."

He leaned in, gently kissing me with his palms framing my face, fingers caressing my cheeks. This kiss seemed to go on and on, and I quickly lost my breath. I gripped his waist to maintain my balance and sense of place in the world, and kissed him back wholeheartedly. Though passion-filled, his kiss and touch remained gentle, almost reverent. None of the grinding, painful kisses from Cameron that I had thought showed his desire for me. I leaned in closer, not wanting this kiss, this embrace, to end.

Gabriel stepped back, breathing heavily. "Forgive me, Clarissa," he gasped. He held me slightly from him, his hands softly on my shoulders.

"There's nothing to forgive, Mr. McLeod," I said. I reached up to stroke his cheek, feeling the bristle from his late-afternoon stubble rasp the soft skin of my fingers. He leaned into my touch like a cat, and I smiled with unutterable tenderness.

The distant slam of a door jolted me out of my reverie, and I quickly lowered my hand.

"My name is Gabriel, Clarissa," he murmured.

I nodded, meeting his gaze. "Gabriel," I whispered, smiling as I saw his eyes flash with a deep emotion. "Gabriel," I repeated in a stronger voice. "I must go."

"Ah, yes, you must," he agreed. "Send word when I may call?"

"As soon as possible," I vowed.

He lifted my hand, quickly kissing my knuckles. I gathered my purse and departed, glancing at him over my shoulder. He stood still, watching me leave, intense longing in his eyes.

CHAPTER 26

"PENNY FOR YOUR THOUGHTS?" Florence asked as she sailed into my schoolroom. My head jerked up. She cocked her head to one side, studying me inquisitively. "What has you so pensive? You seem a thousand miles away." She smiled as she walked over to the chalkboard to begin erasing today's lesson.

"Florence, please don't become angry with me," I said. She turned to watch me with a small frown. I sighed, placing my hands at my sides instead of wringing them in my anxiousness. "I have been spending more time with Gabriel McLeod, and I really like him. I just don't understand why you don't. What happened between the two of you to cause such animosity?" I asked, speaking in a rush of words.

Florence stopped erasing the chalkboard, watching me with wide eyes. She lowered her arm slowly, setting aside the eraser. Her dress was covered in chalk, and her curly black hair was falling out of its bun to the right side, giving her a lopsided appearance. "It's not a topic I like to discuss," she replied.

"Florence, please," I pleaded. "Help me to understand."

"What is the worst thing to ever happen to you, Clarissa?" Florence asked in a low, pain-stricken voice. Her eyes were filled with a devastation I had never seen before.

"My mama's death," I whispered, unable to speak any louder.

"And yet, when she died, you knew she loved you. She loved you," Florence said it as though a statement but in a questioning voice.

"Of course."

"Not everyone is as lucky as you," Florence said, closing her eyes as though to ward off terrible memories. She held herself horribly still, as if protecting against any further pain.

I again thought of my fragile seashells as I watched her. I approached her slowly, reaching out to touch her arm. "Florence, talk with me. Let me share the burden of this memory," I said. I pulled on her arm, leading her to my chair.

She sat with an ungraceful thud, her skirts crumpling around her. I leaned against my desk, crossed my arms, waited for her to speak.

"Do you remember my story about how my family died?" she asked in a hoarse voice.

"Of course," I replied. "I can't imagine such a loss."

Florence closed her eyes tightly, tears escaping from the corners of her eyes. "That is the story I made up to make myself feel better."

I gaped at her. "Florence, what happened?"

"I'm poor," she sniffled, meeting my eyes.

I nodded.

"I have always been poor. But, when I was a little girl, my family was destitute," she murmured. "My mam had a baby nearly every year, and Pa wasn't much of a worker. Liked to drink more than work." Florence stared over my shoulder, a far-off, distant look in her eye.

"When I was seven, we ran out of food. Ran out of money. Ran out of ways to darn our old clothes. They couldn't be darned again. The holes were too big, the cloth too thin. I've never known such hunger. As though my stomach would eat itself from its emptiness," she said, bitterness lacing her rambling recollection. "Pa talked about his next great job. Talked and talked. But never did anything." Her eyes lit with anger, and another tear escaped.

I gripped her hand attempting to show my support yet not wanting to interrupt her.

"My mam became desperate." Florence's voice cracked. She cleared her throat, continuing in a wobbly tone. "She had five children to feed and another on the way." Florence wiped away her tears as they began to fall more readily. "She brought me to the Home one day, leaving me there. Just leaving me there. Promising to come visit." She closed her eyes, shaking her head from side to side, trying to banish the memories and pain.

"The Home?"

"The Home for Little Wanderers. An orphanage for kids like me. Unwanted or orphaned, we were all the same. Alone in this world," she whispered, opening her pain-filled eyes. "I couldn't understand what I had done to be banished from my family. I had always helped mam, tried to be good. Why me? Why?" She took a deep, shuddering breath, exhaling slowly before continuing to speak carefully. "She promised to come back. To bring me home again. But she never came back. I never saw her again. I never saw any of them again," Florence said in an undertone. "I lived at the Home until I was old enough to go into service at age twelve."

"Twelve?" I asked.

"I didn't have to be very old to do some sort of work," she replied, sniffing. "I went to live in the attic of old Mrs. Kruger. I cooked and cleaned and washed until my hands were raw. I hated my life. I prayed every day for my mam to come, to take me away. To take me away and tell me it had all been a mistake. But she never did.

"Mrs. Kruger didn't treat me badly, but I was just so lonely. The house was quiet, so quiet. Mrs. Kruger had no children, her husband was long dead, and she had few visitors. She spent her days reading, writing.

"After about a year, Mrs. Kruger began to read aloud when I cleaned near her. When I began to ask questions, ask her why she believed certain things, she realized I was interested in learning. She hired another maid to help me with the chores and began to teach me," she said in a choked voice. "She taught me more than I ever learned in any school. I learned later that she considered herself a Brahmin. I knew I would never be more than a maid, but she taught me, gave me confidence. Wanted me. *Me*.

"I was her maid, and yet she had tremendous faith in me," Florence stated. "She insisted I go to school. That I become a teacher," she said. "Mrs. Kruger wanted me to have another way besides service to support myself after she died."

"Where is she now?" I asked.

"She died four years ago," Florence whispered. "Right after my world fell apart again."

"Why tell me the other story about your family?" I asked in a tentative voice, not wanting to sound critical.

"What would you say, Clarissa?" Florence asked. "Would you tell people that your family didn't want you, so they left you at an orphanage, never to see you again? Would you?" Florence demanded. "Would you admit your mother lied to you?" She waved broadly at the room. "Would you acknowledge you have brothers, sisters, out there that you will never know?" she asked, her voice breaking. She brushed at the tears that continued to fall.

"I can't begin to imagine what you went through, Florence, so I don't know what I would have said. Yet, I can't imagine living a lie. Creating a lie to live by for so long."

"That's one of the reasons Gabriel didn't like me," Florence choked out. "My inability to feel regret at having created a different past for myself." She shook her head. "You live a lie long enough, it becomes a sort of truth for you," Florence said in a raspy voice. "But you don't know what it does to you to know you aren't wanted."

"You are wanted, Florence," I said. I leaned forward, gripping her hands. "You are wanted here at the school as an excellent teacher. You are a dear friend to me. I can't tell you how many days I would have been lost without you. Mrs. Kruger obviously wanted you, believed in you. And it's not common for the rich to worry about their maids."

Florence sniffed again. "She was eccentric," she said as a way of agreement. "I know all of that is true, but the people who should have wanted me the most, didn't. And nothing can take away that pain. Nothing."

I nodded. "How did you meet Richard?" I asked.

"We should never have met. Yet we did. Mrs. Kruger loved sweets. Always sent one of us out every day to her favorite bakery. One day, her bakery wasn't open. The sign on the door read Closed for Remodel." Florence smiled, remembering the long-ago day. "I panicked, not knowing what I'd do. I stood outside the door, staring at it, like a simpleton, as though I couldn't read the basic note. Richard was behind me, and he leaned over my shoulder, read it aloud and then looked down at me. I can still see the dimple in his cheek, the amusement in his blue eyes. So handsome."

I blushed, thinking of his brother.

"He had been sent out to buy sweets for his aunt, for an important tea," she mused. "But he knew another good baker, so he led me there." She met my eyes, regret, longing, loss reflected in her eyes. "We met. We continued to meet. We fell in love and were to marry." She paused.

"What happened, Florence?"

"I made a terrible error," she admitted. "An innocent error. But an error." A long pause ensued. "I trusted the wrong person."

I waited for Florence to speak, watching her gather herself, attempting to form the words.

"Richard had told me how much he disliked his aunt, yet I couldn't imagine her being as horrible as she truly was. As she truly is," Florence said. "All I could focus on was that he still had family. Brothers. An aunt, uncle, cousins. People who wanted him. People who took him in after his parents' deaths. I thought that showed love. I hadn't realized it was her way of controlling them. Of punishing her sister in her own way, even though she was dead."

I watched Florence, startled by her insight.

"I adored Gabriel. He was the older brother I had always wanted," she said in a low voice. "He looked out for me, took care of me, teased me and treated me as a McLeod. Made me feel as though I belonged. I had spent over ten years not knowing what that felt like, and suddenly I had people who cared for me and treated me like family. Gabriel defended Richard against his aunt so we could have time together. I think that's why it hurt so much when he turned on me."

"Florence, what happened?" I asked, ready to explode with pent-up nervousness and curiosity.

"Mrs. Masterson found out about me. I'm not sure how as Richard and Gabriel were good at keeping secrets. One day their cousin Henry called at Mrs. Kruger's. Came for tea when no one came for tea. He was tall, handsome and charming. He wanted to meet me. See who had so captured his cousin's fancy." Florence looked away. She turned her gaze back toward me. "I was flattered and unprepared to have such attention paid to me. I was going to school by this time, but, at heart, I was a poor simple orphan girl. He knew what to say to make me feel special, to divulge more than I should.

"He had heard inconsistencies in my story, learned about my coming from the Home. He had made inquiries. He continued to call randomly for a few months. I thought him charming, a cultured counterpoint to Richard's rougher manners. Finally, one day, Henry called for tea with Mrs. Kruger—who by this time had warmed to him—with his mother, Mrs. Masterson. Unbeknownst to me, he somehow knew that Richard and Gabriel were going to arrive in the middle of tea." She closed her eyes momentarily before opening them, exuding anger. "I had begun to drink tea with Mrs. Kruger and her guests. Mrs. Kruger believed that, since I was studying to be a teacher, I should begin to learn how to interact in another social realm.

"I remember that day perfectly. I sat at the round table, practicing what it must be like to be a lady serving tea. Imagining in my mind what it would be like to be Richard's wife. And then, looking up, with the teapot in my hand, in the midst of serving Henry, to see Richard and Gabriel striding through the door." She closed her eyes for a moment, as though the memory were too much for her to bear.

"Winnie had let them in," Florence murmured. "Winnie, the other maid. Richard seemed so happy, so confident. He called out a happy 'hello' to Mrs. Kruger, moving to kiss her on the cheek. He was so good to her," Florence whispered. "He and Gabriel were on the verge of moving out, to a new home. He was to start as an apprentice to Old Man Harris. His spirits were high. In a few years, we'd be able to marry," she continued. "We had everything planned. Then he walked through that doorway, moved to the table, with Gabriel on his heels, to find me serving tea to his cousin and Aunt. His hated cousin and Aunt.

"I hadn't realized, until that moment, I was being played for a fool. A complete fool," she said bitterly, shaking her head. "It seemed as though everything was in slow motion, watching Richard realize who it was. Seeing Gabriel turn nearly red with anger. Hearing Henry talk about me as though I weren't present, talking about my past as though it were common knowledge. My real past. Watching Richard and Gabriel realize I had lied to them. I can still see the sense of betrayal on Richard's face. Then Henry mentioned all of his lovely recent visits for tea, and I thought Gabriel would do me bodily damage. Richard just stood there, frozen." Tears flowed from her eyes. "How could I have been such a fool?"

"You didn't know that would happen, Florence," I replied. "You have faith in people. And they betrayed you."

"I lost everything again!" she wailed, rubbing at the tears pouring down her cheeks. "I lost Richard, Gabriel, my dreams for a future. My hopes for a family. I soon lost Mrs. Kruger. All I had was the training to be a teacher. So, I taught. I've learned not to dream. It doesn't hurt when you don't dream," Florence whispered, pulling out a handkerchief to wipe her face and blow her nose.

"Didn't you try to explain to Richard?" I asked, confused.

"Gabriel wouldn't let me near him. Protected him like one of those over-protective mama bears I've read about. I've never seen anyone so mad before," she said. "And not so again, until I saw him recently. He said horrible, horrible things. He accused me of playing with Richard, stringing him along to meet Henry. To meet someone better. As though I would meet someone better than Richard.

"Gabriel's got a long memory, Rissa. Don't forget that, but he's a good man. Just like his brother." Her voice cracked again, as she bent over at the waist, placing her face in her hands, sobbing.

I patted her gently on the back, uncertain what to say, knowing there was nothing to say. Finally Florence stopped crying. "Florence, come for tea," I urged.

"No, thank you, Rissa. I don't relish being near your stepmother."

She blew her nose again. Her face showed remarkably little effect from her crying, a feat I envied.

"Then let's go out for tea," I encouraged. "My treat."

"No, Clarissa," she said in a stronger voice, balling up the handkerchief in her hand, looking at it. "I'm used to being alone."

"Just because you are used to it, doesn't mean you have to remain alone."

She shook her head, patted my hand as though comforting me and rose. "I hope your curiosity has been satisfied."

"Florence," I replied in a low voice. "That's not fair. I care about you. You're my friend."

I saw her blush and look toward the floor. "Forgive me, Rissa," she whispered. "I have a way of becoming prickly when I feel vulnerable." She met my gaze with a melancholic half smile as she continued to sniffle.

I smiled slowly, gripping her hand. "I know exactly what you need," I murmured. "You need to meet my friend, Sophie. Let's call on her for tea."

"Oh, I couldn't," Florence protested, running a hand down the front of her gown.

"You can and you will," I argued, brooking no refusal today. "Let's go."

CHAPTER 27

I MARCHED DOWN THE STREET, almost towing Florence along beside me, my arm hooked through hers. I refused to allow her to walk separately, as I knew she would flee at the first opportunity. Today we climbed over the Hill to Beacon Street. I was hopeful the exertions would clear my mind of the roiling thoughts Florence's story had unleashed. I could not fathom my family giving me away. I did not want to imagine what that would do to my spirit.

We arrived at Sophie's, breathless and in desperate need of refreshment. The green shutters gleamed in the sunlight next to the windows, and we stood in front of the green door. Carriages bustled past on Beacon Street, I heard children playing in the Common, and birds trilled in the trees above us. I grasped the brass knocker, tapping loudly on the door, waiting impatiently for the butler to answer. Florence stood beside me.

"Oh, it's you, miss," the formally attired butler intoned, not waiting for a card. "I will determine if Mrs. Chickering is at home."

Florence and I entered the subdued entranceway, the upper walls a pale mauve satin wallpaper and the bottom half a crisp white wainscoting. "I really shouldn't be here," Florence pleaded, eyeing the door.

"If you will follow me," the butler interrupted any response I might have given. We turned to follow him upstairs into the front parlor. Sophie sat alone on a comfortable settee, reading a book that she set down with a loud *thunk* upon our entrance. Her aquamarine eyes flashed with curiosity upon seeing me enter with Florence. Her emerald-green bombazine dress complimented the yellow satin of the matching parlor suite.

The room, filled with the parlor suite and a smattering of side tables, had a welcoming air with overflowing ferns sitting in a bow-fronted window and books scattered throughout. Instead of walls covered with overlapping paintings, there was one focal painting of a mountain glen, with light sparkling through the branches at dawn.

"Harrumph," she grumbled. "You've finally decided to return." She glared at me in a scolding manner.

"I'm sorry, Sophie. Life has become quite hectic of late," I replied, smiling. I knew she was not truly angry with me.

"And you are?" Sophie turned toward Florence, setting her bright, almost fierce, aquamarine eyes on Florence.

"I am Florence, Florence Butler, ma'am," Florence said, a hint of steel in her tone. "I work with Clarissa at the school."

"And are you a suffragette?" Sophie demanded.

"No."

"No? No?" Sophie gasped out. "What is this nonsense, bringing such a girl by, Clarissa?"

I laughed. "Sophie, she may not have dedicated her time to the cause, but she's forward thinking. Maybe more so than you or I am."

Florence was embarrassed and refused to say any more.

"Well, girl, speak up," Sophie demanded. "What are your thoughts on the vote? On women's rights?" She leaned back against her chair, watching Florence.

"I would like to have the vote," Florence responded. "I would like to have the ability to express what I want."

"What about leaving it to the men in your life to do just that for you?" Sophie challenged.

"Well, as I have no men in my life, there is no one to look out for my interests. And I find that most have a very limited view of charity," Florence said. She reached for her cup of tea, the cup rattling slightly, betraying her nerves.

"Well said," Sophie nearly cheered. "I like this girl, Clarissa."

"I knew you would," I said with a broad smile.

"How come you haven't visited sooner?" Sophie asked Florence, picking up a biscuit to nibble on.

"I, ah, well, I…"

Sophie looked over her clothes with an assessing eye. "You are rather shabbily dressed. Were you afraid your poverty would prevent you from being received?" At Florence's blush, Sophie snorted. "Nonsense, girl," she said. "We need more strong hardworking women like you in the movement. Women who actually know what it is to toil for a living wage, rather than those who sit around drinking tea and gossiping all day long." She eyed Florence again, taking in her slight discomfort at the surroundings. "Tell me, Florence, a bit about your background."

"Oh, I, ah, it's really not that interesting," Florence stammered.

"It's always interesting to me," Sophie encouraged with a small smile.

"Before I started teaching, I worked for Mrs. Kruger as a maid," she said.

"Mrs. Kruger? Old Mrs. Kruger who lived in Chester Square?" Sophie beamed. "She was a fine old woman, wasn't she?" Her tone was nearly reverent as she spoke of her.

"Chester Square?" I asked at almost the same time, incredulous that Florence had lived in the South End, and I had never met her.

"You knew Mrs. Kruger?" Florence asked Mrs. Chickering.

"I did. Though to my everlasting regret, I did not give her the time she merited. I always intended to call, sending my card numerous times but failed to show," Sophie stated. "She had a keen mind, extraordinarily curious about the world. Far too advanced for the age she had been born into."

"Yes, well, she treated me quite well and helped to see to my future," Florence said.

"You were fortunate indeed, dear, to work for one such as her," Sophie intoned. "So now you teach the downtrodden at the same school as my girl Clarissa?"

"Yes, I specialize in the home economics courses, though I am trained in all subjects," Florence murmured.

"Which is a good thing, as I am absolutely dreadful with anything to do with the home arts, and she constantly saves me from being reprimanded by the school board," I interjected.

"Are you telling me that you will not be able to run a successful home and create a pleasing home environment?" Sophie demanded with an evil twinkle in her eye.

"I doubt it would meet my stepmother's standards." I giggled. Sophie began to chortle, too.

"Ah, that woman is insufferable. Count yourself fortunate if you have never met her, Florence," Sophie said.

I saw Florence glance at the clock on the mantel. "I am dreadfully sorry to have to leave," she said. "I have a prior engagement and must go."

I watched her through slitted eyes, not believing her ruse, but decided not to press her. I clasped her hand. "Thank you for joining me today, Flo."

"You are always welcome for tea, Florence Butler," Sophie said. "I should like to discuss Mrs. Kruger more with you."

After Florence's hasty departure, I leaned back against my chair, relaxing. "Thank you for being so friendly and kind to Florence."

"She seems a lost soul," Sophie said, watching me.

"She is. She has no one in this world. No family. Nothing."

"*Humph*," Sophie grunted. "As long as she has good friends, she will never be truly alone." After a short pause, "I am disappointed, my girl."

I raised my eyebrows, certain I had done nothing to disappoint her.

"You were not at the celebration for Mrs. Ward-Howe."

"But I was," I protested, though I did not relish reliving that day.

"Why weren't you on the porch with the rest of us?" Sophie demanded, glowering at me.

"I was informed by Gertrude and Mrs. Cushing that, because I wasn't on the committee, I wasn't allowed on the porch."

"Nonsense!" Sophie hissed. "I can't imagine such insolence."

I shrugged.

"You mean to tell me that you were down in that crowd?"

This time I nodded.

Sophie sighed. "It's all my fault you know. It's because the younger ones dislike me and are trying to show their mettle that they treat you like that."

"Well, suffice it to say, it wasn't my ideal afternoon," I murmured, refusing to dwell further on the memory of the crowd, the jostling for position, the sense that I would be crushed.

"Harrumph," Sophie said, causing me to laugh.

We sat in companionable silence a few moments. "Sophie, I do not have your backbone," I admitted with a long sigh.

"Clarissa, my girl, tell me what the matter is so I can help you dispel it," Sophronia said, her tone expressing she had no doubt of her ability.

"I watch you interact with the other suffragettes and with my stepmother, and I see how strong you are. I see how passionate you are in your beliefs. I am amazed at your ability to communicate them and persuade others to your way of thinking. I do not have such an ability."

"What is this nonsense?"

"Sophie, a few times, when I have been pushed about my beliefs, I back down, rather than start an argument. Isn't that wrong?" I said. "Shouldn't I stand up, express myself?"

"It's not wrong knowing the time and the place to say your piece. And for my part, there's never a better place to speak your mind than with a group of suffragettes. If you can't with them, you can't anywhere," she said with another *harrumph*. She pinned me with a humor-filled look. "And I particularly enjoyed irritating your stepmother."

"How did you have a full life, marriage, children and also suffragism?" I asked. "Do you think your husband would have approved?"

She eyed me over her teacup, taking a dainty sip of oolong. "So this is about a man?" At my faint blush, she chortled. "Ah, dear, I know some of the suffragettes, including Susan, never espoused marriage. But to the right man, it can be wonderful. You simply must take care and choose the correct one."

"You make it sound so simple," I replied, thoughts of Gabriel flitting through my mind. Sophie merely laughed, reminding me that she had raised daughters and must be used to such antics.

"Tell me about your young man," Sophie demanded.

"Gabriel is…he is…" I paused finding it difficult to summarize. "He is the antithesis of Cameron. Dark. Moody. Intense. Loyal. Intriguing." I sighed. "He loves to read, is curious about the world. Dreams of travel and adventure."

"Fascinating," Sophronia said. "What worries you?"

"That he seems to support my teaching and beliefs now, but will that all change if we were to marry, have children? Do men always change?" I asked in confusion and frustration.

"No more than we do, dearest," Sophie replied with a wry quirk on her lips. "We change just as much, though no one likes to admit it. Only you can decide if he is worth taking that risk. Otherwise, if your teaching and beliefs are that important to you, you need to remain single."

"How were you able to have a family and be a suffragette? Did your husband understand your need for, oh, I don't know, *more*?" I asked, leaning forward.

"You must remember, Clarissa, that, though I had a wonderful husband who was very supportive, he died early in our marriage. I have no idea if he would have supported my beliefs, and we were never tested in that way. By the time he died, I had three young children to care for, but he had thankfully left me a very wealthy young widow." Sophie stared into the painting on the far wall for a few moments.

"Never underestimate the importance of financial independence, my girl. I had this lovely house, maids, nannies, others to help me with the day-to-day running of my life. After I finished the worst of my mourning, I had freedom—such a luxurious, rare commodity—to discover what truly interested me. And so I did."

In the ensuing silence, I considered her words.

"Do you know what I find interesting as you talked about your young man?" Sophie asked, watching me with intense but wicked humor in her eyes.

I shook my head, uncertain how I could have amused her.

"I find it fascinating that in no part of that description did you talk about his physical characteristics."

"Oh, well, I could if you like," I stammered out.

"No, I am only remarking that it bodes well that it is not merely the physical that has you enthralled," Sophie replied.

I nodded my agreement.

"It means that you don't want one of those silly so-called happy and 'get with' marriages," Sophronia said.

"Get with?"

"Where you think you're so happy, you get with child every year, and you're dead from exhaustion by age thirty-five," Sophie said. "I hope you would want more than that."

I blushed fiercely at the thought of having Gabriel's child. I nodded again, out of breath all of a sudden.

"And now, my girl," she said with a small chuckle, glancing at the clock, "I am afraid your stepmother would become quite cross if I kept you here any longer."

"Thank you for tea, Sophie," I said. "I will try to call again soon, although things will be hectic with my cousin's upcoming wedding."

"I shall look forward to reading about it in the papers," Sophie said with another of her wicked smiles.

***

I DETOURED THROUGH THE PUBLIC GARDENS, walking along a path that hugged the pond containing the swan boats. The air smelled sweet from the blooming roses, and birds flitted from tree to tree, singing their songs. I exited onto Arlington Street and paused at the street corner as carriages and carts rushed by. I crossed over, passing a small crowd waiting to board an arriving trolley headed toward the South End.

At that moment, someone grabbed my arm and spun me around. I gasped, shocked to be treated in such a way. "Cameron!" I wrenched at my arm, but he would not release me, and I feared he would rip my light jacket. "Let me go."

"No, Clarissa, I must speak with you. I am surprised you felt the need to have Colin protect you at school."

"So it *was* you Colin saw," I said with another angry twist of my arm.

"Yes, he prevented me from speaking with you in a civilized way."

"If you wanted to act cultured, Cameron, you would call at my house. Al-

though it wouldn't matter. I have no desire to speak with you now or ever again."
I stomped down with the heel of my boot, crushing his toes. He cried out in
pain, releasing my arm.

I spun toward the trolley that was just leaving the stop, grabbing onto the
bar to pull myself onto the steps. I tripped but held onto the bar and landed
with a thud on the trolley's floor. I heaved myself to my feet, glancing back to
see Cameron glaring at me. As the trolley moved away, I shivered, for the first
time afraid of Cameron.

***

I SAT IN MY BEDROOM that evening, staring out the back window at the
canopy of trees. A deep unease filled me as I thought of Cameron and his recent
actions. I listened intently to the sounds of the house, hearing Colin and da's
booming voices as they returned from the smithy. Rising from my seat by the
window, I tiptoed to my door, waiting for Colin to ascend the stairs and change
for dinner.

"Colin," I whispered. His head jerked up and he frowned to see me hiding
in my room. He was covered in soot with blackened hands. However, he moved
toward me and I opened the door allowing him to enter my room.

"I have to wash and dress for dinner. What's the matter, Rissa?" He reached
out as though he were going to stroke my arm, but then stopped when he realized he would leave a black smear on my dusky rose satin dress. Instead, he
crossed his arms across his chest and frowned at me.

"I saw Cameron today."

His eyes flashed with anger. "What did he want?"

"To speak with me," I said, taking a deep breath to battle the panic I felt at
remembering my interaction with Cameron. "I had to jump onto a departing
trolley to evade him."

"The bas-. Did he touch you? Did he hurt you?" His hands were now fisted
at his sides.

"Yes, he gripped my arm, but I'm fine."

Colin reached out and pushed my sleeve up. "You'll have a bruise, Rissa."

"I'm sorry, Col."

"For what, Rissa? You've done nothing to encourage him. He's the one who
should be ashamed."

"But you know how things are, Col. If he is acting this way, people will say
it is because I must be doing something to entice him," I whispered, unable to

meet his eyes. "What if my visits to see Gabriel become known? I will seem like a woman vying for the attention of two men. I will be seen as a woman who doesn't know the bounds of propriety."

"You, as a suffragette, must know better than that. And when have you ever cared what people say? Or about propriety?" He chucked me under the chin and I met his gaze. His attempt at levity failed to hide his anxiety at my news. "Now you're so dirty with soot you'll need to wash up for dinner, too."

"Col, I can't tell Da. He'll stop me from teaching. He'll insist I stay at home. I can't be forced to spend my days with Mrs. Smythe."

"I'll talk with him, but you have to be willing to accept what he says. What's most important is ensuring you are safe."

I nodded my agreement and Colin winked before he slipped out the door.

CHAPTER 28

"LUCAS," I CALLED OUT. "Lucas!" I thought I had seen Lucas hurrying up the steps into the Old Howard Theater as I neared Scollay Square the following day, but he did not respond to my call. Uncertain if I would be allowed inside, I rushed toward the theater, holding onto my hat, any rapid movement hampered by my long skirts.

My day had so far been uneventful, and I had been thankful for its normalcy. I felt worn- out emotionally after my recent encounters with Gabriel, Florence and Cameron, and relished a quiet day. Florence had apologized for leaving Sophronia's abruptly, having had an unsuccessful meeting with a society matron about summer tutoring.

I had promised da, after a tense discussion the previous evening in his study, that I would come straight home each day after school. Due to a trolley accident backing up all traffic on Cambridge Street, I had decided I could keep my promise by walking to Scollay Square and boarding one of the underground subway trains. However, after I saw Lucas entering the Old Howard Theater, I decided to postpone my train ride home. Hopefully, he would be able to escort me home and I was curious what he was doing in the West End.

I reached the steps to the Old Howard, a bit fearful about entering the theater unchaperoned on a Friday afternoon. I took a deep breath for courage before ascending the steps, marveling at the three large Gothic-inspired arched glass windows heralding its previous life as a church. As the door squeaked and clunked shut behind me, any resemblance to a church disappeared.

In the dim hallway, I made out plush red rugs and gilt chairs and mirrors, while the faint scent of stale cologne and cheap perfume wafted around me. I heard laughter from the backstage area, imagining the various vaudeville members and burlesque showgirls arriving in preparation for the evening entertainments.

I crept inside and waited for a few moments for someone to catch me skulking in the shadows, but no one arrived. I walked down the dark hallway, belatedly realizing there was a doorway covered in velvet to my right. I poked my head through the curtain into the main theater area.

Only a few electric lights weakly illuminated the stage area, casting long shadows across most of it and the remainder of the theater. I entered into the box nearest the doorway, absently noting the plush red velvet chairs and the flowing curtains on either side of the stage. I focused my attention on the dimly lit stage, where three pianos stood forming a small oval. All three were occupied, two by handsome black men and one by Lucas.

I did not recognize the song they played, and they seemed to be composing and competing with each other as the song progressed. I watched, entranced and fascinated, as I had never seen Lucas so animated and happy. I sat in awe as he kept pace with the other players.

I quickly became lost in the joyous, playful music, so different from the ponderous, plodding church hymns preferred by Mrs. Smythe. After nearly an hour of sitting quietly, they stopped playing. I could see Lucas laughing, before he stood to shake hands with both men and leave.

Through luck or misfortune, he chose to walk up the aisle that would bring him directly past me. He stopped short as he caught sight of me, eyes flaring with concern.

"Rissa!" he whispered. "What are you doing here?" He glanced toward the stage to see the two men watching us.

I stood, reaching out to him, wonder in my voice and expression. "Lucas, that was the most amazing music! I wish I could hear you play like this all the time."

He grabbed my elbow and ushered me out of the theater into the dark hallway. I became momentarily blinded in the unlit hall and tripped over a small wrinkle in the rug, nearly causing us to fall. Lucas kept a tight grip on my arm, leading me to the front and out of the theater's creaky door.

I turned toward Lucas, happiness continuing to fill me at the music I had heard, only to see him glaring down at me.

"What could you possibly have been thinking, Rissa?" he demanded angrily. "Don't you realize that could have been very dangerous for you, to wander into a darkened, almost empty theater?"

"Lucas, I called out to you, tried to catch your attention."

"What if it hadn't been me?" he demanded.

"I would at least have enjoyed the music."

Lucas shook his head, continuing to look away, seemingly embarrassed before he met my eyes. "You liked it?" he asked, with a cautious, hopeful expression.

"No, I loved it," I replied with a full smile. "As I said inside, I wish you could play like that all the time."

"Well, you are almost the only one in the family to think so," he replied with a hint of bitterness, continuing to propel me down the steps. He turned away from the trolley stop, dragging me toward a hole-in-the-wall tea and coffee shop on Cornhill Street off bustling Scollay Square.

The shabby establishment—with tattered upholstered chairs, scarred wooden tabletops and sooted ceiling—was a far cry from the tea shops with polished marble-topped tables I was accustomed to. Today it suited Lucas, away from the linen store and no longer dressed at the height of fashion.

Lucas collapsed into a chair, groaning softly. He watched me for a few moments before speaking. "I wish Father and Mother could understand my desire to play music not heard at church." He sighed. "To play at all," he murmured.

"I doubt they truly understand how much you love it," I said, reaching out to take his hand. "If you don't tell them, or play for them, displaying your joy as you just did, they will never know."

"You saw what happened with Mrs. Smythe."

"I wouldn't judge your parents' reaction by hers," I muttered. "Lucas, what is it that you would really like to do with your life?"

"I like working with my father. I do, Rissa," he said just a bit too forcefully. "It's just that I would prefer to play the piano all day. Be a musician. But that will not happen. I would never make a living on that, and I couldn't do that to Father. He has dreams that the linen shop should go to my son, if the day ever comes to pass that I have a child."

"Lucas, you should be happy," I said, frowning.

Lucas continued to play with my fingers for a few more minutes, before letting them go with a long sigh. He began to tap the tabletop as though it were a piano keyboard with the fingers of his left hand. "Rissa, life isn't always about attaining all of our dreams. There are times you have to compromise on some of them, for your family or for your own well-being."

"Then what is the point of dreams?"

"Just don't become so blinded by your dreams and how you envision your future that you let life pass you by," Lucas said.

"But aren't you just letting life pass you by, by not following your dreams?" I countered.

"I can see that neither of us will win this argument," he replied with a laugh, glancing up to order a pot of tea for me and a coffee for himself from the waitress. "Rissa, I know, and have known, my destiny since I was a young boy. I am to run my father's shop. There is very little I can do to change that. I will have a good living, play piano music in the evenings. Continue to buy cheap sheet music now that it has become available. And I will think myself content."

He looked anything but content as he described his life. I remembered the unadulterated joy I had seen as he had played with the other musicians, and I wished that were Lucas's future. "I just wish," I began, and then stopped, realizing anything I wished for him he would already have dreamt of before. I would never want to cause Lucas pain, so I stopped speaking.

"I know, Rissa. That is what makes you such a good cousin and friend," he replied. He clasped my hand again before leaning away as the coffee and tea were delivered.

"Colin tells me that you've gone to see that Gabriel McLeod a few times at his warehouse." Lucas's eyes, generally so friendly, challenged me.

I gasped involuntarily, confirming his statement. "Lucas…" I began but was cut short by his whispered tirade.

"What on earth could you have been thinking? You know how much this could damage your reputation. You could even be forced to *marry* him," Lucas snarled.

"Don't be ridiculous," I said although I felt a small thrill at the thought.

"Do you want to give up teaching? Do you want to spend all your days at home with Mrs. Smythe?" Lucas continued. "If your da is angry enough, he could make you stop teaching. Or the school board could find you unfit. Immoral."

"Lucas, calm down," I entreated.

"Calm down? Calm down? Clarissa, I thought you were the sensible one. After Cameron, I thought you'd wait, find someone acceptable, someone who wouldn't hurt you. You know we don't think Gabriel is acceptable for you."

"Why am I the sensible one? Can't I have hopes and dreams for myself that are independent of my family's? Shouldn't you want me to find someone who treats me well and seems to generally want and like *me*? And who are you to decide who is acceptable?"

"Sav's making the monumental mistake of marrying Jonas, and there's not a thing I can do to stop her," Lucas said, fire flashing in his eyes at Jonas's name. "I don't want to see you suffer a similar fate."

He moved to push back his chair and stand. I gripped his hand, trying to prevent him from leaving. "Lucas," I called out, but he tore his hand from mine and strode out of the coffee shop.

I sat in stunned silence, uncertain exactly how our conversation had ended so poorly. I jolted as someone sat down across from me, taking Lucas's place.

"Seems as stuffy and pompous now as the first time I saw him," Richard commented with a wry smile.

I sighed, relaxing in his company. "Hello, Mr. McLeod," I murmured.

He smiled as he signaled for a new cup of coffee. He settled his tall, broad-shouldered frame into the chair, his eyes sparkling with merriment. "Is he ever in an agreeable mood?"

"Yes, he's just upset with me at the moment."

"Why should he be?"

"Lucas is simply overprotective of me. Like Colin."

"Then Colin has a strange way of showing his protective nature, leaving you behind with Gabe at the warehouse."

I blushed, realizing I wouldn't easily win this argument. However, I hoped I had turned his attention away from Lucas.

"Rich, leave her alone," Gabriel said, pulling up another chair with a loud scraping noise, sitting next to me. His eyes flashed with pleasure as he looked at me. His work clothes were free of their habitual dust, and he wore a faded black coat with no tie.

"Gabriel!" I gasped, my mind immediately returning to our kiss.

"I hadn't realized you were joining us for coffee, Clarissa," Gabriel said, watching me with warm tenderness.

"I wasn't. I'm sorry to intrude. I was here with Lucas, but he became upset and left," I said quickly. I stopped speaking and bit my lip, worried I might begin to ramble.

"Lucas, the friendly cousin?" Gabriel asked as he shared an amused glance with Richard.

I glared at Gabriel, refraining from responding, causing Richard to laugh. Gabriel leaned back into his chair, seeming completely at ease.

"What upset him?" Gabriel asked, nodding his thanks as a cup of coffee was delivered.

"I discovered something that he keeps hidden from the family, and he seemed upset by that. Then he abruptly changed the topic onto you and me"—I nodded toward Gabriel—"and he became increasingly agitated as he spoke of you until he finally left."

"Something hidden from the family?" Richard asked.

"Don't get any ideas, Mr. McLeod," I muttered. "A secret hobby that brings him tremendous pleasure but of which his parents greatly disapprove."

"A secret hobby?" Gabriel and Richard shared amused glances. "What could that be?" Gabriel asked. Then he and Richard began to toss ideas back and forth in rapid-fire succession.

"Dancing on the stage with a boa?"

"Or the cancan in all its finery?" Richard asked with a wriggle of his eyebrows.

"Singing vaudeville songs?"

"Telling jokes like a comedian with a dancing monkey as his sidekick?" Richard countered.

"Stop!" I gasped, laughing hard. "No, it's nothing like that. He just likes to play the piano." I clapped my hand over my mouth.

"Oh, well, that's rather boring." Richard sighed, shaking his head in disappointment. "I would hardly consider that a secret worth guarding."

"There's more that you aren't telling," Gabriel said watching me.

"No, no more. You two are a menace. I have already said too much," I replied.

Gabriel smiled back, reaching out to hold my hand under the table for a moment. I gripped his hand firmly in return. I thought fleetingly of Florence, realizing this was what she was missing and suddenly comprehended all she had lost.

Another long sigh came from Richard. "Now I am stuck with two lovebirds."

I jolted, letting go of Gabriel's hand. "No, well, yes, but I hope you are not uncomfortable with us," I stammered.

Richard seemed on the verge of laughing again before he ungraciously kicked Gabriel in the leg, his eyes arrested on someone who had just entered the little coffee shop. My back, partially to the door, prevented me from seeing the person.

"Clarissa," Gabriel whispered, leaning casually away and looking formidable and cold, "act as though you can't stand us, and we are bothering you."

I stared at him and Richard in confusion but finally nodded after another fierce glare from him and a grunt of agreement from Richard. I attempted to calm my racing heart, placing a bored, nearly disgusted look on my face. I looked down, not wishing to see Richard or Gabriel—who had recently seemed so happy—now so angry.

A few moments later, a pair of fine, perfectly polished black leather shoes came into my view. I slowly glanced up, noting expensive black satin pants covering wirily thin legs, a garish mauve waistcoat and black jacket. A black top hat remained in place over dull dishwater-brown hair. I raised an eyebrow at the extravagant clothes for a visit to a shabby coffeehouse.

"Henry," Gabriel drawled, thinly veiled menace in his voice, "lovely to see you here. So good to see you've recovered." At this came a small snicker from Richard who refrained from speaking.

Henry fisted his hands, stepping forward as though he wanted to do battle. However, as I looked over his thin, fragile-looking form, I hoped he had the sense to refrain from challenging the muscular McLeod brothers. "If he," Henry said, pointing to Richard, "had even a sliver of decency, he would have ensured I had returned to good health."

"Well, there's no need to, now that you've found us at our favorite coffee shop and shown us to be in such fine form," Richard taunted.

"I almost needed a doctor," Henry whined in a high-pitched effeminate voice. His pale brown eyes squinted together as though he needed glasses but was too vain to use them.

"The key word there, dear cousin, was 'almost,'" Gabriel replied without a shred of sympathy in his voice.

"How can you be so unfeeling to your own flesh and blood?" Henry nearly wailed. "When I think of all that Mother did, taking in you worthless lot after the timely death of your parents, I am appalled you do not do more to express your thanks."

He appeared upset, though I sensed that he relished the opportunity to cause any possible mischief in his cousins' lives.

"Yes, we know all about your mother's charity and generosity, especially when it came to the rod," Richard drawled, reaching out to grip Gabriel's forearm to prevent him from rising.

"It is so appalling, having relations such as you," Henry continued in a loud, carrying voice. From the little I could see, he had begun to attract a small audience.

"If you have a shred of self-preservation in you, you should walk out that door and not cross my path for the next decade," Gabriel ground out in a menacing voice, his arms strung taut as though on the verge of striking.

Henry nodded, seeming quite pleased with the havoc he had wrought. He spun on his polished heel and left.

"Gabe, calm down now," Richard demanded, still holding onto his arm.

He and Gabriel shared a long look, until Richard finally released his arm.

Gabriel let out a low grunt, leaning heavily against the back of his chair.

"The bastard," Gabriel hissed. "What the hell does he mean by the *timely death* of our parents? What right does he have to come in here and stir things up?"

"You know he only does it because he knows he can bother you," I murmured. "He knows your most sensitive subject and finds great joy at poking at it." I smiled at him trying to express my sympathy at having such a cousin.

A fleeting look of embarrassment passed over Gabriel's face. He glanced at me with tenderness, reaching out to grip my hand gently. "I'm just thankful he didn't focus on you," he murmured.

"I agree," I said. "And with that being said, I must head home. I shouldn't tempt fate further and I promised my da." I gripped Gabriel's hand once more and then reluctantly rose. "Shall I see you again soon?"

"Yes, Clarissa, soon," Gabriel responded. I beamed at him before I twirled to leave. Upon reaching the door, I turned back to find him and Richard both watching me. I gave a small wave, before slipping outside the door to home.

CHAPTER 29

I SAT IN THE RUSSELL FAMILY PARLOR on the overstuffed Rococo settee, listening to Savannah and Aunt Matilda argue about wedding decorations. I smiled every few moments in an attempt to act as though I were listening. Instead, I thought about Gabriel. I had been unable to invite him to call as I had promised so he could begin to formally court me. All of my evenings had been filled with wedding preparations for Savannah and I saw no end in sight as a round of prewedding soirees was about to begin. The three of us heard a large whoop of delight from the store, and I bolted up, using any excuse for an escape, bustling down the stairs to the store doorway.

I peered in to see Lucas enfolding a small woman in his strong arms. He almost lifted her off the ground in his enthusiasm. A cane clunked to the ground, and I held my breath. Finally Lucas released the short, plump woman, and she turned with Lucas's aid to face me. Her blue-green eyes shone with delight as she tottered toward me without the aid of her cane.

"Aunt Betsy!" I shrieked, running toward her to hug her. I had to be careful not to crush her in my exuberance. Savannah rushed forward too, although she realized we had an audience with store customers. She ushered us quickly through the doorway adjoining the store into the hallway and rear rooms. The curtains to the store closed behind us, allowing us privacy for our reunion with Aunt Betsy. We took turns embracing Aunt Betsy, with Aunt Matilda the last to greet her sister, tears of delight in her eyes.

"What a joy to see you here, dear sister," Aunt Matilda effused. "And here I thought I would have to remember all the details to write you an in-depth letter. What a joy." She sighed, gripping her sister's arm. We quietly moved to the family parlor.

Aunt Betsy laboriously made her way up the stairs, finally settling in a high gentleman's seat, grimacing as she attempted to find a comfortable position.

I glanced at her with a small frown as I stood over her. "Aunt Betsy, is there anything that I can do to help you with your discomfort?"

"Clarissa, what a dear." She patted my cheek. "No, thank you. I am fine. Just a little sore from my journey." She leaned her head against the chair, closing her eyes and taking deep breaths. After a few moments, she appeared to gather herself and turned to look at me fully.

I once again settled on the nearby settee.

"You look radiant, Clarissa. Any developments in your life?"

I cringed, wishing for Savannah to remain the focus of attention. "Everything is the same, Aunt. I continue to teach. I am very excited for Savannah and her wedding." I smiled at Savannah, hoping to deflect any interest toward her.

"I hear that Cameron is back," Aunt Betsy murmured, watching me. Her pale blue eyes seemed almost green and changed color depending on what she wore. Her rheumatism made her hunch over, making her even smaller than she really was. At barely five feet and slightly plump, she liked calling my brothers and Lucas her giants.

"Yes, he is back, though it really does not affect me." My voice was flat, emotionless. I realized that I had very little feeling left to spare Cameron. My thoughts were filled with Gabriel.

Aunt Betsy continued to study me a few moments, before turning to Savannah. "Savannah dearest, do bring me up-to-date with the newest arrangements," Aunt Betsy coaxed.

Savannah began regaling us all with wedding plans, expressing concerns about the timing of her arrival at the church, worries that the cake would not be fresh enough if it were baked the day before and other such trivialities.

I heard Aunt Betsy murmur, "Yes, I can imagine your concern about the cake, dear. It will be a large cake with so many guests?"

At Savannah's absent nod, she continued to discuss the flowers and the reception, becoming less enthused the more she spoke. As she talked, my mind wandered, thinking back to my wedding day, and I realized what an uncomplicated wedding I had planned. I remembered the unalloyed joy I had felt while waiting upstairs in my bedroom for Cameron to arrive for our simple ceremony, to be had at home, followed by the small reception with plain food, but plenty of time to converse with friends and family. I had never imagined the pain to come.

"The wedding will be in the church, dear?" inquired Aunt Betsy.

"Yes, Betsy," replied Aunt Matilda, rather stiffly. "The numerous guests invited dictated the necessity of using the church."

"That's a shame, dear," murmured Aunt Betsy. "I would have thought a home wedding would have been just the thing." She quietly sipped her tea, watching Savannah.

"Yes, well, adjustments needed to be made, and using the church due to the number of guests Jonas and the grandparents wanted to invite was necessary," Savannah said.

"Betsy, quit stirring up trouble!" Aunt Matilda admonished. "All will be fine with the church. The reception will be in the church hall. We will have cake there, and then Savannah and Jonas will take their leave and go on their honeymoon. Isn't that right, dear?"

Savannah by this time looked ghostly white, and I worried she would soon faint. She nodded vaguely.

"Where are you going on your honeymoon, Savannah?" queried Aunt Betsy.

"Jonas would like to take me to New York City," Savannah said, fidgeting with the edge of her shawl. "If you will all excuse me, I have a headache. I think I will lie down." Savannah rushed from the room.

Aunt Betsy continued to stare at the doorway for a few moments and then turned to look at her sister. "Well, Matilda?"

Aunt Matilda let out a long sigh. "I don't know what is wrong with her. She doesn't seem herself these days. I tell myself it is nerves due to the wedding, but Clarissa wasn't like this before her wedding. Well, her *near* wedding." She threw an apologetic glance in my direction. "I don't know if I should be alarmed. Martin advises me to stay calm as it will run its course."

"Well, someone needs to speak with her, determine if this is truly what she wants," Aunt Betsy advised. "I'd hate for Savannah to be hurt because she is fulfilling someone else's dream."

"What do you mean?" I interjected.

Aunt Betsy shared a long look with Aunt Matilda, holding up her hand toward Matilda. "Let me say my piece, Mattie. She has earned the right to know how *I* feel, at least." Aunt Matilda settled into her chair with pursed lips, upset but unwilling to disagree with her sister.

Aunt Betsy began to speak, carefully choosing her words. "Clarissa, you must know by now that our parents are wonderful people, but very determined to have their way. When your mother, may she rest in peace, and Aunt Matilda married for love, it was my duty to marry well. I, in some ways, felt as though I were the sacrificial lamb for the family. Be that as it may, I did marry well and, thankfully, came to love my husband. Even so, if I had been given the freedom to choose my own husband, I might have had a very different life." Her voice held only a trace of rancor.

"Do you regret marrying Uncle Tobias?"

"No, I will never regret marrying him, as I refuse to regret so many years of my life. I do wish I had been able to have children, but that was my fate. I am now beginning to worry that the past may be repeating itself." With this, Aunt Betsy exchanged a long look with Aunt Matilda.

"Betsy, don't start," Aunt Matilda said with a warning note in her voice.

"Mattie, just because you have rarely been in their good graces since marrying Martin doesn't mean you should sacrifice your only living daughter to them to regain their favor. Think about that. *Please,*" Aunt Betsy implored, leaning forward, her tiny body vibrating a sense of urgency.

"And if Savannah truly wishes to wed Jonas?" Aunt Matilda stated, flushing.

"Then she should receive all of our blessings and support," Aunt Betsy replied with a quiet nod for emphasis. "Now, I think I, too, would like a bit of rest before supper. Clarissa, would you see me to my room?"

She rose, giving me her arm. We left the parlor, with Aunt Matilda deep in thought.

Upon entering Aunt Betsy's room—a simple guest room done in a pale green with a large window, a bed, washstand and sitting chair—I tried to leave.

"No, Clarissa, sit and speak with me for a few minutes. I sense there is much still left unsaid."

I watched her carefully, afraid of revealing too much. "I'm not sure what you mean, Aunt Betsy."

"Clarissa, I know there is much you are not telling me. What is truly happening in your life? How are you feeling about the return of Cameron? I would have thought you would be much more upset about it than you appear to be."

She sat on the edge of the bed, waving me toward the chair. I sat.

"I am coping well, Aunt. I have spoken with him a few times, and I have realized that there is no reason to continue to expend energy or emotion on him," I replied.

"Truly, Clarissa? You seemed so in love two years ago. What were his reasons for failing to show at the wedding?" Aunt Betsy seemed confused, as though trying to decipher a riddle. In many ways, her expression reminded me of Gabriel and the way he watched me. She subtly adjusted herself on the bed to find a more comfortable position, patiently waiting for me to speak.

I cleared my throat, stalling for time. "Well, uh, he felt trapped and felt the only way to escape was not to attend the wedding."

"That doesn't seem right, dear," Aunt Betsy replied. "I remember the two of you together, and I cannot recall a couple more in love. You were perfectly matched. Something must have happened."

"If something happened, as you state, he has not admitted to it. I cannot spend any more time on him," I said in a firm tone.

I met her eyes with a hint of defiance. Embarrassment washed through me again that he had not wanted to associate with my family, like a wave that crested and receded, but always brought pain and discord when it returned.

"Clarissa, I know it hurt you terribly when he failed to show at the house. There was no note, no explanation… You must want to know why," Aunt Betsy persisted, watching me closely, her too-perceptive eyes taking in all my expressions and movements.

"No, no longer," I declared, anger stirring deep inside. "No, Aunt Betsy. It is over for me with him. Don't you understand?" I asked, with a touch of desperation in my voice. "There is no possible explanation for what he did. I will never accept, never believe, anything he says." I blinked back the few tears that wanted to fall.

Aunt Betsy watched me and then gave a short nod.

"Of course, dear. I understand. However, what is it you are not telling me? Is there someone else, then?" At that, I blushed, unable to stop my reaction, and looked away toward the window.

"Ah, so there *is* someone else," Aunt Betsy said, clapping her hands together. "This is good news. Do tell me more."

"Aunt Betsy, don't you want to rest?" I asked, trying to stall her, enjoying the routine.

"Oh, no, I am resting here, talking with you about your new beau. Please, feel free to tell me all about him," she encouraged.

She moved around on the bed to lean back fully on the pillows, stretching out her legs. I moved the chair closer to her, continuing to face her. I leaned forward in my chair, eager for her advice about Gabriel. "I met Ga—Mr. McLeod when I crashed into his ladder in Uncle's store. He fell to the ground and suffered a serious head wound. When I realized he wasn't recovering well, I visited him with Lucas and ensured he received the care he needed.

"Uncle Martin decided to hire him for more projects, and I visited Gabriel at his workshop with Uncle. He is making me bookshelves for my classroom. I have visited his workshop a few times with Savannah or Colin. He recently asked if he could court me properly." I flushed at the words.

Her eyes narrowed when she heard that I had visited his warehouse, though thankfully I never let it slip that I had visited alone. "Savannah agreed to go to the workshop with you? As did Colin?" she asked, watching me intently.

"Yes, she encouraged me to see if this was someone I really wanted to get to know better. Well, until she had an argument with him," I said, flushing as I recalled that scene. "And Colin knows his brother well and likes him."

"Dearest, you ran a terrible risk, as your reputation would have been in tatters had you been seen there by anyone of good standing. I'm sure Jonas would have been very displeased," she admonished. "You must like him very much," she mused with a twinkle in her eyes.

"I do, Aunt Betsy."

"What do you like about him, Clarissa?"

"He's kind, compassionate, responsible. He is hardworking. He doesn't mind my suffragist beliefs, seems to like that I am a teacher. He doesn't appear upset by my clumsiness. Or my family," I said, abruptly stopping.

She squinted her eyes at that last comment. "I beg your pardon? How could anyone be upset by our family?"

"That was one of the reasons Cameron gave for not marrying me," I admitted. "My family. He didn't think we were socially acceptable enough. I think he was more worried about his career, his chance for advancement, than he was about me. Though he never actually worked," I said with a trace of bitterness. "But, if that is the case, then he didn't really love me, did he, Aunt Betsy?" I sniffed, trying to prevent the tears from falling.

"Heavens, Clarissa, what a horrible thing for him to say! How spineless that young man must be. I never realized…. You must know I never would have introduced you had I known…" She appeared lost in thought. "Thank heavens you didn't marry him. I would hate to see you with such a weak man."

She watched me attempting to hold back my tears and spoke with me in a soft tone, like my mama used to speak with me when I had injured myself playing with my brothers. "Clarissa dearest. I can only imagine how terrible his defection must have been for you. I will never truly know what you went through, the pain, the doubts…" She paused. "But, I must say again, I am very pleased you did not marry such a man. You, dearest, deserve the best of men. A strong man, who is proud of you and wants the whole world to know it," she mused, with a faint smile playing around her lips. Her luminescent eyes glowed, and I wondered fleetingly if that had been her dream, unfulfilled.

"Thank you, Aunt Betsy," I whispered, gripping her hand as tears fell. I felt a tremendous sense of relief to be able to mourn Cameron's rejection and move on.

She watched as I tried to compose myself. "I am sorry I have never discussed with you what happened two years ago. I thought it was better not to stir up any more pain. However, Clarissa, I have come to realize I may have been wrong."

"Aunt Betsy, it's all right. I will be fine. I have felt much better these past few months." I scrubbed my face with my hands, smiling as Aunt Betsy handed me a clean handkerchief. I patted my cheeks to attempt to hide any tears I had shed. I glanced out her window, watching the sunlight play on the white lace curtains, its intricate web design projected on the floor and wall.

"No, it is not all right," Aunt Betsy said. "I realize now that although my parents raised me well, they did not instill in either Matilda or myself the ability to give comfort. Only your mother, Agnes, had that innate ability. It is something I have had to learn and I fear I failed you when your mother died. I thought then that if we did not speak of our grief, it would be more easily surmountable. I repeated my mistake with Cameron. I fear my legacy to you will be instilling in you an ability to appear serene while you are weeping inside." She reached out to clasp my hand. "Forgive me."

"Aunt Betsy, I never doubted your love for me."

"I am thankful for that, dearest. I am only sorry that you have had to bear your sorrows alone. Your mother would have been very disappointed in me."

Aunt Betsy watched me contemplatively a few moments before changing the topic. "I would like to meet your Mr. McLeod, though I doubt that will happen without a little help from us. I wonder if we could invite him to one of the prewedding soirees? I should think you'd be able to invite friends." She smiled at me with a mischievous gleam in her eyes.

"Aunt Betsy, I do not want to cause any more gossip," I protested.

Aunt Betsy closed her eyes a few moments, leaning her head fully against her pillows. When she spoke, she opened her eyes to watch me with mild amusement. "Well, your uncle Martin knows him. He built a display for him. Maybe Martin would invite your young Mr. McLeod? An invitation from him would certainly be proper," Aunt Betsy said.

"Do you think he would?" I asked, my eagerness betraying any attempt at indifference.

Aunt Betsy nodded with satisfaction. "Yes, Clarissa, I'll mention something to Martin, something innocuous about the new display and try to see if I can arrange an invitation. If not, would you invite him? I should like to meet him, and you should have time with your new beau in a respectable setting."

I smiled at Aunt Betsy, nodding again my agreement. I gave her a quick hug and a kiss on the cheek.

"Send me word if I need to contact Mr. McLeod," I whispered as I quietly left her room. She nodded, waving me on my way. I felt a lightness of spirit at the thought of seeing Gabriel so soon.

I walked down the hallway to Savannah's room.

"Sav?" I called out softly as I tapped on her door. "Sav? It's me, Rissa. Let me in." I leaned my ear against the door to hear better, but all I heard was silence. I was disappointed as I wanted to say good-bye to Savannah in person, but she seemed determined to be alone. As I turned to leave, her door cracked open, and I saw Savannah's face, streaked with tears.

"Oh, Sav!" I pushed open the door and enfolded her in a big hug. I quickly shut her door again with my foot, not wanting to be disturbed by Aunt Matilda. Sav continued to cry in my arms. I felt inadequate, as I didn't know what to say, so I decided it was better to say nothing and just pat her on the back and rock her as she wept. Finally the crying abated and she moved away from me.

"Rissa, I'm sorry," she whispered, hiccupping. She turned to find a hand-kerchief and blew her nose. I walked to her small chair and sat, pulling my legs up to my chest, hugging my knees as I had as a little girl, wanting to know what had upset her so much.

"Rissa, I am so incredibly nervous about this wedding. I feel like I am not myself. I feel like I haven't been *acting* like myself. Like I no longer know what I truly want, and I hate that. What does it mean?" Sav wailed, tears streaming from her eyes. She scrubbed her face again with her handkerchief. She began to pace the room, and I watched her fascinated. She had seemed so composed, so ready for this wedding. "I've treated you hor-rib-ly," she said, her voice cracking on that last word, causing more tears to pour out.

"Sav, don't worry about me. We'll always be there for each other," I reassured her. "What are you nervous about?"

"I'm worried he won't show up at the church. Then I worry he *will* show up at the church," she whispered. She hiccupped again. "It's complete nonsense. What do I *want*? Why am I wavering so much? I should think I would know what I want by now!" she cried, hitting a pillow on her bed. She sat down with a thump, placing her head in her hands, her long strawberry-blond hair cascading around her. Her shoulders continued to shake with silent sobs.

I leaned in toward her, placing my feet on the ground gentling tracing small circles on her back to try to soothe her. "Sav, some things in life aren't simple, and getting married is the least simple thing of all. You are about to change your life forever, and it is smart that you are really thinking about it and acknowledging how big a change it will be. I think that is why you are feeling this panic," I explained.

"What would Jonas think?" she wailed, looking up to meet my gaze, twin tears tracking down her cheeks.

"Sav, worry about yourself. Determine what you truly want. Quit worrying about him or anyone else," I gently advised. "Besides, he seems astute enough. He is a lawyer after all. I imagine he can tell that you are nervous and anxious. No need to expound on it."

Savannah smiled. "Do you think I am crazy, Rissa?"

"No, Sav, not at all. Completely normal, in fact." I smiled. "Unfortunately there's not much I or anyone else can do for you, Sav. This is a decision only you can make. Only you can decide what will make you happy. It doesn't matter what I think, your parents think, the grandparents think. It really only matters what you think."

"Did you feel nervous before marrying Cameron?" she demanded, eyes fierce, challenging.

"No. And see where that led me," I murmured, feeling a deep sadness pervade me.

Savannah watched me, then looked away, lost in thought. I stood, gathering her in a gentle hug. "It will be all right, Sav. Just decide what *you* really want," I whispered. We shared a long look before I said, "I must go. I will see you tomorrow?" She nodded her assent, and I turned to leave.

CHAPTER 30

I ARRIVED EARLY TO SEE SAVANNAH before the prewedding soiree Uncle Martin and Aunt Matilda had organized. Sav's door stood ajar, though I knocked lightly not wishing to intrude.

"Come in," called out Savannah.

"Hi, Sav." I hoped her recent doubts had vanished for her. Or that she had at least found clarity on the issue.

"Rissa!" Savannah smiled as I entered, turning away from her vanity mirror. "I am so happy you came early."

I sat in the nearby chair and watched her pin up her hair. I studied the forced, cheerful facade reflected in her vanity mirror before turning to study her room. Typically tidy, it was cluttered with trunks and hatboxes, many of the trunks overflowing with clothes made of silk and lace. "How are you today, Sav?"

"I feel quite well. The headache has passed." With that comment, she sent me a telling look in the mirror. I nodded, noting the open door, and general on-going commotion in the hallway.

"I'm happy to hear that. You need to be healthy to fully enjoy your soiree," I replied, trying to affect a fake French accent for *soiree* and failing miserably.

Savannah laughed. "Yes, Jonas became quite worried a few evenings ago when he was unable to see me, yet he was very understanding. I am so fortunate to have found him." She sighed, looking at her reflection in the mirror. She met my eyes, daring me to disagree.

I smiled, hoping that her cheerful mood was more than a well-constructed false front. "Yes, Sav, you are indeed very fortunate," I agreed, attempting to keep any irony or criticism out of my voice. "How long until you are ready to go downstairs to the parlor?"

Sav pushed in one last pin in her upswept hair and turned to me, smiling. "Now."

Her gown was a frothy pink chiffon evening dress with decorative pink flowers at the left shoulder and circling the hem of the dress. She donned long white gloves that reached her elbows and highlighted her slender wrists and arms. She looked very fashionable and beautiful. Even though I wore one of my best gowns, I felt rather plain next to her in my silk burgundy-red evening dress with sheer red lace composing the sleeves from my shoulders to my elbows. I tugged nervously on my gloves, not liking the longer, more formal gloves required for this evening.

We made our way to the formal parlor, and I realized that the guests had begun to arrive. Some of the furniture had been pushed back toward the ornate pink-and-white wallpapered walls to allow for ease of movement around the room. Maids moved discreetly through the room with trays of drinks. As I glanced at the guests, I realized most of them were family. I smiled warmly at Da's brother, Uncle Thomas, as he raised his glass to me. "There's Uncle Thomas," I whispered to Savannah. "Don't forget to speak with him. He is still mourning poor Aunt Elvira."

"It makes you look at trolleys in a different light, doesn't it?" Savannah murmured as she smiled in his direction. "And, yes, I will bring Jonas to meet him as long as you remember to say hello to my grandparents."

"Of course, Sav," I said, searching for Savannah's grandparents, the Russells. Jonathan and Mary Russell appeared humble and demure, yet they had a core of steel that had allowed them to establish one of the best linen stores in the city.

"Where are Jonas's people?" I whispered.

"They are waiting for the grandparents' party on the Hill in a few days," Savannah said as she approached a group of Uncle Martin's friends and work associates.

"Estimably sensible on their part, don't you agree, Cousin Clarissa?" Jonas said as he sidled up to take hold of Savannah's arm. He wore an impeccably tailored black suit, black waistcoat and white tie, and his blond hair was perfectly styled. "I would hate for them to have to meet people who are so, well…" He broke off his sentence as he looked around the room, expressing his displeasure at the company with a raised eyebrow and mock-chagrin smile.

"I wouldn't know, Mr. Montgomery, as most people here are either my family or friends," I replied.

"Count yourself fortunate to be among good society soon," Jonas said on a murmur as he maneuvered Savannah away.

I glared at his retreating back.

I stood to one side of the parlor, sipping a glass of punch. Savannah stood at Jonas's side, talking with family members, slowly moving from group to group. I enjoyed watching her take the lead for once, introducing him to the guests he did not yet know. He appeared more aloof and distant than ever before, rarely deigning to speak with anyone, merely nodding and smiling. I watched Patrick and Colin speaking and joking with Lucas, yet I did not want to interrupt. I sighed, settling into my role as a spectator.

"A penny for your thoughts," a deep baritone voice intoned in my ear.

I started, spilling a few drops of punch on my dress. "A penny? I thought they'd be worth more to you?" I asked, elation filling me at hearing his voice. "When did you arrive?" I reached out impulsively to grip his arm for a moment before flushing and releasing it.

"Just now. Colin invited me." Gabriel stood tall, towering over me. His ebony hair, free of pomade, was recently trimmed. Gabriel nodded toward Colin. Mischief and laughter glinted in his blue eyes. "I had hoped for an invitation from you."

My gaze met Colin's, finding him studying us. Richard had joined his small group and was being reintroduced to Lucas.

I glanced up at Gabriel. "Aunt Betsy was to speak with Uncle Martin about inviting you," I murmured. "And if that failed, she was to send me a note so I could invite you."

"And did you hear from her?" he asked, gazing into my eyes.

"No, I thought you were invited. Hoped you were invited," I whispered.

"Hmm…" he said, lost in thought, turning to study the crowd. "What concerns you, Miss Sullivan?"

My gaze stole toward his for a moment, my heart sinking at him calling me *Miss Sullivan* again. I had become accustomed to Miss Clarissa or Clarissa. "It seems a rather public venue to meet the family for the first time," I replied, watching the room again.

"Well, I am glad Colin invited me. I'm working for your uncle Martin. I thought I should pay my respects to him as his daughter is marrying. It didn't feel right turning down an invitation."

"Oh," I responded.

"And I wanted to see you again," he said so softly that I thought I had imagined the words.

As I turned to look at him, I read the truth in his eyes. I blushed, contained my smile and looked away. However, I could not hide the flash of pleasure and glow of contentment from my eyes. I reached my hand out toward his, and the tips of our fingers met for a moment. "Did Richard mind coming along?" I asked.

"No, he didn't mind. He enjoys seeing Colin." He nodded toward their small circle, smiling as he watched Richard. "And I think he enjoys annoying that cousin of yours."

"How long have they known each other?"

"Years now. I'm not really sure. Time seems to run together after a while."

I glanced at him quickly, noting that he was scanning the room, studying the different groups of people.

"Miss Russell looks well," he said.

I searched the room for Savannah, and saw her with Jonas and Da. "Yes, she is. She's speaking with my da and her fiancé, Jonas Montgomery."

"Your da has been a very astute businessman," Gabriel commented as he studied them.

I shrugged.

"Does my presence make you uncomfortable, Clarissa?" Gabriel asked.

"No, not at all," I said. "Well, yes, it does, but I like your company." I felt foolish as he chuckled.

"Her Jonas seems an important man," Gabriel said, as he continued to study him.

"Well, at least *he* thinks he is. He's a lawyer."

Gabriel looked at me, raising one eyebrow with amusement. "A subtle, yet important distinction," Gabriel murmured.

A breathless Aunt Betsy approached, more stooped than usual and leaning heavily on her cane. Her arrival took me by surprise, as I had not heard her cane.

"Clarissa, dear, I haven't seen you all evening. Why are you hiding in the corner?" she chided. She wore her most fashionable gown of ivory silk chiffon with ivory silk lace netting over the silk skirts. Black lace appliqués were sewn on under the silk lace net around the hem and bodice of the dress. Her black elbow-length gloves matched the flowing black belt at her corseted waist.

I moved toward her and kissed her cheek. "Aunt Betsy, I'm not hiding. This is the best place to watch everyone." I smiled and turned to Gabriel. "Aunt Betsy, may I introduce Mr. Gabriel McLeod. He worked for Uncle Martin to build the new display, and he is building me new bookcases for the school." I turned to Gabriel. "Mr. McLeod, my Aunt Betsy, Mrs. Tobias Parker."

Gabriel bowed toward Aunt Betsy. "I am honored to meet you, ma'am," he said, a smile playing around his mouth.

"And I you, Mr. McLeod. You do beautiful carpentry work for someone so young." She smiled at me and then turned back toward Gabriel. "I was hoping that this would be one event where my beautiful niece would not spend the evening skulking in the shadows. She seems to prefer living on the periphery these days, Mr. McLeod. Have you noticed that?"

"Aunt…" I began, but Aunt Betsy interrupted me.

"I had hoped there would be someone here willing to take a turn about the room with her," Aunt Betsy continued, as though to no one in particular.

"I believe that the choice of whether to remain in the shadows or to enter the light again is a decision only Miss Clarissa can make. Wouldn't you agree, Mrs. Parker?" Gabriel replied.

"Well said, young man. I just hope she makes the correct decision," Aunt Betsy replied. "Oh, there is Sean. I must speak with him and offer my congratulations to him and Mrs. Sullivan. I'm told the baby will be born in November." Aunt Betsy departed as abruptly as she had arrived, her movements heralded by the thumping of her cane.

We remained in silence a few moments.

"Which would you prefer, Miss Clarissa?"

"The light," I responded, looking up toward him with glowing eyes.

He smiled fully at me, flashing his dimple, offering me his elbow. "Let's speak with Richard and Colin. They are a friendly pair to start with." I nodded my agreement.

We walked around the room, from group to group, interacting with everyone. I had not realized how much I had missed listening to the stories, hearing the family news firsthand rather than at the breakfast or dinner table.

When we approached Colin's group, Lucas had already moved away to speak with Uncle Thomas. I had hoped Lucas would speak with Gabriel and that Lucas would be able to ease the animosity he felt toward Gabriel. After a few moments with our brothers, I led Gabriel to meet Da.

"Da, Mrs. Sm…Sullivan, may I introduce you to Mr. Gabriel McLeod?" As I said the name McLeod, Mrs. Smythe nearly choked on her water. I watched her, daring her to be rude to a guest at my uncle Martin's house. "He is the man injured in the accident here a few months ago. He built the display in Uncle's store. Mr. McLeod, Mr. and Mrs. Sullivan."

Gabriel and Da shook hands, and then Gabriel bowed toward Mrs. Sullivan. But when he spoke, he talked with Da. "My brother knows Colin well, sir."

"Yes, Richard, isn't it?" Da responded. With a quick nod from Gabriel, he continued. "Richard was very courteous to my Clarissa recently. We owe him our thanks. He's also a very fine blacksmith."

"Yes, sir, I believe he is. Mr. Harris seems to think so," Gabriel responded with a pleased smile and pride-tinged voice.

Mrs. Sullivan leaned closer to my father, before inquiring in her sugary voice, "How is your dear aunt Masterson? I do count her as such a close, personal friend and confidante."

Gabriel's arm jerked under my hand as I felt him tense. "I am sure you know more of my aunt than I do, ma'am," he replied in a flat voice.

"Oh, how she worries about you boys!" She turned to my da, simpering, "Their aunt took them in when their parents died in an unfortunate accident years ago and raised them as her own. Wasn't that a Christian act?" She touched a lace handkerchief to her left eye as though blotting a sympathetic tear.

Gabriel continued to watch her, with blue ice-chip eyes. "I don't believe religion had much to do with it, ma'am. If you will excuse me?" He bowed and turned to leave.

I thought Gabriel's tension would ease as we distanced ourselves from Mrs. Smythe, but he continued to breathe heavily and stare straight ahead. Soon we had returned to the corner of the room where the night had begun.

"Gabriel," I began. He shook his head, indicating he did not want me to speak. I remained silent and continued to hold his arm, attempting to impart what comfort I could.

Richard made his way toward us. I watched as he jovially maneuvered from group to group, smiling, laughing, yet never lingering. Within a few minutes, he stood on the other side of Gabriel. He continued to smile, outwardly acting as though all was well. However, when he spoke, his voice held a low sense of urgency. "What's the matter, Gabe?"

"That woman brought up Aunt Masterson," Gabriel bit out, anger lacing his words.

"Ah, yes, the beloved stepmama, isn't that correct, Miss Sullivan?" Richard teased. "I remember being shocked by her having tea with the vicious old bat a few weeks ago."

Gabriel let out a sigh, and I could feel him relaxing. "She said Aunt Masterson took us in and raised us as her own," he nearly growled in a low voice.

"Her own servants, perhaps," Richard murmured. "Gabe, you've got to let it go. She's the past, look to the future." He and Gabriel shared an intense look. "You can't keep letting the likes of her and Henry rile you."

"Have you had any word from Jeremy?" I asked.

"Jeremy is in the army," Richard said.

I nodded, expressing I already knew that information.

"We worry about his welfare and hope that he comes home soon, healthy and sound."

"But no news," Gabriel said in a soft voice.

"What will he do when he comes home?" I asked, thinking that they both had good professions by trade.

They looked at me confused and then shared a smile. Gabriel said, "Whatever he wants. He's earned it."

"What is he like?" I asked.

"A bit of a hellion, actually," replied Richard. "You can't deny that, Gabe!" Richard said with a laugh. "He was always getting into trouble. I wonder if the army has tamed him at all. Anyway, tall like us but with even darker hair and more greenish eyes. Not as much of a brooder as Gabe, more outgoing. Livelier. The best of us all, wouldn't you say, Gabe?"

"Hmm, definitely. The most like Da." Again Gabriel sounded wistful, but now there was a small smile playing around his mouth.

"How long has it been since you have seen him?" I asked.

"Three years," Gabriel said. "Richard, we should take our leave now. It's past time."

Richard studied him for a few moments and then shrugged his shoulders, reluctantly agreeing. He turned toward me. "Miss Sullivan, it's always a pleasure to see you. I hope to see you again in the near future." He walked away to rejoin Colin, Patrick and Lucas for a few moments, shaking hands and taking his leave.

Gabriel turned to me, with bleak eyes. "Miss Clarissa." He bowed formally and turned to leave.

Shock cascaded through me at his abrupt departure. I could not believe he would leave in such a way. He had not even kissed my hand! Frustration and the old doubts rose up in me, although I quickly tried to dampen them down. I hoped he would glance back toward me as I watched his retreating disappearance through the door, but to no avail. I stood at the side of the room, flummoxed.

CHAPTER 31

SAVANNAH'S WEDDING DAY DAWNED cloudy and gray. I peered out my window hoping to see a patch of blue, but it was a dismal, dark June morning. As I dressed and primped for the wedding, I fervently prayed the entire time that I would cause no mishaps during the ceremony or wedding breakfast. I donned my new pale green satin dress with tight-fitting bodice, flowing skirts and lace trim. I tilted a matching pale green hat at a jaunty angle and pulled on white elbow-length gloves.

When I arrived at the Russells' home, less than an hour before the wedding, Aunt Matilda was in a state. I rushed to Savannah's room, surprised to find her still in her nightclothes, sitting on the edge of her bed, staring vacantly ahead as though in a stupor.

"Sav," I reproached, as I entered her room, closing the door behind me. "You must get dressed. *Now.*"

Savannah reached out to me, gripping my hand. "I refused to begin preparations until you arrived and I could speak with you. Mother is furious, but I don't care." Savannah spoke in a wavering tone, as though on the verge of tears. "Rissa, I don't know if I can do this!"

"Getting dressed or actually marrying Jonas?" I asked.

"Marrying Jonas," Savannah responded, swatting me gently with her hand. "I feel like I've rushed headlong into something without thinking it through fully. What if this is a mistake?" Savannah peered at me with imploring eyes.

"Sav, I think most brides feel this way on their wedding day."

"You didn't!"

"Savannah, this isn't about me," I said as I took another deep breath, crouching down to face her at eye level. "If you do not want to marry him, then don't. Remember what I asked you last time? What do you want?" When there was no response, I asked again. "Savannah, what do you truly want?"

Savannah stared at me. "You don't like Jonas. Why are you encouraging me to marry him?" She cocked her head to one side.

"I may not like him, but I do want my favorite cousin to be happy." I smiled at her.

"Do you think he'll make me happy?" Savannah implored.

"Sav, I can't answer that. And anyway, why look to him for all of your happiness? Maybe you should start thinking about looking toward yourself…"

"No, none of your liberal teachings today," Savannah interrupted. She breathed in deeply a few times, steadying herself. "Help me up. I need to get ready for the ceremony." She met my worried gaze with a determined look in her eyes. "I am sure, Rissa. It's all planned, everyone likes him. I know my parents wouldn't encourage me to marry a bad man. In times of doubt, I should look to them for guidance, and they've been nothing but supportive. I must banish this sense of misgiving." She took a few more deep breaths and then held out her hand to me. "Help me get ready?"

I smiled, nodding. In the end, we needed Polly's help too, but I greatly enjoyed this last moment with Savannah before she married Jonas. I blinked away tears, knowing that our relationship would change irrevocably once she married him. I sighed, marveling at her in her wedding finery. The long-sleeved cream-colored silk damask with paisley pattern tapered at the waist before billowing out to wide skirts. Waxed orange blossom clusters adorned her left shoulder and waist. Silk and fabric bows decorated the hem, and the lace at her bodice highlighted her trim figure. The lace veil covered her beautiful blond hair done up in a graceful chignon, the veil reaching midback. Quite simply, the dress fit her to perfection.

"How do I look?" Savannah asked.

"Like a fairy princess," I said, echoing what she had said to me on my near wedding day. We exchanged grins in the mirror.

"Thank heavens you are finally ready, Savannah. It wouldn't do to keep the guests waiting too long, not after last time," Aunt Matilda stated as she entered the room, with a pointed look in my direction. I paled at the reference to my canceled nuptials but shook aside any hurt.

"Oh, don't you look a picture," said Aunt Matilda. She paused with her hand over her heart to stare at Savannah.

We hurried downstairs. Uncle Martin watched Savannah descend the stairs, a deep emotion glinting in his eyes. He gently enfolded her in a hug and offered her his arm, to enter the carriages that would take us to the church. They left in the first carriage while I joined Lucas, Colin and Aunt Matilda in the second. Patrick, Aunt Betsy, Da and Mrs. Smythe would meet us at the church.

When we arrived at the church, Lucas and Colin helped Savannah down the steps of the coach. I fussed with her train, and then it was time to enter the church. The organist began to play, outdoing herself with beautiful music. As I sedately walked up the aisle toward the altar on Lucas's elbow, I smiled serenely to the left and the right, not focusing on the invitees. I did beam at Da, Patrick and Aunt Betsy. Thankfully I did not see Grandpapa or Grandmama Thompson.

During the ceremony, Savannah appeared serene and composed, the perfect match for Jonas's calm, expressionless profile. He wore a flawless black suit with white tie and waistcoat, and he held himself stiffly as he stood by Savannah at the altar. I had not noticed even a flicker of joy in his expression as he watched her walk up the aisle. By the end of the service, I had begun to congratulate myself for surviving Savannah's wedding mishap free.

I stepped out behind Savannah and Jonas to follow them down the aisle, blithely reaching for Lucas's arm. I missed the step down from the altar, and, the next thing I knew, I was in the air. I held on to Lucas's arm with all my might, causing him to lose his balance and careen into me, bashing our heads together. I found myself in a twisted heap on the floor, tangled up with Lucas. Savannah glanced back at me with a horrified expression on her face. I saw her lips twitch as though she were trying not to laugh, while Jonas looked at the commotion I had caused and glared at me.

After an appallingly long silence in the church as everyone watched Lucas and me attempt to right ourselves, Da rushed past Savannah and Jonas to heave me off the floor. Lucas rose quickly when he found himself no longer tangled in my skirts. I saw his chest shaking and hoped it was with mirth. I squared my shoulders, gripped Lucas's arm again, ignored his grimace and marched down the aisle with him.

After an interminable receiving line, where I received numerous tongue-in-cheek compliments on my innovative flight from the altar, I moved to a quiet corner. As I stood in my now wrinkled dress sipping sweet punch, I watched Savannah move around the room with Jonas.

"They make a charming couple, don't they?"

I stiffened at Cameron's voice in my ear. "Leave. Leave me alone."

"When have I ever done what was expected of me?" he asked in a joking tone. "I want to speak with you, and I know you will not make another scene after today's spectacle."

I stiffened further as he caressed my elbow. I gave silent thanks for the long formal gloves I wore. "And when have I ever done what was expected of me?" I said in a challenging voice, moving to turn toward him.

His grip on my elbow turned painful, and I stilled my movement. "Listen well, Clarissa. This is the life you should have. That we should have. And we will have it. Someday soon you will forget about that unfortunate attachment to the worthless laborer. You will realize we are to be together. But heed me on this, we will marry."

I shivered at his words and stiffened my shoulders to turn toward him. However, as suddenly as he had appeared, he was gone. My arm was freed, pain flooding my elbow. I massaged it and turned to look for him. I saw him skirting a crowd of high-society people before slipping out a side door.

As I no longer wanted to be alone with my thoughts in a corner, I walked toward Aunt Betsy, forcing Cameron and his words from my mind.

"I had thought there would be more than a few drinks and cake," Aunt Betsy murmured with a forced smile toward an acquaintance across the room.

"As you know, Aunt Betsy," I whispered back, "there were too many guests for a formal meal."

"This is why I suggested a small wedding at home."

"Which would never have been grand enough for Jonas," I said.

"Betsy," Grandmama Thompson interrupted, "good to see you here." She turned to me. "Well, girl, there's no need to demonstrate to decent society you have no wish to wed."

"I beg your pardon?" I asked.

"Seeing as you either flee from the altar or cause your fiancé to flee from you. No man of consequence would want you now," Grandmama said with a sniff of agreement from Grandpapa.

"Maybe she desires more than a man perceived to be more than he is," Aunt Betsy said with a chill to her tone.

"Betsy, don't start," Grandmama warned.

"I, for one, enjoyed the entertainment," Aunt Betsy said with a smile.

"I must hope the wedding reporter had departed by that point," Grandmama said.

"Not very likely, ol' Grandmama," Colin said with an insolent grin as he joined us with a glance around the subdued room. "Only thing of interest to happen all day."

"This is how good society acts, young man," she hissed.

"Then I must give thanks to be so rarely in its presence." He gripped my hand, tugging me away from them. "Insufferable witch."

"Colin!"

"Well, she is, even if she is our grandmother. Come, I think Uncle Martin is to give a speech." We maneuvered our way to a good vantage point.

"Col, Cameron was here," I whispered.

"I know. I saw you speaking with him, but before I could approach you, he vanished. Are you all right?"

"I'm fine. Although I don't know why he thinks I'd ever want to marry him."

"Don't go anywhere alone, Rissa. I worry about him."

"I won't go anywhere but Russells alone. I promise, Col." Colin nodded, accepting my compromise.

Colin turned his attention to the newlyweds. "Savannah seems out of sorts," Colin said, watching her stiffly cut cake with Jonas.

"I think she is trying to act properly."

"She's stuck with him now," Colin said with a shake of his head. "Though I think the grandparents are happier about it than she is." He nodded his head in their direction.

Grandpapa Thompson seemed especially delighted that Jonas was now a member of our family. He clapped Jonas on the back a few times, showing more pride in him than he ever had in any of his grandsons.

Uncle Martin cleared his throat and asked for a moment's attention. The quiet murmurs quickly abated. "If I could interrupt the festivities for a moment," Uncle Martin stated. "I would like to congratulate Jonas on choosing my beautiful daughter, Savannah. May you both be happy in your marriage."

At the polite clapping, I murmured to Colin, "Shouldn't Savannah also be congratulated?"

"Would you congratulate her on her choice?" he asked with a wink. We turned back to Uncle Martin as he continued.

"I would also like to take this time to give my Savannah and her Jonas their wedding present."

He pulled off a sheet covering the sideboard. There was a collective gasp at its beauty. It was even more exquisite than when I had seen it a few weeks before. The mirror gleamed, and the wood shone. The rosewood inlay enhanced the rich mahogany color. Encircling the mirror in a simple interwoven vine pattern with a flower blossom at each corner, the molding highlighted the mirror without overwhelming the simple beauty of the piece.

"It seems Gabriel will have more clients," Colin said with a satisfied smile as he watched the appreciative glances from the wedding guests.

"I should hope," I said.

CHAPTER 32

A WEEK AFTER SAVANNAH'S WEDDING, I sat in the family parlor reading a letter from Florence.

June 29, 1900

> *My Dear Clarissa,*
>
> *I cannot thank you nearly enough for helping me to obtain this summer position. I had quite despaired of finding anything suitable for the summer, and now I will have a decent job with room and board. I count myself very fortunate to have you as a friend. You don't know how I had nearly given up hope. I will even have a holiday at the beach!*
>
> *Thank you, dearest Clarissa. I will write again soon.*
> *Your friend,*
> *Florence*

"Are you reading a letter from your suffragette friend?" Colin asked. He lay sprawled in comfort in his favorite gentleman's chair, his waistcoat, tie and coat removed, and his leg hooked over one chair arm. He and I enjoyed the peaceful quiet of the parlor with Mrs. Smythe and Da out for an early evening stroll.

"No, Sophie is in Newport at an extended house party and far too busy to write me. This is a letter from Florence. One of those snooty society matrons from Savannah's wedding hired her for the summer."

"Good work, Rissa," Colin said, watching me over the top of his newspaper. "I have a story to tell you that might cheer you up."

"Colin, it's not worth the attempt. You know I am rotten company."

Colin watched me with raised eyebrows, as though assessing whether or not to accept my dare. "I went to Austin and Stone's today," he said as he sat up to regale me with his tale.

"You didn't," I gasped, envy flooding me at the thought of seeing the curiosity shows made famous by P. T. Barnum in New York City and then expanded to other cities.

"I did. I went after work."

I moved to sit next to him. "How could you have gone there without me?"

"I'm sorry, Rissa," Colin said. "You must know, I couldn't pass up the opportunity." He shrugged away the rest of his explanation.

"What was it like?" I asked.

"Marvelous. Marvelous," Colin intoned in a dramatic voice, and I laughed, punching him lightly in the arm.

"That's Professor Hutchings," Colin said as way of explaining whom he mimicked. "He's a master showman and everything is 'marvelous, marvelous.'" Colin wiggled his eyebrows.

I laughed again, my spirits lightened for the first time in days.

"Everything and everyone is a curiosity," Colin continued. "I have no idea if any of it is real, but it's a great show." He sighed, closing his eyes as though reenvisioning what he had seen and heard. When he began to speak again, it was in that deep voice. "Behold the world's most magnificently malleable man, the charismatic contortionist come to Boston for your pleasurable perusal. Marvelous! Marvelous!"

I pealed with laughter, my desire to have been there with him increasing as he regaled me with stories. "You'd better tell me no more, or I will die of envy!" I said, sharing a long smile with Colin.

He patted my shoulder. "At least I was able to make you laugh."

I leaned back against the settee, imagining going to Austin and Stone's, the "marvelous," fantastical things I would see. I sighed at the thought, frustrated that it had been deemed unacceptable by Mrs. Smythe.

"I'm surprised at you, Rissa," Colin said, interrupting my musings, with a disapproving expression on his face.

"Why, Colin? I have done nothing of interest for quite some time."

"You had a good man interested in you, and you have ignored him."

"I don't know what you mean," I protested as I tried to hide my flush.

"I spoke with Richard today. Gabe's been very low since the soiree. Look, I know he was a bit rude at the end, Rissa, but I can't believe you won't accept his apology," Colin reproached me, impatience tinting his voice.

"Apology? What apology? I haven't heard a word from him since that night."

"Rissa, I know that Gabe came by the house to speak with you a few days after the soiree, and you turned him away. You wouldn't even come to the door to speak with him."

"Who told you that?" I demanded, sitting up straight on the settee. "Mrs. Smythe," I murmured, staring into space.

"No, Mrs. Smythe didn't tell me, Rissa. Richard did."

"No, Colin, Mrs. Smythe must have turned him away. I never knew he came here," I said. "I must speak with him. Will you go with me to his workshop now? It's not too late, and it's acceptable if you are with me. Please, Colin?"

Colin studied me, seeing my sincerity. He smiled. "Of course, Rissa, I'm always ready for an adventure."

We took a trolley to Gabriel's workshop. I noted absently the continued chaos of Haymarket Square even in the early evening. I was lost in thought, worried about how he would receive me after thinking that I had turned him away. We arrived at the workshop, only to find it closed for the night.

"Oh, Colin! What am I going to do?" I cried, near tears.

"Let's take a quick walk to their house. I know where they live, and it's not far," he said. grabbing my hand and leading me away from the workshop. "Thankfully it is still light."

As we arrived at the North End, the evening gas streetlights slowly flickered on, lending a mysterious, magical air to the streets. The smell of roasting onions wafted from open windows, and men stood on street corners arguing in Italian.

When we arrived at Gabriel and Richard's house, Colin banged on the door. I waited anxiously, worried no one was home, but let out my breath as heavy footsteps approached the door. This time, Gabriel answered the door, appearing surprised to see me, though he quickly masked his expression.

"Colin. Miss Sullivan. Good evening to you both," he said in a cool, flat voice.

"Gabe, may we come in?" Colin asked, urgency lacing his tone.

Gabriel and Colin studied each other for a few moments, and then Gabriel stepped aside and opened the door fully to allow us entrance. He locked the door behind us before leading us to the back room, the room where I had first seen him after I had injured him.

"What brings you by?" Gabriel asked in the same flat tone.

He had entered the back room and moved to the far side of the table, placing as much space as possible between us. He stood with his back against the cabinets, his arms crossed defensively across his chest.

"Hey, Col!" Richard called out from the sofa. He had been reading but looked up as we entered. "Miss Sullivan, nice to see *you* again." Richard smiled at me. He set aside the book.

Colin and I stood in the doorway for a few moments before I entered the room. I moved toward the table, pulled out a chair and sat down.

A tense silence filled the room. I was gripped by sudden panic, momentarily robbed of speech. Richard continued to watch the three of us in apparent fascination as the silence continued.

"The wedding seemed rather interesting, Miss Sullivan," Richard said in a friendly tone.

I blushed, remembering the write-up in the newspaper highlighting my latest public debacle.

A rather rote wedding was made livelier by the bride's choice for attendant. Miss Sullivan, dressed in pale green satin, perhaps overcome by emotions for her fair cousin, the bride, flew off the altar bringing her cousin, Mr. Lucas Russell, along for the ride. The fascinated guests, unaccustomed to seeing anything of actual interest at a wedding, were slow to respond to their distress, probably too enthralled with the excess of petticoats, lace, and shapely ankle and leg visible in the heap representing Miss Sullivan. Miss Sullivan and Mr. Russell, for their part, appeared unaffected by their adventure. As for Mr. and Mrs. Montgomery, they plan to honeymoon in New York City.

"Ah, what a shock to see Rissa appear airborne. And poor Lucas, brought down by bad luck," said Colin.

Gabriel grunted in response, as though remembering his own fall at my hands. I flushed a deeper red, although I continued to meet his bleak gaze, silently daring him to speak with me.

"What do you want, Miss Sullivan?" Gabriel asked.

I took a deep breath to steady my emotions as a deep-seated anger stirred in me. My eyes must have flashed emotion at him as he looked at me. I raised my chin as I responded in a firm tone, "I wanted to inform you that I had been unaware of your visit to my house after the soiree."

Gabriel continued to stare at me, eyes squinted as he studied me.

"Were you now?" Richard called out in a happy voice. "I wonder if that harpy had anything to do with it?" Gabriel glanced briefly at Richard then at Colin. Richard nodded once, rising gracefully from the settee.

"Hey, Col, I have something to show you in the front room," Richard said, pulling Colin out of the room. Colin nodded his agreement, leaving the room, though not before exchanging a long glance with Gabriel.

After Colin and Richard left the room, Gabriel sighed. "Why did you never try to contact me?"

"I was confused. I didn't think you wanted to hear from me. You left the soiree so abruptly. I felt awkward." I looked away, unable to meet his gaze, feeling the old insecurities rise in me.

"Clarissa, I left suddenly because I realized I don't fit in your world. I…" A long sigh escaped him.

I looked up to see him raking his hands through his ebony hair.

"I had to escape that room and the realization that you…"

"That I?"

He met my gaze with bleak eyes. "The realization that you and I are from two different worlds. Worlds that aren't meant to meet or blend."

"You cannot mean that!" I exclaimed. I suddenly felt at a disadvantage sitting. I stood up, although he still remained over half a foot taller than me.

"Clarissa, I do. You were like a blooming rose in that room. I could see it and so could everyone else. You were finally coming out of your shell. I was the one who didn't fit. You come from a well-to-do family. I come from a poor family of nobodies that no one will miss when they are gone."

"Don't speak of your family in such a manner," I chided. "They may have been poor, but your parents were happy, weren't they?"

"Yes, yes, they were," Gabriel agreed, watching me.

"Because they truly cared for each other."

"Clarissa, I know what you are implying. But caring for one another does not heal the malice or ill wishes of society. Nor does it feed a family. Or keep them safe if you are to die."

"Gabriel, why are you letting them win?" I asked, tears running down my cheeks.

"What?"

"Why are you letting the Mrs. Smythes and the Aunt Mastersons of this world win? Why now? Why do you care now?"

"I don't want you to suffer because of me," Gabriel rasped.

"Well, I am, right now, because of you," I replied. I wiped at my eyes and turned to leave. I stopped short, my mind thinking through everything he had said.

"Wait, just wait and let me think," I said, my hand up to keep him silent. I closed my eyes, remembering the night of the soiree. "This doesn't make sense," I stated, turning toward him, glaring at him.

"What do you mean?"

"Why come to the house to speak with me if you truly felt that you didn't belong in my world? Why not just let me go and not speak with me again? Why be so angry with me when I arrived here tonight if you truly felt what you just said to me?" I glared at him.

Gabriel looked down, grabbed the back of his neck with his hand as though massaging sore muscles. He looked up at me with entreating blue eyes. "Clarissa, please just accept what I have said."

"No, not when it makes no sense."

Gabriel closed his eyes for a few moments. He then sighed again, opened them and met my eyes. He spoke in a soft, resigned tone. "Clarissa, your stepmother made it very plain that any further association with me or my family would not be welcomed. She was, ah…very specific in her warning toward me."

"She what?" Colin shouted from the doorway.

I jerked around to see Colin's large figure framed in the doorway, his eyes flashing with ire, hands clenched. "That she-devil. How dare she involve herself in things that do not concern her?"

"Col, can I have a little more time?" I whispered.

"Of course, though not too long, Rissa. We must be returning home. It is getting late," Colin replied, turning to leave the room. I soon heard a low rumble from the front room, most likely from Richard.

I turned back to Gabriel, to find him studying me again with a small smile and warm eyes. "Why didn't you tell me? Why did you treat me so coldly?" I asked.

"Clarissa, I came by the house. I sent you notes. When I didn't hear from you, I realized what she had said must be true. I have been a bear to be around. Poor Richard has been suffering living with me."

"What did she threaten you with?"

"Clarissa, it's not important."

"It is to me," I entreated, reaching out to grab his hand, holding it with both of mine.

He paused, as though to steady himself and then straightened his shoulders. "Your stepmother warned me that, if I did not keep my distance, she would make it known that I had abused your family's trust by taking advantage of you. That I was completely untrustworthy, and that all business dealings with me were to be avoided. I realized it would be the end of my career in Boston. I also understood that if I persisted in trying to see you, my actions would harm you. I couldn't imagine bringing any shame on you, Clarissa. We've done nothing wrong…" He sighed, looking at me.

I stared at him in horror, all color draining from my face. I let go of his hand to bring mine to my heart.

"Yet, I realized I didn't care if it meant I was with you. And I hoped you'd feel the same. It would mean starting over again, somewhere new. With tarnished reputations." He looked at me longingly, reaching up gently with his free hand to push back a wisp of hair that had come loose, and then cupping my cheek with his large hand. "But then I didn't hear from you. You didn't respond to my letters. I realized you must not want anything more to do with me." He finished, dropping his hand, continuing to watch me intently.

I reached out again and gripped both his hands and met his gaze. "You must believe me when I say I never received your letters! How can I ever make amends for my, well she's not my family, but for *her*? And now she's trying to ruin our lives!"

"What are you saying, Clarissa?"

"I am saying I want to be a part of your life, too," I said in a wavering voice. A tear trickled down my cheek as I spoke.

Gabriel pulled me into his embrace. "Clarissa, oh, how I have missed you!"

I hugged him, trying to contain the tears. He continued to hold me against his chest, crooning soft words in my ear for a few moments.

"Well, lovebirds, I hate to break up the reunion, but Clarissa and I must leave," Colin called out from down the hall.

I jerked away from Gabriel, flushing with embarrassment and happiness. I wiped the tears from my face and brushed my skirt in a nervous manner. I turned away hastily from Gabriel but looked back at him over my shoulder and beamed at him. Joy from within lit my eyes.

"I'll keep this picture of you in my mind, always," Gabriel said.

"Ready, Rissa?" Colin called out. I heard his heavy footsteps approaching.

"Yes, Colin." I smiled at him as he entered.

"All worked out then?" Colin asked with a smile. At our nods, he said, "Good. About time. Let's get going, Rissa. Da's going to be mad enough as it is." He started down the hallway again. "'Bye, Gabe!"

I reached out my right hand, fingertips touching the tips of Gabriel's fingers. "I'll see you soon?"

He gripped my hand, pulling it up for a quick kiss. "Yes, my Clarissa, I'll call tomorrow."

I smiled again and followed Colin down the hallway. Richard showed us out, winking at me as I smiled my good-byes.

I held onto Colin's arm, my firm grip preventing him from walking quickly. We strolled to the trolley stop in the warm June evening air. Colin looked toward me frequently but refrained from asking any questions. There were no seats available on the crowded trolley, and Colin kept hold of my arm as I attempted to find my balance in the trolley's jerking movement.

We arrived home to find Da pacing in the family parlor. He had pushed ottomans out of his way so he could walk back and forth, free of impediments, his movements becoming more erratic with each stride. His brown eyes glowed with anger as he stopped moving suddenly to glare at us in the doorway, and he stiffened as though about to enter battle. Patrick, who surprised me by his presence, sat in the rocking chair, attempting to read the paper, although unable to hide his curiosity. Mrs. Smythe sat on the worn scarlet velvet settee, crocheting an unidentifiable blue object.

The parlor glowed from the gentle gaslight, hiding the faded areas on the rose-colored wallpaper. The piano gleamed in the corner by the front window, beckoning me to the relative serenity of that corner of the room. Overflowing vases of pink and white peonies were on every table, their cloying, sweet smell permeating the air.

"Where have you two been?" Da roared at us as we entered.

"Da, don't be so angry. We decided to go on a walk, like you and, uh, Stepmama," Colin replied in a placating voice. "Can you imagine our good fortune to meet Richard McLeod during our stroll?"

Colin sat in his favorite chair, sitting casually with his legs crossed and one arm over the chair's back. He appeared relaxed and cheerful, as though partaking in little more than idle chitchat, but I noted he watched Mrs. Smythe like a hawk. I sat next to Colin in my chair, now uncomfortable and lumpy after its recent reupholstery in a rose floral ecru pattern.

"Yes, wonderful to see Richard," Colin continued. "I hadn't seen him for a few weeks. He invited us for a cup of tea, and we accepted since he has been a friend of mine for quite some time. Seemed churlish to refuse, and Mama always raised us to be polite. Imagine our continued good fortune that when we got to their house, Gabriel joined us, too. Wasn't that fortunate?" He spoke in his friendly, open manner, like he always did, but continued to subtly study Mrs. Smythe. She had set aside her crocheting as we had entered the parlor.

"That's proper then," Da replied. He moved toward the settee and sat next to his wife. He picked up Mrs. Smythe's hand and held it in his. I slowly became more anxious as Colin spoke.

"We had the most interesting conversation with Gabriel, didn't we, Clarissa?" Colin turned toward me. I glared at him and nodded silently.

"Gabriel told us that he had come by the house to speak with Clarissa after the soiree, yet had been turned away. Can you imagine?" Colin asked in feigned innocence, confusion in his expression.

"Turned away?" Da asked with indignation. "Who would turn away such a nice young man? I was very impressed when I met him at the soiree."

"Well, it appears he was informed by our, ah, *step*mama, that he was not welcome here. Isn't that correct, Mrs., ah…Sullivan?" Colin asked, pinning her with an intense stare.

"Well, I never! In all my life. Sean, this is what I mean," she wailed, beginning to cry. "Your children will never like me." She tried to rise, but Da had a strong hold of her.

"No, Rebecca, stay. Explain this misunderstanding," Da demanded in a gruff voice as he glared at Colin. "What did you tell Gabriel McLeod?" Da asked Mrs. Smythe.

She continued to snivel into her handkerchief, wailing slightly. Da waited patiently for her to answer his question.

"Rebecca…" Da intoned again, a warning sounding in his voice.

"Sean, you are too cruel! And in my condition."

She rose to leave the parlor, but Da continued to grip her hand, preventing her hasty departure, forcing her to sit again.

"You will sit down an' tell us what happened," Da commanded in a severe tone.

I shivered.

I saw her blue eyes flash with resentment and rebelliousness, but she eventually seated herself again. She took her time, settling herself, straightening her voluminous cream-colored skirts and blowing her nose loudly. I glanced at Colin, rolling my eyes in exasperation.

"Well, that man, who is a discredit to his family, though no one listens to me, and you should because you will only bring yourselves pain by ignoring my good sense, came by the house a few times. I knew that we are all concerned about the good name of *our* family, because that is my utmost concern, and has been since I joined this family, as I would think you would appreciate, and I politely asked him to refrain from coming here again." She sniffed again, straightening her back, looking affronted.

"There's more to it and you know it!" Colin demanded, finally betraying his anger toward her.

"Colin," Da said in a warning-laced voice.

Mrs. Smythe glanced around the room. "When he returned again, even though he had been advised to keep his distance, I merely apprised him of pertinent information."

"And what would that be, Rebecca?" Da asked, impatience showing in his tone. She appeared taken aback by his manner.

"That I knew about his past and that if he wished to continue to work in Boston, he should keep his distance," she replied.

My eyes widened, and I turned to watch Da closely. His face slowly grew redder, until he resembled a near ripe tomato.

"You did what?" Da yelled at her. He glowered at her with fire in his eyes, breathing heavily. "You threatened a respectable young man, a man who is a friend of this family?"

"I should think *this* family should be more selective of its friends," Mrs. Smythe said.

"You will apologize to Gabriel McLeod. You will explain to him that it was all a mistake," Da demanded.

"I shall do no such thing when I know it to be the truth from my good friend, Mrs. Masterson," Mrs. Smyth replied.

I glanced at Patrick and Colin, noticing their shocked expressions.

"Your Mrs. Masterson must be mistaken. You *will* apologize, and you will cease creating mischief," Da insisted, his soft Irish burr more pronounced with his anger.

Mrs. Smythe merely sniffed and looked away, seemingly unaffected by his rancor.

"Where are the letters he wrote me?"

"Destroyed, of course. No young woman of good standing would wish to receive letters from such a man," Mrs. Smythe said. "I'm just thankful Bridget had enough sense to show them to me before giving them to you."

"In the future, Mrs. *Smythe*, I will decide with whom I wish to correspond and would like no interference with my correspondence. Is that understood?" My face flushed red with my anger.

"I am your stepmama. I must have some say in what I consider best for you," Mrs. Smythe protested. She glanced toward Da.

"In the future, Rebecca, leave everyone's post but your own alone," Da ordered.

I watched shock flit over Mrs. Smythe's face.

"Now if you will all excuse us, your stepmama and I have more to discuss."

Da gripped Mrs. Smythe's elbow, hauling her to her feet, and propelled her from the room. I heard her scolding him for his treatment of her as they ascended the stairs.

I blew out a shaky breath and moved to the settee, collapsing onto it. I stared at Colin and Patrick.

"Did she really deny Da's request?" asked Patrick, shocked amazement in his voice. He picked up the newspaper to begin to read.

Colin rose and began to pace the room. He appeared full of nervous energy but had no other way to vent it.

"Colin, everything will be fine," I coaxed.

Colin glanced at me, shaking his head with exasperation. "Rissa, nothing will be fine as long as she is part of this family. She will wheedle her way out of this and something bad will come of it. Mark my words." Colin let out a long breath, continuing to pace.

Patrick watched him. "Col, what worries you?"

"Rissa is interested in Gabriel, and our loving stepmama is determined to thwart her. That is what worries me. Believe me, she will have a large part to play in what happens in Rissa's future," Colin finished, looking at me thoughtfully.

I smiled at him as I realized his concern was for me. "Colin, things will turn out fine. Now that Gabriel and I are talking again, she won't be able to prevent our being together."

Colin collapsed with a gentle thud into a chair. "Well, I guess you are right, Rissa. There is no use in worrying about what will come. What will happen, will happen, no matter how much we worry about it now."

CHAPTER 33

I WOKE LATE THE FOLLOWING DAY. I had no desire to spend time with Mrs. Smythe, yet I knew we were the only two in the house. I sighed, rolling over to lay flat on my stomach. The scenes from last night played repeatedly in my mind, and I wished I could speak with Savannah. I hated the distance, even temporarily, with her in New York with Jonas.

I sat up abruptly, remembering that Aunt Betsy had remained in Boston, visiting Aunt Matilda. I had not seen any of them since the wedding a week ago. I threw the light sheet off me, the thought of escaping home for the Russells' residence filling me with renewed vigor.

I washed and dressed for the day, donning an eggshell-blue light linen dress. I tied my hair back loosely in a quick bun, not worrying about a more fashionable style. Poking my head out of the door, I quietly listened for Mrs. Smythe but was met with silence.

I crept out of my room and down the back stairs. Mrs. Smythe never liked to use them, relegating that part of the house to the servants. I made my way to the empty basement kitchen, realizing it must be later than I had thought. All breakfast activity had long since ended, and I grabbed the heel of a loaf of bread. I absently ate it as I scribbled a note for Mrs. Smythe, leaving it for her on the front hall table.

I arrived at the store to find Lucas and Uncle Martin manning the front counter, measuring and folding cloth in a lull between clients. Lucas wore a light jacket over his suit, and I knew he was prepared for deliveries. Uncle Martin smiled broadly, his deep brown eyes glinting with pleasure. My mood lifted at seeing both of them.

"Lucas! Uncle Martin!" I exclaimed. "How are you both? How have you been since the wedding?"

I moved toward them, clasping Lucas's arm in my excitement. He patted my hand a few times, seeming as happy to see me as I was to see him.

Uncle Martin eyed me. "Missing my Savannah as would be expected. However, I was not expecting to miss you also, dear Clarissa. Where have you been?"

"Yeah, Rissa. We almost sent Aunt Betsy over to determine if you were under house arrest," Lucas attempted to joke. However, the frank concern in his eyes belied any hint of levity. At that moment, a customer entered, and he turned his attention to her, releasing my hand.

Uncle Martin led me to the family rooms. The darkened formal parlor sat unused since the formal soiree for Savannah. We continued down the hallway, to the stairs. "Let's find your aunts. They will be delighted to see you."

"Uncle, I am sorry to have been absent. I did not want to intrude after the wedding."

"Well, I am sorry that you felt that your company was not welcome," Uncle Martin replied. "We have missed having you here, and I hope your visit today means that you will begin to visit us again regularly."

We walked up the stairs into the family parlor, to find it empty. Light streamed in the windows, the wood furniture gleaming in the sunlight. I sat on the ugly but comfortable Rococo settee, glancing at the paintings on the wall.

"I'll ask Polly to start a pot of tea and find the aunts. Make yourself comfortable, Clarissa dear." He kissed me gently on my forehead before leaving the room.

I heard footsteps accompanied by a gentle *thunk* and knew Aunt Betsy must be approaching. I looked up to see her beaming at me. She leaned heavily on her cane as she stood in the doorway, slightly heavier than when she had arrived a few weeks ago. She wore a cobalt-blue satin dress, her waist cinched with an orange-and-red oriental-patterned belt.

"Darling Clarissa, you have visited us again at last!" She held out her arms to me, and I leaped up from the settee to embrace her in a long hug.

After we settled on the settee, she studied me with her perceptive blue-green eyes. Today they seemed more blue than green reflecting her cobalt dress.

"I thought I would have to come to your house, threaten to move in for a few days to be able to see you," Aunt Betsy joked although I sensed a grim undertone to her voice.

"Aunt Betsy, I am confused. You are always welcome at my home. All you needed to do is come over or write about visiting us."

She patted my hand, as though trying to comfort me. "I did write, a few times." She met my appalled gaze, raising her eyebrows to emphasize her words.

"However, I was informed that you were very busy at present and that, when time allowed, I would be invited for tea. That was five days ago. We all began to worry about you, Clarissa. I even sent a formal invitation for you to have tea here, something I didn't think you needed, which was declined."

I exhaled loudly, sinking into the settee, as shock and a sense of numbness roiled through me. Aunt Betsy watched me carefully, asking, "You did know I wrote you?"

"I had no idea," I whispered, meeting her gaze with stunned eyes. "I thought you wanted some space, some time to recover from Savannah's wedding."

"Clarissa," Aunt Betsy chided, "we would never want time away from you, dearest."

I shook my head with exasperation. "What is she up to?"

"Who, dear, is up to what?" asked Aunt Betsy. "Tell me all over a cup of tea."

Polly entered with the tea tray, and I prepared the cups for us both. Once we had settled on the settee, I related the events from the previous week.

"You visited Mr. McLeod last night?" she asked, taking a small sip of tea, her eyes twinkling over the brim of her teacup.

I blushed, smiling and nodding.

"How did he look?" she asked.

"Handsome. Well, at first he was very angry with me, and I have never seen his eyes so bleak. However, after we finished talking, I have never seen him so happy. He looked wonderful! Well, slightly gaunt and pale, but still wonderful." I realized I was gushing and stopped talking.

Aunt Betsy smiled at me, gently patting my knee. "Oh, Clarissa, that is excellent. I hope things continue to go well for you and Gabriel. I like him. He seems like an industrious young man, and he has the good sense to be enamored with you."

"Colin is worried that Mrs. Smythe will do something to affect our relationship," I admitted. "Last night I was certain that everything would be fine. However, after speaking with you today, I am less confident."

"Clarissa, this simply means you must be vigilant. You are a young woman, who, though respectful of your family, is rather independent. You teach because you want to, not because you need to. If I were to give my advice, I think this is her way of trying to show that she is in control. That you are not as independent as you think."

"Why would she feel such a need?"

"She has recently entered your family and has not been welcomed with open arms," Aunt Betsy said, a mild reproach in her voice. "She may feel this is her way of showing you that she is your stepmother and that she is to be respected."

"I just don't understand why she cares so much about what I do," I insisted.

"You are unconventional, Clarissa. You are educated outside of the home-making arts, and you speak your mind when you want to. You are a caring, kind person, yet you don't suffer fools well. Unfortunately Mrs. *Sullivan* has aspects of the ridiculous about her. Her sugary voice, her preponderance for the the-atrical tears, her use of props to make her seem delicate. That is all an act, Clarissa. My only advice for you would be to not underestimate her."

I shared a long look with Aunt Betsy, realizing I had greatly missed her coun-sel. "How long can you stay in Boston?" I asked.

"Just a few more days. Uncle Tobias is becoming anxious for my return. I believe I will discuss with him having a sideboard or small hutch built by your Gabriel. What do you think?"

"I think that is a wonderful idea! Just ensure that Gabriel doesn't have to spend too much time in Quincy."

"No, dearest, my plan is that I would need to be in Boston, to help oversee any questions and that I would need your help to make sure it is constructed to my specifications." Aunt Betsy smiled at my enthusiastic whoop of delight.

"What's this I hear? Has Clarissa visited us at last?" Aunt Matilda asked as she entered the room. Her honey-blond hair pulled back in a casual bun, she appeared more relaxed than I had seen her in months.

"Hello, Aunt Matilda. It's lovely to see you!" I gave her a quick hug, and she joined us, sitting in her chair.

After quickly explaining the reason for my absence, and noting the frowns shared by the aunts, I inquired after Savannah. "Any news from the honeymoon-ers?"

"We had a short letter yesterday from Savannah. They are in New York City. Jonas appears to be enjoying himself greatly. However, reading between the lines, I think Savannah is less than enamored with the city. She mentioned a few times the noise, the traffic and bustle of the place. What would you say, Betsy?" Matilda looked toward her sister.

"Hmm…I would agree with you, Mattie. I think Savannah is feeling over-whelmed, poor thing. I do so hope they do not decide to settle in New York," Aunt Betsy replied, sighing. She then smiled. "Tobias would laugh at me, what with the railroad now, but it still seems so far away to me."

"Savannah's exciting news is that Jonas has decided they should travel to Paris to see the *Exposition Universelle*," Aunt Matilda effused.

I stared at her dumbfounded. I thought Savannah would be home in a week or two. "What?"

"Yes, dear, the World's Fair, or its equivalent, is in Paris this year, and Jonas wants to take Savannah. Isn't that exciting?"

I continued to stare at her, unable to comprehend that Savannah would be away for so long. "When will they return?"

"Hopefully by September," Aunt Betsy commented. "Barring any problems with the crossings."

"I never thought Sav dreamt of travel."

"She didn't," Aunt Betsy said.

"Ah, to think of all of the fashionable shops she will go to," Aunt Matilda gushed. "The parents will be quite pleased, Betsy, quite pleased."

"Come now, dear Clarissa, let's think about happier thoughts now, shall we?" Aunt Betsy murmured to me.

The conversation turned to my family. "Why don't you come over after supper to visit us? It would be lovely to have us all together again."

"How thoughtful you are, Clarissa," Aunt Betsy said. "I should love to visit the Sullivans and see the changes to Agnes's house. What do you think, Matilda?"

"I see no reason we shouldn't visit. I think Lucas and Martin would also enjoy a change in our evening routine. We shall visit after supper, Clarissa. You will speak with Mrs. Sullivan about our plans?"

"Of course, Aunt Matilda," I said. "And with that, I should leave to speak with Mrs. Smy—Sullivan." I caught Aunt Betsy's amused quirk of her lips at my near misspeak.

I rose, descending to the store, thinking through the news about Savannah. Lucas had a stack of parcels in front of him, and I could tell he was readying for deliveries.

"Can I walk with you, Lucas, as I head home?"

"I would enjoy the company," Lucas said.

"Yes, Lucas," Uncle Martin called out, "great idea to have Clarissa join you. Good for you two cousins to have time to catch up."

Lucas nodded, his large bag nearly bursting with packages to deliver.

"Well, Rissa?" he asked, nodding toward the door, holding it open for me, waiting for me to precede him. "Rissa, please forgive me for being rude at the coffee shop the other day. I did not mean to offend you. It's just that I worry about you."

I gripped his arm as I walked beside him. "I understand, Lucas. However, I need you to trust that Gabriel is a good man. He is nothing like Jonas."

"I don't want to see you hurt again."

"Nor do I, and I am hopeful I won't be," I said. "I have invited the aunts and Uncle Martin to call after dinner. Will you call tonight, too?" I asked.

"Of course. I have a new piece of music I want you to hear."

I beamed at him as I turned down my street, imagining Gabriel's call tonight.

CHAPTER 34

UPON OPENING THE DOOR to my house, I found Mrs. Smythe pacing the hallway, the gold bombazine of her afternoon tea dress brushing the hall stand and chairs with each turn, as though waiting to pounce the minute I entered.

"Where have you been, Clarissa?" she demanded as I opened the door.

I unpinned my hat, and placed both the pins and the hat on the front stand. I studied my hair in the gold-trimmed mirror, stalling for time. As I turned toward her, I straightened my shoulders, smiling tightly.

"Good afternoon, Mrs. Smythe," I said in way of greeting. "As I am sure you received my note, I was with the Russells. They were delighted to see me again after so long."

"You spend entirely too much time with the Russells. Your place is at your father's home, helping me to run it," she snapped. "I expect you to not leave this house again without my express permission, do you understand?" She breathed heavily, one hand over her slightly swelling belly.

"No, Mrs. Smythe, I do not understand nor do I agree. I am of age, and you are not my mama. If I decide that I want to visit my family, I will visit them."

I turned to go up the stairs to my bedroom, but she grabbed my elbow in a crushing grip.

"Do you honestly think your father will take your side in this?" she hissed.

I shook my arm free, walking up the stairs, the picture of her gloating eyes remaining in my mind.

That evening after supper, as we all read in tense silence in the parlor acting as though we were happy to be there together, I heard a knock at the front door. I realized I had been so preoccupied waiting for Gabriel to call, that I had forgotten to inform Da that the family was to visit. I wondered if the caller was Gabriel, but, instead of his deep baritone, I heard numerous voices in the front hall, and realized that the aunts, Uncle Martin and Lucas had arrived.

I rose, walking into the hallway to greet them. Uncle Martin handed his top hat and walking stick to Mary, while Aunt Betsy and Aunt Matilda handed their light cotton wraps to Bridget. Lucas stood holding a folder and gave me a quick wink as he waited to enter the parlor. I slowly walked into the parlor arm in arm with Aunt Betsy, the *thunk* of her cane a counterpoint to each step we took. "Look who's come for a visit!" I exclaimed.

"Hoorah!" cried Da, who jumped up from his chair and clapped Uncle Martin and Lucas on the back, then gave Aunt Betsy and Aunt Matilda hugs. "I am so glad you called. Please, you are very welcome." He ushered them in, and soon the room was full of laughter and conversation.

Mrs. Smythe had remained in her chair, not rising to greet the guests. She sat stiffly, waiting to be acknowledged. However, in the riotous greetings that occurred among the family, she was greatly ignored.

Da and Uncle Martin stood near the fireplace discussing the state of the economy. Aunt Betsy and Aunt Matilda sat on a comfortable settee near me, discussing fashion trends. Mrs. Smythe remained sitting apart from everyone, left to watch us all interact. I felt a pang of pity for her but did not act on it. I thought it was good for her to see how close a family we were, and that it was better not to keep us separated. Colin and Patrick settled into their favorite chairs and soon began discussing politics or sports, I could not decipher which.

Mrs. Smythe spoke in a carrying voice, interrupting the aunts' conversation. "Mrs. Russell, I am sure you are delighted with your Savannah's fortuitous marriage."

Aunt Matilda smiled, almost preening with her joy. "We are. Mr. Russell and I could not be more pleased."

"I am sure you would understand my concern about Clarissa. Wasting away, day after day, with no decent callers. I fear she will never meet anyone worthy of marriage if she continues to work with those unfortunate children."

"Mrs. Sullivan," Aunt Betsy said, her eyes now icy blue, "I am sure you would agree that Clarissa is blooming. She is contented with her life. Aren't you dear?"

I nodded, but before I could speak, Mrs. Smythe continued. "Yes, of course you would think so. You want to believe it. And yet I know how much that young man hurt her a few years ago. If only I had been her stepmother and able to impart all of my wisdom, she would now be a married woman." She sighed, fanning herself as she studied me.

"Cameron, Mr. Wright, has no bearing on my life anymore. I am looking to my future, not my past." I glared at her for suggesting otherwise.

"Oh, aren't you brave, saying such things. I know you want to believe it. I just wish you would give Mr. Wright another chance. He's such a fine upstanding young man from a good family. He would make you an excellent husband."

"How would you know? You never met him," Aunt Betsy demanded.

"Unlike my stepdaughter, I call on other like-minded, sophisticated women for tea. Many of the mothers speak of the quality of his family. On one occasion, I was fortunate enough to make his acquaintance. Such a refined young man." She watched me with a cunning smile. "The sort of man one wishes for in a son-in-law."

"But not in a husband," I muttered.

"I agree. Rissa can do better than Cameron." Lucas scowled at Mrs. Smythe as he joined our conversation. He tapped the folder he carried against his leg. "Care to join me?" He held out his hand, and I rose, walking with him toward the piano.

He sat on the bench and pulled me down next to him. He placed the folder on the piano stand but did not open it. He ably began to play the haunting piece of music he had used to taunt Savannah before her wedding, a Beethoven piece. I ignored Mrs. Smythe's continued exaltations of Cameron, focusing on Lucas's music.

"What's it called?" I asked as he played.

"'Für Elise,'" Lucas murmured. "It reminds me of you because it is calm and gentle."

"I'd think you'd play a piece full of chaos for me," I muttered.

"No, that's not the real you, Rissa." He continued to play even when he glanced up to see Gabriel at the parlor door.

I looked up, eyes flashing with happiness, blushing rosily at the sight of Gabriel entering the room. He stood tall, his broad shoulders tensed as he looked around the room at all present. He appeared to relax when he saw me sitting on the far side of the room. As Lucas continued to play, I watched Gabriel make his way around the room and attempted to wait patiently for him to come to me. I saw him speak with both Da and Uncle Martin. My eyes widened in surprise as he approached the aunts and Mrs. Smythe. He sat beside Mrs. Smythe for a few moments, and it seemed a rather stilted conversation ensued.

Finally he raised amused eyes my way, and I knew he would approach Lucas and me. He rose and walked toward me and soon stood next to the piano bench.

"Lucas, I can hear that your talents at the piano were not exaggerated."

"Nice to see you here, McLeod. I will leave you to talk with Clarissa," Lucas said. He rose, winked at me, and joined Colin and Patrick.

"Miss Sullivan, what a lovely piano. Are you a proficient player?" he asked with wicked amusement in his azure eyes.

I blushed, shaking my head. I scooted over on the bench, allowing him to sit next to me.

"I suppose I should ask you to play, but I don't really want to spend our time together turning sheet music, unable to talk with you. Besides, Colin tells me that you're not very talented. 'Ghastly' was the word I think he used." His voice was teasing.

I laughed, nodding. "Colin does tend to be brutally honest. I am rather awful, though I do try." I met his eyes. His were warm, a fathomless sea of blue that I could become lost in.

"Lucas doesn't seem as angry toward me," he murmured.

"He wants to see me happy but, at the same time, doesn't want to cause me pain by being rude to you."

"I am sorry for any distress I may cause in your relationship with him, darling," he whispered.

I blushed more fiercely at the quiet endearment, finally meeting his eyes.

"I would never mean to cause you pain."

"I am simply thankful he is attempting to like you." After a few moments, I murmured, "Thank you for coming to the house tonight."

"I said I would," he replied, watching me. "Mrs. Smythe seems somewhat distant from everyone."

"Yes, well, she and my da had quite an argument last night when Colin and I returned. Most of the truth came out as to your having come by and having been turned away. Da was furious."

As Gabriel listened, he watched the groups in the room shuffle about until Da sat beside Mrs. Smythe, and Uncle Martin was with Colin, Lucas and Patrick. "She's angry with me because she wants me to focus on acceptable men, like Cameron. Your being here will only annoy her."

"She's met him?"

"Yes, at least once, at an afternoon tea. I haven't seen him since…well, for a while now."

Gabriel tilted his head to one side as he studied me. "Since when, Clarissa?"

"Since he tried to talk with me when I was walking home. Well, and the wedding."

"What happened?"

"Nothing. I pushed him away. Boarded a passing trolley."

Gabriel's eyes had narrowed as I spoke. "Pushed him away? He grabbed you? Touched you?"

"Gabriel, please." I spoke in a low, urgent voice. "He's nothing but a nuisance. Mrs. Smythe likes to anger me, to show me that she thinks you are unsuitable. Nothing more."

"And the wedding?"

"He spoke with me as I stood to the side of the room. Taunted me really."

"How?"

"He seems to believe we will marry. That I will overcome my infatuation with you." I looked at the piano keys, fingering them, but not pressing down on them.

"He seems more determined than I had expected. You'll tell me if you see him again?" The urgency in Gabriel's voice caused me to meet his worried gaze.

"Of course." I smiled in an attempt to banish the topic of Cameron. "What possessed you to sit by *her* tonight?" I was desperate to change the subject.

He smiled. "To show her that I don't scare so easily. I don't know if it worked. I refuse to allow her any control over my life. She seemed startled that I would sit next to her. I think she's not used to having people confront her."

Gabriel turned back toward me, concern in his eyes. "Be careful with her. She has a devious mind, like Aunt Masterson. And even more worrisome, an inability to feel regret or to acknowledge wrongdoing."

"She tried to keep me separated from my family, the Russells, too," I said in a soft voice.

Gabriel's eyebrows shot up in surprise. "I wonder why? What's she playing at?" he asked, glancing toward Mrs. Smythe, studying her.

"What do you mean?"

"I thought her main goal was to keep the two of us separated. However, now it appears that her goal is to keep you separated from everyone you are close to. Why?"

I shrugged my shoulders in response.

He then smiled, with his dimple flashing and his eyes filled with joy, leaning toward me ever-so-slightly. "Enough about her. How are you, Clarissa?" he whispered.

"Happy because you are here." I blushed, looking down.

I heard him chuckle. "I'm happy too, because I am here. I am only sorry that you ever doubted I would come tonight. You had to have known that I would come?" He stated the last as a question.

I looked at him, studying his eyes, which had turned serious. "I hoped you would come but was afraid that you would be unable to."

"Why would I have been unable to?" he murmured, watching me with a confused expression. He leaned closer toward me.

"I worried that the doubts you expressed last night would seem more valid today, and you would decide it easier to avoid seeing me again."

"Clarissa," he whispered as he gazed into my eyes. "Never doubt my feelings for you."

"Hey, Rissa!" Colin called out, causing me to start, jolting me from the moment. My head jerked up, glancing around the room, until I met Colin's amused expression. "Lucas and I are going to take a stroll. Do you and Gabriel want to come along?"

I nodded, trying to gain my ability to speak. "Yes, that would be very nice. Mr. McLeod?"

"That would be lovely," Gabriel replied.

He turned toward the room in general, nodded and took his leave. I followed Gabriel out, gathering my hat in the front hall. Colin and Lucas followed. The men gathered their outer coats, and I put on a light wrap. We made our way to the street as dusk began to fall. This would be a short walk, but I felt instant relief to be out of the stuffy parlor, away from the inquisitive eyes.

I looped my arm through Gabriel's, and we followed Lucas and Colin's lead. They seemed deep in conversation, and I was unable to hear their discussion. I focused my attention on the man walking slowly beside me. I gripped his arm, thankful for the contact.

"I'd give much more than a penny for your thoughts," he teased, glancing down at me, placing his hand over mine on his arm, giving it a soft squeeze.

"Oh, it's nothing exciting. Just wondering what Colin and Lucas are discussing," I admitted.

"I think they are trying to act as though they are having a deep personal conversation so that we can have time alone," Gabriel said.

After a few moments of silence, Gabriel looked down toward me. "May I ask you something, Clarissa?"

"Yes, of course." I had slowly catalogued the subtle changes in the way he addressed me, finding plain *Clarissa* to be my favorite.

"Why did you start teaching? What was your childhood like? I feel like I have told you so much about me, yet I have had to piece together impressions and images of you."

We continued to stroll in a slow manner, managing to keep up with Lucas and Colin. Colin intentionally walked slowly, rather than his usual pace of a forced march. I gathered my thoughts and began to speak.

"My first memories are happy ones. My mama was a wonderful woman who took great joy in being our mother." I paused, smiling as I thought of her. "She was thoughtful, kind, generous, smart. She ensured that we received a good education, yet that we were able to think for ourselves. She rebelled against her parents to marry Da. She did not like conformity. I'm not expressing myself well."

I sighed, searching for the words to explain the essence of Mama. "I don't know how to explain the wonder of her. She taught us what we needed to know to be able to exist in society and the world, yet she wanted to ensure that the rules did not control us." I paused before murmuring, "I remember happiness when I think of Mama."

"What happened to her?" Gabriel asked with intense, curious eyes.

"One day I realized that Mama was not as active as usual. I asked her about it, and she tried to make light of it. However, I realized that Da had become more uptight. Slowly Mama began to fade, and she finally went to sleep one night to never wake up. Colin, Patrick and I had just begun to realize that she was ill, and then she was gone. Some sort of wasting disease," I whispered, holding back tears. Gabriel gripped my hand that was on his arm in comfort.

"I missed her dreadfully in the beginning, unable to do anything but lie in bed and cry. Finally Aunt Matilda and Uncle Martin insisted I return to school. Studying, reading became my salvation.

"After I finished my studies, I again felt aimless. My da was little help. He had become distant after Mama's death, and I couldn't look to him for guidance." I paused, thinking back on those hard years after Mama had died. The anguish, confusion, anger I had felt.

"I hated feeling aimless. I wanted to have a purpose to my days. I began going on long walks, though they were frowned upon by Aunt Matilda and Uncle Martin. Da and my brothers remained clueless. It was as though Da only remembered he had a daughter again at supper, when he was forced to acknowledge me." My throat thickened upon remembering his indifference, his inability to comfort me due to his own grief.

"One day, on one of my walks, I passed a school in a poorer section of town. I was curious to see how the children were learning, so I went in. Even though the children were from poor families, they were receiving a good education. I waited for the end of day, spoke with a few of the teachers, Miss Butler being one of them, and decided I wanted to teach."

"I returned home that night, feeling a connection with my mama, and discussed it with Da, Colin and Patrick over dinner. Da didn't have much to say, though I do remember he seemed mildly surprised I wanted to do anything other than sit at home or dream about marriage. Colin and Patrick encouraged me to try for it if I was interested. I took a teaching preparatory course for a year, and I have been teaching for a few years. That's how I started to teach school. I would have had to have stopped teaching had I married Cameron, but…"

"Why should you give up teaching because you married?" Gabriel asked.

"As a married woman, I should focus on the running of the house. And if the marriage is blessed, children," I said. "Also the school board only likes to hire unmarried women. They think married women are not morally acceptable to teach."

"Should you have been working outside of the home as a young wealthy woman?" Gabriel asked.

"Of course not. Most of my family members were shocked. However, once I started teaching and everyone saw how contented it made me, they didn't prevent me from continuing. Aunt Matilda hoped it would end this year with Cameron's return."

"You seem to value the opinion of your family," Gabriel commented, a slight frown creasing his brow.

"I do. I seek their guidance in most of what I do."

"Is it important that they approve of me?" he asked. I felt his arm tense beneath my hand.

I hesitated, carefully choosing my words. "I seek their counsel, Gabriel, but they do not decide my mind for me. I am relieved that they approve of you, but that has not hindered or enhanced my feelings or regard for you in any way."

"What if your family turned against us?" he asked.

"I like to think I'd be strong, like my mama, and do what I felt was right," I replied, with mild defiance, lifting my chin toward him, meeting his eyes.

"Well, that's good, Clarissa. At this point, no need to go looking for trouble. I think now is the time to bid you a good evening."

I looked up to see that we were about to arrive at my front door, with Colin and Lucas already entering. I had lost sense of our surroundings while speaking with Gabriel.

He lifted my hand off his arm and gave my knuckles a soft kiss. "I will call again tomorrow evening, if that is agreeable?" he asked.

"Oh, yes. That would be fine," I said, my eyes glowing with happiness.

I watched him take his leave, standing on the doorstep in the early evening. Colin eventually returned outside to call me in.

CHAPTER 35

ON ONE BEAUTIFUL SUMMER EVENING, where a light wind blew and there was very little humidity, Gabriel called as usual and asked me to walk toward the park to listen to a concert of the music of John Philip Sousa. Richard had called with him so that he could occupy Colin, allowing Gabriel and me to have time alone.

As we strolled toward the park, I hooked my arm through Gabriel's, enjoying being with him.

"Your stepmother seems more high-strung than usual," Gabriel said, breaking into my pleasant reverie.

"She is irritated on a near daily basis that you are allowed to call. And she had to accept two McLeod men into her parlor tonight," I said. I gripped his arm for a moment, and he met my gaze. "She's irate with my da because he scuttled her plans for an upcoming tea. She discussed the invitation list over dinner tonight, and I can't remember the last time I saw Da so angry."

"Why?"

"The first person on her list was Cameron."

"Cameron?"

I met his worried gaze. "Yes, I think the purpose of her tea would have been for me to have tea with him. See him in an acceptable light again."

"What did your da say?"

"He forbade her from inviting 'that man' into the house. Said he would never be welcomed after how he treated me."

Gabriel nodded his agreement. "And you? How do you feel?"

"Worried," I whispered. "I don't understand her continued insistence that I reunite with Cameron."

"You have allies, darling. Colin, your da. Me."

I nodded, gripping his arm in understanding. "I know. I had hoped to never see him again after seeing him at the school, and yet I keep seeing him or hearing of him at every turn. I want him to disappear."

"Hopefully he will find another woman to pursue soon."

I smiled my agreement. After a few moments, I said, "Mrs. Smythe was also upset with Da for not stopping my visits to see my friend Sophie."

"Sophie?"

"Mrs. Sophronia Chickering, a fellow suffragette."

"Chickering, of the piano Chickerings?" Gabriel asked, seeming astounded. "You are friends with one such as her?"

"They are only distantly related, and she married into the family," I replied. "She is a wealthy widow, with the freedom to do as she pleases."

"And does that appeal to you? Having the wealth and freedom to do what you like?" He watched me.

"Yes. Yes, it does."

"What type of freedom is it that you seek, Clarissa?"

"Freedom to choose my own destiny. Freedom to work at any job I choose. Freedom to do as I please," I said, a touch of defiance in my voice.

"And you don't feel like you have that, living as you do, in a wealthy neighborhood in the South End, with a supportive family?"

I thought I heard a hint of criticism in his voice, which caused me to bristle. "Don't judge me and my life, Gabriel," I replied in a colder voice than I had intended.

"I'm not judging, Clarissa. I'm trying to understand what has you chafing so."

I glanced around, understanding that our conversation was of no real interest to anyone but ourselves. I could hear Richard and Colin arguing ahead about the merits of supporting the Republican or Democratic ticket in the November election.

"You will never know what I truly mean, Gabriel, because you are a man. Simply due to that, you have choices and opportunities I can never dream of. I cannot vote. I cannot choose any profession I wish to study. I cannot…" I paused, at a loss for words to express my discontent.

"You seem especially focused on all the things you cannot do, Clarissa. Why don't you focus on what you can?"

"Because I'm always left wanting more. I feel so constrained," I whispered.

"Hmm…" Gabriel seemed lost in thought. "You say you want the freedom to choose your own profession, your own future. You seem to be succeeding."

"Teaching was one of the few acceptable professions open to me," I snapped.

"Are you saying you don't like it?"

"No, of course not. I just wish I had more choice."

In an instant his mood seemed to change, and his arm was stiff with suppressed anger. He glared down at me as he spoke. "Clarissa, darling, now you are sounding foolish. Do you think my great dream in life was to toil over wood for the rest of my life? Or for Richard to be stuck in a smithy? Or for Jeremy to be in the Philippines in the army?" he demanded, eyes gleaming with anger.

I shook my head, unsure what to say.

"Of course it wasn't," he hissed, "but we work to survive. And we're thankful for the work. And now we will hopefully thrive. But this isn't how I had envisioned *my* life, man or not." He glowered at me before glancing away.

"Gabriel," I began.

"No, Clarissa, sometimes life isn't fair. We can suffer terribly and think life will never be as we want it. But we must learn to play the hand we are dealt," he whispered urgently, anger still in his voice. "You can try to change things for the betterment of your life, but you have to find contentment and happiness as you do it. You must be thankful for what you already have."

"I, I…" I stammered. "I never meant to offend you, Gabriel. I just have this sense that there was more I was meant to do with my life than attend teas and knit."

"Can't you see you already do more?" Gabriel asked. "It's one of the things I admire most about you. You wanted more out of your life, and you ensured you got it. But that is for you to realize. Only you can find contentment with your own life, Clarissa."

His last sentence caused my thoughts to still.

"No, Clarissa," he added, then sighed, the tension leaving him. "I may not understand all of your discontent. But it doesn't mean I won't try to support you." He gently gripped my hand on his arm.

"I'm sorry we argued," I whispered.

"I'm not. An argument's good for a relationship. And my da used to say, 'The best part was the making up,'" Gabriel said with a wicked smile causing me to blush. "Can you come to the museum with me tomorrow? I thought your Aunt Betsy would be a good chaperone."

"I'll meet you there at three," I whispered.

***

THE FOLLOWING AFTERNOON Aunt Betsy and I pulled up to the Boston Museum on Tremont Street. The large white brick building took up nearly half a city block, its four stories appearing more imposing due to the highly arched windows. We arrived a little after three. A carriage accident had backed up traffic and caused our late arrival. I began to help Aunt Betsy from the carriage but was eased out of the way by Gabriel.

"Let me, Clarissa," he murmured. He gently picked up Aunt Betsy and had her standing on the street corner in a blink of an eye. "Easier than trying to make your way down those rickety carriage steps, don't you think?" he said with a half smile and a quick wink. He offered me one arm, the other to Aunt Betsy, and we walked slowly toward the entrance.

We entered the museum, passing through brass doors that led into a large three-storied entranceway flooded with light from the enormous windows. Corinthian pillars rose to the elaborately decorated ornamental plaster ceiling. I glanced up, amazed at the grandeur of the place.

"What would you like to see?" Gabriel asked. "There's the wax museum, the Egyptian mummies, the art galleries," he said, rattling off a few options.

Aunt Betsy patted his arm, noticing an empty velvet-covered bench in the large hallway. "I think I will rest over there and allow the two of you to wander at your leisure. The stairs would be too much for me," she said.

"But Aunt Betsy," I objected, "don't you want to see the museum?" I glanced at Gabriel, concerned.

She shared an amused glance with Gabriel before meeting my worried gaze. "Not today dear." She patted my cheek before turning away toward the empty settee.

"Poor Aunt Betsy," I murmured as I watched her depart. I heard Gabriel chuckle and was surprised at his lack of concern over her rheumatism. "How can you find this amusing?"

"Why do you think we suggested her as a chaperone in the first place?" he said with a mischievous glint in his eyes. "She would allow us time to wander alone." He grinned, seeming delighted with himself.

We made our way upstairs to look at the art exposition. We wandered from painting to painting, though I had trouble focusing on anything but the man walking beside me. He reached out to cover my hand with his. "Have you heard from your cousin?"

"Just a short note telling me about the wonders of New York City," I replied, a hint of resentment in my tone. "And her excitement about traveling to Paris."

"What don't you like 'bout New York?"

"It's too far away," I complained, closing my eyes. "I know Aunt Betsy argues that we have trains now and travel is much easier than before, but it's just too far away."

I opened my eyes, expecting to see mocking amusement in his expression. Instead, I saw compassion and understanding.

"Distance is never easy," Gabriel said in a low voice. "Having the grace to let go of someone we love to find their happiness, their destiny, even if it's far from us, is the hardest," he murmured. "At least, that's what I've found to be most difficult."

"But what if you aren't convinced they are truly going to be happy? If they themselves don't even know what makes them happy?"

Gabriel moved us on to another painting. "It takes longer for some to learn what makes them happy," he said. "And it's not for you or anyone else to decide."

I blushed, looking down for a moment before meeting his gaze again. "I know it's not for me to decide, but it shouldn't be for Jonas to decide either," I argued.

"Is he really as terrible as you believe?" Gabriel asked, blatant curiosity in his voice. We had stopped in front of a painting of a cascading waterfall, the foliage lush and overgrown around the rocks. He now held one of my hands in his, palm up. With his other hand, he began to trace small circles in my palm, making it harder to concentrate.

"Yes," I sighed. "He wants to change Savannah into his vision of an ideal woman."

"Which would be?"

"An immaculately dressed, perfectly coiffed arm ornament who never says or does anything untoward. A woman who creates an inviting home for him, never challenges him, has none of her own thoughts or beliefs," I replied with bitterness. Gabriel studied me as I spoke.

"Cleave unto thy husband," Gabriel murmured. At my nod, he said, "No wonder she became irate with me when I challenged her that day at the workshop. I challenged her vision of her future. Well, at least Jonas chose the correct cousin. You would have broken that mold in a matter of minutes," he said with amused pride lighting his eyes.

"I would never have agreed to marry him."

"No, too much spirit." Gabriel glanced around the room to the other couples and propelled me into motion again. Soon we stood in front of a painting of a distant mountain forest, the pink sunset in the background giving it a romantic hue.

"And what do you want?" Gabriel asked, breaking into my reverie. "What makes you happy?"

"Those aren't simple questions," I protested.

"No, they're not," he agreed. "And they might not be fair. But you seem convinced that you know what won't make Savannah happy. I wonder if you know what will make you happy." He awaited patiently my response.

"I want…" I paused, lost in thought. "I want to teach. I like having some sort of self- sufficiency. I want to have the freedom to voice my own opinion." I paused, clearing my throat. "I want to marry, have children, have large boisterous parties, where everyone plays and ends up dirty."

"What makes you happy?" he asked, leaning in toward me. I felt like we were in a protective cocoon, alone in this small room in the museum.

"A good story, a beautiful song, a sunny day." Another pause. "Time spent with those I care about."

"What more do you want?" he whispered, leaning in farther, his warm breath a caress on my neck.

"I dream of walking alone with you with no need for a chaperone," I whispered. I met his stormy, intensely blue eyes filled with deep emotion.

"Clarissa." He sighed a moment before he kissed me gently. I closed my eyes, gripped his shoulders and kissed him back. He clasped me tightly against him and kissed me with a fierce hunger, causing me to lose all sense of time and space.

Too soon, he leaned away, kissing me one last time, almost chastely, before he broke contact. He pressed his forehead against mine, breathing rapidly. "Forgive me, darling Clarissa," he gasped.

I touched his cheek, smiling fully. "There is nothing to forgive, Gabriel," I murmured.

"I told you, making up was the best part of an argument," Gabriel teased with an impish smile, leaning away from me, and turning toward the door to the small room. He held out his hand to me, and we started to walk sedately through the museum again, hand in hand.

I tried to gather my wits, but I found I could form no coherent thought. I simply wanted to be held by Gabriel again. He squeezed my hand as though echoing my sentiment. After another half hour of traipsing through the museum and looking at the gory mummies, we wandered to the entranceway to find Aunt Betsy.

"Aunt Betsy," I called out, moving toward her. She sat on a bench to the side of the stairs at the base of a large Corinthian pillar. She seemed perfectly content to watch the other patrons as they passed her.

"It's good to see a visit to the museum can put such color in your cheeks, dearest Clarissa," she said, which caused me to blush and Gabriel to laugh.

"Let's go for some tea," Aunt Betsy said. "I have an idea for a project, and I need your help, Mr. McLeod."

We departed the museum, making our way to the Oriental Tea Shop, whose hallmark, a whimsical steaming teakettle, blew steam night and day. The adjoining tearoom with marble-covered tabletops and red velvet chairs with mahogany wood bespoke a place of refined elegance in the midst of the bustling Scollay Square.

After we sat and ordered tea, Aunt Betsy described what she wanted.

"When I saw that glorious sideboard you created for Savannah, I decided you must craft one for me. However, I already have ornately carved sideboards. I am interested in a simpler refined piece in the Eastlake style."

"Of course, ma'am," Gabriel said, seeming to understand perfectly, although I did not understand what they meant. Gabriel reached into his jacket pocket, removing a piece of paper and a pencil. He quickly began to sketch as Aunt Betsy described her vision.

"Ideally I would like it to be smaller than Savannah's, in walnut with rosewood or another wood inlay," Aunt Betsy said.

Gabriel quickly finished his sketch of a simple sideboard, capturing Aunt Betsy's vision.

"Oh, that will be perfect. I will be the envy of everyone in Quincy. I know I shouldn't care about such things, but I do," she admitted with a small smile.

"Now I must return home to Quincy. I had never thought I would be away for as long as I have. My Tobias is starting to fret at my absence. Mr. McLeod, I expect frequent updates, and I expect you to work closely with my niece on any concerns you might have. I have complete faith in her judgments."

I smiled toward Gabriel, feeling a lightness of spirit as our fingertips brushed under the table. I knew his fortunes had turned for the better, and I began to dream of our future together.

CHAPTER 36

GABRIEL ARRIVED AT THE HOUSE a week after Aunt Betsy departed toward the end of July for his now regular evening visit. Tonight we sat in the far corner of the room near the piano, talking quietly. Da, Mrs. Smythe and Colin read on the opposite side of the room with Colin sporadically calling out headlines.

"Gabriel, what's the matter? You seem distressed," I murmured. I leaned toward him, wishing I could take his hand.

He met my gaze, a touch of desperation and sadness hidden in their depths. "Richard and I received disturbing news about Jeremy," Gabriel said. "He is not on his way home due to illness. He's too sick to travel. I fear for him," he admitted, looking down at his clasped hands, gripping them tightly together as though to calm his internal panic.

I reached out, grasping his hands gently. "Gabriel," I whispered. "I wish I had words with which to console you."

"It's comfort enough to be here with you, Clarissa. To be welcomed into your home and to see you every day…" He tried to smile. We shared a long look, hands jerking apart at the sound of a harsh knock at the front door.

I half listened as Colin called out about a polio survivor winning medals at the summer Olympics in Paris, France, before he quickly moved on to updates about the upcoming presidential election. I only paid him half a mind, focusing more on Gabriel. I sensed him stiffen, noting his frozen expression as he watched the new arrival enter the parlor. I glanced toward the door, eyes widening with alarm to watch Mrs. Masterson saunter into the room. She wore all black, the severity of the color highlighting the paleness of her skin and the piercing cobalt blue of her eyes. Mrs. Smythe glanced triumphantly toward Gabriel and me.

"Mrs. Masterson! How wonderful for you to visit us," Mrs. Smythe simpered.

Da looked disgruntled at the addition of an unknown guest but stood and bowed politely. He nudged Colin with his foot, who rose hastily to bow, haphazardly folding the newspaper. Gabriel remained seated, as though rooted in place.

"Mrs. Sullivan, thank you for receiving me," Mrs. Masterson said. She scanned the room, taking in everyone present and the state of the room. "I see that no redecoration has taken place, dear," she intoned, indicating her disapproval, sniffing in disdain as she sat perfunctorily in a worn lady's chair.

She petted the fabric of the chair, expressing her distaste with a gentle grimace as she rubbed her fingers together. She had taken a chair that allowed her to hold a conversation with Da and Mrs. Smythe while at the same time permitting her to see and address Gabriel. My anxiety increased with each moment spent in the same room with her.

Mrs. Smythe and Mrs. Masterson began to speak about inconsequential matters such as the weather and the latest fashion, but Gabriel sat stiffly next to me. His tension continued to mount with every minute he spent in the room with her.

I looked at him with a worried expression. "If she bothers you so much, why don't you leave?" I breathed, barely loud enough for him to hear, not wishing to be overheard.

"I refuse to leave you behind with both of them," he whispered, never taking his eyes off his aunt. Gabriel and I continued to sit in apprehensive silence.

"I hear that your nephew's business has improved since the start of this summer," Mrs. Smythe said. She fanned herself gracefully, a light bead of sweat on her brow on this hot, humid evening. Colin, who had begun to read again, lowered his paper enough to watch the tableau. He glanced toward Gabriel, noted his expression and then focused on the two women.

A long sigh escaped Mrs. Masterson. "Yes, it appears that people are willing to risk their reputations to have furniture made by him. I will never understand mankind," she said ruefully, shaking her head from side to side as though truly concerned for others.

"What sort of reputation does he have that others should worry about tarnishing theirs by associating with him?" Mrs. Smythe asked in an eager, carrying voice.

"Well, you know what they said happened with Old Mr. Smithers?" She and Mrs. Smythe exchanged long looks, and then Mrs. Smythe gasped, "No!"

Colin spoke up in a cheerful voice, folding the paper in front of him as he did. "Ah, what joy to be in the presence of ladies. I find myself confused how you can express so much by saying so little." He smiled in an open, friendly manner to both of them.

Mrs. Smythe watched him warily, but Mrs. Masterson nearly preened under his flirtatious smile.

"I always enjoy a bit of gossip. Do you care to include me?" Colin sat with his legs crossed and looked the picture of a young idle society man.

"What a charming young man," Mrs. Masterson simpered. "Why, you remind me of my Henry." She sighed with pleasure. "I had thought you all uncivilized heathens, but now I realize you must be a true comfort to your stepmama."

I nearly snorted at the last comment and had to act like I had a small coughing fit to cover it up. I glanced toward Gabriel, hoping to share a hidden smile, yet he remained tense, waiting for the impending attack.

"Yes, I like to think of myself as a comfort to those present," Colin agreed jovially, a huff of a laugh escaping. "So, what news do you bring, Mrs. Masterson?" he asked, leaning in, raising his eyebrows in expectation.

"I'm not sure this concerns you," Mrs. Smythe said, appearing to have reconsidered her tactics.

"Nonsense, Rebecca, don't be so greedy. We should share what we know," Mrs. Masterson chided.

"Yes," Colin agreed readily, "we're all family here. Don't keep all the interesting news just to yourselves."

My attention turned to Da, who watched the three of them closely. He refrained from joining the conversation, but I knew he would be suspicious of Colin's sudden, overt friendliness toward Mrs. Smythe. Da settled into his chair, as though unconcerned about their gossip while listening attentively.

Mrs. Masterson leaned forward, as if imparting a great secret. "Well, as everyone knows, there was question of wrongdoing when Mr. Smithers died." Her voice lowered dramatically at the word *died*, and she raised her eyebrows as though it explained everything.

Da, who had watched the exchange between the women and his son with detached interest, sat up straighter. He looked from his wife to Mrs. Masterson, a sense of surprise, then shock, then anger flashing over his face. "And you would believe that of your own nephew? Then you don't know how to judge character, ma'am. You have to be a bleeding fool to believe that, for even a second," Da retorted, anger in his voice. I could tell he was boiling mad as his accent became stronger. Da took a calming breath before continuing, "If all ye wish to discuss is malicious gossip, I would advise ye to find somewhere else to go. An' a more amenable audience."

Colin had sat back in his chair, a look of disgust on his face as he stared at Mrs. Masterson. "I'm sure a sensible woman like yourself must be mistaken, ma'am," Colin said.

"If this is how you are treated, dear, I now see how you have suffered!" Mrs. Masterson cried, gripping Mrs. Smythe's hand. "Oh, how I fear for your darling stepdaughter. How she will suffer with him."

"What do you mean?" asked Mrs. Smythe breathlessly.

She watched Da with trepidation but would not be prevented from her main objective, which I instinctively knew we had not yet reached.

The comment had piqued Colin and Da's interest, though they tried to hide it. Colin attempted to watch them with a detached look in his eyes but failed miserably. Da glared at them but did not prevent them from continuing their conversation.

"He has already enticed her to visit his warehouse, *unchaperoned*. Can you imagine the scandal if that were to leak?" she said in a falsetto whisper as everyone in the room heard her words clearly. "And she met him and his horrid brother for coffee, in a most irreputable part of town. *Alone.*"

My eyes widened with alarm before I closed them. I did not wish to betray any guilt to them unnecessarily.

Gabriel gripped my hand painfully, causing me to gasp. He breathed "Sorry," not wishing to call attention to us.

"Oh, I can only imagine the liberties that he took! He's so unprincipled, so wild. I did my best with them, you must understand," Mrs. Masterson entreated, her voice nearly cracking with her dismay. "Oh, my poor dear sister, married to such a man as his father. And now your dear Clarissa may have a similar fate." She sighed dramatically, dabbing at one eye with a handkerchief.

Gabriel was so tense I thought he was going to fly out of his skin. I didn't know how he remained seated. I kept waiting for him to speak, yet he never did. I glanced at Da and he seemed shocked by what she had said.

Da finally spoke, "I believe it may be a good time for you to leave, ma'am."

He rose, showing her the door. She stood, shaking out her skirts and then glared in Gabriel's direction. She sniffed in disdain as she looked at me before turning to leave the room. She had done her job well; the damage had been done.

Da reentered the room, glancing toward Colin and Mrs. Smythe. "I would like to have a conversation alone, with Mr. McLeod and Clarissa. If you wouldn't mind?"

Colin threw me a worried, guilt-stricken glance but had no choice but to agree. Mrs. Smythe acquiesced, smiling smugly. Da waited for them to vacate the room, then shut the door with a quiet click.

He turned to face us, beginning to pace. He took deep breaths, and I hoped they would calm his sometimes vicious temper. He finally spoke.

"All right, young lady, you have some explaining to do." He stood, breathing heavily, waiting for my explanation. I studied him and realized that though he appeared angry, he was not yet irate.

My mind raced at how I would describe my actions without incriminating Uncle Martin, Savannah, Colin and, at the same time, soothe my da's anger. I sighed, thinking how many people had helped me in this endeavor. I took a deep breath and haltingly began to speak. "Well, you know that I first met Mr. McLeod after the incident at Uncle's store," I said, stalling for time. "We became friendly when he was hired to make bookshelves for my schoolroom. You've heard me speak often enough of the need for bookshelves. A friendship started and…"

"Are you telling me that he also visited your school? Without any of us knowing about it?" Da shouted at me. I gaped at him, not having foreseen that as such a concern. I had focused more on the solo warehouse visits.

"Da," I entreated, holding out my hand toward him beseechingly. "It's not that bad. My friend Florence Butler was there. And one time, he helped me in an argument with Cameron." I heard Gabriel nearly choke at my words and glanced at him. He had closed his eyes briefly and was shaking his head at my folly.

"Do ye think that little butterfly of a girl could help ye if ye needed it?" he demanded, his accent thickening with his ire. "Why would ye feel the need to hide? To skulk around, like it shamed ye? If he's an upstanding young man, why act in a shameful way?" he glowered at me, his anger at top steam. "Young lady, how long have ye been seein' this man without me knowledge?"

"A few months, Da," I said, refusing to feel chastised. "But Da!" I protested before he could explode at Gabriel. "Nothing has happened! All we have done is talk."

"And ye let me, not long ago, defend ye to yer aunt, knowing ye had acted so shamefully?" he venomously spat out. "Ye let me make a fool of meself, knowing ye'd already played the, the…" But there he stopped, thankfully. He took a long calming breath, glaring at me the entire time.

"You should know better, Clarissa," Da said wearily. He shook his head, after closing his eyes as though in resignation. "How could you not know better after what you went through with Cameron?"

"Sir, if I may say something," Gabriel spoke up. I realized that his silence had been pronounced.

"No, you may not. There is nothing you can say at the moment to improve my impression of ye," Da snapped. "Friend or no friend of Colin's. When I think I've been welcoming ye into my home now for weeks an' ye'd already played me the fool…" He exhaled a long breath, glowering at us both.

"Da!" I protested.

"Don't 'Da' me, Clarissa darlin'," he hissed in a dangerously low voice.

I watched him with dawning horror. His reddened face, furrowed brow and ire-infused eyes reminded me of a picture I'd seen once of a wild boar. I dreaded what he was to say and tensed reflexively. "This is my decision," Da intoned. "You will not see him until I give my permission. If you still wish to see him again after that time, then I will consider it."

I gasped in anguish. I couldn't understand why this was happening. Gabriel gently enfolded my hand in his, in comfort.

"Consider it, mind you, I make no promises." He glared at the two of us. "I expected better of you, young Mr. McLeod," Da seethed. "And you, young lady, should try not to act in such a disgraceful manner. I should have listened to Rebecca's recommendations. Taken them more seriously with concerns for your behavior." He watched me with dark eyes, and I feared more than my relationship with Gabriel was at stake.

"This is unfair!" I protested, forcing myself to focus on the present.

"Enough!" Da bellowed. "This is my decision, Clarissa, and you will accept it," Da snapped. He held a steady stare on Gabriel. I felt Gabriel tense, then slowly relax next to me. Da walked to the door and flung it open, nearly ripping it off the hinges. "I believe it is time for you to leave now, young man."

Gabriel squeezed my hand, and we shared a quick, anguished glance before he left. I sat in the parlor, in shock.

I heard the front door close, a deep sadness enveloping me. Da's footsteps approached the parlor again. "Do ye have any more surprises for me, Clarissa?" At my blank stare, his face softened slightly. "If there is gossip, this will help stem it," Da said.

"This is about gossip?" I gasped, incredulous. "When have you ever cared about gossip?"

"Clarissa, do not think about going against me in this. You would regret it," Da growled. He gave me a heated look before he stormed out of the parlor.

CHAPTER 37

August 9, 1900

My Darling Clarissa,

Your da forbade me from seeing you, but he did not mention my writing you. I refuse to be completely separated from you. You mean too much to me. I am sorrier than I can express that my aunt wreaked such havoc on our lives. I fear that she will always try to manipulate me and my life. My main regret is that it has now hurt you and harmed your relationship with your da.

I feel aimless as I wander around my workshop. All of my planned projects have disappeared along with my dreams for expansion, the patrons no longer desirous of my work. The only project I have is for your aunt Betsy, yet I find no pleasure in it because I had imagined making it with your guidance. I had envisioned you, sitting in your chair, reading to me in your quiet, strong voice, full of passion as you delved into the story, enchanting me more each day.

I regret being unable to celebrate your birthday with you, my Clarissa. I hope you had a wonderful celebration. Never doubt how much you are cherished.

I miss you, darling Clarissa. I dream of a time when this separation has passed.

Your Gabriel

August 16, 1900

My Darling Clarissa,

I am more saddened than I can express at our continued separation. Last evening was glorious, and I had dreamt of taking you to a band concert in the park where they were playing Sousa's songs. I remember how much you had enjoyed our first concert listening to his music and wanted to share it with you again. I imagined a night filled with listening to wonderful songs, holding your hand for a few moments and feeling perfect contentment because you were beside me.

New commissions remain elusive. There are numerous new projects within Boston that would be perfect for me and would provide me with months of work, and yet I am turned away once the owner knows my name. I have had hard times in the past, but I begin to worry these may be insurmountable.

Know that you are never far from my thoughts.

Your Gabriel

***

"WELL, MY GIRL, I must say, you are rather poor company today," Sophie said as I sat listlessly in her parlor, the pale yellow of her walls failing to soothe me today. Sophie sat in her favorite buttercream-colored satin-upholstered lady's chair, watching me with raised eyebrows. Her aquamarine eyes shone with concern. "Do you care to talk about it, or do you just want a place to sit and escape your wicked stepmother?"

"Gabriel and I are having trouble," I said.

Sophie's eyebrows shot up, and her lips turned down in disapproval. "I thought that young man was made of sturdier material, and I am disappointed to be proven wrong." She sniffed in disgust, glaring into her teacup.

"Oh, no, it's not Gabriel," I said.

"It's you then?"

"No, no. I'm not explaining myself well." I sighed, feeling a terrible weariness settle over me. "Let me explain." I quickly detailed all that had happened, recalling the horrible parlor scene to Sophie. I finished by describing the last two letters I had received, each subsequent one more gloomy.

"Are you saying they are actively destroying that man's reputation?" Sophie rasped, a formidable glower on her face. At my faint nod, she stood to pace, exuding her rage at the situation by her uncharacteristic jerky movements.

"Why would anyone want to ruin a man's livelihood? For he won't be able to work here again. Not in Boston and not in New England. Not if what you say she said gets around. She will have smeared him among the society folk of this town, and everyone would rather listen and believe the worst of each other than give anyone the benefit of the doubt."

I tried to speak up, but she waved away my words.

"No, my girl, you know what I say is true. No one with any money, any reputation, would seek him out now," she hissed. "And with all of that low-end, mass-produced furniture coming down the line, he needs wealthy benefactors to pay his bills."

She collapsed heavily on her seat, lost in thought.

"He will…" I began but found I didn't have the words to continue. Sophie's certainty scared me. "How can you be sure?"

"I know these people," Sophie said. "I've moved among them long enough. My only good fortune being that I was wealthy enough that I didn't have to care what any of them thought." She harrumphed, appearing thoroughly disgruntled.

"Oh, Sophie, I feel so at sea. I don't know what is going to happen next. And yet I dread the future now, whereas I had been so hopeful," I whispered as tears threatened.

"Chin up, my girl. Never dread what might come. For you are still the maker of your own destiny. No matter who tries to change things around on you, *you* decide what will happen," she said, meeting my teary gaze with her determined aquamarine eyes.

"But what if what happens is something I don't like?" I whispered, thinking about Gabriel's last letter, filled with worry for him and our future.

"Then you act so that it is the future you *do* like, my girl."

"You make it sound so simple," I complained.

"Of course it isn't. Discovering what you truly want, not what those around you are yammering on for you to want, is extremely difficult, but worth it, my girl. And only you have the ability to determine it."

I sighed, sitting back against the settee, holding a throw pillow against my chest, lost in thought. I turned toward Sophie after a few moments, asking, "Sophie, does it bother you that we haven't discussed suffragist topics during my last few visits?"

"This is not wasted time, Clarissa. You are a suffragette at heart, and you are learning about your own freedom as you struggle against the tyranny of some of those in your own family plus your own doubts. That is time well spent, to my way of thinking."

I watched her with an arrested expression, humbled by her belief in me. "Is that how you see me?" I whispered.

"Of course, my girl," she replied, her eyes bright. "I have no need to belabor the history of suffragism or our current inability to mount any real plan of action toward obtaining the vote. You are intelligent enough not to need me for that. No, it has been a joy to have a new friend. An intelligent, insightful friend who wants more out of life than sitting around doing needlepoint or gossiping about the latest hair style."

I laughed, patting my hair, knowing I looked a mess. I had not really considered my appearance in days, not since Gabriel had been forced from my life.

"That's the spirit," Sophie said with a smile of encouragement. "Never let them take away your ability to find joy or to laugh. For it can always be worse, dearest, and the only defense is a good sense of humor and a determination to live the life you want."

I shivered, a sense of foreboding filling me at Sophie's words.

CHAPTER 38

I SPRAWLED MOROSELY ON THE SETTEE, an aching loneliness pervading me. Colin sat nearby, reading the paper again, although he refrained from reading aloud any headlines. I had already thrown one pillow at him to get him to stop reading to me, and I think he feared for the fate of his paper. Ironically now that the room was quiet, I missed listening to his random bits of news.

Da and Mrs. Smythe were out at a supper party, one that neither Colin nor I had been invited to, although we felt no regret at forgoing the Chichesters' company. They were an affable couple, though as interesting as sawdust. I found it remarkable that neither of them had been blessed with the ability to converse. After one miserable dinner at their home—where I counted twenty-three decorative teacups on her sideboard and then catalogued them by color—I was relieved not to be invited back. Colin would argue that would be because, when I left, the number of decorative teacups had been reduced to twenty-one.

Patrick joined Colin and me tonight in the family parlor on a rare evening home from the office. I worried about his long hours, although he believed they would be beneficial for his career. I rose, moving toward the piano, attempting to practice a new piece. I had never been particularly talented with the piano but had decided recently I should try to develop some musical ability. My crowlike singing caused everyone in hearing distance to flee, and I had determined that the piano would be a good alternative. I tried to focus on the sheet music for the song "A Bird in a Gilded Cage" rather than my roiling thoughts. Unfortunately the song only made me think of Savannah.

I hit a wrong note, and Colin jerked his head up, wincing.

"Behold the caterwauling Clarissa, capable of causing considerable auditory damage. Marvelous! Marvelous!" Colin called out from across the room.

"I'm not singing," I protested.

"It sure doesn't sound like the piano," Colin argued. "If you must play, can you at least play something you know?"

I looked toward Patrick for help but saw his nod of agreement as he continued to read. I sighed, pulling out sheet music for "Ta-ra-ra Boom-de-ay."

Colin snickered at my choice of song, and Patrick laughed, so I continued to play. I heard Colin humming the tune, envious of his musical abilities.

Colin sang,

> *I'm not too young, I'm not too old*
> *Not too timid, not too bold*
> *Just the kind you'd like to hold,*
> *Just the kind for sport I'm told.*
> *Ta-ra-ra Boom-de-ay.*

Colin continued to hum, and I looked up from the music, playing the chorus, and laughed at Colin. "Colin! Those aren't the words!"

Colin raised an eyebrow, humming "Ta-ra-ra Boom-de-ay" another few times, smiling and responding, "Those are the alternate words, Rissa. The ones that are popular. Not the innocent words you know," he teased.

I continued to play, feeling happy for the first time in days. A few minutes later, Mary discreetly knocked at the parlor door.

"Excuse me, but there be a Mr. Gabriel McLeod here, an' he's wishin' to speak wit' Miss Sullivan."

I saw Colin and Patrick exchange looks. Colin set down the paper, Patrick laid aside his novel, and both rose to meet Gabriel in the front hall. I sat, as though rooted to the spot, fingers frozen over the piano keys. Colin glanced at me with wry humor but then became serious as he left the parlor. I heard deep voices as they joined Gabriel, yet I could not understand what they were discussing.

I stood, pacing to the bow-fronted window, pushing aside the plush blue velvet curtains. I eventually sat in a Grecian rocking chair, attempting to appear calm, hoping the rocking motion would soothe my nerves.

A few moments later, the parlor door opened and Gabriel entered the room, with Colin a few steps behind. Gabriel held his hat in his hands, tracing the contours of the rim as he watched me with intense blue eyes.

"Rissa, I know you need to speak with him," Colin said. "Patrick thinks it is foolish, but I understand that it is necessary for you. However, you can't be alone with him. You must understand. So, I will sit in the corner reading." Colin walked to the chair on the far side of the room.

I nodded in agreement, unable to take my eyes off Gabriel. "You look well," I whispered. I had thought he would look tired, lost even. Some outward expression to mirror how I felt without him. Instead, he appeared full of life, full of hope.

"And you, Clarissa. You look a picture." He smiled at me, with glowing eyes. He walked toward me, took my hand and kissed the back of it. My breath caught, and I was mesmerized.

We moved to the far corner of the parlor away from Colin, to attain a sense of privacy. We did not sit but continued to stand, watching each other with longing evident in our gazes. Gabriel continued to study me with thoughtful eyes, as though memorizing me.

He spoke in a very soft voice. "Clarissa, I come with news."

I continued to watch him with my stomach tied in knots. I would have wrung my hands if Gabriel had not continued to hold one of them.

He cleared his throat, continuing in the same careful tone. "I have decided to leave Boston. I'm going to live out my dream and travel west."

He watched me, studying my reaction. I felt dizzy, as though all of the air had left me. I clutched his hand to stay upright, and my vision blurred for a few moments. I then met his hopeful eyes with my anguish-filled ones, incapable of adequately expressing the devastation his words had wrought.

"Why must you leave?" I cried.

"Can't you understand, Clarissa?" Gabriel implored, gripping me gently by both hands, gazing beseechingly into my eyes. "I need to make a fresh start for myself. I will never be free from the past here. Aunt Masterson will always try to interfere in my life. Look what she has tried to do to us. Not just to my brothers, but to you and me as well. I cannot live this way. I have a skill that I can use anywhere. I must try to see if I can build a new life."

I had begun to sob, tears pouring down my cheeks.

"You are no better than Cameron!" I blurted out, wrenching one of my hands free, raising it to my mouth to attempt to cover my sobs. I half bent over for a moment, overcome with grief. I realized the unjustness of the words immediately after they were stated and looked up at him with huge shocked eyes. I could not remember ever feeling such agony, not even with Cameron two years ago.

He jerked away from me, as though I had slapped him, looking stricken. "Don't you dare compare me to him," he hissed. "Unlike him, you know what I am thinking. You know what I plan to do. You have no reason to doubt how much I care for you. We will be together again. I promise on all that I hold dear to me, we will," he vowed, still gripping one of my hands.

"Those are empty words, said only to reassure yourself. You will forget me when you are away, having your adventure. I will be alone again." My voice cracked on the word *alone*, and I felt panic nearly overcome me at the thought of being left behind. I wanted to crumble to the floor, but pride made me maintain a semblance of composure. I stiffened my back and attempted to halt my tears, although I knew that would be impossible.

I saw him flush red, with a strong emotion. He refrained from speaking, letting go of my hand, stepping away from me, turning away, massaging the back of his neck. I simply knew I needed to be alone. In a flash, I realized that I would soon have many moments alone. As I stood there in the parlor, not touching Gabriel, but listening to his harsh breaths, I understood that if I allowed him to leave without undoing some of the damage of my words, the harm could be permanent with a distance too great to span.

I felt twin tears continue to track down my cheeks as I reached out to lightly touch his arm. "Gabriel," I whispered, unable to speak louder.

He pivoted to face me once more, looking up at me through his lashes. He vibrated anger, hurt pride, disappointment.

I swallowed in an attempt to dislodge the thickness in my throat. "I am so afraid of losing you. I am afraid of being alone again. I feel like all my hopes for happiness leave with you, and I don't know how to start all over again." I was unable to describe coherently my inexplicable despair.

He pulled me brusquely into his arms, gripping me tightly, his hands biting into my back. "You won't lose me!" he gasped into my ear. "I love you, Clarissa." He leaned away, gripping my face in his hands, his thumbs outlining my cheeks, brushing away my tears, looking into my eyes with a fervent intensity. "I *love* you. We will be together again. I feel it in my bones."

I nodded mutely, still crying, leaning into him and his embrace. I needed him here but did not know how to convince him to stay with me. I took comfort in his embrace, trying to feel the same confidence he did in our future together. I shuddered and sighed, my crying slowly abating. After a few more moments, I was able to speak again.

"When do you leave?" I whispered into his chest.

He nuzzled the top of my head. He kissed my hair, and then murmured, "I think about a week from now. I delivered the bookshelves to your schoolroom yesterday and I wrote your aunt Betsy of my inability to construct her a sideboard. I need to pack up my tools, settle my affairs here. Then I will go. I must travel while it is still summer there. Hopefully to settle before winter hits."

"Will you write me?" My voice sounded plaintive, but I could not prevent that. I was shocked at the sudden life change, and my self-control was depleted.

"Only daily." I could feel his smile. He leaned away from me, bracketing my face with his hands again. "I will think of you every day. Dream of you. Dream of a time when we are together again. I will not forget you," he vowed. His eyes held mine with a searing intensity, a new passion that I had not seen before. I wished we were alone so he could kiss me but heard the soft rustle of Colin's movements and knew that wouldn't be possible.

"I shall miss you dreadfully," I said in a low voice. Two remaining tears escaped my eyes, coursing down my cheeks. He chased them with his thumbs, caressing my face.

"Will you write me?" he asked, pleading in his voice and expression.

"Every chance I have." I smiled more fully at him. "I will write to you as though you are still here with me and keep you informed of my life. I hope the mail service is efficient."

He chuckled, enfolding me in his arms again. "I have no idea, but I am sure we will find out."

I sighed, cherishing the feeling of being in his arms, dreading the moment when he would leave me. I heard Colin gently clear his throat.

"Ahem. Sorry, Gabe," Colin said. "You should be going."

Gabriel eased himself away from me, carefully brushing my cheeks again with his thumbs, and then left the parlor. I sank onto the piano stool, in shock, unable to comprehend all that had transpired.

Colin saw Gabriel out and then returned to the parlor.

"What's the story, Rissa?" He took one of my hands, kneeling down before me to meet my eyes. "I can tell you are distressed but couldn't hear enough of what was said to make out the reason."

I looked at him with bruised, weary eyes, before whispering, "She won."

"What?"

"Mrs. Smythe," I replied. I took a shuddering breath as a few more tears escaped my eyes. I raised my hand to the bridge of my nose, pinching it in an attempt to prevent a headache and to forestall any further tears. "Gabriel is leaving Boston next week. He is going to travel west, have his grand adventure." I paused for a moment and then finished in a barely audible voice, "And forget about me."

"He'll never forget about you, Rissa. Stop thinking that way," Colin admonished. He sank down to his heels and looked to the floor. "I can't believe he'd go. He has his workshop and family here."

"He wants to be free of his aunt, wants to start again," I said, bending forward at the waist, holding myself as though trying to contain the pain that seemed to overflow and seep out of me.

"Hmm…" Colin replied.

The door to the parlor flew open. Da stalked into the room. His frame vibrated with his restrained wrath, and his forehead shone beet red. He was breathing so hard I thought he would not be able to speak.

"I heard that *he* was here," Da bellowed. "Colin, who let him in?"

Colin met Da's glare with a steely expression, upset enough to not react to Da's mood. "Da, calm down and listen for once," Colin snapped. I blanched at Colin's words, although felt too weary to react any further.

Mrs. Smythe sailed into the room, the pale green of her dress billowing behind her with her rapid movement. "Sean, whatever they tell you, they will fabricate what they need to make it seem necessary for that man to be here visiting Clarissa even though you forbade him to come here. I am surprised your children hold your authority with such little regard." Her words baited Da as she turned a taunting, satisfied smile toward me.

"I would be quiet if I were you," Colin said in a very low voice to Mrs. Smythe. He turned toward Da. "Da, will you listen to Rissa?"

Da stopped to study Colin and then took in my expression. I had turned to face him, and the ravages of my recent crying fit were clearly evident.

"Rissa, darling, what's troubling you so?"

"He's leaving, and he'll never come back to me!" I started sobbing again. Colin patted my back and glared at Mrs. Smythe.

"What's got the girl in such hysterics? She really needs to learn to better control her emotions," Mrs. Smythe said with disdain in her voice.

"Gabriel is leaving within a week, and we don't know if or when he will ever come back," Colin ground out. He continued to glare at both of them, having decided that they shared the blame for this debacle.

"Gabriel, leaving?" Da asked in wonder. "He can't leave. It was meant to be just a month or so apart to temper the gossips Rebecca was so worried about. He can't go." He sat down with a loud thud in his favorite chair.

"He can and he is. Because he's sick of people like his aunt and Mrs. *Smythe* trying to ruin his life," I cried.

"Clarissa, no one is trying to ruin his life," Mrs. Smythe retorted with a small sniff. "And I don't see why anyone is so upset. Good riddance, I say. You should have been focusing on more acceptable men in the first place, such as that charming Mr. Wright, though of course no one ever listens to me." She paused, looking around the room, meeting Da's glare at the mention of Cameron. She flushed with anger and said, "If you will excuse me?" and quietly left the room.

"I am sorry, Clarissa darlin', that ye will be alone again," Da said in a gruff voice. Da rose to approach me and then ineffectively patted my shoulder before following his wife from the room.

I fell into Colin's arms, sobbing until I could cry no more. When I calmed, Colin eased me away and handed me a clean handkerchief.

"Rissa, I know you are upset, but I must give you a bit of advice," Colin said warily as he watched me wipe my face.

I nodded for him to continue. My throat felt too raw to speak.

"You must encourage Gabriel in this journey, in this endeavor. He is taking a great risk in seeking to follow his dream, and you need to support him. Say that you will, Rissa," he urged.

"I will, Col, though I don't know what that means," I said. All I envisioned were more nights spent sitting alone in the parlor listening to the insipid nattering of Mrs. Smythe.

"It means showing enthusiasm toward him and his trip before he leaves, not crying every time you are together. It means writing to him, so that he continues to feel a connection with you. It means believing that you will someday be with him again. That's what I am saying," Colin encouraged.

I sighed, closing my eyes, envisioning what Colin said, knowing he was correct. I nodded, whispering, "Thanks for being home tonight."

Colin gently squeezed my hand, and we sat silently for the rest of the evening.

CHAPTER 39

I FELT AS THOUGH I LIVED a waking nightmare. Every time I saw Gabriel, I tried to don a brave face, yet I feared that he was able to see through my brittle facade, to the sadness and despair lurking near the surface.

Due to Gabriel's imminent departure, Da no longer barred Gabriel from my life. Most days we went on strolls during the late afternoon, and Gabriel visited me every evening. I knew that Gabriel spent time with me that he needed to settle his business affairs. Although I felt guilty about keeping him from his business, from his brother, Richard, and from planning his trip, it never stopped me from accepting an invitation. His youngest brother, Jeremy, remained in the Philippines, too ill to travel.

The day before his departure, Gabriel and I sat at the far end of the parlor, quietly talking. Da, Colin and Patrick sat at the opposite end, engrossed in the nightly papers. Occasionally they would discuss an article. However, they had all tacitly agreed to act like Gabriel and I were not in the room. Mrs. Smythe had remained upstairs with a headache.

"What time is your train tomorrow?" I whispered, holding his hand. I watched his face, trying to memorize every feature, every nuance of his expression.

"Ten sharp from South Station," he whispered back, watching me just as intently, tracing patterns on my palm.

"It's been a while since I've been to South Station," I mused with a brave smile. "I shall be glad to go there to see you off."

"Do you think that will be a good idea, Clarissa?" he asked. At my wide eyes and hurt expression, he said, "No, no, please hear me out."

I nodded once in assent, blinking rapidly, trying to hold back tears.

"Clarissa, I know how hard this parting is going to be on me and can only imagine what you will feel. I do not want it to be worse than it is already. Do you want to go to South Station or are you agreeing only because you think it is expected of you?"

I sighed, and a few tears escaped. I blinked, attempting to forestall any more tears. I finally raised my eyes to his, meeting his frank gaze.

"Gabriel, the hardest thing I will have done in my life, other than bury my mama, will be to go to South Station and say good-bye to you. Yet I must go. I must be there and see you one more time." I paused, gripping his hand tightly in mine. I refused to say *one last time* because I needed to believe I would see him again. "Not because it is expected of me, but because I want to go. Do you still want me there?"

"Yes, oh, yes, my Clarissa," he replied. He pulled my hand to his lips and kissed my hand.

"Let us talk of lighter things, Gabriel," I said.

"And what would you suggest?"

"I don't know, but I was trying to change the topic from tomorrow."

"Clarissa, promise me that you will take care of yourself," Gabriel said, suddenly very serious.

I tilted my head, studying him. "I will, Gabriel. I promise," I vowed.

"Take care with Mrs. Sullivan, and I fear that you have not seen the last of Cameron," he said.

I nodded again my agreement.

He smiled gently, the smile that lit his eyes from within that he only used with me. He gently cupped my cheek in his hand and brushed away the track of my tears. "Ah, you wanted lighter thoughts, and all I could think of were more serious ones," he said, mocking himself.

I smiled, feeling cherished. "I do not mind when you are showing concern for my welfare." I leaned my cheek more fully into his palm, enjoying the embrace. He touched my cheek one more time, and then slowly lowered his hand.

"Clarissa, I have something for you," he whispered. He glanced over at the other side of the room, ensuring that we still maintained some privacy.

"Gabriel, you didn't have to bring me anything," I murmured.

"I know, but I wanted to give you something to remember me by," he replied, removing a small box from his coat pocket. "And I realize I never gave you anything for your birthday." He handed the box to me, watching me with his fathomless blue eyes.

My heartbeat quickened as I slowly opened the box. Inside there was an interwoven silver chain with a locket. "Gabriel, it's lovely."

"Well, I don't know as it's lovely. I do know it's simple. Will you wear it and think of me?" he asked.

"Of course," I whispered. "I just wish I could put in on now." I opened the locket to find it empty. "And I wish there was a picture of you here."

"I didn't want to…"

"Gabriel, I want to place your picture in the locket. Do you have a picture for me?"

"In the bottom of the box. I brought one in case," he said with a fleeting smile as he caressed my cheek again. "Keep my locket next to your heart, Clarissa, as that is where you are for me."

I nodded as I carefully placed the cover back on the box. Gabriel glanced at the clock and squeezed my hand.

"I must go, Clarissa. I should spend some time this evening with Richard." He stood, kissing my hand one last time. "Good night, my darling. I will see you tomorrow at the station." He smiled at me, studied me for a moment as though to remember me, and then turned to leave. He paused to say good-bye to my brothers and Da, and then was gone.

I felt a tremendous ache at the thought of him never walking through the door again. Never hearing him call out irreverent advice to Colin in the midst of a cribbage match. Never holding his hand. I sat morosely in the corner of the room, dreading the coming day.

CHAPTER 40

I HAD HOPED the day of Gabriel's leaving would dawn overcast and gray, like my mood. However, it was a brilliantly sunny summer day with a cool breeze blowing in off the ocean. I wondered how the world could appear so perfect when I felt so desolate.

Colin had agreed to go with me, and I hoped he would be able to cheer me as the time for Gabriel's departure neared. The short streetcar ride to South Station prevented me from thinking too much about the impending separation. I attempted to focus on the people we passed outside, the storefronts, the lovely day, anything but what I felt. Colin sat silent next to me.

We arrived at South Station a few minutes before we were to meet Gabriel. I glanced up, marveling at the three arched entranceways placed at an angle of Sumner and Atlantic Avenues. The white pillars above the archways led to a large clock with an eagle spreading its wings. I paused, taking in the grandeur and the elegance of the building. We were jostled a few times as travelers hurried past, rushing to their trains.

I gripped Colin's arm, attempting to maintain my composure and entered the main waiting room. I paused again, looking with awe at the coffered ceilings and the marble floors.

"Col, I don't remember it being this big. What if we can't find him?" I asked as I glanced into one of many oak alcoves. "What if he has to depart without saying good-bye?"

"You said by the flower merchant," Colin murmured, guiding me in that direction.

I scanned the passing multitudes, hoping to glimpse two tall, broad-shouldered, black haired McLeod men. We approached the flower sellers, with still no sight of Gabriel. I clutched Colin's arm tighter with my anxiety, causing him to grunt with pain.

"Clarissa," Gabriel breathed deeply into my ear from behind. I twirled around, feeling a wave of emotion wash over me at the sight of him. I studied him for a moment. His black hair was freshly cut and casually styled, he was clean shaven, and he wore his best suit. I let go of Colin's arm and reached out to Gabriel.

"Gabriel," I whispered, incapable of speaking in a stronger voice.

He smiled at me with sad eyes. Two fingers gently traced my cheek and jaw before coming to rest on my upper arm. "You came," he said.

"I told you I would," I said, echoing words he had said to me recently. I attempted a brave smile, wanting him to feel joy as he started on his journey. "When does your train depart?"

"In about fifteen minutes. Richard's with my trunks. I need to make sure I don't lose them," he said, glancing over his shoulder as though trying to see Richard.

"Let's find Richard," I said, pulling his arm in the direction he had looked. I glanced at Colin to see him following us. We darted between rushing men and strolling women, evading the crowds with ease. I felt as though we were in our own cocoon sheltered from the outside world.

We approached Richard, who nervously eyed the clock. He attempted a smile, but no joy reached his icy-blue eyes. We ensured the trunks were checked to Chicago and then stood around with very little to say.

I watched as Gabriel turned toward the large clock, sharing a look with Richard.

"I should make my way to the train," Gabriel said, the steam engine puffing and hissing. Sunlight glinting off the sparkling windows prevented me from seeing the interior of the train. The end of each car had a small balcony, with steps leading down to the platform. A conductor stood at the base of the steps, checking tickets as riders boarded.

As we approached his train car, Colin and Richard fell back a few paces to give us a moment alone. Gabriel looked at me intently, taking in every aspect of my appearance. I closed my eyes as he tucked a piece of hair behind my left ear, tracing my ear and earring. I opened my eyes, unable to hide my misery at his leaving.

"Clarissa, love," he breathed, saying no more. I nodded, knowing there was no more to say. "You have my locket?"

I smiled, touching my chest. He covered my hand, leaned down, touching his forehead to mine.

"Never doubt, we will be together again, Clarissa," he whispered.

"All aboard."

I jerked back, eyes widening to realize the moment of separation had arrived. We stared into each other's eyes for a fleeting second and then everything seemed to occur in double time.

Richard rushed forward, pulled Gabriel in a hard embrace before propelling him toward the train. Gabriel stood near the train's steps, allowing others to pass as Richard spoke in his ear, one arm slung over his shoulder. I realized again how close they were and appreciated that this separation would be extremely difficult for both of them.

I stood still, trying to maintain my composure, gasping for breath as I watched Gabriel move farther from me.

As the whistle sounded, Gabriel's head jerked up, meeting my eyes. I saw a reflection of my own anguish mirrored there in his azure eyes. He rushed toward me, grasped my cheeks gently in his large hands and kissed me.

"Until the next station meeting, my Clarissa," he whispered. Then he was gone, rushing up the train stairs and out of view. The train slowly heaved into motion, taking him away.

End of Book One

AUTHOR'S NOTES

Thank you for reading *Banished Love*. Never fear, dear reader, the second book in the series, *Reclaimed Love*, will soon be forthcoming with the next installment of Clarissa and Gabriel's story. I hope you will continue to join me on their journey.

Would you like to know when my next book is available? You can sign up for my new release e-mail list, where you'll be the first to know of updates and special giveaways at http://www.ramonaflightner.com

Follow me on twitter: @ramonaflightner

Like my Facebook page: http://facebook.com/authorramonaflightner

Reviews help other readers find books. I appreciate all reviews. Please consider reviewing on Amazon, Goodreads or both.

Most people learn about books by recommendations from their friends. Please, share *Banished Love* with a friend!

Look for *Reclaimed Love*, Book Two in the Banished Saga, in Fall 2014.

ACKNOWLEDGEMENTS

It is impossible to write a novel without the aid of numerous people. Over this three-year journey from idea to publication, I have accrued many debts and if I inadvertently omit thanking you, please know I am deeply thankful.

You joined me on my numerous research detours and expressed enthusiasm every time I said, "Wouldn't that be interesting for research?" Thank you to my wonderful, supportive family who continues to live with and be supportive of my frequent disappearances to write, read or edit.

You read and critiqued early copies, gave me invaluable insights into plot chasms, and continue to be my most vocal cheerleaders. Thank you, mum and dad.

Thank you, Sheila, for understanding I'd rather write than cook and for always sending me home with a carload of food. You are always interested in a research outing, a wonderful gift for a curious author. Thank you.

Thank you, Barry and Natalie, for your enthusiasm, support, and unflagging belief in me.

Kathleen, you read early pages, believed in my book and have been one of my greatest cheerleaders. You kept my cat and garden alive while I created another world. There are not enough ways to say thank you.

Thank you, Margo, for reading and editing an early draft. Your delight in my characters and the story I created gave me much needed confidence.

The Ladies of Eastie- Susan, Katie, Candace, Jamie, Laura, Eileen, Tina Marie, Eloisa, and Melissa- thanks for all of your support, faith in me, and encouragement!

Your boundless enthusiasm about my series and writing has provided energy and inspiration on the days I did not want to write. Thank you, Courtney.

Thank you Jerry, Eileen, Katie, Danny, John and Bonnie. You've helped me with research and your unflagging confidence in my book and abilities has kept my spirits high through this journey.

Thank you, Brendan for all of your musical expertise and guidance.

Thank you to my wonderful editors at Bubblecow, specifically Gary and Deb. Your advice, edits, and enthusiasm about my book were invaluable.

Thank you to my amazing cover designer, Derek Murphy. Thank you for listening to my input and for creating such a beautiful cover.

BANISHED LOVE:
READER DISCUSSION QUESTIONS

1. This novel presents several social problems still confronting 21st century America. Is it possible to resolve some of these issues or is each one an unavoidable component of our lives?

2. Which of the many themes in this novel resonated most with you? Surprised you?

3. How does the way Clarissa chooses to cope with her problems characterize her?

4. Family life and duty to one's family form important elements of this novel. Discuss how these elements limit/guide Clarissa's actions.

5. Note the different ways the female characters choose their mates. Would some of these be unlikely or inappropriate today?

6. Are there parallels between the marriages of the older generation and the situations faced by Clarissa and Savannah? In what ways do Florence's circumstances enrich and inform the possibilities of the younger women?

7. Note the role risk plays in this novel.

8. Is Cameron characterized in ways other than through Clarissa's thoughts and comments?

9. In what ways does Cameron's pursuit of Clarissa affect her relationship with others? Help the reader know them?

10. What does America share today with the past described in this novel?

11. How does the setting of Boston affect the plot?

12. There is a sequel to BANISHED LOVE. What do you think the future holds for Clarissa? Savannah? Florence? Gabriel?

Made in the USA
San Bernardino, CA
30 January 2014